NICO VINCENTY

DEATH BETWEEN THE STARS

Q435
DEATH BETWEEN THE STARS
4.5K
Nico Vincenty

AUTHOR'S NOTE

Death Between the Stars is intended for an adult audience. If you have concerns about things you may find in its pages, I encourage you to read the following list of sensitive topics. In this book, you will find references to suicide, bodily injury, death (on and off page), blood and gore, sexual content (on page), discussions of homophobia, discussions of death and murder, coarse language, claustrophobia, and possession. Read with care.

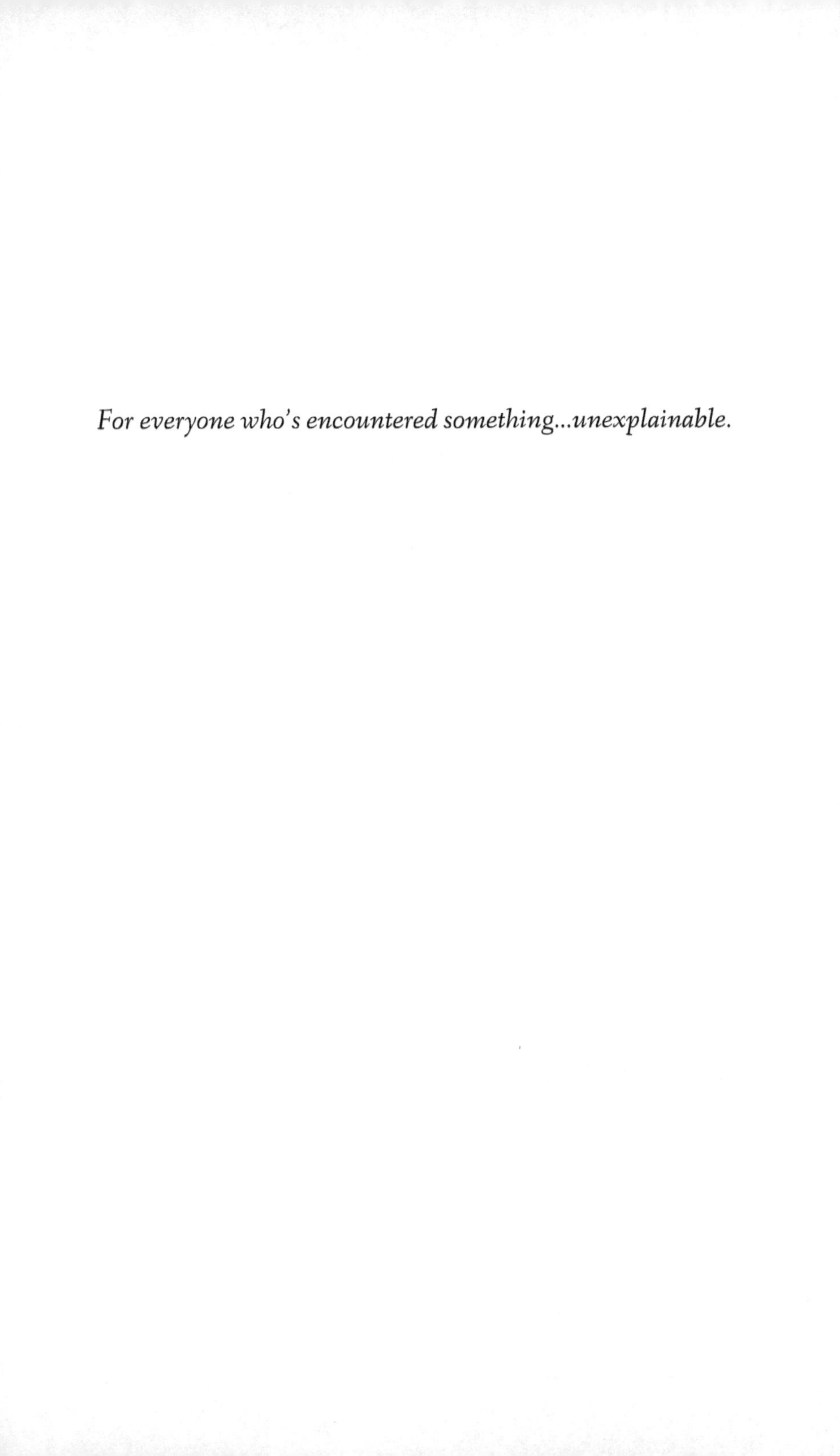

For everyone who's encountered something...unexplainable.

DAY ONE

CHAPTER 1
KORINNE

*From camera 14.9.12: [a door opens halfway, then closes
again]*

THREE MORE DAYS, and then Korinne would never have to
talk to a ghost she didn't believe in ever again.

She grabbed the side rail of the land craft as it went over a
particularly egregious bump, her head nearly hitting the ceiling
and her stomach following along with it. If that happened one
more time, she'd assume the AI running the vehicle chose the
path on purpose to mess with its human occupants. Next to
her, her best friend and business partner ignored all the discomfort and clapped her hands.

"We're almost there," Magnolia sang, her bracelets clicking
as she pointed to a white spot in the middle of the long, blue
grass. A squat, rectangular shuttle waited there, ready to take
them to their destiny.

"Thank God," Korinne said, her friend's joy almost enough
to squash the nausea.

Her friendship with Magnolia started like all great relation-ships: by accident, involving a party and too much alcohol. By the end of the night, they'd had an argument, a bet, and an idea for an interstream show. Flash forward five years, and the silly show they started as a joke paid for their rent, their bills, and Korinne's graduate school. They'd seen a lot of really cool—and really gross—places over the years, and now had the biggest and best opportunity a ghost hunter could hope for: the generation ship *Arkana*.

It would make for one hell of a series finale.

The atmo-station drew closer. Now Korinne could see rust coating the scaffolding around the shuttle. A puff of smoke appeared and dissipated every few seconds, and she could've sworn a spark or two flew from the engine. Despite the mild danger of the situation, she grinned.

The land craft found one more pothole to drive over before slowing a few meters away from the atmo-station. Through the clouds, Korinne spotted the *Arkana* lurking in low orbit, its white lights flashing on the dark gray hull. The cylindrical ship floated sideways, its conical nose pointed toward their destina-tion. Conceptually, she knew it to be ten kilometers long and three and a half kilometers across, but the pictures in her text-books didn't give its size justice. Korinne wondered exactly how many of the thousands of square kilometers she could explore over the next three days.

Magnolia jumped out of the land craft first. "There it is!" The breeze caught the ends of her wavy lavender hair and sent them dancing. "Can you believe the restoration council said yes to us doing this?"

"Considering you're the one who asked them, yes, I can." Korinne exited the vehicle with less ambient enthusiasm, slowed by the same awe and nerves she got on a first date. Hopefully her time with the old ship went better than her last awkward encounter at a coffee shop. "If I die, I swear to every god I'm coming back to haunt you."

"Ha! Got that one on camera," Magnolia said.

Korinne turned to find her pointing at the comm pad strapped to her chest, the camera on the tablet recording their every move.

She lifted one pierced brow. "So?"

"So, it's video evidence of you agreeing ghosts are real." Magnolia's violet eyes twinkled, both in mirth and thanks to the extra light reflectors gifted by her alien heritage. She wasn't fully Vaelish, but her grandfather's genes definitely dominated the Earther ones.

Korinne scoffed. "My spirit is so strong, I'd invent ghostlihood just to haunt you. Put me down in the textbooks as the first ghost ever created." She walked backward toward the waystation, her eyes on the camera. "The only way I'll believe in ghosts is if I become one myself."

"Lies, you told me a full body apparition would suffice," Magnolia said. Her attention shifted to the ship, and the light of all three suns brought out the lavender tint of her skin. "This is the one–I can feel it."

"You said that about the crash site in Nueva Playa, and about the hospital in Bolvardy, and the school in—"

"You've made your point, thank you," Magnolia said, apparently not wanting to hash out the same conversation they'd had a million times. This trip, their grand finale, would serve as Magnolia's last chance to prove her point—and Korinne's last time dealing with all the obnoxious equipment she swore provided undeniable proof. What they did afterwards...

Well, Korinne wasn't quite ready to think about that.

While it was always the plan to finish the show when she finished her Ph.D. in Earth and *Arkana* Studies, the looming threat of the unknown had her wondering if maybe her lumbar could handle a few more nights sleeping in haunted places. Then again, where else could they go that would compete with a generation ship that carried humanity to the other side of the stars?

Ah, the ship. Thanks to the right technological advancements, the *Arkana* was done floating in Vaela's orbit. It could now make one last trip to another goldilocks planet in the system, where it would actually get to land this time. There, a whole team of specialists waited to restore it next to its sister, the *Covenant*. It held centuries of history and a wealth of knowledge about times long gone and nearly forgotten.

Not to mention, it was incredibly haunted. Allegedly.

For the first time in fifty years, the *Arkana* would host humans once again. Well, a few humans and one partial alien.

Hustling the last few meters, Korinne and Magnolia boarded the shuttle with just their comm pads and hip bags of equipment. A red alarm flashed on the main screen, and an artificial voice warned of their upcoming flight.

"I know, we're late. I'm sorry," Korinne said, pulling up a message on her handheld and keying in the code it gave her. When the light turned green, she turned to Magnolia. "The bots are all set?"

"Looks like it," Magnolia said from where she looked at her own handheld. She swiped a few times before nodding. "Cameras are mostly in place, map has been uploaded, and our luggage is waiting in our rooms."

"Damn. We're really doing this," Korinne said as the shuttle rumbled to life.

Magnolia clapped her hands before wrapping her arms around Korinne's shoulders. "We really are!"

Korinne stiffened at the contact, though really she wanted to melt into it. Magnolia, probably misinterpreting the reaction, let go and put a respectable distance between them. That was fine, Korinne told herself. They had a job to do, and she couldn't let something silly like *feelings* get in the way of it.

Instructions flashed on the screens, telling them to find their seats and buckle up. As the shuttle rose, Korinne watched the object of so many late nights grow closer and closer. As they approached, the wide expanse of the ship's hull managed to block two of the three suns from view. Scrapes and gashes decorated the gray outer covering thanks to hundreds of years worth of collisions with space debris. If the outside of the ship showed that much age, Korinne was nervous to see the state of the inside. Along the side, faded paint displayed the words *Loss of Self for the Success of All*, the ship's motto singing loud even after all this time.

The shuttle stopped, and a cool voice instructed them to wait for the airlock. It hissed as it connected, sealing them from the cold emptiness of space. Excitement had Korinne shifting from foot to foot. Here it was, her magnum opus, the thing she'd been working toward ever since she started her graduate degree. If the next three days went well and she successfully defended her dissertation, she'd finally qualify to work on the restoration crew.

"Ready?" she asked as the doors slid open.

"Ready," Magnolia said, matching her smile.

They checked the comm pads in their chest harnesses, making sure they were stable and recording. Magnolia gently carded her fingers through Korinne's short, dark curls as Korinne ignored the tingles that rose everywhere she touched. In return, Korinne made sure Magnolia's makeup wasn't smudged in any places—not that it ever was. Then, it was time to go.

Their steps echoed in the quiet bay as they walked onto the ship. Faded paint on the walls and floor gave directions and safety instructions. The metal doors and glass windows told of old techniques from a faraway place. The whole setup was so similar to interstream period pieces that Korinne almost expected to see her favorite characters come around the corner. Magnolia paused and placed her hand on the gray plastic wall, which looked positively ancient compared to the common polymers they used now.

"Come see this, Rinne," she said in her dreamy way. "You can really feel the history."

"I think that's called tetanus. I read an article about it once," Korinne said, though she followed Magnolia's instructions.

Magnolia removed her hand so she could smack her arm. "Korinne!"

"What? It's a real problem," she said.

"You have to be nice. Ghosts could be listening." But Magnolia didn't touch the wall again. In fact, Korinne caught with her eyes and comm pad camera as Magnolia stealthily wiped her palm on her floral skirt.

"Nothing's listening except the germs coating the place." Korinne cleaned her own hand with much more gusto; the black fake leather pants had taken worse hits before. "The only sentient beings here are you and me."

As if to spite her words, their bots, Bitt and Efex, rolled through a side door and buzzed their displeasure. Magnolia shot Korinne a glare before patting the bot's tallest cameras, which their manufacturer had designed to look like binoculars. Their "eyes" came to Korinne's waist, and their compact cuboid bodies housed more power than one might expect. After all, they dragged in everything the women would need for this journey.

"Don't listen to her," Magnolia said as Bitt chirped. "You two count."

Efex grumbled, and Bitt reached out with a telescoping arm

to poke its broad side. Efex, of course, reached back with its own arm to poke Bitt. The two went back and forth until Korinne stepped between them.

"Hey now. No fighting, kids. We've got a job to do, and the ship is about to take off." She needed them to cover a lot of ground over the next three days, which meant limited time for robot squabbles. Efex let out a low whistle and wheeled past them toward a cargo closet. It took two slaps of its robot hand for the door to slide open, and it sighed a very human-sounding sigh when it found the closet full.

"I know, existence is a struggle," Korinne said, trying not to laugh and making sure to capture the whole ordeal. Their merch of Efex and Bitt sold the best out of everything in their online shop, so she had to get enough footage to satisfy all their adoring fans.

Efex lined up at the wall. When Bitt rolled next to it, it slapped Bitt again. Magnolia whistled before they could start all over.

"Behave, please!" she said. Both bots made noises almost like an apology, then deployed their stabilizers. Korinne bit back the feeling of being the second-favorite parent. "Thank you."

Once they were settled, Korinne gave a wicked smile. "Shall we?"

Magnolia beamed. "We shall."

Korinne gestured for her to go first, and Magnolia curtseyed before moving to the main ship door. She placed her palm on the pad with gusto, really hamming it up for the camera. They waited. And waited.

"Uh, Mags?" Korinne said, trying to keep herself from laughing.

A line appeared between Magnolia's lavender brows. "Yes?"

"It only reads pressure, not your prints."

"Oh, hells." Magnolia slapped her hand against the pad again, and a green light blinked. "Victory!"

Magnolia raised her arms high until the door creaked open. The metal-on-metal squeal made her quickly drop her hands to cover her ears. Korinne did the same, the sound so loud she swore she felt it in her teeth.

"Holy shit, I should've brought oil or something. That was terrible," Korinne said once the door stood open.

Magnolia glared over her shoulder. "She just needs some tender loving care, Rinne."

"That's literally my goal, to fix her up."

Magnolia's eyes lit up. "Oh, right!"

She spun and placed her hands on either side of the frame to prevent the door from sliding closed again, addressing the comm pad on Korinne's chest.

"In case you didn't know, after her time on the ship, Korinne will then be eligible to defend her dissertation on structural internal changes to the *Arkana* and how they correlated with societal standards of its occupants."

Korinne blinked. "You remember my dissertation topic?" Magnolia had said it word for word.

"We may have been drunk, but I distinctly remember the discussion. Besides, I could never completely scrub off the pro and con list we made on the wall. Anyway, as part of this adventure, she'll get to observe as the captain lands the *Arkana*. Who knows, maybe he'll need a second set of hands?" She wiggled her eyebrows.

"Doubtful," she said. "There's professionals for that."

"You took a class on it, you'd be fine. Let's go!"

Korinne, who planned to edit that sidebar out later, yelped as Magnolia grabbed her wrist and led her through the door, where they found men in helmeted exosuits waiting.

"Whoa, what the hell?"

Korinne pulled Magnolia behind her. They were supposed to be alone on the ship this week; that was the agreement. Just them, the bots, and the captain. Who the hell were all these guys?

"Rinne, look." Magnolia pointed at the men's feet, which levitated several inches in the air. The suits were, in fact, empty and hanging. No inhabitants, just old tech left behind when no one needed to space walk anymore.

Korinne let out a breathy laugh. "I think that's the first time I've gotten scared on one of these trips," she said.

"Please, we've been scared loads of times before," Magnolia said.

Korinne raised a brow, then bowed her head and spoke to the comm pad. "Note to editing Korinne, add in a compilation of Mags getting scared at nothing here."

Magnolia swatted her backside and stepped out from behind her. "You're the worst."

Korinne rubbed the stinging flesh. Damn, Magnolia could hit when she wanted to. "I'm just giving the people what they want."

Past the airlock antechamber, the area opened into a large hallway lined with rusty metal and several branching pathways. On the floor, different lines ran down each hall and occasionally turned toward closed doors. More faded letters spelled out the ship's motto again, *Loss of Self for the Success of All* ghosting across the surface.

"Huh, that's weird," Korinne said as she eyed the empty hallway. "I thought the captain was supposed to meet us here."

"Yeah, that's what his message said. Maybe he got busy? We *are* running late," Magnolia said as she, too, searched for someone who wasn't there.

"I mean, we're not *that* late," Korinne grumbled, as if she wasn't the reason for their tardiness.

Overhead, the ship-wide speakers crackled as the captain came online. "Ladies, thank you for joining me. Please find your seats. We're taking off in five minutes."

Korinne pointed at the speaker. "See? We're right on time. Now, where are we sitting?"

She didn't care for the smile gracing Magnolia's beautiful face.

"The inner ring seating deck," she said.

Somehow, that was worse than Korinne expected. "You mean the same place that blew up during the original liftoff?"

"Exactly! The perfect spot," Magnolia said, far too cheerful. "What are the odds the engine blows up twice?"

If Korinne were superstitious, she'd find some wood to touch after such a proclamation. "Statistically? You really want to know?"

Magnolia ignored her and instead focused on pulling up the map on her handheld. "Not in the slightest. Come along now."

She dragged her over to the elevator and pressed the button. It took an agonizingly long time for the lift to arrive. Though it had been the height of technology back in the day, the elevators travelled quite a bit slower than the ones they were accustomed to. At least they went every direction in the cylindrical ship, which would help with travel time to their various planned locations.

Magnolia pressed the proper buttons for their destination. The elevator carried them as fast as it could to the innermost ring of the ship and dropped them off in an empty cargo area. Blue emergency lights lit their path, but not much else, forcing them to grab flashlights from their bags. Instead of the wide open areas the outer rings boasted, the inner rings held narrow hallways arranged in a grid, each branch marked with a letter and a number. Engine sounds roared above them, so loud Korinne had to shout into the comm pad and hope her words came out clear in editing.

"Originally, this level was for folks who boarded mere minutes before the ship took off. We all know the story: people bought their space, but when the time came, didn't claim their seat for one reason or another. With each person who didn't show, someone from the lottery line got a seat. The next level out was also used for this, but I assume we're sitting here because so many people lost their lives in this area that day."

"Exactly," Magnolia said. "More than likely, when we take off again, those spirits will have their say one last time."

"So you're really risking our lives just to try and prove your point?" Korinne tilted her head to the side. It wasn't like Magnolia to do something so dangerous, or potentially creepy. She really was going all out for this last trip.

"Of course I am," Magnolia said. "If I die convincing you ghosts are real, then I'll die happy."

Magnolia punched another panel, and the door slid open with an almost human-like scream. The dark, narrow room stretched further than their flashlights reached. Plastic seats with dangling seat belts lined both walls. The ones situated away from the door showed little signs of the passage of time, but the closer chairs had burn marks and dark stains that looked suspiciously like blood.

Magnolia took over the history portion. "They were able to fix the engines without stopping liftoff thanks to engineering redundancy, but they couldn't address what happened here until forty-eight hours after. Even then, it was more about repurposing rather than fixing. I bet so many spirits linger here, since people died so fast and so young. Do you feel that? Something's definitely different as soon as you walk in the door."

"Yeah, there's a hole in the wall," Korinne said, pointing to her left.

Parts of the wall sank in, and black tarps covered a number of empty spaces. She knew they'd be visiting this area at some point, but figured it would be later, once the ship was safely traveling. Not right as the engines fully kicked on for the first time in decades.

"Why didn't they fix it at the time?"

She gave the leading question as Magnolia circled the area, trailing her fingertips over the tops of the chairs.

"They didn't have the resources," Magnolia explained, perfect as always with her recitation of the research Korinne compiled. "There were some supplies set aside for disasters, but with the extent of the damage, they decided it was better to clean the area and repurpose it for storage. This opened up other areas as living quarters."

"And what did they do with the bodies?"

Korinne had to add that question. It was morbid, yes, but the more macabre they got, the more viewers liked it.

"As the first losses of life during the trip, they chose to bury them at sea. Or, well, at space." Magnolia sounded a little too sad, a little too honest.

She opened her mouth to try again, but Korinne cut her off; she liked when they showed some realness to the audience instead of perfect presentations.

"I feel like space debris would be a pretty awesome afterlife. Way better than going to the reclamation tanks," she said.

"They wouldn't still be attached to their bodies, Rinne," Magnolia said, as if that were obvious.

"Oh, right," Korinne said. "Some of them are probably still attached to these walls."

"Korinne!" Magnolia put a hand to her chest, but Korinne laughed.

"They're not here anymore, Mags," she said.

"Don't disrespect the ghosts!" Magnolia was getting worked up now, which was exactly what Korinne—and the viewers— wanted. Five years, and she still fell for it every damn time.

"That's literally my job. Disrespecting 'ghosts' is my strongest skill." She made sure to lay on the air quotes extra thick.

"You're going to get us in trouble someday," Magnolia said, eyes wide.

"A girl can only hope," Korinne replied. "All right. Which one of these rusty buckets are we strapping ourselves into?"

A man cleared his throat, which sent Korinne's heart rate right into overdrive. Magnolia squealed, and Korinne hoped to every deity she didn't believe in that the comm pad picked it up.

"Holy hells," Magnolia said, gasping as Captain Armand stepped into the light. "Captain, Sir, why would you sneak up on us like that?"

"Didn't sneak," he said with a shrug. He was a slender, older man, and dressed the part of the first ship captain with a white uniform and brass nameplate. It certainly was a choice, but people did odd things when they knew they'd be on camera. She appreciated his dedication to accuracy at least. "I came to warn you—now's your last chance to change your minds."

"Oh no, we're not changing our minds," Korinne said. They'd worked way too hard to turn back now. "We're not scared of an old ship. You said it can fly, and we believe you."

"You sure?" He looked at Magnolia this time. She stood to her full height and nodded once.

"Absolutely," she said. "There are stories to be told, and we want to hear them."

The captain huffed a laugh. "You'll hear something, all

right. Anyway, we have a pretty simple procedure for takeoff. Strap into the seats, and make sure you pull the all the belts tight. You won't hear the countdown as the engines fire up, so you'll just have to stay ready. I'll announce over the intercom once we reach cruising velocity and it's safe for you to get up. The flight pattern itself is on autopilot, so if you need anything, let me know and I can help."

"Aye, aye," Korinne said with a half-assed salute. Magnolia caught her hand and shoved it down. He gave them one long, lingering look before leaving them with their decisions. With nothing left to stop them, they took their seats and buckled the seatbelts around the comm pad holsters.

Magnolia took a deep breath. "This is going to be amazing," she said.

Korinne triple checked her seatbelt, then turned to Magnolia, her eyes alight. Her friend gazed back with equal excitement. On impulse, Korinne reached out and squeezed her hand, letting out an uncharacteristic squeal. This was, far and away, the best way to end their series.

The rumble increased, the chairs beneath them vibrating until numbness settled in Korinne's legs. A low creak sounded, followed by a loud crash. The ship lurched. She grabbed her seatbelt and fought to breathe.

This was fine, it would all be fine. The ship wasn't going to burst into a million pieces. They were going to take off, hang out for a few days, then relax on a beach somewhere on the *Arkana's* new planet.

"Is anyone with us right now?" Magnolia called out to the air around them. Oh, right, they had a job to do. "My name is Magnolia! This is Korinne!"

"Fuck!" screamed Korinne as the ship jolted again.

"You're probably scared, huh? You've experienced this before, right? When the ship took off the first time?"

Another quake went through the ship. It shot up, sending Korinne's stomach into her shoes. Something low growled in the background, different from the ship sounds.

"If you're here with us now, please communicate." Committed, Magnolia pulled a palm-sized light from her bag. Normally, she would put it on something sturdy to give the ghosts ample breathing room, but the shaking ship prevented that. "This light only needs a little energy. If you're here with us, please turn it on."

"Mags, for real?"

The ship jumped again, then shoved them to the left. The shaking grew so violent she couldn't form words, only gasp for air.

As the ship rumbled to life, the light in Magnolia's hand flipped on and off, on and off. Viewers would call it ghosts, but it was probably due to electromagnetic interference, or Magnolia fighting to keep a hold on it. Easily explainable either way.

The ship lifted and pulled out of orbit. It leapt forward, shoving Korinne deep into the hard seat. For a few agonizing minutes, she fought the pull. The straps dug into her skin, and a jolt went through her as one strap partially tore. It couldn't be long now; she just needed it to hold a little longer.

The velocity evened out, allowing her to breathe. Her skin tingled as the pressure of the belts released. The engines quieted, as did the light in Magnolia's hand.

They were officially off.

CHAPTER 2
MAGNOLIA

*From camera 15.3.20: [a light sparks in front of the
engine room as the engines kick on]*

MAGNOLIA HAD NO DOUBT the *Arkana* held more
spirits than the rest of their adventures combined, and it was
too easy to imagine wading through them as she unclipped
from her seat and followed the blue floor lights back to the
elevator. The engines rumbled just right to make it sound like
whispers followed them down the hall. But like a real trooper,
she only complained about the goosebumps on her arms once.

As a kid, she could always tell when there was someone
else in the room, someone no one except her could see. Only
her Vaelish grandfather took these declarations seriously and
encouraged her to seek it further. The rest of her family—all
Earthers—asked her to keep those sensations to herself. But
even he changed his tune after she had a bout of a mysterious
illness that he called a "soul sickness," presenting her with her
Grandma Josie's old pendant to "protect her from the spirits".

When he passed, he left one instruction: keep it on, and don't listen to the voices.

As a teenager, she tried taking it off once. But that led to a suspiciously timed bout of nightmares, odd scratches, and the same weird illness she'd experienced as a kid, so she decided it was in her best interest to keep it on. It obviously kept dark spirits at bay, which made her feel brave when she and Korinne visited these terrifying places.

Watching their first episodes now made her cringe. Too excited by the camera, she'd really leaned into her "ghost senses." After that led to nothing but mean comments, she'd decided to focus more on collecting hard evidence via nice, expensive equipment. All of which she lugged onto the ship for this final adventure.

"Which spot are you most excited for?" Magnolia asked.

Korinne smirked in a way that made her heart stutter. "The hospital, of course," she said.

Magnolia's heart palpitated again, but for an entirely different reason.

"Why the hospital?" she asked, her mouth dry.

"'Cause even the thought of it makes you look like that."

Magnolia sighed and pressed the button for the elevator. "Why do you always torture me?"

"I'm contractually obligated, of course."

As they stepped on and Magnolia pressed the right buttons, Korinne pulled her comm pad out of its harness and stopped the recording, which was in direct opposition to Magnolia's goals. What if they heard or saw something on the way to their rooms? She needed the equipment on at all times because, so help her, she would prove once and for all that ghosts were *real*.

"Hey, turn that back on," Magnolia said.

"Why? It's just gonna record the floor," Korinne replied.

"You never know when something might pop up," she said. Then, because viewers loved the dramatics, "In fact, I think I read that your room is the most haunted place on the entire ship. It was a multi-generational murder house or something. So keep it rolling."

"Hey now," Korinne said, brandishing a finger. "I can accept the soft evidence of your machines, but I draw the line at fake history."

"Please? It's automatically backing up to the hard drive, you don't have to worry about space," Magnolia said. She gave Korinne her widest eyes and poutiest lip.

After a few seconds, she gave in. "Fine, I'll keep it on. But if I don't capture a full apparition in the next five minutes, you owe me five credits."

"Deal." She probably owed Korinne around a thousand credits, but thank the gods she never collected.

"Very well. Your wish is my command, my liege," Korinne said with a fake bow.

"You're obnoxious," Magnolia replied.

"I love you too, dearest."

Something shifted in Magnolia's chest, and she rubbed her sternum to dissipate the sensation. She had to keep herself focused, so she didn't do something completely stupid. There was a lot of ship to cover, a lot of video to go through, and a lot of secrets to solve before they landed on the new planet, Capa Emphara. She couldn't afford distractions, even cute ones with pretty brown eyes and a bad attitude.

"Ah, shit," Korinne said, startling her. "I think Efex is stuck."

"What?"

The bot never had problems before—it was just Magnolia's luck for it to start now. On the screen, a white dot blinked at Efex's location. Sure enough, it sat stationary, evidently struggling with one of the last cameras. She scanned the area until she found Bitt's location, but its dot inched steadily down a hall eight rings out.

Korinne sighed and tapped the screen. "Efex? You all right?"

The dot turned green, indicating Efex was chirping, or at least trying to. No sounds came from the speaker.

"Is your volume up?" Magnolia asked.

"Of course..." Korinne trailed off, then clicked the wheel for settings. When she found the volume on, she continued, "Of course it is."

Magnolia stifled a smile and touched the screen again. "Efex? Can you send a ping?"

The light blinked green at irregular intervals, but no noise came and no ping landed in their messages. Magnolia let out a frustrated sigh; they'd paid good money for these bots, and they were supposed to last at least a decade. Perhaps it was the comm pad? Korinne must've had the same thought, because she tapped Bitt's name.

"Bitt, can you hear us?" she asked. Bitt's high chatter came through loud and clear, and it sent a ping.

Yes, is there a problem?

Its dot stopped moving on the screen.

"No problem," Magnolia said. "Just checking things. Sorry for interrupting."

Another ping came through. *It's okay!*

The cheery bot continued on, returning to its task. Korinne frowned.

"Should we ask it to check on Efex?" she asked.

Magnolia shook her head. "No, let's go check ourselves. I don't want to interrupt and then find out it's just some silly malfunction we can easily fix."

Or, if it was interference from a ghost, she wanted to

capture the evidence herself. Could she be lucky enough to win on the first day?

It took a deceptively long time to reach Efex's location thanks to distance and road blocks. The mid-level rings had wider walkways and open areas, but also more damage. Broken columns and collapsed walls slowed them around every corner, but they arrived to find the actual room relatively intact. Magnolia didn't mind the obstacle course—the more terrible a location looked, the more people loved it.

Efex had stopped in a dark cafeteria complete with long metal tables and benches bolted to the floors. It wasn't one of the most active places on their list, but it did have a few consistent reports back when the ship allowed visitors. As soon as they passed through the sliding doors, a charge raced through her. Her pendant even grew warm on her skin, and her subconscious went haywire in a new and exciting way. Oh, they *definitely* needed the camera in here.

"There it is," Korinne said, sweeping her flashlight to the far corner. Efex sat there unmoving, its lights flashing yellow and red. "Efex? You okay?"

Nothing. A cold stone settled in Magnolia's stomach. Usually, Efex wouldn't shut up, and its silence freaked her out. It didn't even turn its binoculars their way.

"God damn it," Korinne muttered, crossing the room in as long of strides as her short legs could make. Magnolia followed, both to film Korinne assessing the problem and to give her space to scan the area. Unfortunately, no matter how many times she pointed her flashlight at the dark areas, no ghosts appeared.

Efex had both of its hands out, grasping a camera on a tiny tripod. It hadn't turned it on yet. In fact, it hadn't even activated the magnets on the bottom of the stand. Its telescoping arms periodically moved backward and forward in tiny intervals, as if caught in the final placement.

"All right, let's see what's going on here," Korinne said.

Korinne sat next to the bot and pressed a few buttons, but got no response. Magnolia, useless when it came to most electronics, let her mechanic work while she continued her search. The hairs on the back of her neck rose, but no matter how hard she looked, she found nothing but tables and shadows.

With a sigh, she turned back. "Anything?"

Korinne had Efex's back panel open, its wires and motherboard on full display. Oh, it would be so embarrassed when it came back online.

An annoyed breath escaped her. "Not that I can see." She poked around a little more. "Everything is connected, all the circuit lights are on, communications parts are online... I'm at a loss."

Magnolia joined her on the metal floor and did her best to understand what was in front of her, but she only saw a mess of wires and screws. Out of the corner of her eye, she spotted Korinne's grin.

"What's the diagnosis, doc?" Korinne asked.

"Hmm," Magnolia said, tapping her chin. "I think something might be messed up."

Korinne snorted. "Well, you're not wrong."

She reached in with a screwdriver and carefully moved wires this way and that, trying to see past them. Like a good assistant, Magnolia held the flashlight *almost* where Korinne needed it and waited patiently for instructions. The back of her head tingled the whole time, like she was being watched. As bad as she wanted to be dramatic about it, she swallowed it down. They could fix the bot first, and then she could freak out properly where the camera could capture it.

"Mags?" Korinne paused her search and turned.

Magnolia jumped. "Yes?" she asked. Korinne wore her concerned expression, which usually didn't come out until much later in their investigations. "What?"

"You're like, super tense," she said.

Magnolia made a conscious effort to relax her shoulders and unclench her fists.

"Sorry, this place just has a really weird vibe," she said, gesturing behind them.

Korinne twisted around to face the supposedly empty room. "Do you want to take a break for a second? We've been running around a lot this morning. It might be good to stop and get our bearings."

Magnolia shook her head and gritted her teeth; she would *not* be done in by this final trip, and especially not on the first day. "No, I'm okay. Thank you, though," she said, even if she really did want to go lay down for at least a good hour after rushing and taking off on an actual spaceship.

"Okay, well, if you need me to go over there and"—she threw her hands out in a few wild punches—"you just let me know."

She made that joke every time, and every time it made Magnolia laugh. "You can't fight ghosts, Rinne."

"What? Bullshit," Korinne said. She put down her tools and stood. "Watch me."

"Rinne!"

In Magnolia's opinion, it was way too early to antagonize a whole gaggle of ghosts. But Korinne didn't care, because she didn't think they were real. Antagonizing ghosts was her favorite pastime.

"Fuck off, ghosts." She performed a wild array of punches and kicks in a phenomenal display of athleticism.

"You missed one," Magnolia said, pointing to her left. Dutifully, Korinne jumped in that direction, swinging her arms like a cartoon character. Magnolia laughed again as the stress dissipated. Now, the room seemed like just a room, with old tables and nothing more. No lingering spirits waited to eat her soul when she wasn't looking. "Thank you, my knight in shining leather," Magnolia said as Korinne settled back down next to Efex.

"These pants aren't leather, they just look like it," she said, her problem-solving face back on as she analyzed the inner workings of the bot.

"Knight in shining fake leather, then," Magnolia amended. She leaned in close, as if she could offer any illuminating information. Then she whispered, "By the way, I caught all of that on camera."

"Good," Korinne whispered back. "I'll use it for my highlight reel. Ah!"

Magnolia jerked back. "What?"

"Found it!" Korinne said.

Magnolia put a hand on her forehead and forced an inhale. "I swear, sometimes it's like you enjoy scaring me," she said.

"Only sometimes? I need to be more obvious then." Korinne frowned, and her eyes narrowed as she poked around with the screwdriver. "Okay, you're not lighting up, but why?"

She was back in her zone, and all Magnolia could do was hold the flashlight. The silence stretched, and the levity Korinne provided moments before slowly dissipated, replaced again with discomfort. Magnolia glanced over her shoulder; was she imagining things, or were the shadows moving? The temperature dropped a few degrees, and pressure built in her chest. A sting erupted under her pendant, sharp enough that she checked to see if she was bleeding.

"What the hells?" She turned completely but stayed seated, making sure the camera on her comm pad could catch whatever she might see. She'd never deny having a certain instinct for ghostly presences, but these sensations seemed excessive, even for her.

"Mags, what—oh," Korinne said.

"Just looking for something," Magnolia said.

"Right, carry on. I'll just prop the flashlight here."

It took a few seconds before Magnolia realized she needed to change her tactics. Watching wouldn't be enough, not anymore. If she wanted results, she had to go after them. She flipped the comm pad camera to the infrared setting and cleared her throat.

"Did you have anything to do with this?" She directed the question to the room. Something in her tone of voice must've clued Korinne in, because she didn't answer except to say,

"If they did, tell them to either fix it or fuck off."

"They can hear you just fine, darling," Magnolia said. Sometimes she wished ghosts couldn't hear her, if she was honest. "If you messed with our bot, please come fix it. It was very expensive, and we need it for this trip."

A shadow shifted in her periphery. Oh, something was *definitely* in the room with them. She held her breath and tried not to stare at the door, where it felt like she could sense a presence just outside her vision. It had been decades since she felt like this; was the ship so haunted that it dialed her instincts up to an eleven? She checked the screen of her comm pad, but the temperature fluctuations it caught held no pattern, no sure outline of a person.

"Can you fix the bot?" Magnolia asked again.

"You talking to me or the ghost?" Korinne muttered.

"The ghost. I have full faith in you," she replied. She held her breath, feeling like she stood on the edge of a cliff. "Damn, these ghosts are going to be a problem, I can feel it."

"And that, folks, is what we call foreshadowing to a self-fulfilling prophecy," Korinne said. The jab was for the viewers, and Magnolia snorted despite herself.

"Rude," she said, so her response could be included. Then, she added, "That was a good one."

"Thank you, it came naturally. Here we go!"

Something clicked, and Magnolia spun back around. Machinery whirred as Efex came back online. Its little lights blinked in rapid succession, then maintained a steady glow.

"Good morning, sunshine," Magnolia said. The bot made a noise that almost sounded like a groan.

Korinne gently closed its back panel. "How did you end up with your robot brainstem turned off?"

Efex let out a long, drawn-out noise. It sounded like a human thinking, though Magnolia knew it was running diagnostics. A ping landed on their handhelds.

No interference found.

"What's the last thing you have recorded?" Magnolia asked.

It beeped a few more times, then a file arrived. She opened the video, leaning over so Korinne could see too. In it, they watched as Efex held the camera on its stand. Before it could bolt it down, a loud crash sounded from behind it. It rotated its camera to see the room, but nothing out of the ordinary showed on video. Another bang echoed through the room with no apparent source. Then, darkness as Efex went offline.

"Well, I don't care for that one bit," Korinne said, and Magnolia had to agree. "Did you see anything in that?"

"No, we'll have to go back and check it frame by frame. Probably just stuff falling, but I couldn't see anything that would've sent the bot offline." The camera caught no shadows or human-shaped things where they shouldn't be. "Efex, you're sure you can't find anything with diagnostics?"

It squealed so loud, Magnolia thought her skull might

burst. She clapped her hands over her ears, wincing as she accidentally hit herself with her flashlight. Almost as soon as it started, it stopped. Another ping came through.

No interference found.

"Oh yeah? You're just gonna act like that didn't happen?" Korinne asked, massaging her temples. Magnolia understood her ire; the interruption wasn't just annoying, it was painful. And almost a sure sign that something was deeply wrong with their very expensive bot besides a ghost messing with it.

Efex beeped a curious noise, and Magnolia patted its head.

"I know, buddy. You're doing a great job," she said. It cooed and turned its binoculars under her hand.

"How about you go sit and run a full panel of diagnostics?" Korinne said.

Efex let out a sound somewhat akin to a huff and pinged them.

I'll finish this and hand off to Bitt.

"Good idea. We'll check in later."

Korinne stood and dusted off her not-leather pants, then offered a hand to Magnolia. She allowed herself to be heaved to her feet, then daintily shook the dust from her skirts as her mind spun. If the ghosts could damage the bots...that wasn't good.

"I wonder if the gravity generators are messing with the tech. We should check on Bitt too," Korinne said, leading her toward the door.

"I don't think it was the ship," Magnolia said. The presence from before continued hovering in her periphery, but disappeared any time she looked straight on. "There's a lot of weird energy around here. And electronics hate ghosts."

They passed through the door, and a shudder ran down Magnolia's spine. She spun, hoping to lay an eye—and a camera —on whatever energy lingered, but once again found nothing.

"Did you feel anything there?" she asked Korinne.

Korinne stopped and took stock, then shook her head. "No, sorry. No drafts or anything, no vibrations, no sounds." She did her due diligence, examining the area. "Anything specific?"

"Just when we went through the door," Magnolia replied.

Korinne walked back over to the door and glared with narrowed eyes. "Haunted door, you think?" she asked, and once again Magnolia felt her unease melt.

"Definitely," she said. Only Korinne could calm her frazzled nerves like this.

Korinne nodded, and casually walked through the opening. When nothing happened, she backed out. After a dramatic pause, she completed the cycle another three times at varying speeds until she had Magnolia giggling.

"They're not biting for me," Korinne said. "Come on, ghosts. Fuck me up. You're gonna mess with my friend but leave me alone? Weak. I've met specters with more gumption than you."

"I think specter is just a synonym for ghost," Magnolia said.

"According to the dictionary, yes," Korinne said. "According to some very opinionated commenters? Absolutely not, and we're frauds for suggesting as such."

"Eh, people will find any reason to call us frauds. Might as well have some fun in the meantime," Magnolia said.

Efex rolled up to them, then stopped halfway out of the door. Its gears turned, and a low noise echoed from its machinery. It almost sounded like a growl. But since when did their bot growl?

The sound stopped. Efex, seemingly unaware, rolled out of the room completely. Magnolia made eye contact with Korinne.

"Yeah, it's definitely a diagnostic cocktail for you, buddy," she said.

It rolled by, and Magnolia leaned down to pat the spot where its brain sat. The metal, usually hot from all the processes beneath it, was ice cold on her fingers. When she touched it, the shadow appeared in the corner. When she let go, the shadow disappeared.

"Its temperature is off," Magnolia said, because addressing the bot instead of the shadow would be an easier conversation.

"Huh?" Korinne said. She came up and touched the same spot. "Weird. Must be because it was offline for so long. It'll warm up again soon, I'm sure."

Magnolia touched the spot again. This time, no shadow appeared, and already the metal felt closer to its usual temperature. Perhaps she could give Korinne that one.

"All right, where to next?" Korinne asked, already moving on.

Magnolia suppressed a shudder and tried to focus. "Let's grab the rest of our stuff from the rooms and get this show on the road. We've got a lot to do."

Something here was very, very wrong. And she was going to figure out what.

CHAPTER 3
CASSIE

From camera 1.19.72: [three thumps sound, like a ball bouncing]

THESE GIRLS WERE FUCKING IDIOTS.

Granted, Cassie was also a bit of an idiot. But how was she supposed to know her little ghost hand would fuck up that robot? She hadn't seen any technological upgrades in... How long was it? She couldn't tell anymore. Time worked differently after death. The point was, these girls were dumb. These little shits would be stuck on the ship while it traveled, and Cassie knew better than most that there was no escape in space.

The first ten or so years after the Earthers went down to Vaela, while the ship hung in orbit, they had a ton of ghost hunter visitors to amuse Cassie. But she supposed some higher ups shut it down, because until a couple of months ago, the ship just floated empty in space, miles away from anyone living.

Then the show started. She'd watched the mechanic crew fix up the engines. Then, she'd seen the captain plan the path they'd take to the new planet to reunite the ship with its sister. This hadn't surprised her; she'd assumed they'd figure out what to do with the ship at some point or another. But then the two robots came in with a metric fuck ton of stuff. Cassie had to do her due diligence and see what the silly-looking cuboid things did, spending most of the morning watching them roll around and put hundreds of little cameras up. Cameras she understood; these bots, she didn't. So she got a little too curious and accidentally short-circuited one.

It turned out to be a blessing in disguise, because then she got to meet the two dumbest women in the galaxy, who thought running around on a haunted spaceship talking at ghosts for three whole days was a good idea.

They weren't the first ghost hunters to investigate the ship, just the first ones in a long time. And with the ship actually powered up, they'd probably see a lot more stuff than the ones who came before them.

Now, if only Cassie could figure out how the hell the purple one—Magnolia?—managed to look *right at her* so many times. She was on stealth mode, she checked! The dark and surly one didn't have a clue, that much was obvious thanks to her putting on a show for her girlfriend and pirouetting through like, ten half-materialized ghost friends and scaring them back to the in-between.

"Think they can handle it?" Cassie asked her companion, a white, three-legged terrier named Baxter. Baxter wagged his tail harder, nearly losing his balance. "Yeah, we'll see."

They followed the girls to their rooms, but once Baxter realized neither one of them planned to pet him, he bounded off. Cassie leaned just outside the door, eavesdropping as they discussed their plans and flirted back and forth. The one in all black—Korinne, if Cassie overheard right—said they needed to cover as much area as possible.

Cassie scoffed and stuffed her hands into the pockets of her gray jumpsuit. "Oh, so you're like, really dumb." Even in all her time dead, she hadn't met every ghost on the entire ship. More than a few mischievous characters wandered the halls, including herself. But ghosts could only do so much damage, and it had been a long time since Cassie got to watch living people freak out.

Yeah, she'd stick around for a minute, just to see what they found.

Baxter chose that moment to come back and bring his pink ball with him. He dropped it at Cassie's feet, and with all his energy and excitement, it made an audible *thump-thump-thump*.

Inside the room, one of the women gasped. "What was that?"

Magnolia sounded nervous. Must be her genetics; the purple people who first visited the ship always did seem to understand the ghost situation better than the Old Earth descendants like Cassie.

"Probably nothing," said Korinne. "This thing is gonna creak and pop a lot, remember that."

"You say that, but I'm definitely going to assume every sound is a ghost," Magnolia said.

Baxter pawed Cassie's ankle, right where the bone stuck out. She bit back a grunt and moved her foot away.

"Now is not the time to play," she hissed. Baxter looked up with his one eye full of pleading, and she sighed. "Okay, fine. I still don't understand how you managed to bring a ball with you into the afterlife."

She grabbed the ball—slobbery, even in death—and chucked it. It sailed down the open hallway and passed through the floor. Perfect. Baxter shot off after it; he loved a hunt—the more difficult the better.

Cassie decided to get a little closer and phased into the room with the two women. Tingles shot through her as her spirit separated into minuscule particles and slipped between the atoms making up the door. It wasn't comfortable, but she'd gotten used to it over the past however many years.

Korinne sat in front of Magnolia discussing the cameras and all the technical stuff associated with them. Such a waste of time—no matter how fancy the camera, it wouldn't be powerful enough to catch anything unless the ghosts used enough ship energy to make it happen. And they rarely decided to use their resources like that.

Cassie wandered around the room. The women certainly made themselves at home, with piles of pillows all over the bed and a whole army of lotions lined up on the nightstand. Where there weren't pastel pillows and soft blankets, there were empty boxes where a million cameras started their journey. Cassie let out a long-suffering sigh. People never learned.

Magnolia looked right at her. Again.

Oops, did she accidentally sigh out loud? With so much energy readily available for the first time in a while, Cassie would have to get used to controlling it. The last thing these girls needed was to randomly see a blonde woman with half of her head caved in.

Something about Magnolia made her nervous. She looked familiar, even though they hadn't had visitors since long before she was born. A weird sensation curled in the back of Cassie's head when her attention landed on her, a feeling that made her want to avoid Magnolia completely.

Too bad she was stubborn as hell. And after decades of boredom, she didn't mind trading a little discomfort for some entertainment. Those few years the higher ups allowed people to visit served as great fun for Cassie, who thought that since she died so young, she was allowed to get up to some shenanigans in the afterlife. It was only fair, she reckoned.

It felt like an hour before Magnolia looked away and they finished the recording, grabbing their equipment and heading to an outer level. And Cassie, obviously, went with them.

God, it was so much quieter in the outer levels. She always forgot that. The inner levels were a lot louder, which got old very fast. Was that her unfinished business? Just a good night's rest?

No, she'd tried that. But any time she fell asleep, she woke up disoriented and in the same place she died, which was pretty annoying. If she could just remember something from her life, anything besides the name of one single woman, maybe she could figure it out. But no, she and someone named Rose stayed in the dark.

The women turned down a different hallway, and Cassie jogged after them as fast as her limp allowed. As she rounded the corner, three kids greeted her, staring with freakishly wide eyes.

"Ah! God!" Cassie exclaimed, clutching her chest even though she had no heartbeat. Past the kids, Korinne and Magnolia continued down the empty hall. The kids' attention shifted to the women, and Cassie clapped her hands, dragging their attention back.

"Who are they?" one asked. He flickered out for a second, then back in. All this time, and he still couldn't figure out how to manage the energy right.

"Don't worry about them," she said. "Go find your tía."

Usually if the kids manifested, so did Silvia. But it had been a long time since Cassie last saw her.

The second kid wrinkled his nose. "What was that word?"

"Your auntie. Remember Silvia? Fuck, of course you don't—"

The third kid pointed, and the first disappeared completely. "You said a bad word!"

"No shit, I said a bad word," Cassie said. More people came out of the metalwork, all just as confused and ephemeral as the kids. She shoved the remaining two toward one of the more qualified adults and tried to continue pursuing her prey.

"Miss, do you know how to get out of here?" a man behind her asked.

"Uh..." Cassie paused, and even in those few seconds, the man flickered three times. Not worth it to explain it all. "Sure don't."

"Oh. Sorry Ms. Malone. Do you know who does?" The man furrowed his bushy gray brows, which deepened his wrinkles. Cassie looked down and once again cursed herself for dying in a stolen jumpsuit, the name *Malone* stitched in red on the iron-on patch. She didn't remember her real last name, but she knew that wasn't it. Hell, she didn't even remember what the jumpsuit signified.

"No, sorry." She hoped her smile was real enough, then turned on her heel and strode away.

The more energy flowed through the ship, the more ghosts appeared. Most of them faded almost as soon as they woke as others stole from them. Cassie, luckily, learned how to siphon from a professional, and thus had no trouble staying present as the others oscillated between the layers of the afterlife.

She dodged another ghost asking questions. "Go ask the first mate! I saw him by the Commons." It was a lie, but an effective one. The ghosts murmured to each other and wandered in that direction, away from Korinne and Magnolia. Half of them faded as they did, blinking back to sleep.

Good. Back to business.

It took a few tries, but she eventually found the women again, this time in a dark hallway. She remembered what the engineers said when they came to fix things up: they'd shunt power to the most important parts of the ship and keep the rest dark to preserve energy. Little did they know that would also keep too many ghosts from bugging the living passengers.

The lights the women set up made Magnolia's eyes flicker oddly, kind of the way Baxter's did. They also made it difficult to read the map on the wall, which had faded with time. Great, so the paint could fade away and move on, but she couldn't. Typical.

"Okay, here we go," Magnolia said, running her hands through her lavender hair.

"Hold on, you've got something there." Korinne leaned forward, reaching toward the other woman's face.

"What? Where?" Magnolia went stock still, eyes wide and lips parted.

Korinne poked her. "Oh wait, just a nose."

Magnolia tried to swat her hand away and missed by a mile. "Rinne! This is serious!"

"I know, you just make the cutest face when you're annoyed," Korinne said with a laugh.

Magnolia closed her eyes and took a steadying breath. "You're insufferable."

"Don't be too mean, I'll fall in love with you."

Cassie scoffed. "Oh my God, you make me want to die all over again." She had to turn away, the interaction both annoying her and sending a pang through her chest.

An eye glinted in the dark, and Cassie stopped. What could possibly be out here, and was it going after the two women bickering next to her? The thing in the engine room was supposed to be sealed, she'd watched Jocelyn do it. And even then, surely it couldn't reach down this far—

The eye moved, swaying left and right as it drew closer. Strong energy came from it, but Cassie couldn't name the emotion beyond profound triumph. A predator, catching sight of prey and knowing it would win. She took one step back, then another, preparing to what, fight? Then, the creature stepped into the light.

"Baxter, holy shit." The dog hobbled out, tail wagging. "What took you so long? Normally you're faster than that."

Baxter, of course, had no explanation. He dropped his ball and sat like a good boy, waiting for his sweet reward of attention. Because she was dead, not cruel, Cassie leaned down and scratched his cheeks, which earned extra tail wags against the floor. The first few made no sound, but his excitement overcame the partition between their world and the previous one. Three thumps echoed into the open central space.

"Shh, did you hear that?" Magnolia asked.

"Hear what?" Korinne said.

"It sounded like footsteps, maybe? I don't know. It was just a few of them."

Once again, Magnolia looked *right at them.* How did she keep doing that?

"Hello, is anyone here with us?" she asked.

Korinne perked a pierced eyebrow. "What would you even do if someone answered?" she said.

Magnolia shrugged. "Probably shit myself," she said honestly, and Cassie couldn't help but laugh. At least these two had a sense of humor, unlike most of the people who'd visited back in the day. "I'm Magnolia, and this is Korinne. Does anyone want to talk?"

"Not really, I'm still sussing you out," Cassie said. She picked up Baxter's ball and threw it again, and the dog soundlessly ran off.

"Sounds like they're not in the mood," Korinne said.

Magnolia dug into her bag and produced a narrow, palm-sized box with two antennae on it. A small screen took up half of the front. "Maybe we just need to make it easy for them."

She flipped a switch, and the tiny box let out a surge of energy that made Cassie feel like she could run through walls. Well, technically she could already do that. But it made her feel like she could've when she was alive. She was glad Baxter had run off, otherwise, he definitely would've caused some problems with a spike like that.

"Ah yes, the Mad Lib box," Korinne said.

"It's not a Mad Lib box," Magnolia muttered.

"Right, sorry about that, dearest."

So these two were dumb *and* disgusting. Their affection made something squeeze in Cassie's gut, but she ignored the sensation.

"Rinne, please, this is why people are always speculating in the comments," Magnolia said as she stood. Korinne cocked her head to the side.

"Oh, so you don't want to keep going with the whole 'will-they-won't-they' situation we've been playing up for two years?" she asked. If she noticed the emotion crossing Magnolia's face, she didn't show it.

Wait, did that mean they weren't together? They sure as hell acted like it. Maybe they were pretending not to be, for the cameras?

"That was the point of the line," Magnolia said. Korinne kept her face neutral, but Cassie didn't miss the slight pause before she answered.

"Right, of course."

"You're obsessed with each other," Cassie said. "What the hell are you two doing?"

Magnolia didn't hear her question, and instead raised her voice to talk to all of one ghost in the vicinity. "This is a Parabox. It'll make it easier for you to communicate. If you say something, the box will repeat it, as well as show it on the screen. Go on, give it a try. Can you say our names?"

"Our names," Cassie parroted. Her energy surged, but the box made no sound. "Uh, excuse you. Our names."

The box buzzed. "Names," an electronic voice said.

"Okay, smartass," Korinne said as Cassie barked a laugh.

"Oh, shit," Cassie said.

The box buzzed again. "Shit."

This time, Korinne laughed too. "I think this ghost is messing with us."

But Magnolia had grown very still. Cassie wandered closer to look at the machine; sure enough, her words appeared on the tiny screen.

Huh. Maybe she could fuck with them, just a little.

"Can you tell me your name? Since I told you ours?" Magnolia asked.

Cassie used her most intimidating voice. "Bill."

The box, of course, used the same electronic voice. But instead of saying the name, it said, "Real."

"Real?" Mags asked. "Yes, I believe you're real. It's Korinne who's the problem."

"No, not real," Cassie said. "I said Bill, you son of a—"

"Sunset," the box said.

"Sunset?" Magnolia looked to Korinne, who shrugged.

"Don't look at me, no sunsets in space," she said.

Cassie groaned. The box, of course, said, "Bug."

"This isn't making any sense," Magnolia said.

Korinne stepped away, scanning the area with the tablet strapped to her chest.

"It never does," she sang.

"I think you need a new one," Cassie said.

"Done," said the box.

"Fine, I can take a hint," Magnolia said, and switched the thing off.

"Guess they're not in a conversational mood today," Korinne said.

Cassie scoffed. "I'm always ready to chat, it just depends on the company." This was one of her favorite games.

"C'mon, Mags. We gotta get this intro done, then we can start all the fun stuff."

Magnolia didn't move right away, instead staring in Cassie's direction. She could tell Magnolia didn't *actually* see her, otherwise there would be screaming and crying and possibly throwing up. Brain matter had that effect on people. But she was really damn close, and that was weird.

"Okay, you're right," Magnolia said, turning back to Korinne. "Intro time."

"Oh, this ought to be good," Cassie muttered. Baxter trotted back up and dropped his ball at her feet. "You're back just in time."

"All right, when you're ready," Korinne said, positioning herself in front of Magnolia and the map.

Magnolia cleared her throat and shook her shoulders before pasting on a smile. Tension in her jaw kept it from reaching her eyes. Could she tell Cassie was here? Did it make her uncomfortable? Usually, the ghost hunters had a certain level of nervousness, but she seemed different. God, where had she seen her before?

"Hi there, and welcome back to *That's the Spirit*. If this is your first time seeing us, my name is Magnolia, and I'm joined by my partner in crime, Korinne."

"What's up?" Korinne said.

"Today, for our final episode, Korinne and I are here on our longest and most haunted investigation yet." Magnolia came alive as the recording started, signs of nervousness fading.

"We're on board the *Arkana* now, the generation ship which brought Earth's humanity here to Vaela."

"Where your grandma floated down from the heavens and met your grandpa," Korinne said.

"Exactly." Magnolia tossed her lavender hair.

"Called it," Cassie said.

"We're here to go with the *Arkana* as it takes its final trip to Capa Emphara, where it'll land and join its sister ship, the *Covenant*. It's a three day trip, which will give me ample time to prove to Korinne once and for all that ghosts are, in fact, real."

"Bullshit," Korinne said at her cue. Cassie reached out and flicked her ear, but the gesture did nothing except make one dark curl wiggle.

"Almost five hundred years ago, the *Arkana* left the Milky Way and survived the journey to our current system, Falgan. The trip itself took how many years, Korinne?"

"Four hundred and twelve," Korinne said. How did she know that so fast? Cassie didn't even know that, and she'd been alive on the ship for nineteen of those years.

"That's a long time to collect ghosts," Magnolia continued. "Due to equipment failure, the *Arkana* couldn't actually land on Vaela, and as such has been kept in orbit for the past sixty years."

Cassie scoffed. "It couldn't land 'cause Jocelyn sabotaged the landing sequence. But sure, whatever you say."

Wait, Jocelyn. *That's* who Magnolia reminded her of. They didn't exactly look alike, but they had similar vibes.

"The ship's council has kept strict watch over visitors since then, as well as how resources were distributed on the planet's surface." That much was true at least. "It's been fifty years since any member of the public has been allowed on board, but we're lucky enough to join Captain Armand on the *Arkana's* last voyage."

"It was probably closed 'cause it's a disaster zone," Korinne said.

"This week," Magnolia said, continuing as if she hadn't been interrupted, "we're going to spend a lot of time collecting evidence by visiting the most haunted areas on the ship. But there's also a few challenges we'll be doing based on the poll you guys did last month."

Korinne chuckled. "Some of the challenges are pretty diabolical. Think you'll be brave enough to visit the portal to hell in the engine room?"

"Yeah, no. You should definitely *not* do that one," Cassie said as a cold shiver went down her spine.

"Of course I will be," Magnolia said, unaware of Cassie's concern.

These girls were getting dumber by the second.

"We'll also be looking into one of the most famous murder cases from this ship," Magnolia said. "That's right—over the next couple days we'll be walking through the last moments of the mysterious death of Cassie Malone."

Cassie stopped, mouth open.

"What the *fuck?*"

CHAPTER 4
CASSIE

From camera 11.19.4: [someone screams]

NO. No, no, no. This was not happening.

"Why Cassie Malone, Rinne?" Magnolia asked, though she sounded far away.

The two of them shifted, putting the focus on Korinne. She looked almost as uncomfortable as Cassie felt.

"Lots of mysterious deaths happened on the *Arkana*. Cassie, however, was the very last passenger to die before the ship found Vaela. By that, of course, I mean before the Vaelish people welcomed Earthers, as opposed to shooting us out of the sky," Korinne explained.

"Yes, appease your purple overlords. I'll make sure the leaders know of your respect," Magnolia said with a laugh.

Panic gripped Cassie. She knew her death was weird, yes. The people who found her body said as such. But mysterious? What was mysterious about it? She thought it was pretty obvious—she'd done it to herself.

"They found her at the docks, which by itself isn't unusual, but they found her there long after any scheduled shuttle times. But what has everybody confounded, is that her body was packed tight into a space that... Let's just say someone had to really force her into it. There was no way for her to get there herself. But her killer left no trace, no evidence, nothing that could lead us back to them." Korinne's voice grew solemn, respectful even.

"Fuck you, I could get anywhere I wanted," Cassie said as anger overtook her shock. Somehow, she managed to keep her energy low enough that the girls didn't hear her. "You're really going to use my death like this? For some stupid show?"

"Unfortunately, Cassie's killer was never brought to justice," Korinne continued. "In fact, we only know her name was Cassie because the owner of her jumpsuit, Willa Malone, said it when she reclaimed her clothing. However, she didn't give any more information than that, not even her last name."

"Wait, what?" Cassie knew she was in someone else's jumpsuit, but she didn't realize they didn't know her last name. She'd assumed they'd figured it out eventually. Now she kind of regretted not attending her own autopsy the way she did her funeral.

"Why wouldn't Willa share Cassie's real name?" Magnolia asked. Cassie, honestly, had the same question. Was *this* her unfinished business?

"Well..." Korinne had the decency to appear sheepish. "Besides injuries, they also found evidence of a homemade explosive on her hands. Likely, Malone didn't want to be implicated in whatever Cassie was caught up in."

"Oh," Magnolia breathed.

"Oh shit," Cassie said. Explosives? Since when did she play with explosives? This *had* to be her unfinished business. Had Rose been in on it? Was that why Cassie remembered her name? It wasn't Rose's jumpsuit, so evidently she was involved in another way.

"Yeah. So Willa Malone never told anyone Cassie's full name, and by that point in the trip, the record keeping wasn't nearly as accurate as when the voyage first started," Korinne said.

"We were hitting the stir-crazy part of the journey, huh?" Magnolia asked quietly. Korinne nodded.

"Toward the end, humanity was this close"—she held up her forefinger and thumb pressed together—"to pretty much giving up on the whole thing. When Vaela showed up on the radar, Cassie's death fell to the wayside."

"I know, I was there," Cassie said through gritted teeth. "Everything else was so much more important. No one cared who I was, or how I died."

She understood, she really did. From birth, they taught the ship passengers the concept of the greater good. *Loss of self for the success of all.* They needed complete obedience in order for humanity to succeed. But it only seemed to matter that certain passengers followed it. She never understood that better than when she died.

Korinne spoke again. "And so, while it's too late for us to do anything about Cassie's killer, we can at least figure out who she is and tell her story. We can remember her, even if the others didn't at the time."

"No, that's so not necessary," Cassie said, her anger fading as panic rose. She took one step forward, and startled as something zapped her. Something attached to Magnolia. The other woman looked up and clutched the silver pendant hanging from her neck.

"Did you hear that?" Magnolia said, scanning the area.

"No, I was busy doing my song and dance," Korinne said, doing awkward jazz hands for emphasis.

Magnolia's shoulders tensed, almost like she expected to turn around and find Cassie staring at her.

"I swear, it literally feels like someone's standing right here next to me," Magnolia said.

Cassie tried to swallow the feelings down; the last thing she needed was for them to see her. This was a mistake; she needed to leave these girls to their own devices and *go*.

But maybe...

Maybe they could help her. If she remembered how or why she died, then maybe she could overcome whatever hold the thing in the engine room had that kept her stuck here.

Despite the decades, the memory of her ghostly awakening stayed fresh and painful in her brain. She'd uncurled and climbed out of that shaft on the side of the loading dock, a place no one could even reach, let alone stuff a body. The world seemed so dull, and all she felt was confusion and fatigue. She'd been lucky enough to have two people there at her awakening—one living, one dead—to help orient her and teach her to siphon energy from the ship.

Magnolia paused, then made a visible effort to calm herself. "Never mind, I'm probably just freaking out because of the whole ambience. Good job, you nailed that one on the first try," she said, going up and giving Korinne a high five.

"You sure? Wasn't too melodramatic?" Korinne seemed genuinely concerned, and if they were investigating anyone else, Cassie probably would've appreciated the sincerity. As it was, she wanted to punch Korinne in the mouth.

"This is stupid," Cassie said.

"No, not at all. Very respectful." Magnolia pulled out her handheld and scrolled for a second. "Do you want to go over what we know already about Cassie, or do some more exploring and B-roll stuff?"

"I am begging you to do anything besides talk about me,"

Cassie said. Anxiety simmered in her gut. What if they didn't figure out why she was at the loading docks that night? Or worse, what if they did? Why the hell was she handling explosives?

"Let me get through Cassie first," Korinne said, consulting her handheld. "Get all the intro stuff in one spot, then we'll dig in when we find her room."

"God damn it," Cassie said. "Wait, my room?"

"Okay, sounds good," Magnolia replied, standing just right to record Korinne properly.

"No, go back to the room part," Cassie said, stepping over to look. On instinct, she reached out to swipe the screen of Korinne's handheld and scroll through the information, as if her ghostly appendage could do anything.

The handheld sparked, and the screen went dark.

"Shit!" Cassie gathered the surge of energy from it and sent it into the floor. Had she learned nothing from her time with the robot earlier? These two were idiots, and she was right there with them. She took a few limping steps back, as if that would undo the damage.

"What the hell?" Korinne said. She tapped the screen, but it stayed black. "Damn it, I knew I should've gotten a new one of these before this trip."

"Odd timing, don't you think?" Magnolia asked. Her eyes lit up, and she rummaged in her bag. She brought out the Parabox again and flipped it on. "Maybe she's here with us and wants to talk!"

"Like hell am I doing this again," Cassie grumbled.

"Hell," the box vocalized. Magnolia's eyes went wide, and her jaw dropped. Korinne scoffed and dug through her bag.

"It's just a coincidence," she said as she found an external battery pack and attached it to her handheld. "Put that away. I probably remember the majority of Cassie's story. I can always patch it later during editing."

"Just give it a second." Magnolia's attention shifted, her eyes falling way too close to Cassie's location. How did she keep doing that? Did she have the same sight Jocelyn did? "Cassie, are you here with us?"

For once in her death, Cassie stayed silent.

"Cassie?" Magnolia tried again. She looked at Korinne, who shrugged.

"What?" she asked.

"Do your thing," she said, waving her hand to goad the other woman.

"What thing?" Korinne asked.

"The thing where you antagonize!" Magnolia said it in a loud whisper, as if ghosts had hearing problems. Well, her right ear wasn't as good as her left due to the whole head-smashed-in thing, but it still functioned decently enough.

"I'm not antagonizing a woman who got brutally murdered. I do have some standards," Korinne said. "If we find her murderer though, I'll let him have it for sure."

The words made Cassie's brain itch. Something about the statement felt off, but she couldn't figure out exactly what.

"That's very thoughtful of you," Magnolia said, putting a hand on her heart. Hot damn, these two were annoying. Magnolia fiddled with the pendant hanging there, evidently thinking. "Cassie? Are you sure you don't want to talk? Or do we have someone else here?"

"Are your ghost senses still tingling?" Korinne asked.

"Didn't you say people often feel a presence here following them?" Magnolia said, a deflection if Cassie ever saw one.

Cassie held her breath, wondering if the stars would align and Baxter would come trotting back up. She glanced over her shoulder, but the dog was nowhere to be seen. Damn it. She was too good at throwing that damn ball.

"Come on, let me get my presentation done," Korinne said, fidgeting with one of the many silver rings on her fingers.

Magnolia sighed, but did so. "I don't know why the first few still make you nervous, you do a great job," she said as she set up again.

"I do mediocre at best. You're the much better presenter," Korinne said, matter-of-fact.

"I am not," Magnolia said.

"The people say you are. They say you're hotter too," Korinne added, smirking as Magnolia blushed.

"You don't have to flatter me," Magnolia said, though she had a certain glow from the compliment.

"Not flattering, just stating facts," Korinne replied. God, what the hell were these two *doing?*

"This is almost as painful as dying," Cassie said, deadpan. "You two are ridiculous."

"You're better than you think. Now go on, tell me all about Cassie." Magnolia stopped fiddling with her necklace and focused on Korinne, though she kept glancing in Cassie's direction.

"Stop that, it's weird," Cassie said, moving a few feet over just to get out of her line of sight.

"Okay, so, as for how something like a name can slip through the cracks," Korinne started, "passengers on the *Arkana* utilized wristbands for things like credits and personal information. This was great at the beginning of the trip, but by the end, wristbands traded hands a hundred different times, and information wasn't always updated. They had passengers whose entire jobs were fixing access permissions."

"Wow, it really was kind of lawless by those final days, huh?" Magnolia asked.

"You have no idea," Cassie said. She didn't have any idea either, but she had a feeling, and that had to count for something.

"Oh, it was terrible. Brewing rebellion, religious extremism, class wars, the whole thing. Humanity was not built to withstand generations in a flying metal can," Korinne said.

"So what did Cassie's wristband tell us?" Magnolia asked.

Cassie looked down at her arm, but found nothing but smooth, pale skin. That's right, they'd had wristbands. At times, they'd felt like handcuffs.

"That's the problem—she wasn't wearing one," Korinne said. "Not on her wrist, not on a keychain, nothing. Not even in her pockets."

"Oh no, so she really was kind of a ghost," Magnolia said. She sounded so sad that it pissed Cassie off.

"I'm not some pitiful creature," she said, stalking over to Magnolia. "Shit happened. Stop feeling sorry for me. I wasn't the first to die under mysterious circumstances, just the last, apparently."

Magnolia gasped and clutched that stupid pendant.

"What?" Korinne asked.

"It just got really cold," Magnolia said.

Cassie got right up in her face. "I'm telling you, leave it alone."

Magnolia released a shuddering breath, which manifested as mist. Oops, maybe she did turn it up a little too much.

"Whoa," Korinne said.

"Please tell me you caught that on camera," Magnolia whispered. This time, it wasn't cold enough to see her breath. Good, one crisis averted.

"Of course I did, I'm not an amateur," Korinne said.

Magnolia shivered again and rubbed her arms before

training her eyes on her partner. "Okay, I'm fine now. That was weird. Keep going."

"You're a terrible liar," Cassie muttered. It was so easy to tell when living people weren't telling the truth, how did others not see it?

"You sure?" Korinne asked.

Magnolia nodded, a little too emphatically. "It's passed now."

Korinne paused for a second, then inhaled. "Okay, class is back in session." She cleared her throat and stretched out her arms, but that barely distracted Cassie. Her attention stayed with Magnolia, who looked about ready to crawl out of her own skin. She gulped, and Cassie watched as her throat bobbed, right above that necklace.

One good thing about being a ghost, she could straight up creep in people's personal space without it being an issue.

Cassie bent over until she was at eye level with the necklace and inspected the pendant. It was perfectly round, with an almost sun-shaped thing at the bottom and two lines going to the top. On either side of the lines, there was something not quite like wings filling in the space. She'd seen it before, but couldn't remember where.

"The hell is this?" she asked, more to herself than to Magnolia. She vaguely sensed Korinne continuing her talk; now she was onto the part about the rebellion, and how class disparity affected the passengers. None of Cassie's business, that was for sure.

In a moment of brave stupidity, Cassie reached for the pendant. For the first time in a long time, warm metal touched her skin.

Wait, touched?

A force flung Cassie away from Magnolia and into a bright white light. Was this it? Could she finally leave this damned ship and pass on to the next life? She spread her arms wide, waiting to land in Heaven or Hell or whatever spiritual stop ended up being the correct one.

No such luck. She landed with a thud on the metal floor of the *Arkana,* five rings out from the girls. Pain ripped through her as the pieces of her broke apart, and she couldn't stop her scream as she clawed at any energy she could find. A little more, and she could stay together.

The blue lights around her flickered and faded as she siphoned from them. One by one, she brought her atoms back together. She hadn't felt pain like this since...since she died.

"You have one hour until the last ship leaves."

Cassie coughed as everything settled. Almost as fast as the pain came, it left, leaving her a panting mess on the floor. She looked around, searching for where the strange voice came from. No one, dead or living, appeared in her field of vision. She was, allegedly, alone.

"Hello?" Silence. "So this is what the ghost hunters feel like."

For someone who didn't need oxygen, it took Cassie an inordinate amount of time to catch her breath. Some things stayed so ingrained in her psyche that, even after death, her hands felt clammy and her heart rattled against her sternum. In all her years, she'd never heard that voice before.

Or...had she?

"One hour until the ship leaves," she murmured. One hour until the ship leaves? The captain hadn't said that before take-off. Cassie squeezed her eyes shut and replayed the words, trying to place the voice.

The memory hit like an asteroid.

"You have one hour until the last ship leaves," an older man said. He was pale, with oily, graying hair. His blue eyes bore into her, and a smirk played on his lips. The expression made

Cassie's palms sweat and her muscles tense. "Plant the explosive in the conference room, and I'll make sure you're on it. You can go to the *Covenant*."

Once again, she settled into the present, blinking rapidly to clear the last pieces of the vision away. No, not a vision. A memory. After decades of emptiness in her mind, her memories were coming back. And that man... She knew him. She'd seen him at some point during her afterlife. When?

"Shit," she said. She forced herself onto her side, then all fours. The movement made her world spin, which was pretty fucking stupid considering she didn't have any blood. God, what was happening to her?

One hour until the last ship leaves, one hour until the last ship leaves, one hour until the last ship—

Cassie shook her head. Okay, so she knew that at some point before she died, she wanted to jump ship and go over to the *Covenant*. She could continue on with that knowledge. And maybe, when the *Arkana* landed, she could pop on over to the sister ship. Then she could be free.

The fog in her brain cleared, and she pushed herself to her feet. Magnolia definitely had more than just vibes in common with Jocelyn. If she had even an inkling of that same power, then maybe Cassie could get *all* her memories back. No more living in the dark about who she used to be.

With one great breath, she jumped up, passing through the levels until she found the girls again.

"You sure you're okay?" Korinne asked. She had a hand on Magnolia's arm and tenderness in her voice.

"Seriously, I'm fine. Something just shocked me, and it surprised me." In Magnolia's defense, she certainly sounded better than Cassie felt. Had the interaction hurt her too, or had it just been a shock, like she said?

"We can do this later, if you want. Take some time for a break."

"Seriously, Rinne. I'm good. Let's keep going."

"If you're really sure," Korinne said. At Magnolia's nod, she dropped her arm and stepped back to her position. "For this investigation, you'll notice a theme for the spots we've chosen. That's because we'll be walking through Cassie's last day on the ship, as far as we know. And we'll start by finding her room and revealing her real name."

"Wait, seriously?" Magnolia asked as Cassie jolted. "You already know?"

Korinne smiled, whatever discomfort she had gone as she bragged. "Seriously. It took a lot of digging—like, a *lot*—but I found it."

Emotions warred inside Cassie. She didn't want this attention, didn't want the pain that would come along with it. But if it also came with knowing...

Cassie paused. Her name. She could have her name back. Did she dare?

"Well shit. What do I have to lose? Not like it'll kill me."

CHAPTER 5
MAGNOLIA

From camera 5.25.11: [a door to a jail cell shakes]

"NICE WORK," Magnolia said, coming up and giving Korinne a high five.

"Almost like I'm a professional or something," Korinne said. "Are you sure you're okay? You got like, super pale there for a second."

Magnolia waved her off, not wanting to relive the last few moments. Her stomach felt vaguely unsettled, and her chest kind of hurt, as if a joint popped halfway out. She kept stretching, trying to relieve the sensation.

"Just a little spell. I'll get the first aid kit to check me out later. It's weird. I always knew the ghosts were around, but like... I don't know. It's like I can feel them here."

"That's the feeling of millions of credits hitting our bank accounts when we drop this video," Korinne said, going up and putting her arm around Magnolia's shoulders. She dug into her pocket and pulled out a fruit bar. "Need a snack?"

Korinne truly understood her as a person.

"Gods, how did you know?" Magnolia asked, taking the bar and tearing open the wrapper. It was her favorite greenberry flavor, and her favorite brand.

"I pay attention, duh," Korinne said as Magnolia took a massive bite. "Now, are you ready to go to Cassie's room? Or are you rethinking that break?"

"We don't have time for breaks," Magnolia said with her mouth full. She felt better already. "We only have three days, and a *lot* of ground to cover. Did you really figure out her real name?"

"I'm pretty sure. Dug through enough tracking information from around that time to figure it out—but I'll tell you the whole thing when we get there," Korinne said. She was such a little tease.

"Well, what are we waiting for? Let's go!"

Magnolia wriggled from her grasp and gave her a brilliant smile, which only grew as the faintest blush appeared on Korinne's cheeks.

"Anything for my liege," Korinne said.

Every time. "You just had to add that in."

Korinne laughed to herself as she led Magnolia to the elevator. Magnolia let her go first; even if she was excited for their next location, she needed Korinne to take charge for a few minutes. Her pendant burned on her sternum, hot enough to make her consider taking it off. But if it was working that hard, she *definitely* needed to keep it on.

"You know," Korinne said as they reached the elevator, "I actually do want to find proof of ghosts."

"Really?" Magnolia asked, pendant momentarily forgotten. Five years, and Korinne had never said anything like that. She built her whole internet persona on picking apart their experiences, but they agreed at the very beginning to stay as true to their personalities as possible. Inevitably, some parts blurred when they got in front of the cameras.

"Yeah. I mean, it's not likely, but it would be kind of cool," she said. "I'd take losing a bet for something like that."

Well that explained it. "Oh yeah, just 'kind of cool' to prove to the solar system that ghosts are real?"

"Most coolness would be negated by how absolutely insufferable you'd be," Korinne said, because of course she had to poke fun. Viewers loved it, and usually Magnolia did too.

The elevator arrived, and they boarded. She opened her mouth, then closed it as a chill came over her and a shadow appeared in her periphery. When she turned, she saw nothing but the dingy off-white of the elevator walls. If she closed her eyes, she would've sworn there was a third person in there with them.

"What?" Korinne asked, her voice colored with concern.

Magnolia thought about telling her, but ended up shaking her head. "Nothing."

Korinne paused, probably waiting for Magnolia to expand, but ended up saying, "If you say so."

After a short trip, the elevator slowed, and the doors slid open. Korinne didn't wait, walking with confidence as she entered the residential hallways. Magnolia followed along, catching the moment with her comm pad and glad Korinne's camera faced the wrong way to see the silly smile she knew she had. It was just so endearing, seeing Korinne in her element.

Both of them clicked on a flashlight and hooked it to their belts, the beams illuminating more metal hallways. Another map decorated the wall in front of the elevator, detailing which rooms lay in which direction. The ink, once black, had faded to a gray similar to the wall. A line of doors extended in either direction, further than the light reached. More hallways cut through periodically, dark maws waiting to swallow them whole. Magnolia pushed down the feeling of dread; how many ghosts waited for them in those dark corners?

"Let's take a second here," Magnolia said, gesturing to the map.

"For what?" Korinne asked. She shifted her weight back and forth, an excited tick that Magnolia definitely caught on camera.

"You're practically buzzing with fun facts. Get a few out here so you can focus better when we get there," she said. Korinne knew her favorite snack bars, Magnolia knew her subconscious habits. More or less an even trade.

"The extra fun facts can wait until tomorrow, that way I have an outfit change for the tangential history lessons," Korinne said. She pulled out her handheld and breathed a sigh of relief as it turned back on, fully charged. She opened the document and skimmed through her notes.

"'Outfit change'? You brought something besides black tank tops and pants?" Magnolia asked. If Korinne owned other things, she hadn't seen them.

"Underwear and socks, of course. Those have some color on them." Korinne flicked her gaze up for a split second to give Magnolia a smirk.

It took a moment for Magnolia to answer as she squashed a few errant thoughts. "Well, that doesn't count. Unless you're planning on prancing around the ship in your underwear."

Korinne dropped her hand and gazed at the ceiling. "Shit! Oh my God."

"What?" Magnolia asked, moving to her side and trying to see the screen. Were they in the wrong place? Did the information not save?

Korinne let out an exasperated sigh. "We should've been doing this in bikinis the whole time," she said.

Magnolia choked. "What?" she squeaked as images of tiny black swimsuits entered her brain uninvited.

"Think of the views!" Korinne said. Exponentially more, probably. But also exponentially more harassment in the comments. "Damn it!"

"Darling, if you were running around in a bikini, I fear I'd get nothing done." She could feel the back of her neck heating at the very idea.

"That's all I had to do to get your attention?" Korinne asked.

"You always have my attention," Magnolia said. She grabbed Korinne by the shoulders, looked her dead in the eye, and said the sexiest thing she could think of. "Now, tell me some historical fun facts before you lose your mind."

"Yes, daddy," Korinne said with the most infuriating grin.

If she blushed any harder, Magnolia might combust. "Focus, please. I believe we're only a few feet away from Cassie's room?"

"Yes," Korinne said, stepping back and seamlessly switching to presentation mode. She'd warmed up now. "So for context, the outermost level of the cylinder was named level one, and there's fifty levels in total. These inner ones were packed with small residential rooms built for one or two people, while the outer ones had bigger apartments for families. For genetic diversity, families were allowed either one or two children, depending on the population and resources at the time of application."

"People had to apply to start a family?" Magnolia asked, a perfect leading question. It was an easy game at that point in their career.

Korinne nodded. "Everything from water consumption to marriages was very strictly controlled by a small group of experts. As you could probably guess, that didn't always sit well with the general population. Things were good the first hundred or so years, but about a hundred and seven years into the journey we start seeing signs of dissent."

"And they still had so far to go," Magnolia said. Her heart ached; what must it have been like to have to ask permission to be with someone you loved? To have a certain allotment of food and water and space to yourself?

"They really did. By the time we get to Cassie's era, there was a lot of noise. Which is what leads me to believe Cassie was part of a certain group led by one Etienne LeBeau."

"Oh, no." Magnolia placed a hand on her chest, and while many viewers commented on her so-called over-the-top reactions, she'd stopped caring a long time ago. Magnolia simply *felt* so much, and the rest of the galaxy could learn a thing or two from her.

"Yes. So, let's find her room and see if we can find any evidence of that—or the contrary."

Korinne pulled up the map on her handheld and typed in her desired location. A line traced the hallways on the screen, their own location a blinking red dot.

"This way."

She didn't rush her steps, and Magnolia followed behind, dutifully capturing everything. There were no open doors, but some of the room placards had faded notes written on them or old family names scratched into the metal. While the *Arkana* took off in pristine condition, it landed with over four hundred years of human history memorialized on every square inch.

"Is it magical, finally being here?" Magnolia asked softly.

Korinne rewarded the question with a massive smile. "I don't know if I'd describe it as magical, but it's definitely pretty fucking cool."

"Humor me, come on," Magnolia said.

"I can't. I have a reputation to uphold," she said. They went to turn into a hallway, but her light flashed over something round and colorful. "Oh! Art!"

"What?"

Korinne ignored Magnolia and backtracked down the wrong hallway. Sure enough, someone had painted over the doors and walls in bright colors, creating a great swirling galaxy circling a black sun. It wasn't their current solar system, and didn't look like any they learned about in science class.

Just something from the heart, then.

"Amazing," Korinne said, tracing over every line and curve. In the top right corner, someone put an artistic rendering of the initials *AB*. A signature. "I love fine art, but nothing speaks to the human experience like graffiti. All right, putting a note to check the database for this later."

"It's beautiful," Magnolia said, coming next to Korinne to admire the work. "How did they manage to get it done without alerting the neighbors?"

"Your guess is as good as mine on that one," Korinne said, taking note of which rooms the art covered. "Either they were very sneaky, these rooms were empty, or they had permission. We may never know. But what we do know"—it was time to get back on track—"is where Cassie's room is. Quit distracting me, Mags."

"Right, I'm so sorry I pointed out that art to you," Magnolia said, laying on the sarcasm as Korinne directed them back to the correct hallway.

"Want."

The whisper barely reached Magnolia's ear, and she spun around. The dark hallway stared back at her.

"Rinne, did you say something?" Magnolia asked. She turned to find Korinne a good twenty feet away, having continued on their mission while Magnolia had a small existential crisis.

"Huh? No. Why, did you hear something?" she asked.

"I thought so, but maybe not," Magnolia said, suddenly doubting the whole thing.

Korinne punched something on her handheld. "I time-stamped it, we'll check it later in editing."

"Perfect. Sorry about that, let's keep going."

The trek seemed so much shorter on the screen of her handheld, but it took them another ten minutes of walking before they reached the final turn. The entire time, Magnolia couldn't shake the feeling of someone following them. She even swore she heard footsteps at one point. But any time she turned, she found nothing but empty hallway.

"Okay, L13-R42. Here we go," Korinne said.

They stopped in front of the door and made sure the comm pads were secure and recording. Korinne pulled out another energy bank, a cable, and a screwdriver.

Magnolia once again looked back from whence they came. If she squinted, she could almost see the outline of a person. She grasped her pendant, the silver hotter than it should be just from laying against her skin.

"What are you doing?" Magnolia said to the shadow.

"Are you talking to me?" Korinne asked.

"Yes," she lied, proud of herself for not jumping when Korinne responded. She couldn't look away from the spot behind them.

"For the record, I hate when you do that," Korinne said.

Magnolia finally tore her eyes away to look at her friend. "Do what?"

"Look past me like you're watching something. You awaken some primordial fear in my hindbrain," she said.

"Aw, I bet you say that to all the girls," Magnolia cooed.

"Of course not. Only you can initiate my fight or flight response." She turned back to the task at hand. "To answer your question, the captain has limited where energy goes in the ship for the trip. So, if we can't have homegrown power…" She pried open the face of the palm pad and plugged in the power bank. A second later, it lit up. "Store bought is fine." She pressed the palm pad, and the door inched open.

"No passkeys?" Magnolia said. That seemed like a massive safety hazard.

"There used to be, yes," Korinne said. "But I had the captain turn them all off, of course. I don't have time to hack every room we want to go into."

The door got stuck halfway open. None of the inside lights had enough juice to turn on, but that was fine. Part of being a professional ghost hunter meant lugging around an inordinate number of flashlights.

"Okay, let me get this part done before we go in," Korinne said, straightening. Magnolia positioned herself right so the comm pad camera focused on her. Gods, Korinne looked so excited.

"Go for it," Magnolia said, giving her two thumbs up.

"If I'm right, then we're outside the room of the woman known as Cassie Malone. For years, people tried to find her real name and any idea of who she was. Most people thought 'Cassie' was short for 'Cassandra,' which was an incredibly popular name at the time."

"For my favorite scientist Dr. Cassandra Fuentes, who was able to manufacture a vaccine for the influenza outbreak a hundred and twenty years before the *Arkana* found Vaela," Magnolia said, entirely too proud of herself.

Korinne paused. "Since when do you have a favorite scientist?"

"Since you told me all about the badass who saved humanity," she said with a shrug.

Korinne blinked, evidently dumbfounded. "I told you about her like, three years ago."

"Yeah, and?" Magnolia cocked her head to the side, waiting for Korinne's reply.

"And that's super cool," she finally said. "Wait, why am *I* not your favorite scientist?"

"You're my favorite sociological scientist, Rinne. She's my favorite biological scientist," Magnolia said. Every new subject Korinne studied, Magnolia picked a favorite. She just didn't always voice it, mostly so she could drop the information on her at random times and make her make that face.

"Right, of course." Korinne shook her head, trying to get herself back on track. "Anyway, Magnolia is right. Many babies were named some variation of Cassandra for a long time after Dr. Fuentes saved everyone. But our Cassie? Her parents apparently had an interest in either astronomy or Old Earth Greek mythology. Her name was Cassiopeia. Cassiopeia Whitlock."

Elation and relief filled Magnolia in equal measure. After all this time, the woman would have her name back. She could only hope it gave her some measure of peace in the afterlife.

"Welcome back, Cassiopeia."

CHAPTER 6
CASSIE

*From camera 1.2.15: [the elevator dings and the door
opens to an empty lift]*

CASSIOPEIA WHITLOCK.

So, that's who she'd been. It felt like a puzzle piece sliding
home, another part of the mostly-blank picture of her life.

She waited for some deeper understanding to manifest, or a
sense of freedom from the thing keeping them captive. Nothing
came up. Nope, not her unfinished business then. Damn it.

"All right, let's go see Cassie's little nook," Korinne said.

"Don't insult her room," Magnolia said. "She didn't exactly
have options."

Cassie didn't know it had been an insult until she said
something. She was born and raised on a generation ship, every
passenger spent their entire life trying to carve out a *little nook*
for themselves.

"I wasn't—would you prefer I call it cozy? Compared to

other places we've investigated, this is definitely cozier," Korinne said.

Cassie grimaced, and was glad they couldn't see her face. Cozier? She didn't even know her.

"Cozy works," Magnolia said.

They squeezed into her alleged room, and Cassie slipped in behind them. Her subconscious registered them talking, pointing out all the "cool artifacts" and "layers of history," but the words didn't sink in. Her focus stayed on the sight in front of her as bits of memories shuffled behind the veil between the afterlife and the one before.

She hadn't made the bed. That was the first thing Cassie noticed, how the gray, standard-issue blanket sat rumpled beneath the cords across the mattress, the ones they used when they cut the gravity generators at night to save power. The pillow lay on the floor, and one corner of the sheets had escaped their hold. How much of it was her, and how much was turbulence of the *Arkana* over time? Something told her to give herself more credit than the ship.

According to the girls, resources ran thin by the end of the journey. If that was the case, where the hell did Cassie get all these trinkets?

Stuff cluttered almost every available surface, and as she looked, the items became less foreign and more familiar. There was a watch, passed down through a family. Cassie traded something for it, but couldn't remember what it was or to whom she traded it. A glass jar of black stuff might've been a plant once, but what good was a plant in a room like this? Everything seemed to be in its proper place, but nothing felt right.

"Oh, a tablet," Magnolia said as she analyzed Cassie's desk. Nosy.

"See if it turns on," Korinne said.

Panic gripped Cassie's insides. "No!" she said, even though no one could hear her.

"I don't think we'll be that lucky," Magnolia said. She picked up the tablet and pressed the power button, as if any battery could hold a charge for multiple decades. To Cassie's horror, Magnolia found the charger and plugged it in. Could technology last this long?

"You don't need to see what's on there," Cassie said, coming to stand shoulder to shoulder with Magnolia. Unbeknownst to the living girl, they both watched the tablet for signs of life. When the screen stayed dark, Magnolia sighed and rubbed her arms, stepping away as Cassie went dizzy with relief.

"Well, you tried, and therefore no one can criticize you," Korinne said.

"Let's check the wall screen. It might have the answers we want." Magnolia placed the tablet back down and sent a furtive glance Cassie's direction before going to Korinne's side.

Oh, right.

The name felt right, but how could she figure out if they were in the right spot? Her answer came in the form of a pile of faded, threadbare clothes in the corner. Korinne and Magnolia focused on the wall screen next to the door, and Cassie moved to take a closer look. If she could find a name patch, then she'd know if Korinne was right. She leaned over and checked the pile every which way, then spotted the edge of a patch sticking out from a fold.

Cassie glanced back at the girls. They were trying to get power to the wall screen, which apparently required more juice than anticipated. Korinne was correct, the captain limited power to this area, but there was no way to cut it completely. Cassie dug into the ship until she found the thin current trickling through the floor.

Cassie gathered the energy, reached out, and shoved one of the cloths to the side. It only moved an inch, maybe two, but it was enough to show the letters *-tlock* stitched on the name badge.

"Did you see that?" Magnolia asked, and Cassie froze.

"No, I'm looking at this," Korinne said. "I think I've almost got it."

"Something moved in that corner." Magnolia pointed *right at Cassie*. Or maybe right at the pile of clothes, which was also in her vicinity.

"Stop looking at me," Cassie said, making sure to expel any energy she didn't need before shifting away. Luckily, Magnolia's attention stayed on the laundry.

Magnolia took one hesitant step toward the corner, then another. Cassie tapped her fingers against her thigh. It would be so easy to scare her right now, with all her attention on that one little spot. Should she? She shouldn't. She was on a mission now—she didn't need to mess with these two. They were there to help her.

Magnolia leaned over the pile.

Do it, something deep and internal whispered to Cassie. A thread of mischief thrummed in her heart.

Magnolia reached with a tentative hand.

Cassie gathered energy again and shoved a cup. She barely had enough to overcome the magnets holding it to the desk surface. It fell with a clunk and rolled off the desk, clattering to the ground.

Magnolia jumped so high Cassie swore she nearly hit the ceiling. Korinne spun around, her flashlight scanning until it found the cup. And oh, Cassie laughed. She laughed so hard her stomach hurt and tears formed in her eyes.

Ah, fucking with ghost hunters. It was nice to have time for her hobbies again.

"Don't say it," Korinne said, going back to the wall screen.

"But that had to be a ghost!" Magnolia said.

"It's an old room opened for the first time in sixty years, Mags. I doubt anything in here qualifies as stable."

Cassie snorted. "I don't think it qualified as stable even when I was alive," she said.

"Bingo!" Korinne threw a fist in the air as the wall screen lit up. "Now all we need to do is fudge a few permissions and..."

"We're just going to ignore that cup?" Magnolia asked as Korinne tapped on the wall screen.

"Yep, because I was right."

The screen displayed an identification file with the picture of a baby-faced preteen. With the cherub cheeks and shorter hair, Cassie could barely recognize herself. No wonder the people looking through the files didn't see it.

"That does *not* look like her," Magnolia said.

Korinne pulled up her handheld and scrolled to find—

"Holy fuck, is that my death certificate?" Cassie said, moving closer to see. "God, they didn't even fix my hair. No wonder I look like this."

"Oh, that's her all right," Korinne said, holding the handheld up next to the wall screen. "Look, same color and shape of the eyes. Same ears. Same birthmark at the edge of her collarbone."

Cassie touched the bone and felt the bump of a tiny mole, one that matched the spot on the girl in the picture.

"Hot damn, you really did find me," said Cassiopeia Whitlock, staring at one of very few mementos of her life.

"She was so young in this picture," Magnolia said, and she sounded so goddamn sad.

"You don't have to be weird about it," Cassie said. "Everyone's young at some point."

"Age of adulthood was thirteen on the ship because they needed workers," Korinne explained.

Magnolia made a face. "Disgusting."

"Just for work. Trust me, one leader tried to institute thirteen as an age for other things and he got assassinated like, so fast," Korinne said.

Cassie fake gagged, not that the girls could appreciate the humor. The story sounded familiar, though any facts surrounding the situation escaped her. She didn't think she was someone who paid much attention to history class, anyway.

"Let's see what else is on here," Korinne said. Before Cassie could stop her, she flipped to a different application. "The main purpose of these screens was for ship-wide announcements, but passengers could also upload personal things to them. Things like..."

"Pictures," Cassie said. There was something on there, something they shouldn't see.

The first picture showed a crowded cafeteria, with a live and intact Cassie cheek to cheek with a tall man in a doctor's coat. He had deep brown skin and eyes, and a completely shaved head. Cassie stared at it, willing herself to remember, but nothing came.

"Oh look, you can actually see Etienne LeBeau here," Korinne said, pointing to the background. There sat an older man with graying hair, slicked back to hide a bald spot.

The same man who told her she had an hour left until the last ship to the *Covenant* left.

"Oh, shit," Cassie whispered. "Oh, no. That's not good."

"Did you want to talk more about him here?" Magnolia asked.

"Nah, we'll do that up at the jail later. Better ambience," Korinne replied.

She flipped to the next photo. Five people stood in different jumpsuits, arms slung around necks and waists. In the middle stood a woman with short dark hair and a playful scowl. Her uniform fit snugly, showing off the muscles of her arms and legs. A uniform which fit Cassie in length, but not width. On her chest, just big enough to read, the name *Malone* shone in red thread.

Cassie stared at the picture, at Malone in particular. She knew that woman; this time, half-baked memories rose, more sensations of joy than actual pictures. They'd been close, she and this woman who gave her the uniform. Cassie saw her once more after death, at her own funeral.

"Think they were together?" Magnolia asked.

A jolt of panic shot through Cassie. A denial sat on her tongue, heavy and true. No, she and Malone weren't together, not romantically. But they were close, questionably close, according to some people around them. And Cassie had her uniform. How did she get it?

"I don't think so. This was during a time with a resurgence of religious extremism. So while same-sex relationships weren't illegal on the *Arkana* like they were on the *Covenant*, it was frowned upon," Korinne explained. "Actually, this all happened right before the *Arkana* and the *Covenant* split to go to different planets. More than likely, this was when the last diplomatic envoy from the *Covenant* visited, probably encouraging some of those ideas."

"Ugh, I hate when the extremists get going," Magnolia said.

"You have no idea," Cassie said. A deep-rooted fear whispered from her chest, and she swallowed it down.

Korinne continued flipping through pictures, and Cassie saw more familiar faces with no names attached. She saw herself, smiling and happy.

The picture changed again, this time to a beautiful girl in white. Dark curls were piled on top of her head in an elegant pattern, and she sat posed with three quarters of her face toward the camera. Her hands, one flesh and one a metal prosthesis, sat in her lap. She was the perfect picture of poise. Cassie's nonexistent blood rushed in her ears.

"Whoa, buddy, who's this?" Korinne said, tapping the file. "This came from the *Covenant*!"

"Rose," Cassie said, recognizing the only name she remembered after death. "Holy shit, that's Rose."

Now, if she could just remember anything about Rose, that would be rather helpful. If she was on the *Covenant*, how did they meet? What did they mean to each other? Why did it hurt so bad to see her face?

"She's so pretty," Magnolia said.

"She's more than pretty," Cassie said. "She's..."

But what was she? Cassie didn't know. There was nothing but recognition and pain attached to that face.

"I can probably get a name, the *Covenant* kept better records than the *Arkana*." Korinne pulled out her handheld. "I've got a friend who works on it—"

"No." Cassie stepped forward and smacked the handheld again. They couldn't know about Rose. She knew that in her dead, broken bones. Three things happened in quick succession.

The screen went dark.

Korinne groaned and cursed the technology.

And Magnolia looked Cassie dead in the face, her eyes wide and lips parted.

How could she see her? Yes, she had a little extra energy, but not enough to fully form. How did this happen?

Cassie pushed the energy into the floor and held her breath.

"Did you see that?" Magnolia asked.

Korinne looked up from where she plugged the battery pack into her handheld again. "See what?"

Cassie waited for the screams, the excitement, the drama. But Magnolia simply gulped and shook her head.

"Nothing. Probably just a trick of the light," she said. "This place may drive me crazy."

Cassie relaxed. This was enough for one day. She needed them to move on, to talk about something besides her.

"The next part's easy," Korinne said.

"Finally, something else," Cassie said.

"Really?" Magnolia asked.

"Yeah, we're just headed to the docks," Korinne said.

"You can skip that part," Cassie said. "Super boring. Trust me, I've been there a million times."

"I thought they said we couldn't visit the place where they found Cassie?" Magnolia asked.

"They did," Korinne said. "But there's another docking bay that looks more or less the same. We can at least set the scene for viewers so they understand how weird her death was. I'll get Bitt to meet us there."

"You know," she said to no one in particular, "the fire suppressants never worked quite right after that day. Add that in."

"Perfect, that sounds like a nice, safe option," Magnolia said.

"It is. And then we can hit the hospital," Korinne said.

"I'm going to pretend I didn't hear that," Magnolia said. She stopped halfway through the door. "Oh, but—"

She went back to Cassie's desk and unplugged the tablet.

"Whoa there, that's not yours," Cassie said.

"Gonna plug it in back in the rooms?" Korinne asked.

"That's the plan. Cassie deserves to be remembered, and there might be something here that helps," Magnolia said.

"There's nothing there you need to know," Cassie said, trying to figure out a way to get her to leave it behind. But what was her option, fully appearing and telling them not to? That would open up an entire can of worms. If somehow the ancient thing turned on again, she could simply shut it down. She at least had the power to do that.

"Let's take it with us, then. I'll mess with it later." Korinne's handheld lit up, as did her face. "Excellent! Okay, we're back in business. A few more minutes of footage in here and then we can go."

"You don't want to bag and tag everything while we're here?" Magnolia asked, and Cassie once again wondered if she realized how she looked at Korinne.

"That'll be my job after all this is done with," Korinne said. "Gotta get this job done first before I can look ahead to that one."

"Right, of course."

Ew, she sounded so sad again. Why? It was obvious to Cassie that they'd been together a long time. How she knew that, she couldn't say. After all, the only people she really knew were ghosts.

Cassie held still as they took another slow sweep of the room, collecting footage with the tablets strapped to them. She had no interest in visiting the docks; they never gave her answers before, and they probably wouldn't give her any now. She thought about touching Magnolia's pendant again, but hot damn, that had *hurt*. Would she have to go through that every time just to get a new memory? There had to be an easier way.

She stared at the wall screen, and Rose stared back at her. Her picture came from the *Covenant*, but did Rose herself come here too with that delegation Korinne mentioned? If so, why hadn't Cassie found her ghost yet, or remember seeing her after she died? Had she gone back to the sister ship, leaving Cassie alone? Was *that* her unfinished business?

She'd known Rose well enough to get a picture of her, which meant they had at least some communication. Communication that would've been recorded. Encrypted, yes. But recorded.

The tablet. She had to let them turn the tablet on and see what answers it held. Some amnesiac part of her wanted to guard whatever was on it, but Cassie's curiosity far outweighed whatever fear her subconscious held. After all, what could they do to her? She was already dead. And until the tablet turned on, she had another option, someone who'd seen almost everything over the years. Someone who'd been there the moment she woke up as a ghost.

"Let's get this show on the road," Korinne said.

"It sure is going somewhere," Cassie muttered.

They left for the docks. Cassie left to visit Lottie.

CHAPTER 7
KORINNE

From camera 50.3.1: [someone whispers something unintelligible, and the screen goes black]

KORINNE MADE an effort to slow down after they left Cassie's room, more so to bask in her win than anything else. Over sixty years had passed since Cassie died, and now they finally had a name for her. She had her identity back, thanks to Korinne and about seventeen different databases of information. It had been a struggle to keep the information secret from Magnolia since she did most of the compiling and organizing, and victory had Korinne flying high.

Magnolia linked their elbows, and Korinne squeezed, not even worried about the affection. She'd done it, she'd taken a decades-old mystery and found the answer. Cassiopeia Whitlock had her name back. Korinne held no delusions of grandeur when it came to solving her actual death; after all, there were no witnesses, no evidence, nothing besides a coroner's report. Whoever killed her would take that secret to the grave.

"I still can't believe you found her name," Magnolia said with a well-timed squeal. "Rinne! That's huge!"

"I'm just glad I was right," she said as a wave of humility overtook her. "I mean, could you imagine the time wasted if I was wrong?"

"Please, you're never wrong, my smart girl," Magnolia said, reaching out to tap Korinne on the nose. Heat pressed into her cheeks at the compliment.

"I mean, I'm wrong sometimes," she mumbled.

"Maybe, but I can't think of any specifics," she said. She seemed to be feeling better now that they were on the move, no longer startling at shadows or staring over Korinne's shoulder like something waited to attack them.

"Think we'll get the tablet to work?" she asked.

"We can only hope. I'm surprised it was still there, didn't they pretty much gut the ship when they reached orbit?" Magnolia said.

It wasn't a leading question for the show, but a genuine one. Korinne loved those. "Everyone was responsible for their own rooms. If Cassie was the only one living there, no one would go back for her stuff."

Magnolia slumped and leaned her cheek against Korinne's shoulder. "That's such a sad thought. How many of those rooms hold forgotten memories like that?"

"More than a few, I'm sure." Korinne smoothed her stride, so as to not jostle Magnolia's head. "Don't worry, I'll find them all if I nail my dissertation."

She brightened at that. "*When* you nail your dissertation. I'm so excited for you. You'll finally be living your dream," she said.

For some reason, the thought made Korinne's heart seize. She was excited for the next step in her journey, but what would that mean for their friendship?

"Are we doing the right thing, ending the show?" she asked.

Magnolia stopped and pulled away so she could put her hands on her hips. "Don't tell me you're getting cold feet about finishing school," she said.

"What? No, I'm going to finish for sure," Korinne said. "I didn't come this far to not finish."

"Has being here changed your mind about wanting to join the project?" Magnolia asked.

"No, if anything, it's solidified it," she said. It was true; finally being here and seeing the ship made all the stress worth it. She had no doubt she wanted to spend her time bringing the stories from the passengers back to life and sharing those stories with whoever visited the ship in the future.

"Then what is it?" Magnolia said. When Korinne didn't answer immediately, she continued. "This has always been the plan, darling. We go until you finish school, and then you land your dream job."

"I mean, maybe I could do both," she said.

Magnolia scoffed. "You can barely do it all right now."

"And what about you?" Korinne said. What she really wanted to ask was, "What about us?"

But Magnolia shrugged. "It's been fun doing all the admin stuff, but I agree that it's time for us to move on. Who knows, maybe a nonprofit will need help getting organized or fundraising. I'm good at stuff like that. Hells, maybe I'll just start making jewelry or something."

"Or maybe this episode will make us enough money to spend our days sipping drinks on a beach and neither one of us will need a job," Korinne said.

"Now your head is in the right place," Magnolia said. She resumed her position, and they continued down the hall. "Change is scary, but it's a good thing too. You'll see. You'll get going restoring this place, and you'll forget all about the days you spent chasing after ghosts."

"I could never forget this time with you, Mags," Korinne said. Oh no, that sounded way too sincere. "The neck pain alone from sleeping in weird places will plague me for at least a decade."

"Something to remember the good old days by," Magnolia said, pulling Korinne closer for a moment.

"And we'll still hang out, right?" She voiced her true fear, the one that kept her up at night wondering if this was all some grand mistake.

"Oh, absolutely," Magnolia said, and she held so much certainty that Korinne's doubt faded. "I'm going to come bother you every day at lunch so you can tell me all the stories, and make friends with your coworkers so we get invited to the cool parties."

"Ah yes, the super cool parties that anthropologists are known for," Korinne said. A warmth spread through her chest at the idea that she would still be part of Magnolia's life when all was said and done. And maybe, if she could be just a tiny bit braver, things could end a little differently.

"I've been around enough academics at this point to know there are some absolute ragers being thrown, and we'll be invited."

"You and I have apparently met very different brands of academics," Korinne said as they rounded the last corner. She slid her handheld from her pocket and set a timestamp on the recording with a note to edit out the entire conversation. She probably wouldn't need a reminder, but she didn't want to take any chances.

Bitt waited outside the docking bay and gave a happy chirp at their arrival. Magnolia patted its binoculars as Korinne hooked the power bank up to the palm pad and fired it up again. The door opened reluctantly, the oversized area beyond dark except for the low lights lining the edges of the dock. Someone had left the outer airlock doors open, and the clear inner doors showed off the vast emptiness of space.

Bitt turned on the bright lights located in its binocular eyes, flooding the area ahead of them. More metal flooring covered the spacious area leading up to the dock itself, which was a wide, flat rectangle with deep, empty spaces on either side.

"So shuttles would come through there, and the jets would fit on either side?" Magnolia asked the leading question, pointing to the areas.

"Yep," Korinne said. "Those openings span an entire ring's width. The *Arkana* used shuttles to take supplies from one side of the ship to the other, but also to go visit the *Covenant* before they split apart."

"Oh, gods, imagine if you fell," Magnolia said with an appropriate gasp.

"Luckily, that was pretty rare. Passengers usually wore magnetic boots 'cause they never knew if or when the gravity generators would give out."

"Oh, so you could dangle over the edge by your shoes, even better," Magnolia said. "How close together did the two ships travel?"

Another perfect question. "The *Covenant* left Earth about three months after the *Arkana* did. Its engines were a little bit better, so it was able to catch up after about six months of space travel. They flew in tandem until the split."

"Aw, that's cute. Just two little buddies flying through space," Magnolia said with a laugh. "Gods, and look at that view."

"Yeah," Korinne said as they both looked out of the airlock. "Really drives home how big space is, and how much of a last resort this trip was."

Korinne led the way into the room, Bitt's lights sending her shadow ahead of her. Their footsteps echoed in the empty expanse, and she shone her flashlight up to find it barely reached the ceiling. She did her best to take some slow turns and scan the area, but the extra footage of the area wouldn't help them much in post-production. Really and truly, they were in a big metal box with a thick pane of glass protecting them from outer space.

"Don't get too close to the edge, Rinne," Magnolia said, stopping a healthy distance away from the dock.

"I won't," she said, walking right up to it. She tried to see the bottom—ignoring Magnolia tittering about safety hazards—but her flashlight wasn't strong enough to reach it. She scanned the sides and saw the three-by-three cutouts underneath the edge. The squares lined the area on both the dock and the solid ground next to it. Open pipes sat tucked inside, ready to expel fire suppressant if needed. At least the light could reach those, which was what Korinne really needed.

"Okay, that's enough. You're making me nervous," Magnolia said.

"Sorry," Korinne said, stepping back. "Bitt, come over this way so we can see the blocks underneath."

Bitt rolled over to the spot Korinne pointed to, and she lined herself up so its camera caught her and the cutouts. Its lights showcased the cramped block and its position two feet below the surface. Magnolia stepped closer to see the spot Korinne pointed to and covered her mouth with her hand.

"That's where they found her?" she asked, voice muffled and reflective eyes glinting in the light.

"That's where they found her," Korinne said.

Now that she saw the area with her own two eyes, it was even more obvious that foul play was involved in Cassie's death. Not for the first time, Korinne got a little pissed at her ancestors for not valuing human life the way they should've. Someone got away with a murder, and an innocent woman was dead. How many more victims went without any answers, like Cassie?

"There's no way she could've gotten in there by herself, accident or no," Magnolia said. She stared hard at the squares, and Korinne could see the wheels turning in her head as she tried to picture it. "No, there's no way."

"But it also raises the question, how did someone get her in there?" Korinne said. If someone didn't know her, they might've thought she was implying paranormal interference. Really, she just had a hypothesis.

Magnolia opened her mouth, closed it, then furrowed her brows. "I don't know," she said. "It's not too far from the floor, but it is a bit of a reach. And to hold a whole body like that and get it into that space? I mean..." She trailed off and grimaced. Korinne knew where her thoughts went, because she'd gone through the same process before. "Why didn't they just drop her?"

Korinne spun one of her rings around on her finger, delaying the answer to another genuine question from Magnolia. Sometimes they had ideas for conversation beforehand, but this wasn't one of those moments. Her stomach curdled, and she steeled herself by thinking that, if she hated adding this part in, if it put too much attention on Cassie's possible murderer and not on the woman herself, then she could simply edit it out later.

"I have a hypothesis," Korinne said, too quiet.

Magnolia grimaced. "And what's your hypothesis?"

"We know there's a chance she was involved with Etienne LeBeau," Korinne started. "She was found with explosive residue on her hands, but there's no record of any explosions taking place that day. I have no evidence to corroborate any of this, but... I think he might've killed her and left the body where she would be found as a way to send a message."

Magnolia paled. "A message to who? The people in charge?"

Korinne shook her head. "To the people who followed him, to make sure they stayed in line."

"Oh, I hate it," Magnolia said, putting her hands over her stomach. "If she was trying to get out, and he did that... Rinne, that's terrible."

"I know. And like I said, there's no evidence to support this. It's just an idea. Actually..." She changed her position so Bitt's camera could fully see the area. "Note to editing Korinne, take that part out."

"Note to editing Korinne," Magnolia said to her own comm pad. "Let's see what Cassie's tablet shows us before you take this part out."

"I don't know if I want to broadcast to the galaxy that she was involved in a rebellious scheme," Korinne said. "If that's the case, I think we should just reveal her name and leave it at that."

"That's a good idea," Magnolia said. "But we should still check the tablet. If it comes out that she was involved, we'll decide what to do with that information then. Otherwise, we'll just find other things to celebrate her life."

Korinne let out a breath as relief seeped into her. "Okay, yes. Good plan." Doing any sort of presentation involving true crime required sensitivity, and Korinne wanted to remind their audience—and herself—of that. The passengers on the ship were real people, with hopes and dreams and ideas. They deserved to be remembered with respect and dignity.

"Anything else you want to add about this spot?" Magnolia said. For the first time since they left Cassie's room, she turned to look at one shadow or another. Korinne really hated when she did that.

"Nah, anything else I'll add in post-production. Want to try the light real quick?" she asked.

"Oh, great idea," Magnolia said. She fished through her bag and found the palm light from takeoff, flipping it on before she placed it on the ground. "Hello? Is anyone here with us?"

"I feel like they would've said something before now," Korinne said.

"Maybe they're just polite," she said. "Hello? I'm Magnolia, this is Korinne. Are there any ghosts here? Any dock workers? Cassie maybe?"

"Oh, I hope she's not here," Korinne said. "That'd be so embarrassing, like talking about someone and not realizing they're right behind you."

"This light is super easy to mess with," Magnolia said. "If you touch it, it'll make it brighter. Want to give it a try?"

Nothing. The light maintained a steady glow. Next to them, Bitt made a noise that sounded suspiciously like a giggle covered up with a cough, which was impressive given its limited tonal capabilities.

"Guess they're scared of the dock too," Korinne said.

"It's really easy, just touch it," Magnolia said, talking to a random area of darkness now. Korinne squinted, but couldn't make out any shapes amongst the shadows. "I promise, I've seen a bunch of ghosts do it."

"Oh, so that's what you're into?" Korinne asked. "Noted."

"Korinne!" Magnolia said, hair flying as she whipped her head around.

"Listen, the eight percent of our viewers that are ages fifteen to eighteen are gonna find that hilarious," she said as a laugh escaped her.

"No, they won't, it was way too much of a reach," Magnolia

said. "If you're going to make a sex joke, at least make a good one."

"Right, sorry to disappoint you with the lack of cleverness," she said, trying to stifle her giggles. Magnolia was right, it wasn't that funny. The dumb jokes never were. It was her reactions to them that brought all the entertainment.

"Ignore her," Magnolia said to the room beyond. "Go on, give the light a try. Let us know you're here."

They waited a full minute, which felt roughly like two hours. "I don't think they're biting, Mags."

"Ugh, fine. I know when to admit defeat," Magnolia said as she picked up the light. Korinne thought to dispute the fact considering she'd spent the past five years doing anything but admitting defeat, but decided to let it lie.

"There's probably just not enough ghosts in this area," Korinne said. "Let's go somewhere we know has a ton of reports."

"You don't even believe the reports," Magnolia grumbled.

Korinne slung an arm around her shoulders. "No, but you do. So the next stop is a spot that's sure to get all your ghost senses tingling."

Magnolia bit her lip. "I feel like I'm going to hate whatever you're about to say."

"Probably," Korinne said. "'Cause the next stop on our Cassie tour is the hospital bay."

Korinne really hoped the comm pad camera caught the expression on Magnolia's face.

"Oh, so you just really want to make me scream?" Magnolia crossed her arms over her chest.

"Always," Korinne said, adding a wink for good measure. "You can scream now, or you can scream later. It's your choice. I'm ready when you are."

"You're really playing this whole thing up, huh?" she said, gesturing between them. Korinne grinned back.

"We're practically the only two people on a three day long spaceship trip. The romance novel writes itself," she said. "But I digress. Was that a yes?"

Magnolia hesitated. "I was really hoping you forgot. Why do you always want to do the scariest things?"

"It's not me who wants it, it's the people." She showed the screen of her handheld, where the list their assistant, Zavir, made had *Hospital* in bold letters with very detailed bullet points underneath. "It's all right here. What do you think?"

Magnolia wanted to say no—it was all over her face. Fortunately, Korinne knew she was genetically incapable of backing down from a challenge. She bit her lip and tapped her fingers against her arms, all while Korinne's smile slowly grew. After the longest pause, Magnolia straightened and looked down her nose at both Korinne and her comm pad camera.

"Fine. Just for that, I'm going to stay calm and collected so the viewers are disappointed and you're extra bored while editing the footage," she declared.

Korinne made a valiant effort to smother her laughter with a cough. "Yes, I absolutely believe that," she said, earning a cute glower.

"You'll see. You'll be so bored you'll cry," Magnolia said.

"For sure," Korinne said. "It'll be worse than all the data entry I did in undergrad."

"It'll be so dry you'll wish you had some data to enter," she said.

"Well then, let's get this boring part over with so we can do something more exciting."

Magnolia glided toward the door, Bitt following after her. Korinne hoped she'd hold onto that bravery the rest of the trip, and quit looking for people hiding in shadows.

CHAPTER 8
CASSIE

From camera 15.3.20: [the engine room door shudders]

WHILE MAGNOLIA and Korinne waxed poetic about dock structures and unrealistic physics, Cassie went after a few answers on her own—answers she hadn't cared about since the first few days after her death.

She traveled through the ship much faster than her living buddies, passing through floors and walls with nary a particle out of place. She pulled up to the water reclamation area, then stopped to straighten her clothes and fix her hair, remembering too late half of it was caked in blood and brain matter.

For the living, there had been a heavy price to enter the gambling den nestled near the water reclamation tanks. In death, the ghosts just paid with time. Cassie didn't bother doing the special knock on the door she'd seen some people do, instead passing through it and into the bustling room. Most of the ghosts there went in and out of their visible forms, conserving their energy to prolong the games. They sat at the few old tables left, playing with cards, tiles, chips, or any combination of the three. Like Baxter's ball, they somehow brought these things over from life.

"Sorry, Miss, there's a line." A wall of a man with graying blond hair put up a hand to bar her passage.

"I'm not here to play," Cassie said, pasting on the sweetest smile she could muster.

"Get in line!" a skinny old lady snapped. She jerked her gnarled thumb behind her. Sure enough, a whole line of ghosts waited for their turns at the tables.

"I'm not playing," Cassie reiterated, keeping her eyes on the bouncer and ignoring the grumbles from the line. "I'm just looking for Lottie, where is she?"

The bouncer perked a brow and crossed his thick arms over his wide chest. "She's in the middle of something, kid. Come back later."

Annoyance flared, and it took everything to swallow it down. "It'll just take a minute, it's important."

He didn't budge. "It can take a minute later," he said.

"Frederick, are you bothering my friends again?"

The gentle, feminine voice somehow soared over the volume of the den, an effective trick. Cassie scanned the area until her eyes landed on a tall woman lounging on a faded couch, one leg crossed over the other. Her long, dark hair fell in gentle waves, and even in death, she sported perfect make up and painted nails.

"You said you didn't want to be disturbed," Frederick said. At least he had the wherewithal to look abashed, though he still managed to glare at Cassie from beneath his heavy eyebrows.

"Well, there are always exceptions," Lottie said. She dismissed the man next to her with a wave of her hand, then smiled at Cassie. "Come here, Cass. It's not often I get to see your beautiful, bloody face."

Cassie smiled at Frederick, wide and sarcastic, before weaving through the tables to the couch. Energy flowed freely, making it easy to become corporeal enough to relax on the furniture.

"How did you get electricity here?" Cassie asked. Lottie smirked and tapped the wall with her knuckle, the sound reaching the material plane.

"Back ups and more back ups. They never wanted the water reclaimers losing power, so it's written into the code," she said.

"Ah, location is everything, huh?" Cassie said. Beneficial in life, and certainly in death. Lottie nodded and picked an invisible piece of lint from the pant leg of her maroon suit.

"Yes, it is. Now, to what do I owe the pleasure of your visit? You're not here to play, but it doesn't feel like this is a social call."

That was why Cassie liked Lottie. She didn't beat around the bush or make Cassie play weird social games from a time she didn't know. When she'd first woken as a ghost, she'd gotten in a lot of fights with others because she accidentally did something rude. But Lottie always seemed to understand.

Cassie leaned in close. "What do you know about my death? Or even my life, for that matter?" she asked.

Lottie's perfectly drawn brows lifted. The table nearest to them grew quiet as the ghosts shamelessly tried to eavesdrop. Lottie noticed, and in a sweeping motion, stood and pulled Cassie with her.

"Let's retire to the lounge, shall we darling?"

She pushed her toward the back door, a saccharine smile plastered on her face. Cassie tried—and failed—to match the expression until they were past the wall.

"Sorry," she said once they were alone. The lounge didn't have much in the way of comfort with a singular bench bolted to the floor, but the ghosts out in the den didn't need to know that. They just knew this place was for Lottie and Lottie alone.

"No apologies necessary, baby," Lottie said as she sat. "I just don't need the others stirring up trouble, that's all."

"So there is something weird about it? Tell me," Cassie said, belatedly adding, "please."

Lottie hummed like a disappointed parent. "So you only want to visit me when you need something?"

Chagrin crawled up Cassie's neck, hot and red. "I didn't mean it like that," she mumbled. She swallowed the awkwardness. "It's just... A memory came back earlier. First one I've gotten."

"Wow, that took a while," Lottie said. "I got my first one back just thirty years after death. It popped up out of nowhere?"

"No, I touched something and it like, shot me back," Cassie said, trying to explain as well as she could. "Hurt like hell, like I was getting burned to death or something."

"You didn't die by fire, baby," Lottie said, patting her hand.

"I know, but there's something weird about it. I thought it was suicide this whole time, but these girls are saying I was murdered—"

"Ugh, they always call the mysterious ones a suicide," Lottie sneered.

"Charlotte!" Cassie snapped. "This is serious. Something feels off about the whole thing. About my death, about why I'm stuck here—"

"Well, we know why we're stuck here," Lottie said. She glanced up in the direction of the engine room and pointed.

"Well, yeah, that thing is why we're stuck here, but why do you and I and all the others in here fully form while others are just, I don't know, half-assed remnants?"

Lottie pursed her lips. "That I couldn't say. But I know that most of us fall under the 'mysterious circumstances' tab."

"So the whole 'unfinished business' myth is real?" Cassie asked. If that was the case, then she'd have to stalk Korinne and Magnolia the whole time until all her memories came back. Then, when the ship powered down and the thing in the engine room went to sleep for good, she could be free.

It took Lottie a second to answer. "I don't know if I'd call it 'unfinished business'. With the few deaths I witnessed, there was always so much pain surrounding them, so much heartache—more than usual."

Pain. Cassie certainly understood that very well.

Lottie reached over and took her hand. "Tell me about your memory."

The strange voice of LeBeau, the bone-deep desperation flooding her system. It all felt so fresh, so real.

"It was someone telling me I had an hour before the last ship left," she said. "I think I was trying to get to the *Covenant*."

Lottie tapped a red nail against her equally red lips. "Yes, I remember that time. The ships were about to split, to see which of the two planets fared better. But no one really wanted to go to the *Covenant*, they were much stricter there compared to here."

"Yeah, but..." She paused. "I don't know. I remember this girl, Rose. But I don't know who she was. A sister that went over there?"

"Oh, no. Siblings weren't allowed during your time," Lottie said. "Try again."

"A friend then?"

"You're a terrible liar," Lottie said with a laugh.

"Am I? I don't know! That's the problem," Cassie said.

"Calm down, Cass. It'll all come back sooner or later.

Might take you a few hundred more years, but what else do we have besides time?"

Cassie had never felt more impatient in her whole, entire death. "But you do know who Rose is?"

"I know *of* Rose. It was the first thing you said when you woke back up. I have my suspicions, but I wouldn't want to influence you," Lottie said.

So much for those answers. It was all up to the girls and her tablet now. She decided to switch directions. "How much do you know about Etienne LeBeau?"

Lottie scoffed. "That piece of trash? He wanted a revolution, but all he did was get good people killed. And for what? A failed rebellion. I never understood what people saw in him, including you."

A chill settled in Cassie's chest. "I think he's the reason I died."

"I wouldn't be surprised," Lottie said. "He got what was coming to him, though. That sister of his sure did a number on him. True comeuppance if I've ever seen it."

"Jocelyn? What did she do?" Cassie asked, desperate for any nibble of information Lottie could give her.

"Sacrificed him to the thing in the engine room, the one that keeps us stuck here," Lottie said. "Almost ruined the whole ship to do it, but hey, that's what they built those escape pods for, right? Always had to be sure to have enough lifeboats."

Cassie's jaw dropped. "She did that? To her own brother?" She knew Jocelyn as someone sweet and caring, someone who'd been there when she first woke up as a ghost. Yeah, she'd sabotaged the landing sequence, but since Cassie was so newly dead when it happened, she hadn't thought to question it. If Jocelyn thought it needed to be done, it probably did.

Lottie seemed unconcerned. "Well, if your brother threatened to blow up enough of the ship to send it crashing to the ground with an unchecked soul-eating monster aboard, you'd do something drastic too."

"How did she even know about the thing in the engine room?" Cassie asked. As far as she knew, only the ghosts knew about it, and even then, some remained blissfully unaware.

"I mean, she wasn't the first person to recognize all the spirits on the ship, just the first to do something about it. But you'd have to ask her on that one," Lottie said. "All I know is she managed to seal it enough to keep it from going after the living. It's why she sabotaged the landing sequence."

"And how do *you* know that?" Cassie asked. How had she missed that was a better question.

Lottie lifted one shoulder. "We talked. She's the one who brought me to your second awakening."

Cassie had always wondered about that, and never thought to ask. But with the ship's current trajectory and imminent landing, she had more important things to worry about.

"And it's sealed? For sure?" she asked.

"More or less," Lottie said. "Don't worry your pretty little crushed head about it. The Malevolence in the engine room might be leaking a little bit, but it should be fine."

Leaking? Since when? "That's not good, Lottie. We've got living people on the ship right now, and they're taking it to land next to the *Covenant*," Cassie said as heat curled in her abdomen.

Lottie took way too long to answer. "They're real?" she whispered, which made Cassie balk.

"Of course they're real, are you serious? Why would you think they're not?"

Lottie's eyes unfocused for a second before she seemed to come back to herself. "I'm just not always sure anymore, not after things being dark for so long."

"Dark? Things here were never dark. Quiet, maybe, but not

dark," Cassie said. It felt like they were having two different conversations. "Lottie, focus. Is the thing in the engine room trying to escape? How can we keep it there?"

"Keep it there?" She laughed then, loud and forced. Doubt snaked through Cassie's heart. "Oh, Cassiopeia, what that thing does isn't up to us. Jocelyn did the best she could, but some things are too strong."

"You just said she sealed it, that she sacrificed her brother," Cassie said, her voice small.

"Oh, she did," Lottie said, a dark laughter escaping her. "Man's still stuck here, wasting away in that cell. Wasting away like we all are. Human souls aren't meant to last this long, I don't think."

"What do you mean by that?" she said. Wasting away? No, she just started getting her memories back. She was too young to start wasting away, she hadn't even hit a hundred years yet!

"I've been stuck here a long, long time, Cassiopeia," she said, uncharacteristically solemn. "Maybe it's time for us to all accept our fate. Everything they said in life about ghosts was a lie. This isn't about unfinished business, or righting our wrongs. This is just an onerous pit stop on the way to an actual afterlife." She paused, tilting her head to the side. "Or maybe, removed from Earth, this is how God punishes us. Forever entombed by our own hubris."

"I have no idea what you're talking about now," Cassie said. Never had a conversation with Lottie gone like this. Normally, she knew everything. Cassie put a hand on Lottie's shoulder and felt a stab of heat from her, even through her suit jacket. She jerked her hand back. "Lottie?"

Lottie shook her head, and her dark waves fell into her face. She stayed there for so long Cassie almost said her name again. But she snapped back, blinking rapidly as the tiniest bit of red smoke cleared from her eyes.

Oh, *fuck* no.

"Don't mess with that thing, Cass." She sounded tired.

Cassie swallowed against her dry mouth. "Okay, I won't," she said, because she couldn't think of a better response. She tried to surreptitiously analyze Lottie's face and body, but based on the smirk the other woman wore, it wasn't sly at all. If only she were just checking her out, not searching for signs of some cosmic horror bent on capturing souls.

"Thank you for your help." Cassie stood and forced herself to move away in a slow, controlled manner. Lottie didn't join her, instead staying on the bench and tracking her every move.

"Of course. Anytime," Lottie said. Cassie waited a beat, wondering if she would say or do anything more, then turned to leave. Before she could slip through the wall, Lottie called her back. "Oh, and Cassie?"

Cassie paused, took a breath, turned. "Yeah?"

Lottie looked at her for a long moment before saying, "Careful which stones you overturn. You never know what you'll find hiding underneath."

Cassie, who'd never seen a stone in life or in death, nodded. "Right. Thanks."

Propriety forgotten, Cassie practically ran out of the den. She ignored the players and the bouncers, instead wholly focused on escape.

This whole mission was a fail. Instead of coming away with answers, she came away with more questions. But at the very least, she had an idea of where to go, because apparently there was someone here who knew the Malevolence even better than Lottie, even better than Jocelyn.

"Okay," she said, trying to calm the anxiety rolling in her stomach as the vision of Lottie's red eyes replayed in her mind. "Okay, maybe it was just a fluke. Just a trick of the light. What does Lottie know anyway? She couldn't even tell me who Rose was."

Rose, with her dark hair and sharp features. Seeing that picture in her room brought up all sorts of feelings, most of which Cassie didn't want to sort through at that moment. Where did she fit into all this?

She let out a loud groan, energetic enough that, if the girls were nearby, they'd probably hear her. Good thing they were off gallivanting in some other portion of the ship with their flirting and their cameras and...

...And her tablet. Her tablet, which might turn on and tell her more about Rose. Her tablet, which might have answers that led to more memories.

Damn it. It was as good a time as any to find the two idiots again. Where were they going again after the docks? Right, the hospital.

Well, at least she'd be visiting another friend.

CHAPTER 9
KORINNE

From camera 19.1.5: [Korinne lays on a gurney; next to the camera, a scalpel slowly spins ninety degrees]

THE *ARKANA* HAD half of a ring dedicated to medical practice of all sorts, especially contagious diseases. Humans persisted, but nothing persisted harder than viruses and bacteria. Add in advanced but untested equipment and a bunch of people stuck in confinement, and the hospital bays ended up being one of the busiest areas of the ship. Korinne had seen pictures before; if any place got to Magnolia, it would be there.

The entrance to the bay had no standing door, just the panel off its track and lying flat on the ground. Inside, the wide room leaned into every gruesome stereotype of a haunted hospital. Rusted gurneys sat magnetically bolted to the floor, and stains littered the tiles, never quite scrubbed out. It was one of the few places that had this type of flooring instead of metal due to the likelihood of falling fluids.

"Oh, I hate this. I regret this immediately." Magnolia

wrung her hands and shivered. Korinne very nearly put her arm around her shoulders, but ultimately kept her hands to herself. "There's got to be so much unrest here."

"Well, yeah, look at these beds." She tapped the leg of one with the toe of her boot, and the whole thing shook. "No way to rest on this thing. Bet there's a shit ton of spirits wailing about cricks in their necks."

"Rinne! Respect!"

"Right, sorry, these beds are very fragile. Very sensitive." She said it like a joke, but meant it with utter sincerity. There was no saving most of these gurneys, no matter how much rust they removed. The restorers would have to build replicas once the ship landed on Capa Emphara.

"So many people died here," Magnolia whispered. "Gods, and when you get to those illness years..."

Years two through four. Years eighty-one through eighty-five. Year two hundred and three. Those were the worst ones. Korinne knew each by heart, but learned long ago their audience *hated* when she spouted too many dates.

"Yeah, those were rough ship-wide," she said. "There were eight epidemics in all during the trip, with thousands dead. The ones on the *Covenant* were even worse."

"Is there anyone here with us right now?" Magnolia asked the air. "Does anyone want to talk?"

Korinne went to check the camera Efex placed in the room earlier, making sure it could watch Magnolia do her thing. The screen showed most of the room in focus, capturing a few beds, equipment caches, and the edge of the circular desk in the middle of the room. The desk held a long line of screens, the glass either shattered or dark on all of them. Only one gap in the circle allowed for entry and exit, which didn't seem like a good idea in case of an emergency. Korinne left the camera and slipped through the narrow opening to investigate the computer towers, hoping she could get enough power to turn one on.

"As per usual, no ghosts have anything to say," Korinne said, playing her part. For the videos to make more money, they had to be extra dramatic. It was a miracle she'd lasted the last five years. Well, not a miracle. It was all thanks to Magnolia.

"Fine, you try," Magnolia said in the most perfectly petulant tone.

"All right, sure," she said, and cleared her throat. "What's up, ghosties. It's me, your girl."

"All this time, and you still haven't managed to find a better conversation starter," Magnolia muttered.

"Yeah, well, it never gets less weird to talk to nothing." She flicked her hand at the air around them. "But I do it because you're pretty and you ask nicely."

"If you don't hush, I swear—"

"Here, ghostie ghosties." A click of her tongue, like calling a cat, sealed the deal. "Anyone? Anyone?"

Magnolia flinched. "Now you're just being ridiculous."

"I'm always ridiculous, Mags," she said, flipping her black curls from her eyes and giving Magnolia a dazzling smile. "Now, do your thing. I'm gonna keep trying to turn on this computer."

"Why?" When she leaned against a gurney, it groaned, probably as a threat. "It's not like you have log-in information. There were no universal chips back then."

"No, but I am armed with some old school software." Korinne flaunted her handheld. "Or, malware I think it's called? I mix up the old hacking stuff. I'm better with the physical."

"I'll say," Magnolia remarked, and the accompanying wink nearly ended her.

Korinne's jaw dropped. "Remember what I said about you

being mean? It's even worse when you're complimentary." She tried so hard to keep her tone light, and sent a kiss her way as a bonus.

Magnolia shook her head. "Ridiculous."

Did Korinne imagine it, or was there a blush on her cheeks?

For a few more minutes, Magnolia attempted to commune with the ghosts, and Korinne tried to restart the ancient technology, but neither of them managed success.

"Ugh, okay, fine." Korinne stood, admitting defeat. "Bring it back in."

"Time to get to work." Magnolia fixed her hair, then reached out and corrected a few of Korinne's curls before settling a few feet away. She cleared her throat and pasted on that camera-ready smile.

"Tell me everything," Korinne said, giving her two thumbs up.

"After Cassie's body was found, they brought her to one of the nearest hospital bays, just like this one. There, they would've done three full vitals checks before declaring her death. Usually, staff would attempt life-saving measures, but as we could see in her autopsy photos, Cassie was gone before she even left the docks."

"At least they gave her the respect of the vitals checks," Korinne said. "Wouldn't want to have someone wake up in the reclamation tanks again."

That got a full body shudder out of Magnolia. "Can you imagine waking up in one of those as the machine starts to eat you?"

"You don't have to imagine it, we'll see the reclamation tanks tomorrow," Korinne said.

"Oh, don't remind me. I was feeling so brave a few minutes ago, and now it's all just drifting away," Magnolia said as she clutched her pendant.

"Don't worry, I'll protect you from everything, just like I always do," she said. "No one's getting eaten or anything."

"I certainly hope not," she said, so quiet, Korinne wasn't sure she meant to say it out loud. It was a prime opportunity for some fake flirting, but if Magnolia wasn't going to take the bait, then she would roll right past it too.

"Do you want to go first, or me?"

"You, of course. I need to clear my head." Magnolia shook out her hands, as if the ghosts clung to her. This trip certainly seemed to affect her more than the others, and Korinne wondered if this was all a grand mistake.

"I'll make sure they're nice and riled up for you," Korinne said, like an asshole. Before Magnolia could say anything she continued with, "Just kidding. I'm gonna lay down and be nice to all the little ghosties hanging out in here."

Magnolia rolled her eyes. "Doubtful, but I appreciate you trying," she said.

Korinne scanned the room to find the sturdiest gurney. To be extra enticing to all those ghosts allegedly present, she found a few forgotten tools—just as rusted as the gurneys—and sat them on a tray next to her place.

She paused, hands on hips, and admired her work. "All right, I think I'm ready."

Magnolia hesitated at the door and eyed the setup. "What are you doing?"

"I'm setting the scene for them. You know, being nice." With a flourish, she lay on the gurney, ignoring the way it shuddered and squeaked. "Come on, ghosts! Are you mad? Are you pissed you're dead? You can take it out on me!"

Magnolia gasped. "Rinne! That's not being nice!"

"Sure it is! I'm giving them an opportunity to let out some otherworldly frustrations. Don't worry, these big baby ghosties won't mess with me," Korinne said, putting her hands behind her head and getting comfortable.

"Fucking hells. Five minutes! Good luck." Magnolia tossed up her hands and stomped away, far enough that Korinne couldn't hear her footsteps or her muttered curses.

"Hello, ghosties," Korinne sang, tapping one foot against the other. If Magnolia was that stressed by the setup, their viewers would freak out when they saw it. She could practically hear all the people typing up comments about her disrespect. "How's it feel being dead, hmm?"

Nothing.

With Magnolia gone, Korinne didn't have to worry about scaring her. That left plenty of room to do what she did best: say silly things to try and either make a ghost appear or make their viewers freak out.

"Must suck, right? Being dead? I mean, especially being stuck here all the time. Are the nurses here too? Oh, God, what about the food? Hospital food is the worst. Wait, do ghosts eat? Is your unfinished business just a good meal?"

Silence.

Korinne sighed. "You know, I don't think you're real. Magnolia does, though. She says she can feel your presence or whatever. Just stresses her out more than anything when we do these things. So if you could stop doing whatever bullshit you're on and let her rest, I'd appreciate it. You can mess with me instead. Hear me out, appear right now so that we can just call it a night."

Nothing but the tapping of her foot.

The gurney groaned as she rolled to a different position. Despite the years and the probable mold, the mattress wasn't all that uncomfortable. She could stay here longer if she needed to.

"Look, I'm just laying here, with fresh kidneys ripe for the taking," she said. She was tempted to take a five minute nap, ghosts and cameras be damned, as exhaustion from shitty sleep the night before set in.

Too bad Magnolia would come back and think she died of ghost poisoning or something.

"Come on, get freaky. I'm ready and willing."

Still nothing. Korinne watched the time tick down, adding a few more jibes and insults in an attempt to make something rise from the ether of the universe, but nothing deemed her worthy of their time.

It felt like a thousand years before she heard Magnolia's shoes on the metal floor as she hurried back to the hospital. Because she was bored and had too much time to plan, Korinne spread out on the gurney and made herself look as dead as possible.

"Oh, no, she's quiet. Rinne?" Magnolia stopped at the door and must have spotted the gruesome scene, because she exclaimed, "Korinne!"

In a flurry of hair and dress, Magnolia arrived at her side, her eyes wide and luminous in the low light. She grabbed Korinne's face with cold hands, and she looked so scared Korinne had to cut her farce short.

"What?" she asked.

Magnolia yelped. "You jerk!"

She dug her bony fingers into Korinne's ribs, causing the other girl to screech and scramble away. One of the gurney legs broke with a loud *crack* and sent Korinne tumbling. Magnolia fell with her. Their limbs tangled in a mess of knees and elbows until they landed on the floor. With all the movement, Korinne's flashlight got pinned beneath her, leaving them in darkness. It hurt like a bitch, considering most of Magnolia's weight was on top of her.

"Are you all right?" Magnolia asked. She'd landed so close Korinne could feel her breath on her cheek.

"Yeah, I'm fine. You?" She shifted her hands and found they'd wrapped around Magnolia's waist. Reluctantly, she let go.

"I'm okay," she said, moving slightly to one side and putting more pressure into Korinne's hip, which in turn sent more weight into the rail underneath her.

"Ouch, shit," Korinne said as the metal bit into her. Her pants probably saved her skin from a scrape, but she'd be so pissed if the fall ruined her favorite pair.

"Sorry," Magnolia said, rolling back the other way just as Korinne tried to pull her other knee up, making Magnolia land smack in between her legs. Both stopped, the air between them charged with something completely unrelated to ghosts.

"We've got to stop meeting like this," Korinne murmured, and Magnolia let out a breathy laugh.

"Do we now?" she replied. She put a hand on Korinne's shoulder, then her ribs. Korinne inhaled sharply, but Magnolia only used the touches to find the floor. She pushed up and away, leaving Korinne cold. With enough space to move, Korinne fished her flashlight out from underneath her.

Magnolia hovered over her on hands and knees, her lavender hair just long enough to tickle Korinne's collarbones. Her eyes sparkled in the low light.

"Makes for good ambience," Korinne said, raising a brow.

Magnolia sat back and reached her hands out. Korinne grabbed them, but halfway up, Magnolia let go.

"Ouch, Mags, what the hell?" she asked as she smacked back against the floor.

"I remembered I'm mad at you! That was mean, don't do that to me," Magnolia said, gesturing to the collapsed gurney.

"Don't do that to you? You *tickled* me! Don't do that to me!" Korinne clambered to her feet and held her torso tightly, wary of a second attack.

"I thought you were dead!"

"Why would you think I was dead?" She did, in fact, want Magnolia to think she was dead, but not at the expense of getting tickled.

"Because you were splayed out like a Vaelish sacrifice!"

"You know I don't know what those look like!"

"You're a historian, how could you not know?"

Korinne groaned loudly and ran a hand through her short curls. "That doesn't mean I know all the history about everywhere. We've been through this."

"And yet you never seem to learn about your own planet, where my ancestors came from." Korinne thought Magnolia sounded a little too sincere, and so turned down her ire. She made a fair point; Korinne hadn't studied Vaela properly since high school. After that, it was all about Old Earth and the *Arkana*.

"You're right. I promise I'll read so many books about it when we're done with all this," Korinne said. A shiver went down her spine at the thought of her dissertation, and how many long nights she spent staring at grainy pictures. She didn't have the brain power for another Ph.D., but she could at least learn enough to not accidentally hurt Magnolia's feelings.

"Thank you," Magnolia said. She picked up Korinne's flashlight and handed it over. "Go on, give me my space."

Korinne laughed. "You're really pushing me out? Are you that excited to spend time alone with all the angry ghosts?"

"Not particularly, because I have the distinct feeling they are *very* angry. But so am I, and I want to get it over with." She held herself ramrod straight and put on a brave face, but Korinne could tell she was scared. They'd hit plenty of haunted places before, haunted hospitals even, but none of them had the history of the *Arkana*. None of them made Magnolia bite her lip like that, or clutch her skirts.

"You must be some sort of masochist to constantly put your-self through this." Even if Korinne thought the whole existence of ghosts was bullshit, Magnolia believed it, and it obviously distressed her. For a second, she thought to stop the experiment. But that wouldn't do at all, not with millions of viewers waiting for her response.

"It's my lot in life," Magnolia said. Instead of the gurney, she opted for a rickety stool, which creaked with every movement. She sat tall, prim, and proper, and crossed one leg over the other. "Go on now, I've got work to do."

"Hold on, we have an addition," Korinne said. She dug into her bag. "I promised you jewelry."

Magnolia narrowed her eyes. "What?"

It took a bit of rummaging, but Korinne found what she wanted: magnetic handcuffs.

"Ah ha!" She brandished the cuffs, and Magnolia paled.

"No," she said.

"Yes." Korinne opened the correct document on her hand-held and showed her the screen. "Suggested and voted on by our lovely viewers. They want you restrained."

"This is too far," Magnolia said, and for the first time, Korinne thought she'd truly say no to a challenge. She faltered and moved the cuffs back toward her bag.

"If it's too much, then it's too much. We don't have to do it." She laced her words with as much sincerity as possible, knowing at times it was hard to tell if she was serious or joking. "For real, we can let it go. Angry comments fuel the algorithm just as well as positive ones."

She was one hundred percent serious when she said it, but the words seemed to give Magnolia pause. They stood silent for a long minute before Magnolia held her hand out.

"Give me the cuffs," she said. Surprise rocked through Korinne.

"Really?" she asked. This had been the one challenge on the list she thought wouldn't fly.

"Really," Magnolia said.

Korinne held the cuffs out but didn't let go, even as Magnolia grabbed them.

"You're sure?" she said.

"I'm sure." She had that look on her face now, the one that probably got them this opportunity to begin with. "Just come back right at five minutes. Not a second later, okay?"

"Yes, my liege. It's set for both of our fingerprints, so if you need to bail, do so." Korinne ran her thumb over the fingerprint lock and it popped open. She then let go and watched as Magnolia hooked one end to the gurney and the other to her wrist. Pride welled in her chest at Magnolia's bravery. Season one of the show, she would've been hyperventilating at the simple idea of handcuffing herself to something. Their audience better appreciate it, or Korinne would be responding to comments in a very ill-advised way.

Magnolia didn't look happy, but she did look determined. Korinne saluted her, gave her one last look, then wandered far enough away to give Magnolia solitude.

"She's probably freaking out right now," she said to her comm pad, passing the time by once again talking to no one. "Not gonna lie, it's definitely a freaky spot. They really leaned into it with the scalpels and blood stains and biohazard signs."

The ship shifted and tilted for a second, then righted itself. Korinne paused, waiting for Magnolia to call out, but heard only ship sounds.

"Did I feel anything? No. Did I hear anything? Also no. I mean, nothing out of the ordinary. But that's not exactly unusual."

Another awkward pause. Thank God for post-production

editing. The ship shimmied and shook for a second, and she waited for it to quiet before continuing.

"Thing is, a metric fuck ton of people died in that room, so Magnolia is gonna lose her mind—"

Right on cue, a crash sounded and Magnolia screamed. If she didn't sound so terrified, Korinne would've congratulated her excellent execution of dramatics.

As it was, her heart leapt into her throat, and she took off.

CHAPTER 10
MAGNOLIA

From Korinne's comm pad: [Magnolia screams]

MAGNOLIA HAD NEVER CHANGED her mind so fast.

"Oh, gods," she said, her voice wavering. "I hate this. Oh, I hate this so much."

She gave an experimental pull of the cuffs, but they stuck hard to the gurney. Her heart skipped a beat, and she forced herself to take a deep breath, then another. This was fine, she could do this. She just needed to stay calm.

"Okay." She looked at the camera, staring into the eyes of the future viewers. Brandishing a finger like a weapon, she said, "Don't tell Korinne I did this. It's just so I don't have a panic attack so severe that my heart stops beating."

As long as she knew she could escape, then she could last the requisite five minutes. Excuse in tow, she ran her thumb over the fingerprint lock.

The cuff didn't budge.

"Shit." Magnolia tried again, but once again the cuff stayed closed. "You're kidding me. Oh, that's just cruel."

Korinne wouldn't do this to her, which meant it was just another piece of equipment failing at the time she needed it most. First Efex, now this? What was next, the comm pads themselves?

"Okay, that's fine. This is fine. I'm fine." If she said it enough times, maybe it would come true.

Shadows appeared in the corner of her eye, two of them this time. On her chest, her pendant heated. She closed her eyes and prayed to every god that the camera would pick up something.

The temperature around her dropped, and she felt the two distinct presences come closer to her. Magnolia let out a shuddering breath, a cloud of vapor rising.

"Is, um–" Damn, it was super cold now. "Is someone here with me right now?"

Silence answered her, except for the general creaks and groans of the ship. The hair above her ear twitched, and she spun. The cuff bit into her wrist as she reached the end of it, but no visible ghost greeted her on the other side.

"Magnolia, you have to give them a way to answer." With trembling fingers, she dug through her bag and found the Parabox. If she focused on that, she didn't worry about how the cold made her nose hurt and how it felt like someone squeezed her heart from the inside. "Okay, let's try this again—"

"Hurt," the box said as soon as she turned it on, its tiny electronic voice making her jump.

"I'm sorry you're hurting," she said. Pretty par for the course for the hospital, but she kept that thought inside. Korinne might be brave enough to antagonize a ghost, but she sure as hell wasn't. "My name is Magnolia. Can you tell me your name?"

"Pain," the box said this time.

"Yes, I'm sure you felt a lot of pain." It took a gargantuan effort to keep her breaths even and her heart rate below a thousand. "I'm so sorry about that."

"Cake."

"I—what?" Cake? What did cake have to do with the hospital? "Did they serve you cake here? Was that the good part?"

"Balls."

"Now I feel like you're just fucking with me." Magnolia gave another tug on the cuffs; nope, still stuck. "This is your chance, you know. Tell the world your story. What's your name?"

Silence.

"Oh, sure, now you want to stay quiet." The cold dissipated, and she let out a sigh. "Thank you, that cold sucked. Did Korinne remember to turn thermals on with that camera? Gods, I hope so."

She shook out her hand—singular, since the other remained occupied by a fucking handcuff—and willed warm blood into it. She should've gotten a thicker jacket than the flowy cardigan she currently sported.

Magnolia checked her watch. Great, only three and a half minutes to go.

Across the room, a cabinet opened on silent hinges. She paused and waited.

"Was that you, or the ship?" she asked. Never mind that only one cabinet opened and no others. Once again, she received no answer. Just as she opened her mouth to ask another question, another cabinet opened. Then another. Then the whole row flew open in succession with such speed that some doors snapped closed. Magnolia jumped and grit her teeth, doing her best to pretend she wasn't scared out of her mind.

"Okay, good job. Thank you for alerting me to your presence." That was neutral, right? It wasn't antagonizing? She held up the Parabox. "You want to talk about it?"

"Kill."

"Well, that's not very nice," she said, her voice barely escaping past her heart in her throat. "Don't kill me, that would be a terrible mess for Korinne to clean up."

"Die."

"Yes, you did die."

Wrong thing to say, apparently.

Cold air blasted her, and something flew across the room. Magnolia couldn't see what it was because she was too busy ducking out of the way. The cuffs, holding tight to the bed rail, yanked her shoulder in an awkward direction. She tugged at them again, but all that did was shake the already precarious gurney.

"I'm sorry, I'm sorry!" she yelled, covering her head with her other hand. "That was insensitive, I know. I apologize."

"Stop," the Parabox said.

"I'd love to stop right now," Magnolia said as fear flooded her. "This was a terrible idea. Fucking hells, this was *such* a bad idea."

"Don't."

"Don't what? I can't do anything! I'm stuck!"

Three cabinet doors slammed shut, and Magnolia yelped. The cold hit her once more, then retreated.

"Holy shit holy shit holy shit—"

A vibration went through the floor. The ship shuddered, then threw her to the side. She fell, her left hand still held above her by the cuffs. Almost as soon as it came, it stopped, leaving her in silence and stillness. Her pendant swung back and forth as she stayed on her hand and knees, trying to catch her breath.

"Okay," she whispered. One strong swallow and another breath. "Okay, we're okay. You're fine. Everything is fine. Half of that was the ship, not an angry ghost trying to eat you. These ghosts are just playing."

One inch at a time, Magnolia stood. Once upright, she rested her hand on her hip and continued her calming techniques. All the cabinet doors remained stationary, the room felt neither cold nor hot, and no mysterious objects flew at her head. The two shadows didn't even show up now; she was alone, with just the ship to talk to.

"Is anyone here with me?" She wasn't proud of how her voice shook, but she kept her head up. Gods, Korinne would have a field day when she saw the footage later. "Anyone want to say anything?"

"Run," the Parabox said.

Magnolia waited, staring at the word on the little screen.

"That's it?" she asked, like a fool. When nothing answered her, the fear started transforming into bravery. Maybe it really was all just from the ship doing something weird, and these sensations were just her being tired. She jiggled the cuffs. "I can't run, obviously. Thank you for the advice, though."

The Parabox had nothing to say. Magnolia checked her watch—two minutes to go. This had to be the longest five minutes of her life.

"Hello?" she said. In the quiet, she realized her wrist hurt. Actually, it hurt a lot. She looked down to see the skin rubbed raw and bleeding in a couple of places. "Oh, now that's annoying. Damn it, I should've seen that coming."

Now that she'd seen it, she couldn't unsee it, and the pain bloomed further.

"Okay, maybe I can call Korinne—"

The cold returned, but only on her sternum, as if someone placed their hand there. Magnolia stilled. It wasn't the same as before; sure, earlier there was an intense chill, but this felt deeper, colder. As if Death itself held her heart in its hand.

"Hello?"

Something flung her pendant back. The chain choked her, and in the darkness, someone appeared.

Magnolia's breath caught. Burns coated the person's entire face. Skin hung in melted chunks, and wide, lidless eyes stared intently. Blood dribbled from the bare muscles of their forehead. A rattling breath escaped the gaping area where their mouth used to be, and cold drifted over her. She froze, caught in their stare. Was this...a hallucination?

Just in case it wasn't, Magnolia flung a hand out and screamed.

She screamed so loud it hurt her ears and her throat. A burst of light left her palm, and the face disappeared. Sharp pain lanced her wrist as she tried to run, and the cuffs held her tight. The magnets holding the gurney gave up, and it tipped over, hitting the ground just seconds before she did. A panic so strong her lungs spasmed rose in her as she screamed again and again.

"Mags!"

Heavy footsteps sounded from behind her, and Magnolia tore her eyes away from the darkness to find Korinne sprinting into the room. She slid onto her knees, bumping into Magnolia's side. Without any prompting, she reached up and ran her finger over the sensor. The cuff broke open, and she scrambled out of it.

"Oh, gods," Magnolia choked out. She sat up so fast she collided with Korinne, their foreheads smacking together with a terrible *thunk*.

"Shit!" Korinne fell back, her hands on her forehead and her eyes squeezed shut. "Damn, you have a hard head."

"There's—there's a—"

Magnolia turned, but nothing waited for her. There was no sight of melting flesh or shaking bones. No ghost, no noises, no cabinet doors moving. It was just an empty room with old equipment.

"Mags, what happened?" Korinne took her by the chin and forced Magnolia's eyes back to hers. "Are you okay?"

Magnolia tried to hold it together, she really did. But before she could think too hard about it, she threw herself into Korinne's arms and wept.

"There was a face and all the cabinets and something flew at my head..." Her words barely made it through her tears, and Korinne's arms tightened around her.

"Hey, you're okay. Nothing's gonna get you now." Korinne repositioned slightly so she could cradle Magnolia to her chest. It was like she built a little cage of safety with her body, and Magnolia sank into it. "You're okay, nothing's there."

"Yeah, anymore." Magnolia felt herself trembling, and Korinne gently stroked her hair as she held her tight. "It was so real, it was right there," she whispered, afraid to admit it out loud.

"Want me to fight it?" Korinne asked. For some reason, the offer renewed Magnolia's tears, and she once again devolved into a shaking, sobbing mess on Korinne's shoulder. The other woman continued her gentle words and warm hold, letting Magnolia get all her feelings out.

She didn't mean to cry for so long. Hell, what she really meant to do was run as fast as she could out of the room. But things weren't as scary when she had Korinne; her partner turned haunted places into dark, empty rooms, ones where she didn't have to be afraid. The last dregs of fear buffered from her system, and after a few minutes the tears stopped as well. With as much composure as she could muster, Magnolia sniffled and loosened her hold on Korinne's shirt.

"Sorry about that," she said. She sat back, and Korinne moved forward, staying close. There were wrinkles in her tank top where Magnolia gripped too hard, and she reached out to try and smooth the fabric.

"Don't apologize. Are you okay?" Korinne gently tucked one lavender lock behind Magnolia's ear, her dark eyes searching her face. "What happened?"

Now that she'd calmed down a little, embarrassment seeped in. "I don't know, I think I just..." She looked around the room, trying to both find an explanation and ignore how close Korinne's face was to hers. "I thought I saw a ghost," she said.

"Close up or far away?" she asked, much more sincere than Magnolia anticipated. Her eyes snapped back to Korinne, who looked neither mocking nor annoyed. Only concerned.

"Oh, um, up close," Magnolia said, her voice scratchy. Korinne nodded for her to continue. "Their face was all burned, I couldn't really tell anything about them, and they were just"—she held her hands up a couple inches from her face—"right there." She dropped her hands, energy spent. What had that weird light been? It was almost like it came from her.

"Yikes, no wonder you screamed so loud," Korinne said, reaching forward to gently rub the muscles on the sides of her throat. Magnolia didn't realize someone could have tense muscles in those spots until that moment.

"So you believe me?" she asked.

"Of course I do." Korinne paused, glanced at her own hand, then pulled her arm back.

Magnolia sighed as the unspoken part hovered between them.

"You believe that I *think* I saw something," she said, voice flat.

"It's not up to me to decide what you did or didn't see," Korinne said with a wince.

"But you don't think I saw a ghost," Magnolia said.

Korinne opened and closed her mouth a few times before deciding on what words to say. "That's what we're here to find, right? So just 'cause I wasn't here to see it doesn't mean that it wasn't a ghost," she said. Magnolia gave her a wry smile.

"You've gotten better at that professional-talk-around thing," she said.

Korinne grimaced. "That might be the meanest thing you've ever said to me," she muttered.

"Just trying to make you fall in love with me," Magnolia tried to joke, though it didn't come across as strong as she wanted.

"Ha! Too late," Korinne replied with an exaggerated scoff. She reached out to wipe one last errant tear from Magnolia's cheek. "Do you want to check the camera? See if it caught anything?"

She should feel excited and hopeful that there was a camera recording the terrible encounter, but after so many fails, Magnolia couldn't quite muster the energy.

"We can check it later, I just..." She trailed off, and the ensuing silence pressed on every part of her. How could she explain how scary it was, when there likely wouldn't be any photographic evidence?

"Oh, shit," Korinne said, startling Magnolia.

"What?" Adrenaline flooded her system again, and she turned this way and that, trying to see the whole room at once. "What is it?"

"You're bleeding, Mags." Korinne pointed to her hand. Sure enough, multiple cuts lined her wrist where the cuff tore her skin, and a bit of purple blood dribbled out. Once she saw it, the searing pain came through.

"Ow," Magnolia said. Then, with a little more feeling, "Ow!"

"Yeah, forget the camera. We need to get that cleaned up."

Korinne heaved herself to her feet, then took Magnolia's hands and helped her up. She wobbled slightly, and her knees threatened to give out, but through sheer spite she managed to stay upright. These ghosts could terrorize her, but she would continue on like a professional.

"I hate this place," she murmured. In solidarity, Korinne took her hand and held it tight as she led her out of the room.

"I know. But you're doing great, and your hair looks fantastic," she said, throwing a wink at her. "Just think, only two more days and then it's nothing but food, drinks, and chairs on the beach."

"No, it's two more days until we sit like shrimps and edit for a thousand hours." She noticed Korinne didn't let go of her hand. Well, if she wanted to be affectionate, Magnolia certainly wasn't going to stop her. Especially after she got bullied by ghosts.

"Shh," Korinne said. "We don't have to edit immediately. The interns have to scrub through all the blank footage first. Our only job will be relaxing in the sun with something tasty in hand."

"Unless the beach is haunted," Magnolia didn't quite have the same humor as usual, but at least it was coming back.

"If we stumble upon a haunted beach, I will build the thickest salt circle the universe has ever seen just so you can have some peace and quiet," she said.

They reached the elevator, and Korinne pressed the button, the lift taking forever to arrive. Only when they boarded did Korinne seem to realize the hand-holding situation, and casually let go. Magnolia tried not to let her feelings get hurt by it and stuffed her hands into her pockets, seeking the same warmth.

Maybe then her shivering would stop.

CHAPTER 11
CASSIE

From camera 19.1.5: [a flash of red]

CASSIE STARED, open mouthed, at her friend. Even in the darkness of the hospital, she could see his lidless eyes on display.

"Dude," she said after a minute. "What the fuck was that?"

"What?" Jensen turned to her, one of his hanging pieces of flesh swaying with the movement.

"It was supposed to be 'funny ha-ha' kind of haunting shit, not 'scare the living daylights out of her and make her cry' shit!" Cassie put her hands on her hips and leaned back to watch the girls walk down the hallway.

"I mean, is it not funny to pop up and scare somebody? You're the one who said to try getting close to her!" Some muscles tried to raise his eyebrows, but most of them were too charred to work. Cassie gave him an unamused look.

"Yeah, get close to her, not show her your nightmare fuel," she said, poking her own cheek.

"Hey!" Okay, he was right to be mad about that. That was kind of mean.

"Sorry, I know getting burned to death really sucked," she said. Jensen remembered his death in full detail and was one of few people who made Cassie glad she didn't remember her own.

"Yeah, it did. You know I was actually pretty good looking before all this? Stupid. Now I can't even get a date with dead guys. I might actually be stuck in hell." He leaned against the counter and crossed his arms.

"Still, no reason to terrify the girl. It's supposed to be more physical stuff for the cameras," Cassie said, gesturing to the one in the corner.

"Maybe they should be scared," he said with a shrug. "I don't know, Cass. Sometimes it's hard seeing people. *Living* people. They take so much for granted, and it just... It makes me so angry." He mimed choking someone, which made Cassie freeze. She'd never seen Jansen act like this, and in sixty years he'd never said anything about feeling angry.

"You okay?" she asked, head tilted to the side.

The muscles in his jaw, nice and on display, clenched. A little bit of blood leaked out.

"No. I'm dead, and I'm tired of it. All we do is sit here all day and watch people run around," he said, his eyes flashing red. Red, just like Lottie's. The fuck?

Cassie blinked, but the red remained. "Dude, we haven't seen people in like, decades," she said.

He shook his head, the red light fading.

"Whatever. Guess I'll just go apologize to that girl, hmm?"

Cassie didn't miss the sarcasm.

"Don't worry about it now. I'll make sure they don't come down here and bug you again," she said.

"They have to," he spat, throwing his arm in a wide arc.

White bone showed as he did so. "Their stupid cameras are still down here."

Well, he had her there.

"Fine, next time just go hide and I'll deal with them." It was the best she could do. Sure, having an accomplice made it a lot easier to mess with people, but she wouldn't do it if it left someone in tears—or, apparently, got Jansen all twisted up.

"Whatever." He didn't bother saying goodbye, he only leaned back and fell through the counter, disappearing into whatever abyss he chose to rest in. Cassie stood alone in the middle of the hospital, staring at the spot where he'd disappeared.

"What the fuck was that?" she muttered.

Well, she got into a bad mood sometimes too. Maybe Jansen just needed a break. Startling people was one thing, but Magnolia damn near peed herself with fear. Cassie wasn't going for that.

And what the fuck was going on with his eyes?

"Fool me once," Cassie said, jumping up through the ceiling. Two people in a row having red in their eyes? Lottie saying the thing in the engine room was stronger than they could imagine? Yeah, she needed to take this seriously. For a second she thought to go to the source and check the engine room herself, but that sounded like trouble. If only she had an alternative...

Wait, she did. Lottie said Jocelyn sacrificed her brother, and that his soul was still here. If anyone would know what was going on with that thing, it'd be him. Selfishly, Cassie wanted the visit anyway, because that asshole probably had at least one answer about her life.

Did she dare? Did it matter?

Cassie paused. Where had that thought come from? Of course, it mattered. Sure, she was dead and stuck here, as they all were. But that didn't mean she wanted Korinne and Magnolia to join them. Did she? No, she didn't. She just wanted to mess with them, scare them so bad they *almost* died—

What? No.

She slowed her ascent and stopped in front of a door with a window. Bit by bit, she siphoned enough energy from the ship to materialize.

In the glass, her eyes glowed red.

Cassie gasped and shunted the energy away. No, she wouldn't succumb to the Malevolence. She wouldn't! She would keep those two girls safe, even if it killed her all over again. No one else would be hurt by that thing ever again, she would be sure of it.

With all the power of positive thinking, Cassie pushed down the negative thoughts and the vague feeling of despair building in her chest. After a deep, useless breath, she took more energy and looked again. This time, no red reflection stared back at her. Good, so it didn't have a true hold on her. That meant she still had time to figure out how to hold it back and protect Korinne and Magnolia.

The answer was obvious. While she couldn't go to the source, she could go to the next best thing. She had to go talk to LeBeau.

The original flight commanders apparently didn't anticipate a need for a prison, as it only held about ten small cells. Iron bars covered each entrance, with a slot around waist-high for food. No warden waited at the front, but plenty of ghosts occupied the cells. All of them reached through the bars as Cassie passed.

"Hey, you girl—"

"Just open the door, I'll make it worth your while—"

"Can you at least get me some more water?"

Cassie only stopped long enough to see what they looked like, then passed by with a wave.

"Nope, get it all yourselves!" she called over her shoulder. Funny, how none of them tried to escape when they could literally walk through walls. Most of them faded as soon as they talked to her, but their feelings of shame and guilt lingered enough to leave a sour taste in her mouth.

One by one, Cassie checked the cells, but never saw an aged face with slicked back hair. Maybe she was wrong, and this LeBeau guy wasn't stuck here with the rest of them. Where else would his sister put him?

She arrived at the second to last cell on the right, and felt a shift in the energy. Something was different here—darker. She paused, girded her loins, and stepped up to the bars.

"Ah, I wondered when I'd get to see you again."

Etienne LeBeau sat with his elbows on his knees, calm and confident, the picture of a perfect inmate.

"You," Cassie said.

Etienne spread his hands wide, inviting.

"Me," he said, like they were old friends reuniting.

Cassie stalled the anger threatening to overflow. The last thing she needed then was her eyes going red. "Word around the halls is it's your fault I died." She still couldn't remember the day, or the situation. But that's what Korinne and Magnolia implied, and they obviously knew what they were talking about.

"Not in the slightest," Etienne said. "It's your own fault you died, because you didn't listen to me."

"Bullshit," she spat.

He had the nerve to smile, cocking his head to the side.

"And how do you know? Do you remember how it all happened? Because I do." The most infuriating smirk graced his once-handsome face, a smoldering glint in his eye.

"What? How?" Her resentment continued to burn, and a hot curiosity added to the flame. How could he remember things, and she couldn't? "Tell me how."

He laughed, he actually *laughed*, and Cassie nearly reached into the cell to punch his face and steal his energy. But that was the kicker, she realized. Why would he, out of all people, stay in his cell after death?

Etienne leaned back, putting his hands behind his head. "I remember everything for the same reason I'm stuck in here." He nodded to the cell door, where someone had carved a small symbol into the metal. It looked oddly similar to Magnolia's pendant.

"The fuck is that, some kind of curse or something?" she asked. Was Lottie right, that his own sister sacrificed him?

"Certainly something. My sister decided one life sentence wasn't enough and locked me in here with nothing but the Malevolence for company." He scowled at the symbol and spat on the floor.

"You've got friends next door, don't be so dramatic," Cassie said.

"It sees you, you know. Watches you. It's gotten a taste of your soul," LeBeau said.

"That's gross," Cassie said, trying in vain to stay chipper when ice had settled into her gut.

His eyes glinted red, just like Lottie's and Jansen's had. But with him, the red stayed. It didn't fade like Cassie's did.

"I wouldn't be so flippant," LeBeau said, his voice low. "You don't know what it's capable of."

"Sounds like not much." Cassie tapped the symbol carved into the wall, and a spark of energy zipped through her. Her vision went white for a moment, then a bite of a memory popped up: Cassie lying in bed, reading a poem on her tablet. Since when did she like poetry?

"It stings, I know," LeBeau said in reference to the symbol, mistaking Cassie's experience for whatever pain he got from it. It hurt, yeah, but it also brought a memory. Belatedly, she realized the anger simmering in her had dimmed some, as if the magic soothed it. And if it could do that... A dangerous thread of hope pulled tight in Cassie's chest.

"Your sister, is she still around?" she asked, trying in vain to sound nonchalant.

If Jocelyn had this kind of power in life, then surely even as a ghost she could help get Cassie's memories back and clear whatever hold the Malevolence had on her. Hell, maybe she could also protect the girls and be sure they all made it to Capa Emphara in one piece.

"No, she abandoned the ship, just like the rest of them. Convinced them all to leave me up here to die." He stood and came to the bars, holding them tight. Cassie fought every urge to step backward. "You could've done something important, Cassie. If you'd just followed orders, everything would've gone as planned. We would've made real change for the better. It's all your fault the rebellion failed."

"See, that's the funny thing about the afterlife," Cassie said. "I may not remember much, but I remember everything that's happened after I died. We didn't need that rebellion, we found a planet and got off the ship without me doing whatever you wanted me to do. So you can stop telling yourself that lie. We all turned out just fine without your stupid fucking plans."

LeBeau clenched his fists, and she gave into the instinct to step back. It was too easy to imagine him reaching through the bars and grabbing her. He noticed, and a grin spread across his face.

"Talking such a big game with this barrier between us." He let out another laugh, this one humorless. "I see. It only took *dying* for you to grow a spine." He sighed heavily and shuffled back to his seat. While he tried to do so with poise and power, his age and malnutrition showed. His death must have been slow and painful, which was almost bad enough for what he deserved.

"Look, I'm not here for a social call. I just want to know what happened." Maybe, if he told her that, then more memories would pop up.

LeBeau chuckled. "Oh yeah? And why should I tell you?"

Cassie blinked, her mind whirring. She should've known he wouldn't give the information up easily. So much for the cautious optimism she'd been working on.

"Why not?" she said, the only response she could come up with. "Not like it would kill you."

"You have to give me something first," he said, all humor gone from his voice. It would border on menacing if Cassie didn't know he was full on cursed to stay in the cell.

"Oh sure, let me just get my band and transfer some credits over." She held up her naked wrist and poked at it. "Beep boop beep. There you go, my whole bank account is now yours."

"I need energy," he continued.

"You need an attitude adjustment," she replied.

His eyes blazed with a spark of red. "Bring me enough *living* energy to bust out of here, and I'll tell you everything I remember about your life. Your name, your job, your dreams, everything. I'll tell you why you were down at the docking bay that day." He held her gaze, and a shiver went down her spine. She didn't like the way he was looking at her.

"What's wrong with borrowing energy from your little friend? Isn't it all powerful?" she asked.

"It doesn't work, obviously," he sneered. "Just as dumb in death as you were in life."

"Okay." Cassie clapped her hands together and pointed at him. "You're clearly a fucking asshole, and I'm gonna continue blaming you for everything. Thanks for wasting my time, good luck getting out of here."

She turned on her heel and stomped toward the door. Behind her, she heard LeBeau scramble to the bars of his cell.

"Cassie, wait!" Oh, he changed his tune *really* fast if he didn't get his way. No wonder his rebellion failed. Cassie kept walking, but he called her bluff. "Don't you want to know all about Rose?"

Her steps faltered. Rose? How would he know about Rose? Why did he get to know about Rose and she didn't?

No. This man didn't get anything from her. Not in life, and especially not now in death.

"I'll figure it out on my own. Thanks for nothing, fucker!"

With ease, she passed through the doors, ignoring the cries of the prisoners around her. If she couldn't get her memories back through LeBeau, fine. She'd just go about it the old fashioned way. And clearly Lottie was wrong about the Malevolence. It was obviously still there, but if it wasn't leaking enough to let LeBeau out of jail, then clearly it wasn't that big of a threat. He even said it wasn't all powerful, which had to count for something.

But maybe she'd keep an eye on the girls tonight, just in case. At least she didn't have to do that alone.

She stopped and put her hands around her mouth.

"Baxter!" she called. That *had* to be loud enough. A few seconds later, he dropped through the ceiling and into her waiting arms.

"How did you know I'd be right here?"

Baxter panted and wagged his tail, which smacked against her broken ribs.

"Want to go keep an eye on our new friends?" she asked, and his joy was worth the pain. "Good. Let's go."

CHAPTER 12
MAGNOLIA

AROUND HALFWAY THROUGH the long elevator ride, Magnolia's shivers and heart palpitations slowed as her subconscious packaged the experience into a tiny box for the back of her mind. It also helped that she had Korinne next to her the whole time, though she was uncharacteristically quiet and scrolling madly on her comm pad. She was so calm and so confident of their safety that it made Magnolia believe it too. As she glanced at her friend out of the corner of her eye, a well of affection filled to the brim in her chest.

"Hey, Korinne?" she said softly.

Korinne turned to her, brows drawn inward and one hand reaching out to touch Magnolia's wrist. She didn't take her hand again, but the contact was comforting, nonetheless.

"Yes, dearest?" she replied.

Magnolia took a deep breath, deciding what to say. "Thank

you for coming to save me, even if you don't think it was ghosts." While she wished Korinne truly understood, the unwavering support did more for her than any beliefs could.

"Of course," Korinne said, throwing an arm around her shoulders and tucking her into her side. "You're my partner. If you're in trouble, I'm coming to get you no matter what the situation is."

Magnolia wrapped her arms around Korinne's waist and laid her head against her shoulder, squeezing tight and trying her best not to get blood on her shirt. She soaked up the heat of Korinne's body and her loyalty.

"I don't know what I'd do without you," she said.

"I got you, Mags. Always," Korinne murmured, and Magnolia nearly cried all over again.

The elevator arrived at their floor, and they walked to their rooms. The entire walk, Magnolia fought the urge to look behind her. The sense of being watched, of being *followed*, never quite left her. At the doors, Korinne nodded her head toward hers.

"Come inside, I've got all the first aid stuff," she said as she punched the panel.

"Oh, it's okay, I can do it." Bumps and bruises weren't unusual in their line of work, since they usually wandered around in dark, uninhabited places. Normally they had a first aid person on staff, but Magnolia had both the knowledge and supplies to take care of it herself.

Korinne rolled her eyes. "Come on, it'll take two seconds."

She didn't wait for a reply, instead going into her room and pulling out the red box. Magnolia hesitated, then followed. Korinne gestured to her bed, which had only the basic bedding necessities.

"Sit there."

"Yes, doctor," Magnolia said as she gingerly sat on the edge of the bed. The sheets were black, of course, and softer than she anticipated. But the softness didn't make up for the lack of pillows. "Remind me to buy you good bedding when we get back home."

"Hey, this isn't my normal stuff, this is just the travel stuff." Korinne sat next to her and cracked open the box. She pulled out disinfectant wipes and a roll of self-adhering wound gauze before gesturing for Magnolia's hand. "My stuff at home is way better than this, you know that."

"I've seen your room. It could use some more coziness."

She hissed as the disinfectant stung the cuts on her wrist. Upon further examination, they were deeper than she originally thought. Damn, she really fought those handcuffs with everything she had. She was lucky her wrist didn't break.

"My room is cozy. Just in the hibernating bear way, not the pastel fairy way," Korinne said. She delicately turned Magnolia's hand over and continued to wipe away blood and germs. After a few more silent swipes, she said, "I'm sorry, Mags."

"What? For what?" Magnolia tried to think of something Korinne did or said, but found nothing worthy of apology.

"For the cuff. I should've vetoed it. It was dangerous, and I'm sorry I did it anyway." Korinne looked at her through her lashes, then returned to her task.

Magnolia leaned forward so she could catch Korinne's eye. "Don't apologize, it wasn't your fault," she said. "I'm a grown woman, I could've said no. You were ready to respect that."

Korinne swallowed and avoided her gaze. "Still. I'm sorry you got hurt."

She finished with the disinfecting wipes and moved on to wrapping Magnolia's wrist in the gauze. It had something infused in the cloth that created a cooling effect on the cuts, and she sighed in relief.

"Oh, that's good," she said as the wrap soothed the pain.

Korinne's hands faltered, nearly dropping the roll. Magnolia laughed. "Good catch."

"Just testing my reflexes," she said. She finished wrapping and cut the gauze. "There you go, all done."

"Thank you," Magnolia said. An underlying anxiety simmered in her stomach, but now, far from the hospital, it was almost back to her baseline nervousness. She rubbed her eyes. "Gods, I hope I can sleep tonight. Today was too much."

"Well, if you can't, you can always stay in here with me," Korinne said. "You'll have to supply your own pillows though, I've only got the one."

Magnolia opened her mouth to turn her down, then thought about it. "You know what, this might be the one time I have to give in and take you up on that offer," she said.

Korinne cracked a smile, then sat up a little straighter. "Only took me five years, but I'll finally get you in my bed," she said, earning a laugh.

"Korinne, we've shared a bed before," Magnolia said. Korinne bowed her head, talking to her comm pad.

"Note to editing Korinne, don't provide any context for that comment," she said, making Magnolia dissolve into giggles.

"Some of the hotel rooms only had one bed!" she said.

"Note to editing Korinne, leave that part in."

"Rinne, oh my gods," Magnolia said. "Don't even get me started on the undergraduate days."

Korinne blew out a long breath. "Damn, we've been working together a long time, huh?"

"Yes, we have," Magnolia agreed. Once again, her affection boiled over and threatened to choke her. "Best job I ever had, with the best coworker a girl could ask for."

Korinne's smile faltered for a second, then returned. "Can't argue with that. It's been a good ride, Mags. Glad we got to take it together."

"Me too." She gripped Korinne's fingers for a second, then forced herself to her feet. "I think I'm spent for the night. We'll get back to it tomorrow."

"Sounds good, I'll see you at two in the morning for a snuggle," Korinne said as she unclipped her comm pad harness.

"Perfect, I'll bring the good pillows," she said with a smile.

She left Korinne's room, but stopped as someone said, "Give." Magnolia looked around, but no one was in the hallway with her. Had Korinne said something as she walked out, and she misheard it?

"Give," the voice said again. No, that wasn't Korinne. Maybe she was watching a video?

Magnolia pressed the palm pad, and Korinne's door slid open. She looked up from her comm pad, still in the same position Magnolia had left her.

"Mags? You okay?" she asked.

"Yeah, did you say something? Or turn on a video?" Magnolia asked.

Korinne shook her head. "No, why?"

Gods damn it all. "Just thought I heard something. Probably just thinking too hard."

"Well, if the thoughts get too loud, just pop back over, okay?" she said.

Magnolia adored that girl. "I will, thank you."

She tried leaving again and this time actually managed to make it to her room without any weird whispers. She fully expected the quiet to drown her, but apparently just having Korinne next door was enough to keep most of the suffocating fear at bay. She removed her harness and plugged her comm pad into the charging station that allowed it to stay upright and record the room.

"Oh!" she said as it clicked home. Glad she remembered, she opened her bag and pulled out Cassie's tablet. It had a bigger screen and thicker body than the comm pads they used now, and the gods only knew what kind of software it ran. But surely if she could turn it on, they could find a way to hack it.

The charging cable from Cassie's room had burn marks on the side meant to plug into the wall, so Magnolia began digging through her bucket of cables in an effort to find one that matched. It had a different port compared to the adapter most electronics used, but considering all the gear she'd purchased over the years, certainly something had to have a matching dock.

"Ah ha!" There, at the bottom of the bucket, sat a tangled cable with the same shape. She had no idea which piece of equipment used it, or if she even had that tool anymore. The important thing was that she had the charger.

With all the optimism in the world, she plugged in Cassie's tablet and let it rest on her desk. She waited a few seconds to see if it turned on, but the screen stayed dark. It probably needed some time to reboot after sleeping for over sixty years. She'd let it rest and check it again in the morning.

Since she had everything set, Magnolia took the hottest shower the ship would allow and settled in to do some editing. The sensation of someone outside the door never left, but some-thing about it felt...reassuring? She didn't know how to describe it. Whoever was out there didn't scare her. She thought about grabbing the Parabox and going outside, but the idea of hearing that voice again after the incident at the hospital sent a shiver of fear down her spine. No, she wasn't quite ready to try and communicate yet.

But perhaps she would set up a camera and motion detector before she went to sleep, just in case.

CHAPTER 13
CASSIE

From camera 45.8.1: [the sound of someone sighing]

"HOLD ON, YOU TWO THINK..." Cassie trailed off, watching in confusion as the girls settled in for the night. They thought they were just coworkers? They each thought the other saw them platonically?

Oh. *Oh.*

These idiots didn't *know.*

"You can't be serious right now," Cassie said. A memory tickled the edge of her brain, something just beyond her reach. A certain brand of anxiety built in her, making her feel like Korinne and Magnolia were on borrowed time. How could they not know? They needed to know.

Her mischievous side flared to life again, this time having nothing to do with whatever turned her eyes red.

If she could trap them in a small space, they'd have to confess their feelings, right? She added it to her list of things to do. Get her memories back *and* get those two dumbasses to figure out their feelings.

All while dealing with the leaking Malevolence.

Cassie huffed.

"Piece of cake," she said, and set herself up for a long night.

CHAPTER 14
MAGNOLIA

From camera 1.1.1: [something clicks on the floor]

MAGNOLIA GOT a solid few hours of sleep before the motion detector went off.

She rolled out of her pile of blankets and pillows before tapping her watch to silence the alarm. Still in her silky pajamas, she stuffed her feet into some sneakers and grabbed her bag. At the last second, she strapped on her comm pad, practically ripping it off of the charging dock. There was a camera up, yes, but it only faced one direction, and their rooms sat in the middle of a very long hallway with lots of space for ghostly activity.

"Hello?" Magnolia whispered as she stepped out, the low sound echoing through the empty space. She clicked on her flashlight. "Is anyone here with me?"

She listened for signs of ghosts, but also for sounds from next door. Silence surrounded her except for the soft creaks of the ship. A certain pressure squeezed her subconscious, harder than she'd felt at any other sites they'd visited. She scanned up and down the hallway, searching for any sign of what might've set off the alarm. Yes, she could just run the video footage back, but where was the fun in that?

"Hello?" She tried again, taking slow, careful steps one way.

Something brushed against her ankle, and she jumped. She flashed her light down, but found nothing except gray floor.

Ever thorough in the way Korinne would be, she examined the area for anything that might've set off the motion detector. No matter where she looked, she couldn't find any debris or pieces of ship falling apart that would explain the sensor activating. In her mind, that left one explanation.

She knew, in her heart of hearts, that ghosts filled the ship. That had to be why she kept seeing things, or feeling such odd sensations. In the other places they investigated, there were reports of only a few hauntings. Here, there were centuries of lost souls wandering the place between this life and the next. The presence of so many ghosts was overwhelming all her senses, both conscious and not. Gods, if only she could see them.

Magnolia had a bad idea.

She clutched her pendant, the silver circle already warm. How bad had the soul sickness been, really? Surely not that bad, otherwise her grandfather would've done more than just give her a little necklace. She was older now, and probably way more resistant to ghostly interference. If she only took it off for a second, then that wouldn't be enough time for the ghosts to do any damage.

She tapped her sternum a few times. What could it hurt?

Before she could think any harder about it, she pulled the pendant off.

At first, nothing happened except for a slight increase in

the pressure. She clutched the pendant in her hand, not willing to completely let go. Going without it made her feel naked, which in turn made her more nervous. It was a silly idea, a stupid idea, one that would never work. She moved to put her pendant back on.

Then, she saw the first one.

A man came down the hallway toward her. Magnolia gasped, her eyes wide. He didn't seem to notice her as he walked, his focus instead on the tablet in his hands. The longer she stared, the more she could see. He had dark hair, and his skin was light brown. If she really concentrated, she could make out the pattern on his blue shirt and hear the *swish* of his olive green pants. He stopped long before reaching her, turning and placing his hand against the palm pad to a room. She blinked, and he was gone.

"Holy shit," Magnolia whispered.

A ghost. She'd really and truly seen an *actual* ghost.

Her heart soared, and victory thrummed in her veins. It hadn't been a fluke earlier in the hospital. And she wasn't going crazy seeing all those shadows. It wasn't the environment, or bias, or desperation. She could actually see these ghosts!

Two more ghosts appeared: a woman with a short afro, and another woman with a sharp bob. They wore matching uniforms, but left through another door before Magnolia had time to parse the colors.

She turned and saw three more winding their way through the hallway. None of them seemed to notice her, just going about their daily business. Too late, she thought to turn completely so the comm pad could record. An inner voice that sounded suspiciously like Korinne said the camera probably wouldn't capture any of it, but she had to try anyway, just in case.

The hallway sprang to life. Ghosts walked this way and

that, too many for Magnolia to count. Her breath caught in her throat, and every habit she'd built over the past five years of ghost hunting flew out of the airlock. There was no greeting, no reaching out, no offering her name. Hells, she couldn't even speak. Tears sprung into her eyes as soaked in the validation, even if she was alone in this triumph.

So many ghosts. And she could see them all.

The temperature dropped, and she spun back around in time to see a woman appear about ten feet away. She inhaled, and panic rose in her chest. She was so close, she was going to see her, she was going to *run into her*.

Magnolia took one step to the side, but didn't dodge fast enough. She braced for impact. The woman's shoulder clipped her own, and energy rushed into her. Something powerful buzzed underneath her skin. For a split second, she saw the woman in absolute clarity, from the gray streaks in her brown hair to the specks of gold in her blue eyes.

And the woman saw *her*.

"Hi," Magnolia said, like a prepared and professional ghost hunter.

The energy built, and the woman opened her mouth to reply, but before she could make a sound, she flickered and faded. The power, however, remained. Magnolia's heart raced, her muscles coiled, and she felt like she could run a marathon. She felt so strong, the idea of soul sickness was like a faraway worry. With this energy, she could do *anything*.

Sound erupted around her. Magnolia twisted as she caught pieces of conversations, the shouting of children, and the pounding of magnetic boots. Sometimes the sound accompanied a visual, and sometimes it just echoed, a whisper of the past. She tried to stay out of the ghosts' way, but every time one brushed against her, more energy flooded her system. This was what her grandfather wanted her to avoid? It wasn't scary at all. It was beautiful.

A ball bounced by her, and a white terrier with three legs chased it. A dog? Since when had there been a dog on the ship?

He pounced on the ball, which shoved it through a wall. The dog followed it with reckless abandon. Magnolia watched, waiting. A few seconds later, the dog emerged victorious, trotting with his tail high and the pink ball in his mouth. He spotted her and upped his pace, tiny sparks emanating from his feet as he ran. It was real light, not ghost light, though Magnolia wasn't sure how she could tell the difference.

The dog abandoned the ball just before he reached her in order to jump on her legs. He passed right through, sending a tingle through her shins. His one eye showed so much disappointment that Magnolia's heart squeezed.

"Hey buddy," she said, her mind whirring. If she gave him some energy, would she be able to touch him? Hells, would that make it so the cameras saw him? She had to try.

The dog bounced as he realized her attention was on him. Magnolia knelt and held her hand out, and he readily attempted to bump it with his head. Not quite knowing what she was doing, she tried to push with her hand, hoping it would do the trick. A purple spark ignited where they met, just like when she tried to shove away the ghost in the hospital. The dog hopped again as her energy hit him. Now she could see the brown of his eye and his little silver name tag engraved with *Baxter*.

A wave of fatigue hit, and the sounds of all the other ghosts disappeared. Magnolia caught herself before she collapsed, suddenly exhausted. A headache bloomed behind her eyes, and nausea rolled in her stomach. Baxter, excited that she was down on the floor with him, ran around her a few times before trying to lick her face. Despite feeling like she'd been hit by a bus, her sacrifice somehow wasn't enough energy to make his attempts at affection anything more than puffs of cold air.

"Okay, that didn't work quite as expected," she said as her vision cleared and her vitals normalized. Perhaps her grandfather had a point. The discomfort remained, but it dissipated enough for her to continue. "Let's try something else."

Baxter was obviously excited to play. Magnolia sat back on her heels and dug into her bag to retrieve the small light. Just by picking it up, the touch sensors along the side turned it on, the brightness increasing further as she set it on the floor. Baxter watched with curiosity as she tapped the side a few times, taking the light to a medium setting.

"There you go," she said. "Maybe this can help. Go on, touch it."

She tried to take hold of the pink ball, but didn't have enough juice to actually grab it. Baxter followed her hand anyway, so she wiggled her fingers over the light. Sure enough, he took the bait and hit it with a paw. The light flickered brighter, and he dimmed to the point that she could no longer read the name on his tag. He cocked his head back and forth, his eye never leaving the bulb.

"Silly boy," Magnolia said, once again waving a hand over the light. She didn't miss how utterly wild it was for her to be playing with a ghost dog. "You're supposed to take the energy, not give it."

Baxter tapped the light, and once again faded as the light brightened. He jumped back and dropped into a play bow, his tail going at a wild speed.

Magnolia turned the light to its brightest setting, thinking that might be the problem.

"Take it, buddy," she said. "Take the energy. Then maybe I can pet you for real."

Baxter, with full confidence, pounced on the light. It lit brighter than she thought possible, then the bulb popped. When the stars in front of her eyes faded, Magnolia found nothing but darkness.

"Damn it," she muttered as a curl of smoke exited the light. Good thing she had extras in her suitcase. "Baxter?"

Nothing. No ball, no sound of claws on the floor, no brushes against her. Why had he given his energy instead of taking it from the light?

She sighed and sat back, the harness of her comm pad clicking in the silence. With trembling hands, she removed it and scrolled back to the start of the recording. Second by second, she watched the entire interaction with Baxter go down.

Thousands of credits she'd spent on this comm pad. It had the most sensitive camera and a long list of features no one needed except military personnel. And yet, all it captured was the light dimming and brightening, dimming and brightening. None of Baxter's sweet face, or the sound of his tag jingling. Nothing but light and her own voice.

"Gods damn it," Magnolia said as tears threatened. As high as she'd flown with her win, the agonizing weight of defeat threw her right back down. She eyed Korinne's door, contemplating waking her and telling her the whole story. After all, she told Korinne *everything*.

But then... Would she be comforting? Or would it be another moment like the hospital, where Korinne did everything in her power to be supportive except believe her? Magnolia could hear her justification: anecdotal evidence is the lowest form of evidence.

But it still counted, right?

Magnolia took a steadying breath. It counted to her, yes,

but she and Korinne agreed at the start of this venture that while stories were good, they weren't definitive proof.

Fine. Maybe she just needed to put a little more oomph into it next time.

Fatigue settled into her bones. Okay, maybe next time she needed to stock up on a few snacks before donating her energy to a ghost. Then she could give enough to make them visible, and all her problems would be solved.

Magnolia pulled on her necklace again, her skin sore where the edges bit into her palm. She flexed her fingers a few times and sighed with relief as the pressure in her head abated to a more manageable level. With her first successful experiment under her belt, she could prepare for a second one.

A tingling started between her shoulder blades. Magnolia paused, then pushed herself to standing, pretending not to notice. As normally as she could, she turned back to her room and went to the door. A shadow stood at the end of the hall. One single ghost, after all the others she'd seen. Annoyance drifted off of them in waves, and in Magnolia's chest, nervousness mixed with elation. Even with her pendant, she could sense the ghost's presence and feel their emotions. Which meant she could tell this one was rather pissed off.

Magnolia gulped and pressed her palm to the pad next to the door. As before, it slid open three-quarters of the way. She had to move sideways in order to fit through, giving her ample opportunity to face her phantom stalker. Their head wasn't shaped quite right, and they listed to one side, as if supporting an injury. A spike of fear went through them, so she dropped her eyes and fully entered her room, closing the door behind her.

In the quiet, Magnolia smiled. This was how she'd win the bet, and how she'd prove to everyone ghosts were real. It would take a little work and a lot of risk, but she had full faith she could do it.

One at a time, she placed her multitude of pillows back in the way she liked, then straightened her blankets. Her watch read four in the morning, long past the witching hour but way too early for her to get up and get started on the day. A few more hours of sleep and she'd be ready.

She didn't have a plan set in stone yet, but she had the beginnings of one. All she needed was a little more time and a little more trial and error. With that one glorious thought, Magnolia nestled back in bed. If she wanted to win this thing tomorrow, she needed to be well rested.

The rest of the night, she dreamed of a white terrier running around a field, and a strange blonde woman throwing his ball.

CHAPTER 15
CASSIE

From Magnolia's comm pad: [the light pops]

CASSIE STOOD, glaring at Magnolia's door.
  "Dude, my fucking dog!"

DAY TWO

CHAPTER 16
KORINNE

From camera 21.2.7: [a chair falls over]

KORINNE WOKE BRIGHT AND EARLY, which kind of sucked. She'd gotten pulled into some preliminary edits and stayed up far later than she intended. If she was honest, she was also waiting to make sure Magnolia got to sleep and didn't need her in the middle of the night, finally giving up around two in the morning.

She sighed and rubbed her hands over her face as guilt chewed at her insides. Why did she think the cuffs would be a good idea? She should've vetoed it and deleted the comment the moment it showed up in the forum. The hospital was scary enough on its own. With the ship rocking and causing the cabinets to open and close like that, it was no wonder Magnolia got all worked up. Hell, if they'd done that during her own solo investigation, it might've freaked Korinne out too. And now, Magnolia had cuts all over her wrist and probably some emotional damage.

"We'll do better today," Korinne murmured. Their viewers were important, yes. But not more important than Magnolia's safety and well-being. They had two more days—well, a day and a half, really—on this trip. She could protect her for that long.

She pulled out her handheld and checked their itinerary. They still had the funeral room and the human reclamation tanks, both of which might tear Magnolia's soul from her body. There were a few more challenges as well, but none of them held the same fright factor as the first two.

Then, if she was lucky, she could run around unleashed, exploring the object of her studies while Magnolia got to take a nice, long nap.

With no other distractions, Korinne pushed herself to the edge of the bed, then took a moment to stretch. She exchanged her pajamas for a black tank top and jeans, then reached for her black lace-up boots, fully prepared to go grab some coffee from the dining room.

A noise sounded outside her door. She paused. Were those... footsteps? It couldn't be later than six o'clock, and Magnolia normally slept at least another hour or two. Was she up early because of what happened yesterday? Korinne waited, boots in hand, for her to knock on the door. But the knock never came.

A grin spread across her face. Magnolia didn't need any more scares this trip, but a little surprise wouldn't hurt.

Shoes tossed and forgotten, Korinne padded across the tiny room and pressed the palm pad. It inched open, which killed the surprise somewhat.

Except Magnolia wasn't there. The door opened into an empty hallway.

She furrowed her brows. She'd heard footsteps, hadn't she? But there was no Magnolia in sight, and her door was closed.

Korinne went and pressed her ear against the metal to see if she could hear Magnolia moving around, but was met with absolute silence.

Huh. Weird.

"Mags?"

No answer. Irrationally concerned now, she pressed on the palm pad. The door opened three-quarters of the way to put a sleepy Magnolia on display, nestled in her pile of pillows and blankets. She lay curled on her side, her hair splayed around her like a lavender halo. The whole scene was so soft it made Korinne's chest ache.

"Good morning, gorgeous," she said, stepping into the room.

"What time is it?" Magnolia rubbed her eyes instead of looking at her watch.

"A little past six. Thought I heard you walking around and tried to scare you, but I guess it was just the ship."

Magnolia's eyes snapped open, and she sat up. "Footsteps? Outside the rooms?"

"Yes?" Why was she so excited about this?

"Did the motion detector go off?" She checked her watch then, probably for alerts.

Korinne thought back to their set up, but couldn't remember putting a motion detector outside of their rooms... even though she was definitely supposed to.

"No, I just heard it," she said.

Magnolia scrambled out of bed, nearly tripping over the blankets and pillows, and ran outside. Korinne, unsure what the hell was going on, watched the whole thing happen. Surely something that sounded almost like footsteps wasn't that exciting?

"Damn it," Magnolia said, hands on hips. It was then

Korinne noticed the silky pajamas, and placed her hand over the camera of her comm pad.

"Nothing?" she asked. A pang of guilt went through her as she thought of the day before.

"Nothing," Magnolia said, coming back inside and face planting on her bed.

A few errant pillows fell onto the floor. Korinne picked them up one by one and laid them along Magnolia's back and legs until she had her entire body covered. Magnolia let it happen, her only response a groan muffled by her face in yet another pillow.

"You'll get 'em next time," Korinne said as she perfected her masterpiece. "Now, are you going back to sleep? Or are you ready to get moving?"

Magnolia let out another excessively long groan, then pushed herself up. Her movements upset the delicate balance of pillows, returning them to the floor. Damn it, Korinne had worked hard on that.

"Come on, let's get some food in you."

She gave Magnolia time to get dressed in the cutest pair of floral overalls she'd ever seen, then brought out another box of her favorite snack bars. Neither one of them were really breakfast people, but Magnolia surprised her by eating three of the bars instead of her normal one.

"Guess I have to give you a better dinner tonight," Korinne said. "You never wake up hungry."

"Burned a lot of energy yesterday," Magnolia said, tearing open a fourth bar. "I'll be better prepared today."

"That's my girl," Korinne said. "Don't worry, the first stop is an easy one."

"Hmph, we'll see about that," Magnolia said. "Where are we at in the Cassie tour?"

"The funeral room," Korinne said. "The one with that weird circle etched into the floor."

"Oh, goodie, I love cryptic floor etchings. At least this challenge is for you while I get a break."

Korinne tried to remember what the document said, but their assistant, Zavir, purposefully left a few things off both of their documents so they could film legitimate reactions. He was a damn good assistant for it, but she didn't really care for the surprises. Surprises messed with plans, and she had nearly every minute of this trip spoken for.

"Do I want to know?" she asked.

Magnolia grinned. "I'll wait until we have better ambience to tell you."

Great, so she got to wait for an obnoxiously long time to hear her fate. She knew, logically, that it would take time to shuffle from one spot to the next in the massive ship. She just wasn't used to it taking twenty minutes to go to the next place on their investigation list, though it did give her time to start checking through the cameras the bots set up—one of which had gone offline.

"Shit," she mumbled.

"What is it?" Magnolia asked, looking up from her handheld.

"One of the cameras went dark. I'll have to send a bot to fix it," Korinne said. She opened the channel to check on Efex. When it checked in with a clean diagnostics report, she sent the location.

"Probably a ghost messing with it," Magnolia said. "We've had way too many equipment malfunctions on this trip."

"Probably a bad battery. We were bound to get a couple of them with how many we bought," Korinne replied.

The elevator slowed, then changed direction, sending them

to the left. Good, that should've been the last turn before their destination.

"Could you imagine living here your whole life?" Magnolia asked. Korinne finished with the camera diagnostics—no answers, of course—and put her handheld away.

"Honestly, sounds terrible," she said. "I mean, I'm glad humanity found a new home and all, but being stuck in here for your entire life? Having to follow the sacrifice of your ancestors, whether you wanted to or not?" A shudder went through her. "I'm surprised we managed."

"Me too," Magnolia agreed. "Though, if you never knew what it was like to be outside, would you even miss it?"

It was a common question posed in every philosophy or psychology class Korinne took throughout her schooling. But somehow Magnolia made it feel more genuine than a bunch of stuffy graduate students.

"I think you would," Korinne said, speaking of the general *you* and not Magnolia specifically. "Grass is always bluer and all that. What did your grandmother say?"

"Nothing really," Magnolia said with a shrug. Both of them had grandparents who arrived on the *Arkana*, but Magnolia's grandmother was the only one who lived long enough to meet her grandchildren. She continued, "I tried to talk to her a couple of times for school projects and stuff like that. She always said she didn't want to remember that part of her life, which—I mean, if things were as precarious as you say, I don't blame her. She passed right before my grandfather did, so we kind of ran out of time on that front."

"Damn, I'm sorry, Mags. I didn't realize you lost them both so fast." She knew Magnolia's Vaelish grandfather was the one who got her into ghost stuff, and apparently said he could talk to them too. Must've been who she got it from. "I think he'd be really excited about all the stuff you do."

Magnolia blushed hard, her cheeks turning a dark shade of plum as her eyes got glassy. Thickly, she said, "Thank you, Korinne. That's really sweet of you to say."

"It's the truth." She reached out and rubbed her cheek with her thumb, and Magnolia leaned into the touch.

The elevator slowed, and this time completely stopped. The doors opened too quickly in Korinne's opinion. Back to work. She dropped her hand and put a little more space between them, clearing her throat.

"Are you ready to hear your challenge?" Magnolia asked, trying and failing to sound casual.

Korinne saw right through it, and knew exactly what it meant. Magnolia always did get too excited about one thing when it came to their investigations.

"Not doing it," she said before Magnolia could finish.

"You have to!" Magnolia said. She flipped the handheld around so Korinne could see her doom spelled out on the screen. "See? It's on Zavir's list."

"I hate the stupid SonoWave," Korinne whined. "It always gives me a headache."

The SonoWave was a blight upon her ghost hunting existence, and she made sure everyone knew it. If she wanted to be screamed at constantly, she'd go back to working in retail.

"You only have to do it for five minutes," Magnolia said, still trying not to laugh.

"Ugh, that's five minutes too long."

"Better than handcuffs," Magnolia said, and Korinne had no comeback for that. She continued reading the document, and her eyebrows shot toward her hairline. "Oh. The viewers want you to lay in the circle scratched onto the floor. That's terrifying."

"What? It doesn't even have any sigils carved into it. Boring." The ship had a hundred more exciting places for them to visit, and they had ten other pieces of equipment that didn't give Korinne a migraine. She let out the longest sigh she could manage before relenting. "Fine, only because I still feel guilty about the handcuffs."

Bitt waited at their destination, its binocular eyes glowing as it recorded everything. They walked the last few meters to the room, but before Korinne could open the door, Magnolia slid her arm around her waist. "You have to be nice, that spot is supposed to be super haunted," she said quietly. It was just for the drama, Korinne knew that. But her closeness still made heat collect in her torso.

"This whole ship is supposed to be super haunted," she whispered. "I can't be nice the whole time."

"Of course you can, you're always nice to me," she said, and Korinne literally bit her tongue to keep herself from spitting out a truth neither of them was ready for.

"Well, yeah. You're real and I want you to stick around," she said instead, sliding her hand around Magnolia's shoulders in a moment of indulgence. "Ghosts can fuck off for all I care."

"Rinne!" Ah, music to her ears. Magnolia wriggled out of her grasp, and Korinne let her.

"Come on," she said, laughing. "Let's go lay in a circle, I guess."

She patted Bitt on the head, then hooked up her energy bank to the palm pad. The door opened halfway, then ground to a stop.

"That's gonna look great in post-production," Korinne said as they slipped through the entrance.

The funeral room lacked any decoration to denote its purpose, save for the dirty outlines of a few religious artifacts on the wall. It sat one ring inward from the human reclamation tanks, which to many people meant ghosts wandered between the two areas with a certain degree of freedom. Then, of course, there was the circle on the floor. Someone had taken six laps around the middle of the room, carving a thin line into the metal the entire time and leaving behind yet another unsolved mystery.

"Ready?" Magnolia asked.

"Ready as I'm gonna be," Korinne said, taking her place.

"I promise I won't make you use the SonoWave ever again after this," Magnolia said, her smile a shadow behind the light of her comm pad.

"Don't lie to me, Mags, my heart can't take it," Korinne said.

"A promise is a promise. And you know I always keep my promises." Her tone was light, teasing, and Korinne swallowed any feelings it invoked.

She leaned her head left, then right, sighing as her neck cracked and the crick in it almost went away. After shaking her arms out, she straightened and put on her camera face. Magnolia placed herself just right, then nodded.

"Legend has it," Korinne started, standing just outside of the circle, "that a certain flavor of witches carved the circle into the floor. Some say it was to create a portal for souls to cross over, others say it was to keep the souls stuck here."

"I don't think they needed help with that," Magnolia said. Whether out of instinct or dramatic effect, she glanced toward the door. Somewhere down the hall, a bang sounded. "See?"

"That was nothing," Korinne said. "Normally, this room was used for many years as a place where people could pay their last respects before bodies got shipped to the reclamation tanks to be broken down into their component parts. Unfortunately, no one really kept records of funeral attendants, so we have no way of knowing who came for Cassie. Based on the photos on her wall screen, I imagine it was a pretty full house."

Unless, like Willa, her friends wanted to avoid being associated with a possible criminal.

"Anyway, we're here outside this circle—which was created for either nefarious, assistive, or benign purposes—to see if I can entice some ghosts to interact with us. Mags, what do you think it does?"

Magnolia paused, chewing her lip as she stared at the circle. "I want to think people were trying to help, but I don't know. Feels weird to put this where funerals happened."

"So your vote is nefarious?" Korinne clarified. Magnolia nodded.

"Yes. Isn't yours?" she asked.

"I think people got bored and wanted to fuck with their shipmates," Korinne said. "Either way, they say you're not supposed to step in the circle, that there's demons or bad luck or whatever waiting in there."

"So of course," Magnolia said, directed toward their invisible audience, "you all chose for her to not only step into it, but to lay in it for five minutes. Risking life and limb and spiritual safety."

"I'll find a way to soldier on," Korinne said. "What reports have we gotten here, hmm?"

Magnolia squeezed her eyes shut, her nose wrinkling as she thought. "The usual—cold spots and scratches, particularly when people have bare shoulders."

"Good thing I am completely unscratchable," Korinne said, flexing her arms. "All right, now—do I really have to use the SonoWave?"

"I'm not making you use it, the viewers are," Magnolia said. "If you didn't gripe about it so much, they probably wouldn't have selected it."

"Once again I have no one but myself to blame," Korinne said, digging through her bag to find the offending object. It was a small black box the size of her cupped hands, with two nubby antennae on top. A small light between them usually glowed green, but turned red when something interrupted its electromagnetic field. It also screamed like a mother fucker.

"Don't forget to explain it," Magnolia reminded her. Korinne breathed a sigh.

"Thank you, I almost forgot." She was always too eager to get tasks done, but had to remember the lead up steps in case this video was the first one a viewer saw. "This is the Sono-Wave. It works by passing an obnoxiously loud sound wave between these two antennae. Alleged ghosts can make noise by diddling their ghosty fingers in between."

"Why do you always explain it like that?" Magnolia grumbled.

"Because if I have to use it, I deserve to have a little fun with it," Korinne said. She directed Bitt to the corner so it could record the entire room, catching all the angles the comm pad on her chest couldn't. This was especially important when a cabinet door in the corner opened of its own accord.

"Oh look, they're coming to see you already," Magnolia said, though she didn't sound quite as excited as usual.

"Perfect, maybe that means I can end my sentence early." Korinne went to the edge of the circle, then looked over her shoulder back at her partner. "Sure you don't want to come in here with me?"

"Not even a little bit. Have fun!" Magnolia stepped back through the door. "And remember, be nice!"

"I'll try," Korinne said as the door closed. With a groan, she lowered herself to the floor and stretched out. It was wide enough that she couldn't reach the edges if she lay smack dab in the middle, not that she had a particularly impressive wingspan.

"This ground is so hard." She adjusted her position, but the metal didn't magically become more comfortable. "Looks like this is as good as it's going to get."

After one more complaint, she turned off her flashlight and turned on the SonoWave. Five years, and she never got used to the screeching wail the tiny machine let out, the undulating pitch reverberating through the small room and ricocheting off her poor eardrums.

"Fuck!" Korinne let out her traditional response to the thing and started her timer. Five minutes—she could manage five minutes. "Okay, if someone's here, go ahead and appear so I can turn this stupid thing off."

She waited, cringing as the howling continued. Of course, nothing.

"My name is Korinne," she yelled over the machine. "Is there anyone here with me? If you touch that little box, it'll alert me to your presence." No one could say she didn't give it a good try on these investigations. The wave box stuttered and dropped in tone for a second, and she rolled her eyes.

"God, they're gonna have a field day with that," she muttered. "Okay, was that just the electromagnetic field from the ship, or from a ghost? Never mind, you can't answer that. Touch the thing twice for yes, once for no."

The machine tone dropped once, then went higher three times.

"Three wasn't an option." Damn it, the ship was going to interfere with the SonoWave way too much. So now, not only would it annoy her, it would also waste her time.

The tone beat twice. Not an unusual occurrence, but a timely one. God, Magnolia—and the viewers—would lose their shit over that. But as with all good science, Korinne wanted repeated results.

"That's more like it. Follow directions if you want to participate." Korinne checked her watch. Shit, only forty seconds passed. In the time it took her to look, the box hit three high notes and two low ones. Somehow, the variation in the tone made the whole thing worse. "All right, same rules. Two for yes, one for no. Were you a resident on the ship?"

The high pitch continued without change. Korinne waited a respectful amount of time before continuing.

"Did you work in the funeral room here?" she tried. "The man in black? Sorry, I don't know your name." It was in her notes somewhere, she'd add it in post-production.

The tone dipped twice. After a beat, it dipped twice again. Almost right, but not quite. Didn't mean the believers who watched their videos wouldn't count it as irrefutable evidence.

"Still want to be in charge even though you're dead, huh? I get that."

The tone beat once, then twice, then once again before returning to a consistent high pitch.

"You have to stay consistent, otherwise, this isn't fun." She could feel a needling headache starting behind her right eye, and it hadn't even been two minutes. "Did you run the funeral room?"

No response this time, just the wail. She took a breath to continue, but the machine beat once, interrupting her. "Okay, now you're just being obnoxious."

Two more beats. Was the box broken? It never changed this much. If the answers were more consistent, it would make her question a thing or two. But considering the variability and the fact they were on a spaceship, she had to factor in confounding variables.

"At this point, I think I need a control for the experiment. With all the wonky stuff on the ship, it could give me false positives." She lifted her head and lobbied the explanation at Bitt, who dutifully recorded the whole event. Even with more "responses," there was nothing clear or concise enough for her to call it pure evidence. She waited a full minute, expecting the noise to drop, but it stayed at a pitch that made her teeth hurt.

"Are you still here?" she asked. Over halfway done now. The pitch didn't change. "Hello?"

She got four beats from that touch of disrespect.

"Oh yeah, the ship is definitely interfering." One beat sounded. "No? Just you?"

High pitch, another singular beat, then the high pitch again. Korinne checked her watch; a minute and a half left, and she was so tired of talking to no one with a screaming box.

"Not just you then? Is there someone else here? Someone deep and dark and dangerous, tied to this little circle on the floor?"

The SonoWave didn't change for a long moment, then beat twice. Before she could respond to that, it beat once, then repeated the pattern.

"Are you—"

Twice, then once. Twice, then once.

"Don't interrupt me, asshole," Korinne said, just in time for it to cycle again. And again. It continued until the time between the intervals disappeared and she was left with a steady, low tone. She let it go for a solid thirty seconds with no change before giving up.

"Don't tell me something else broke." Korinne sat up and crossed her legs underneath her, picking up the box. Its little light, red now that there was alleged *paranormal interference*, burned bright in the dark room.

"What the fuck?" She hit the side of the box, but it maintained the wrong tone. Even a good shake didn't change it.

"Maybe I just need to..." She thought to turn it off and turn it back on, but when she flipped it off, the noise continued. "Oh, absolutely not."

With her crimes in full view of Bitt's camera, she opened the back panel and pulled the wires. She plunged into silence and darkness.

"Finally, some peace," she said, laying back down. But of course, she landed on something sharp. "Ouch, shit!"

Korinne brushed at the back of her shoulder, but nothing came off her skin. She swiped at the floor and felt something small and metal bounce away. With a clear space, she lay back down and took a breath.

"Rinne, your time isn't up yet!" Magnolia called through the door.

"I know, but the machine was messing up." Korinne checked her watch again. "I was short twenty whole seconds, I think everyone will forgive me for that."

The door slid open, and Magnolia's flashlight momentarily blinded her. Korinne held her hand over her eyes.

"Damn, Mags, watch where you swing that thing," she said, blinking the stars away.

"Are you okay? Did anything happen?" Magnolia asked. Korinne held up the SonoWave and shook it, the wires clacking together.

"Just this stupid thing malfunctioning. I don't understand, electronics worked just fine for the entire original voyage. The gravity generators and all that shouldn't mess with our stuff this much," she said.

"Maybe it's not the gravity generators, maybe it's ghosts," Magnolia said, eyes wide.

Korinne felt her expression go flat as she stared at the camera.

"Be serious, Magnolia," she said.

"I am," Magnolia said. "We've seen more stuff happen in the past twenty-four hours than in entire investigations."

"Yeah, all *explainable* stuff," Korinne pointed out. "Things falling over don't count this time. We're on a spaceship that's hundreds of years old, flying for the first time in decades. Stuff is gonna break. We can't blame everything on ghosts."

"What about all of our equipment breaking?" Magnolia asked.

"We're stuck on a ship built completely differently compared to our standards. Who knows what wonky machinery is messing with it?"

Magnolia pursed her lips, probably trying to come up with another argument. "Fine. Then get out of that circle and let's go do something else—this place gives me the creeps."

Korinne stood but stayed in the middle of the circle, holding out a hand. "You sure you don't want to join me?"

"No, thank you," Magnolia said, her voice tight.

"Look, I'm fine, nothing got me." Korinne waved her arms and legs to prove their functionality. "No ghosts or spirits or demons or whatever trying to snatch my soul into another dimension."

"You can take that risk, I'm certainly not—oh." Magnolia stopped, her flashlight pointing at something behind Korinne. Ghosts weren't real, but the sensation still initiated a survival instinct that had her whipping around.

"What?" Her shadow kept the majority of the room in darkness, so she turned on her own flashlight to find the open cabinet from earlier. However, now it wasn't alone. Every cabinet door sat open, displaying their empty depths. "Huh, we must've turned or something."

"Rinne," Magnolia said, just above a whisper.

"Yeah, I know—why didn't they open before? We've been flying for hours. But honestly with this stuff it's always fine until it's not, you know what I mean?"

"No, Rinne, the doors are weird but... You're bleeding," Magnolia said. She stepped up to the edge of the ring, but didn't cross it.

"What?" Korinne looked over one shoulder, then the other. Out of the very corner of her eye, she could see something red on her right shoulder blade. "Oh, yeah. I laid down on the floor and something scratched me. That's what I get for the 'unscratchable' comment earlier."

"Did you see what it was? You might need antibiotics or something," Magnolia said.

"No, it was dark. But I swiped it away, somewhere over..." She squatted and skimmed the area along the bottom of the cabinets, stopping when something sparkled in the light. "Here we go, this is more or less the right direction."

"What is it?" Magnolia asked. She refused to even walk *around* the circle, staying at the front of the room.

"Let's see." Korinne went over and grabbed a shiny thing no bigger than her thumbnail. "Some kind of button?"

She turned the silver, dome-shaped thing over and found it hollow on the back side, with a raised circle in the middle. It looked like a covering. She checked the open doors of the cabinets; sure enough, there were several silver buttons placed evenly throughout, and one naked screw head. When Korinne placed the button over it and pushed, it clicked into place.

"There we go, mystery solved," she said, though she wasn't quite sure how something so smooth managed to scratch her. "See, everything has an explanation."

She turned to smile, but Magnolia wasn't looking at her. Something outside the room had caught her attention, so Korinne walked over to look over her shoulder and see what could possibly be more interesting than her problem solving. When she got to the door, she found Magnolia staring very hard at an incredibly empty hallway.

"What are we looking at?" Korinne whispered, and Magnolia jumped.

"Don't sneak up on me like that," she said.

"I'm literally one of three people on this whole ship, I

wasn't sneaking," Korinne said with a laugh. Magnolia pouted, but dropped the subject to go back to the hallway.

"Damn it, now it's gone," she said.

"What is?" Korinne asked.

"There was..." She paused and swallowed. "Oh, you're going to make so much fun of me."

"Well now I won't, 'cause it would make me feel like an asshole," Korinne said. "Out with it, what did you see?"

"I just... I could've sworn I saw someone standing over there. I stared at it to see if the shadows moved, but it never did," Magnolia said.

"Until I interrupted?" Korinne said.

"Correct," Magnolia's shoulders slumped, and she let out a sigh.

She was right, Korinne really did want to poke fun at her for it, but she swallowed down the instinct.

"I probably scared it away. You know how ghosts are terrified of me," she said. "We've got one last stop, want to take a break before we hit it?"

Magnolia shook her head. "No, let's just get it done," she said.

Korinne, who'd been expecting a different answer, nodded. "Away we go, my liege. The reclamation tanks await."

Magnolia grimaced. "Oh, this is gonna suck."

CHAPTER 17
CASSIE

IN CASSIE'S DEFENSE, the issue with the SonoWave was *not* her fault. Maybe Korinne was right and the ship also fucked with the electronics. The cabinets though? Those were all her.

"You missed out on a good time, Howard," Cassie called to the shadow in the corner of the room. Weird that Howard didn't try the SonoWave—he was usually pretty engaged with that sort of stuff. He'd been moving around the room and even into the circle with Korinne, but as far as she could tell he hadn't messed with the machine. She couldn't be positive though, considering he didn't bother to fully form.

"What's your deal? You okay?" With all the red eyes going around, this change in character worried her. Howard didn't answer. Unease built in her gut, some instinct warning her of a coming storm. For a second, she wondered if this shadow was Howard at all. "Howard?"

Nothing. The shadow hung there, and even though it

didn't have eyes Cassie could tell it was staring at her. Alarm bells rang in her head, and she took one step back toward the door, then another.

"Okay, talk to you later then," she said, phasing through the door and going after the girls.

CHAPTER 18
KORINNE

From camera 15.3.20: [something crashes in the engine room]

"ARE you sure you don't want to go get cleaned up first?"

It was sweet of Magnolia to ask, but Korinne wasn't worried about a little scratch. She'd take care of it later when they went back to their rooms. There was no reason to waste time now going all the way there just to come all the way back.

"Nah, I'm fine. Doesn't even hurt." That was the truth.

Magnolia narrowed her eyes. "You promise?"

"I promise. Come on, it's our last stop on the tour. We've seen Cassie's room, the docks, the hospital, and the funeral room. All that's left is the human reclamation tanks."

Magnolia shuddered. "I hate the sound of that."

Something clicked in Korinne's mind, and she realized that maybe Magnolia had concern for both of them, not just her. After all, she'd been flinching and jumping at basically every sound for the past ten minutes.

"Do you want to head back?" Korinne asked. The elevator slowed, changed direction, and picked up speed again. Magnolia startled then, too. "I can do this one solo, if you want. You can get a nap in."

"Oh no, I'm okay. Just please don't handcuff me again," she said, and Korinne forced a grin to cover up the guilt still gnawing away at her.

"Not unless you ask me to," she replied.

Magnolia barked a laugh. "I swear, you're asking for trouble in the comments sometimes," she said.

"Just sometimes?" she said. "All the time."

That's all it was, Korinne reminded herself. Just silly statements to get people all riled up and hypothesizing on the extent of their relationship. Nothing more than that. Because even if she had some stupid feelings for her best friend, the friendship was way more important.

Magnolia cleared her throat. "Do you ever think about..."

The elevator stopped, and Korinne turned to find Magnolia picking at a thread on her floral overalls. Her heart rate kicked up, and she held her breath as she waited for the rest of the sentence.

"Think about what?" she asked when Magnolia didn't continue. The door slid open, and Magnolia shook her head.

"Nothing, never mind," she said, stepping off quickly.

"You can't leave me hanging like that. Tell me your thoughts," Korinne said, jogging to catch up and falling in line with her.

Magnolia waved the comment away. "It's really nothing. Just hypotheticals about the night we met." At Korinne's raised brow, Magnolia continued. "Did I ever tell you I almost didn't go to that party?"

"What? No, you didn't tell me that. What were you going to do instead?"

"Go to bed early," she said primly.

Okay, that had to be a lie. "Seriously?" Korinne asked.

"Seriously!" Magnolia giggled, which was entirely too adorable. "I was supposed to do this fundraiser run the next morning."

"A run? As in, jogging for an extended period of time? You?" she said. Never had she seen Magnolia go above a walk unless she absolutely had to.

"Yes, exactly that," Magnolia said.

"You hate running," Korinne pointed out.

"I do, but my friend made a convincing argument. And it was for a good cause, kids with cancer or something like that," she said through her laughter. "But the forecast said a huge storm was coming, and so they postponed the event. I was so excited about the cancelled plans I decided to go to the party."

"Damn, one storm saved our entire careers," Korinne said, shaking her head. "You know, I almost didn't go either."

"What? But it was at your house," Magnolia said, shocked.

"Yes, it was, and I was so pissed at my roommate for throwing a party at the last minute that I almost went and stayed with a friend," Korinne said. She couldn't wait to move out of that house. "But then she bribed me with snacks, so I stayed."

"Wow, so it really was fate that brought us together." Magnolia reached out to take her elbow and pull her close. She rested her head on Korinne's shoulder, basking in the glow of their luck.

"Or a storm and a plate of chips and dip," Korinne said, putting her cheek against the top of Magnolia's head.

"Shh, you'll ruin the moment," Magnolia said.

"I won't, but that certainly will." Korinne pointed to the door ahead of them, where a plate displayed the words "Reclamation Center" in bold font.

"Oh, boy," Magnolia breathed, her voice shaky. "Yep, definitely ruined the moment."

"Don't worry, I'll protect you." Korinne untangled her arm and reached up to tug one of Magnolia's braids. "Ghosts can't beat me in a fight, I'm currently undefeated."

"Oh, absolutely. None of them can handle all that." She gestured to Korinne's body, and Korinne struck a pose to show off her muscles.

"That's right. Do you know how strong you have to be to drink a million cups of coffee a day and carry a laptop to eight different libraries? What can ghosts lift, hmm?"

"My heart rate," Magnolia said. "My blood pressure."

"Whatever, I can do that too. They're not special," Korinne said.

She meant it in a "put her in scary situations" way, but the commenters could speculate whatever they wanted. Before Magnolia could respond, Korinne smacked the panel to open the Reclamation Center door. It wouldn't do to linger at this point, it would only devolve the conversation—or Magnolia's sanity—further.

"Okay." Korinne addressed Magnolia's comm pad, entering her presentation mode. "You might be wondering why I didn't have to use my fancy device to power up the door. That's because when they originally built the ship, they put in a few special safeguards in the case of electrical issues so certain important areas wouldn't completely lose power."

"Gods, could you imagine?" Magnolia said, her hand on her abdomen. "All the bodies in there and the electricity turning off? That would be disgusting."

"Exactly," Korinne agreed, trying not to let the gross idea take hold. "And so the original engineers made sure that, no matter what, a minimum amount of power would stay on for important places such as the captain's station, the agricultural area, and both reclamation areas. Can't run out of water, and can't have bodies decomposing."

They walked through the door, and low-level reserve lights hummed to life along the floor, lending a blue glow to the room. Rows upon rows of metal coffin-like boxes lined the area, the ceiling so low even Korinne felt the squeeze of claustrophobia. No other lights came on, keeping most of the room shrouded in darkness. They clicked on their flashlights, which helped marginally.

"Oh, I hate this," Magnolia said. She whirled every direction, the beam of her flashlight shining into every dark corner in record time.

Korinne, unbothered by the alleged spookiness of the situation, wandered between the reclamation tanks. Studying these had been one of the coolest and grossest parts of her degree. They even got the opportunity to see a replica in action as it broke down an entire cadaver in less than ten minutes. She could see why the area would freak Magnolia out, though. It wasn't as gruesome as the hospital bay, but it had a certain cemetery vibe that could lead wandering minds to worry about what hid in the depths of the tanks.

"What? This is super cool," Korinne said, grabbing the lid of the nearest tank and prying it open. Two seconds later the stench hit her, and she dropped the lid to cough. "Oh, ew, that one smelled terrible."

"Huh, looks like we're not getting as much power as those fun facts said we should," Magnolia said. She went to one of the boxes and put her hands on the lid. "This thing isn't on. No wonder it smells like that."

"Yeah, imagine getting a face full of it." Korinne pulled the neck of her tank top over her nose and mouth to breathe, trying to avoid the last of the fumes. Cold air hit the skin of her waist, sending goosebumps across her torso.

"You just want to show off your abs." Magnolia shifted to let the camera linger on the vision; if this moment made it through edits, they could guarantee at least ten more comments.

"Note to editing Korinne, cut this out," Korinne said, squashing down the intrusive thought to pull her tank top all the way up and effectively flash Magnolia.

"Note to editing Magnolia, make a back up of this," Magnolia countered.

Korinne narrowed her eyes. Magnolia stared back, a gentle smile on her face.

"I think I've been a bad influence on you," Korinne said.

Magnolia shrugged. "You could be much, much worse."

Korinne was not proud of the strangled noise that escaped her throat. She tore her eyes away from the shit-eating grin Magnolia sported, instead focusing on the reason they were there: the tanks. They each measured about seven feet by four feet, with thick metal walls and a variety of tubes exiting the bottoms. A panel sat on one end, with a number of buttons and dials.

She looked up to find Magnolia distracted, her brows furrowed and lips pursed as she pressed buttons on the side of the tank next to her. Korinne sat on the nearest lid, letting the comm pad record Magnolia's scientific examination. If anything, she could claim she needed this footage just in case something scared her. In actuality, the sight of Magnolia tinkering made affection burn in her chest.

A second later, the tank powered on.

"I fixed it! You just press—Korinne!"

"What?" Korinne swung her legs against the tank and pretended she hadn't just been staring for no good reason. "I needed to sit down for a second."

"Oh, gods," Magnolia said, pinching the bridge of her nose. "Your disrespect is going to stress me out."

"This isn't disrespect. It's a tank, not a coffin." Korinne leaned back on her hands, the perfect picture of casual relaxation. "Besides, it's not like anyone else is using them."

"Right, fine. Everything's fine." Magnolia took a few calming breaths, then settled herself in the proper filming position. "Why don't you tell everyone what usually goes on in this room?"

"Oh, I would love to." Korinne hopped off and paced the narrow rows between the tanks. "The trouble with generational travel was the occupants would have no access to any outside resources once they took off. Therefore, these machines were built to recycle human bodies during the trip, so our component parts could help further humanity and all that. As for ghost stuff, we get all the usual players here. Things get cold, or people get scratched, all that stuff you hear about every haunted spot."

"But...?" Magnolia led.

Korinne paused for one dramatic beat. As far as she knew, Magnolia had only heard the basics of the story, and the details would definitely shock her.

"But we also get reports of a man screaming. And, if we allow that ghosts are real, then we'd assume that man is one Onan Kohli, who was wrongly placed in a reclamation tank while still alive."

"No!" Magnolia said. Sometimes Korinne kept a few fun facts to herself, if only for Magnolia's genuine reactions. "I thought you were kidding when you said that earlier. He really was alive?"

"Unfortunately yes," Korinne said. She didn't respect ghosts, but she at least respected their memories. "Onan was in a coma after an accident. He worked in the engine room, and a piece of machinery broke and fell on him. They allowed three days of life support before declaring him clinically dead and withdrawing treatment. Meaning, they thought there was no way he would wake up again, even if his heart was technically still beating."

"Three days?" The devil was in the details. "They only gave him three days to wake up?"

"Limited resources," Korinne said, hating how often historians cited that reason for some of the more questionable happenings on the ship.

"That's terrible," Magnolia said, one hand on her chest.

"Yeah, there were tough medical protocols on both the *Arkana* and the *Covenant* limiting how much treatment clinicians could give, otherwise they risked running out of supplies. Some things could be recycled or manufactured, but not everything, and not quickly or easily."

"And so poor Onan ended up down here, and woke up during the process?" Magnolia said, her voice quiet.

Korinne nodded. "Even though he'd been unconscious the whole time and all his vitals declined by the hour, he woke up in the reclamation tank." She touched the corner of one tank, taking note of the number painted on the side—a big, blocky five. "Afterwards, the ship council enacted the Kohli Protocol, wherein everyone sent here to the reclamation tanks had to be actually deceased before the process began, not just on the way there."

"You'd think that would be common sense," Magnolia grumbled. "I mean, shouldn't it be obvious?"

Korinne thought of some of her professors and gave a humorless laugh. "Well, when you have people who aren't experts in a subject area making rules for that field, trouble comes around." She walked past a few more tanks before finding the one she wanted. "Here we go, tank number eleven."

"Is that...Onan's tank?" she asked.

"It is," Korinne said as she dug into her bag.

From the far corner, they heard a sharp click, then the whirr of a tank turning on.

"Rinne, how likely is it that a tank would turn on by itself?" Magnolia asked, her voice shaking.

Korinne paused her rifling and turned toward the sound. "Uh, I mean, not zero," she said. She momentarily forgot her search and beelined through the tanks until she found the right one. "Huh. That's weird." She looked all around the edges. "Yeah, I don't know why it turned on."

"What number is it?" Magnolia pulled out her handheld, likely to consult their notes.

"Forty-eight," Korinne said as she checked the number on the tank. It didn't ring any bells. "Do you remember anything about it? I can't think of anything specific."

"Let me check... No, nothing."

The next tank, forty-nine, also turned on.

"Weird," Korinne said, staring at it. She put a hand out and felt the vibrating metal. Yep, definitely on. "They might be on a timer. The mechanics fixing up the engine probably didn't think to check out here since it'd be a programming thing instead of an engineering thing."

"Maybe don't stand too close to it—it might explode," Magnolia said. She shot her flashlight to the left, but it illuminated nothing but a blank wall.

Korinne wished she would stop with the paranoid flashlight waving; it made something tingle between her shoulder blades. "It's not going to explode, the wiring isn't *that* bad." She jogged through the room, back to eleven. "But just in case, I should hurry for this next part."

Oh, Magnolia was going to hate this.

"No, Rinne, don't tell me you're—"

"Hopefully this one smells better," she said, prying open the lid to eleven. Yes, Magnolia would hate it. But the viewers would *love* it.

"Rinne, do not do what I think you're about to do."

"It'll be fine! Look, it doesn't even stink like the other one. Some of them actually got cleaned before we left the ship." She opened the tank entirely, then returned to her bag. Finally, she found the Parabox.

"All right, this is going to be fun."

"Korinne—!"

"Don't worry about it!"

Without a care in the world, Korinne hopped into the reclamation tank.

CHAPTER 19
MAGNOLIA

MAGNOLIA HELD HER BREATH, frozen with shock and fear. With all the unstable machinery, how could Korinne do this? This was bad, this was so bad. Magnolia hated it all so much. Even the ghost in the room—she could absolutely feel it now, their emotions pushing on her chest—disliked the stupid idea of jumping in a reclamation tank.

Korinne fucking *giggled.* "I'll have you know, I really, *really* wanted to scream just now and scare you, but figured that would be too mean."

"It absolutely would be too mean," Magnolia said, stomping over to the tank.

Korinne lay on a metal grid, legs crossed at the ankles and hands folded behind her head. The Parabox rested on her chest, silent for now. The inside of the tank had holes matching the tubes on the outside, as well as a drain in the bottom.

"See? Everything's fine. It's only a little stinky." She settled in further, which made Magnolia nauseous. "These things are honestly kind of genius. The grid underneath me gently heated the bodies while an acid cocktail got funneled through these holes, liquifying everything and sending it out to be sorted."

"Korinne, there were so many dead people in that thing," Magnolia said, trying to keep her energy up even though panic threatened to choke her. Her ghostly companion agreed with the sentiment. "You're going to need the longest, hottest shower this ship has ever seen after this."

"Don't worry, I factored in time for that," Korinne said.

"Good." It took everything not to throw up. "You had your fun, you can get out now."

"All right, ghosties, anyone here with us right now?" Korinne asked.

Really? *Now* she chose to take their job seriously?

"My name is Korinne. If you're a ghost, you should say something. It'll make us a ton of money if you do."

"Korinne I am so serious right now," Magnolia said.

Another tank kicked on a row closer than the others. Magnolia whirled around, expecting to see something, anything to validate the sensations plaguing her. The empty room mocked her, and the pressure on her chest increased as the ghost following them inched toward her.

A shadow materialized next to the running tank, as if feeding on its energy. It felt different than the first one. The first one felt friendly, almost like they were part of the team. The second one didn't exude the same mercurial emotions humans had. It didn't seem fully conscious, with a primal undercurrent of want and anger. It made the hairs on the back of her neck stand up.

A whisper reached her ear, almost sounding like the word *want.*

"Hide," the Parabox said, and Magnolia nearly screamed.

"Korinne, I don't like this," she said instead. Her skin buzzed and her hands trembled. The first ghost appeared at her shoulder, sending goosebumps down her arm. The second stayed at the edge of the tank, watching. Waiting.

"Beach," the Parabox said.

"See? It's a beach day," Korinne said. "Nothing to worry about at the beach."

"Uh, there are so many things to worry about at the beach," Magnolia pointed out. "Do you know what sort of creatures hide in the ocean?"

"Ah! Hide!" Korinne pointed to the box, where the word remained on display.

The box spoke again. "Endorse."

"See? The ghost endorses me," Korinne said.

"Bullshit," Magnolia said. The second spirit didn't move, but the vague sense of anger increased. How could she make Korinne take this seriously? "Rinne, get out of there. You're going to get hurt."

"Is there anyone who wants to talk? I'm right here, ready to pass on your message from beyond the grave," she continued, ignoring the fact that Magnolia was so nervous she wanted to crawl out of her own skin.

"Korinne—"

"Mags, introduce yourself," Korinne whisper-yelled.

As soon as Korinne got out of that tank, Magnolia was going to throttle her. "Korinne—"

"No, I'm Korinne," she said.

"Okay, I'm Magnolia—seriously, can you quit playing around and get out now?"

Korinne sat up, which only made Magnolia feel marginally better. "Mags, take a deep breath." She spoke gently, legitimately trying to soothe her. There was no malice, no patronizing, but somehow that made it worse. Especially when the second ghost at the back of the room flared with heat.

"Something just feels off. I keep seeing"—another form out of the corner of her eye, another empty space when she turned her flashlight on it—"I keep seeing things, and feeling cold spells, and these things keep turning on."

Right on cue, another reclamation tank lit up, something mechanical clunking rhythmically in its depths. The darkness stood there now, but Magnolia hadn't seen it move. Tears prickled the backs of her eyes, and she wanted nothing more than to sprint out of the room.

The chill stayed at her shoulder, and Magnolia heard a voice distinctly whisper, "No."

"Gods!" She whirled around, searching for a speaker and finding none. It had been so clear, much clearer than the words she thought she heard before. "Rinne, please tell me you heard that."

"Depends on what you mean," Korinne said, still patient.

"It was so clear," Magnolia said as the word tumbled around in her head. "You seriously didn't hear it?"

"What was it?" she said, resting her forearms on her knees and looking at Magnolia with the utmost intensity.

"I heard a voice." She swallowed and gathered her nerves. So many things were happening in such a short time. She wanted out of this room. "It said 'no,' but that's it."

The Parabox buzzed with the word, "Bargain."

Korinne got out her handheld and tagged the time. "We'll check the audio later, see if the comm pads picked up a voice phenomenon."

"Execute," said the Parabox.

"Wow, this thing is really going off," Korinne said. "Onan, is that you? Do you want to execute me?"

"Oh my gods, Korinne," Magnolia said as her stomach clenched. Why would she tempt it?

"What? It's just a question," she said, so nonchalant, as if some dark force wasn't moving closer with every passing second. It stood only one row away now.

"Can you at least get out of the human-body-recycling-machine *before* you antagonize a potentially angry spirit?" Magnolia requested. Another tank turned on right next to the shadow, and she swallowed a cry. The darkness slid into the space right next to them. Cold spread through her entire body. "Seriously, Korinne. Please."

"Force," said the box.

Korinne sighed. "All right, all right. Only because you asked so nicely."

She placed her hands on the sides and went to heave herself up, but caught the edge of the lid wrong. It tilted, slowly at first, then rapidly fell onto her head.

"Ow, shit!" Korinne let go of the sides to grab her skull, and the heavy door slammed closed.

"Korinne!" Magnolia scrambled to open the tank. The top didn't budge. Next to her, the first ghost vibrated with fear.

"Holy shit it's dark in here," Korinne said, her voice muffled. How could she be making jokes at a time like this?

The reclamation tank next to theirs kicked on, and Magnolia almost wet herself.

"It's stuck," Magnolia yelled, pushing the lid again. It shifted a heartbreakingly small amount. Korinne made it look so easy, opening it earlier. "Was it always this heavy?"

"It's not that hard. Some kind of latch must've triggered," Korinne said. She was oddly serene for such an alarming situation. Did she not hear the other tank? "I'm checking in here, but I can't see anything."

"Fucking hells," Magnolia said. She readjusted her grip and

shoved. The lid moved an inch, which wasn't even enough for air to get through. Never mind the risk of the thing turning on, Korinne could run out of oxygen. She lowered herself to get more underneath, then pushed again. It raised another inch.

"It's kind of hot in here," Korinne commented, which was less than encouraging.

"I'm trying," Magnolia grunted as she really laid into it. A dark shadow appeared in the corner of her eye, and a feeling of despair nearly overwhelmed her. It made her want to give up and cry—but when had she ever done that in her entire life? Her pendant warmed against her skin and Magnolia turned with a hand out, as if she could fight a ghost. The lid slammed shut as a white light pulsed from her palm. The angry ghost darted to the back of the room, freeing her heart from its clutches.

"Stand," the Parabox said. Cold touched Magnolia's arm again, on the opposite side from the dark spirit. The nice ghost, there to help her.

"Seriously? I think this ghost is making fun of me," Korinne said.

"Oh, *now* you think it's a ghost," Magnolia said. The ghost next to her found that funny.

"Brink," she heard the Parabox say, its tiny voice faint. "Limited. Hell. Fool. Pair."

"Okay, I'm turning this off," Korinne said. How the hells she could stay so unperturbed was beyond Magnolia, because she was about to pass out from fear. "Okay, Mags, let me get into position. Count to three, and we'll both push."

"You weren't pushing this whole time?" Magnolia exclaimed.

"It's very tight in here! I figured you'd free me, but looks like it's gonna take both of us. Just a second." Bangs and thuds sounded from the box as Korinne readjusted, likely hitting the sides with her elbows.

A vibration started beneath Magnolia's feet.

"Rinne? Hurry," she said, as calm as possible. Which was to say, not calm at all.

"Working on it," Korinne said, her voice strained. "Okay, I'm—"

Reclamation tank eleven turned on.

"Oh shit!" Korinne said.

"Push!" Magnolia didn't bother with a countdown. She threw her weight into the lid. It shifted, first one inch, then two. Then it hit a hard block.

"My shoes are melting," Korinne yelled. "Shit! And my pants."

"I'm trying!" What happened to those tales of superhuman strength appearing in times of need? Of mothers lifting cars off of babies and shit like that? Magnolia held her breath and prayed to any deity listening for boundless power.

The door shifted another inch, enough for open space to appear beneath. Magnolia shifted her hands, the metal edge digging into her skin as she pushed. Beside her, the sensation of *someone* strengthened until she could practically see another person standing there, helping her open the lid. Her pendant warmed and she desperately willed it to stop. It could shunt the angry ghost to the back of the room—she needed this one to stick around.

"Ow, shit!" Korinne said, her voice loud now that the lid was partially open. Magnolia pressed harder. With a wretched squeal, the lid opened halfway, enough for Korinne to scramble out and collapse onto the floor. Magnolia followed, running her eyes and hands over her entire body, looking for injuries.

"Are you okay?" she asked, breathless and lightheaded.

True to what Korinne said, the knees and shins of her pants were left in tatters, and the skin underneath red. The toes of her boots reached a similar fate, nearly eaten through.

"I'm okay," Korinne said, chest heaving. "I'm okay."

Magnolia grabbed her by the shoulders and roughly pulled her to her chest, holding her tight. With her adrenaline crashing, fear and relief mixed to form tears.

"I was so scared," Magnolia said. Gods, this was the worst investigation they'd ever done by far. She leaned back and cradled Korinne's face in her hands. "What hurts?"

"Just my shins and hands a little," Korinne said softly, said hands gently touching Magnolia's waist. "No worse than a sunburn, I promise. There wasn't any acid, it just got really hot."

"Gods." Magnolia pulled her close again, if only to convince herself Korinne was actually out of the tank. "That was too close."

"I'm okay," Korinne said, though it sounded like she was trying to convince herself. "I'm okay."

"You're okay," Magnolia agreed.

Korinne put her forehead against Magnolia's shoulder and breathed, her body trembling. Next to them, the tank vibrated as it continued the decomposition cycle. Magnolia felt the first ghost standing behind her, close enough for a chill to run down her spine. Was it merely curious, or was it protecting them from the darkness on the other side of the room?

Korinne pulled away and took a shuddering breath. "I should probably go put some ointment on these burns," she said, assessing her palms. She wasn't bleeding, but her skin appeared angry and red.

"No more stupid shit during this trip." Magnolia meant for it to be a request, but came out as more of an order. "Promise me."

"I promise." Korinne's voice wavered on the two words. Her tan skin was a few shades paler than usual. "No more stupid shit. I'm so sorry, Mags. I'm a fucking idiot."

"It's not your fault," Magnolia said automatically. Did she agree with Korinne's decision? No, but now was not the time to play the blame game for something that had clearly been an accident.

"Yes it is," Korinne said, with more vehemence than Magnolia expected. "I willfully climbed into the tank. You told me not to. It's one hundred percent my fault."

"But you didn't close it," Magnolia said. "You didn't turn it on."

"Not on purpose, no," Korinne said. "But that doesn't mean I didn't do it. God, I'm such an idiot." She ran her hands over her face, heedless of the burns.

"Hey, don't talk about my best friend like that. Accidents happen," Magnolia said, because even if she wanted to rip out the part of Korinne's brain that sparked the idea, it wasn't like she did any of it deliberately. This had been her shtick for the entirety of the show: silly and borderline stupid things to entertain the audience. They had to know at some point it would come back to bite her in the ass.

Korinne paused her pity party to look at her, dark eyes searching. She opened her mouth, then closed it, then tried again.

"Right. Accidents happen," she said. "I'm just going to make sure no *more* accidents happen for the next"—she checked her watch—"twenty-six hours."

Magnolia smiled, her own shaking slowing. Behind her, the ghost moved away, giving them space. "I don't think you can just decide no more accidents will happen," she said.

"Of course I can, I just did," Korinne said. They sat in silence, the moment drawing out long enough for Magnolia to notice how close their faces were, as well as how close she was to losing Korinne. Korinne continued to hold her gaze, and Magnolia decided they were going to have a long, long conversation once they landed on Capa Emphara.

"Do you think you can stand?" Magnolia asked.

Korinne blinked as the spell broke, then nodded. "Yeah, I can."

Magnolia rose, then took Korinne's wrists and pulled her to her feet. "There you go."

"I need to shower. And change," Korinne said. Somehow, her clothes looked even worse now that she was upright. It would've been funny, if the rips didn't put the irritated skin on display.

"Yes, let's do that. Can't have you running around the ship indecent," she said, trying to bring some levity back to the situation, even if her heart continued at a thousand beats a minute. She couldn't look away from the injuries. "You know what the sight of your knees does to me."

"It's true, my knees are known to make many a man or woman crumble." Korinne adjusted her bag, and Magnolia leaned over to close the lid of the tank. While no one else would be visiting this area for a long while, she wouldn't be able to rest if it remained open. It continued to vibrate as it ran through the cycle, and the scent of charred fabric lingered in the air.

As the lid clicked into place, Magnolia noticed hand prints on the metal. Two pairs of them. Had she left that many marks on it? No, she couldn't have, she held the door nearly the whole time. She'd only dropped it the once.

Magnolia paused, glancing over to find Korinne distracted by her handheld. She moved next to the tank, making sure the spot was in full view of the comm pad. She put her hands where they'd been previously, noting how the edges of the marks lined up perfectly. Then she laid her palm over the other print.

The size didn't match up.

CHAPTER 20
CASSIE

From camera 65.3.19: [someone crying]

CASSIE WATCHED THE TWO LEAVE, a sense of foreboding swirling in her gut.

She'd turned on the first reclamation tank, yes—one on the outer edge, close enough to scare them, but far enough to prevent danger. They needed content for their show after all, and Cassie was only too willing to oblige. Plus, if she kept them here, then they wouldn't go wandering around the rest of the ship where who-knew-what waited for them.

But after the whole debacle, Cassie wondered if she'd made a mistake. The thing in here with them didn't seem to be the same kind of ghost as her. It held no form and had no identifying factors. Even if she'd met it before, she couldn't recognize it. Magnolia had managed to push it away with a force that looked very similar to Jocelyn's, an even stronger push than when Jensen scared her. If she could repel the energy... Maybe Cassie didn't need the old ghost seer after all.

The spirit shifted, and the edges of it ebbed and flowed. It didn't really have a form, but it certainly radiated emotions. Well, not emotions, plural. One singular emotion.

Anger.

Deep, guttural, raging anger. Volcanic anger. An anger so deep, Cassie wondered if it wasn't a ghost at all, but one of those poltergeists or whatever-the-fuck previous ghost hunters called it.

"What the fuck is your problem, dude?" Cassie asked. She felt more than saw as it turned its attention on her. An instinct that transcended life and death woke in her chest. The worst part? It felt familiar.

Whatever this thing was, Cassie had encountered it before. Was it after her death, or before, when she was alive?

"Okay, just be cool," she said, holding her hands up. It shifted toward her. As if she had that stupid word box, words appeared in her consciousness. *Want* and *give* and *pain* flitted through her brain as the starving blight reached a snarling red tendril toward her.

"No thanks!"

She jumped, fully intent on passing to the next level up. Instead, she hit the ceiling and slammed back to the ground. "What the fuck?"

More vague ideas of words. *Hunger* and *anger* and *mine*. The spirit moved closer, and the anger it expressed toward the two living women evolved into something more rotten as its attention latched onto Cassie.

She tried to pass through the floor. Nothing.

The shade inched closer, more red tendrils stretching toward her like long, burning fingers. Cassie did what every self-respecting person would do: she ran, the old fashioned way. A tendril shot out at her as she did, and she contorted her body to avoid it. This sent her into a reclamation tank, the metal corner biting into her hip. If she had a pulse, she'd be bleeding for sure.

"Shit." Cassie spun in an effort to avoid both the tank and the shade, but was only successful on one. A tendril touched her, light as a feather, and slid along her forearm.

Pain erupted in Cassie's chest. Her breath left her in a rush, scattering the dirt along the floor. She collapsed to the ground as every muscle spasmed. It felt like her skull got crushed all over again. Voices overlapped as bits and pieces of memories popped into her mind.

The shade continued to inch forward. If it could do that with just a touch, what would happen if it full on grabbed her?

"Fuck!" She forced herself to rise, crawling on hands and knees toward the door as snippets of her memories bombarded her.

"It's not your fault, love," the tender voice said.

"These things take time," the gravelly one—LeBeau—said.

"No wristband means no pass." That voice was new, and incited a pain so deep a dry sob wracked through Cassie's chest.

On and on the fragments slammed into her, but she kept her eyes on the door. The further she got from the shade, the easier it was to breathe, until she finally broke free of its hold and tumbled into the hallway. Even if everything hurt, she forced herself up and broke into a run. She leapt, and let out a cry of relief as she passed through the ceiling. Up and up and up she went until she no longer felt the shade's eyes on her.

"Fuck," Cassie said, collapsing onto her hands and knees. She didn't need oxygen, but gasped for breath anyway. Her forearm ached where the shade touched her, and when she looked, she found a raw, gaping wound. Black necrotic tissue lined the edges, and the gouge ran deep enough to see her bone. "Well, that's new."

She poked the wound and hissed as it stung. The thick,

tough edges of it shriveled further the longer she looked at it. Since when could ghosts get wounded? And how the hell could she fix it?

Energy. She just needed a little bit of energy and she could heal. Warmth flooded her as she siphoned from the ship and directed the flow to her arm. As soon as it touched the wound, pain flared again, this time coupled with a sense of fear and anguish. Cassie stopped the flow and was once again left gasping.

"What the fuck?"

Give.

The shade's words—if she could call them that—spoke over the new memories in her mind. It wanted her pain, her fear, her heartbreak. The bits and pieces of her life it gave to her painted a terrible picture of the one memory she didn't want back.

"Oh. This is bad," Cassie realized. "This is like, super bad."

But what did it matter?

Cassie grit her teeth. No, she wouldn't give in to those thoughts, wouldn't fall victim to whatever the Malevolence was trying to accomplish. She was going to save herself, and those two women, and everyone else stuck on the ship. Which meant she could no longer do this alone.

For the hundredth time, Cassie forced herself to her feet. She went to the elevator and climbed up, laying on top of it and soaking in the steady stream of energy. As she rested, she scanned the area, trying to use whatever ghosty senses she got in the afterlife. How much danger were they all in?

A red light glowed from the innermost level. At first, Cassie thought it was just emergency lights. But most of the emergency lights on the *Arkana* pathways were blue, not red, because the last thing a ship needed during such an event was to incite further panic. Another piece returning from her life.

Cassie pushed off the elevator and sent herself toward the girls' rooms. It was time. She needed to communicate with them face to face. She needed to tell them what was going on.

Or maybe just one of them—the one who already believed in her existence.

CHAPTER 21
MAGNOLIA

From camera 1.1.1: [someone whispers "fuck"]

"ARE YOU SURE?" Magnolia asked, her heart still rattling against her ribs.

"I'm sure," Korinne said with a laugh. "I'm fine, Mags. I can shower by myself, I promise."

Logically, Magnolia knew this. Emotionally, she didn't want to let Korinne out of her sight.

"Okay. But if you start feeling woozy or something, please call me," she said.

Korinne smirked in full view of the comm pad. "If you wanted to see me naked, you just had to say so."

"Korinne!" Magnolia choked out. Her cheeks burned like the surfaces of the suns. "I only feel like I have to supervise you because otherwise you might, I don't know, try to crawl into the drains or something!"

Korinne laughed, but it seemed somewhat forced. Good, Magnolia managed to strike a nerve then. Maybe Korinne would do as she promised and think twice before doing something ridiculous just for the cameras.

"No drain spelunking, I promise," Korinne said, holding a hand over her heart. "I'm just going to shower and then we can go get lunch."

"Fine. But you're still on thin ice," Magnolia said as heat continued to radiate through her.

She received one more infuriating smile before Korinne closed the door. Magnolia wiped her sweaty palms on her pants and waited in case Korinne changed her mind and called for her. When no such call came, she accepted her friend's independence and went into her own room. The door slid shut with its customary creak, leaving her alone with no Korinne and no signs of ghosts.

Try as she might, Magnolia couldn't figure out an argument against ghostly interference in the whole debacle. There was no explanation for the handprint, nor for how Magnolia suddenly opened the lid on her own when she previously couldn't. The whole thing was right there on video. Even if the ghost itself didn't show up, she *had the print*.

She'd never been so glad she bought the comm pad harnesses. That said, it felt good to take it off and let her torso breathe for a second.

Her pendant slid along its chain as she settled into bed, the metal warm from where it sat on her skin. Or was it warm because it was working so hard? She didn't think she'd noticed the temperature of it this often in all the years she'd been wearing it. It had helped whenever the one spirit moved too close in the reclamation tanks, pushing it back and calming that odd feeling of despair it gave her. Was that the pendant doing its job, or did all these sensations mean it was starting to fail? For the millionth time in her adult life, she wished she could call her grandparents and ask questions. After all, even if her grandfather gave her the pendant, it had been her Grandma Josie's to start with. What did they know that she didn't?

Something moved outside her door. Magnolia held her breath, and it was all too easy to feel like she sensed someone on the other side. Probably Korinne, done with her shower and coming to check on her. Well, Korinne couldn't check on her if she checked on her first. Magnolia jumped up and smacked the pad.

The door creaked partially open to put the empty hallway on display. Magnolia poked her head out and looked both ways. No signs of Korinne, or any of the ghosts she saw in the middle of the night. The feeling, however, persisted. Someone was there. Magnolia sensed it with every fiber of her being. Luckily, it wasn't the scary one from before.

"Hello?" she tried.

A whisper of a feeling swirled in her heart—the ghost's hesitation. Her pendant warmed, and energy buzzed in her fingertips. If she concentrated, it reached toward where her subconscious perceived another person.

"We can talk, if you want," Magnolia said in the direction of the spirit. A spike of panic emanated from them. "No? Okay."

She lingered, waiting to see if the ghost decided to try something. When it made no move, she gave up and closed the door. If a ghost didn't want to show themself yet, so be it.

Unless...

Baxter had needed energy to fully form. Was that the problem with this ghost? Energy continued to tingle in her hands. A grin formed on Magnolia's face as she realized exactly what she needed to do.

Bolstered by unfounded confidence, Magnolia slammed her hand against the door pad. Before she could think too hard about it, she whipped her pendant off but kept hold of it, just in case. She had to be smart while she was being stupid.

The door creaked open, and the empty hall greeted her.

Except it wasn't empty.

A blonde woman stood in front of her, blood coating her forehead and part of her skull caved in. Magnolia's eyes widened, and the other woman's did in return as they realized they were, in fact, looking at each other.

"Oh, uh, hey," the other woman said. Her voice was low and raspy, like it wasn't used often. Like she was...

"A ghost?" Magnolia asked. Stupid question of the century, of course she was a ghost. There were only three people on the ship, and this woman certainly wasn't one of them. Especially with that head wound.

The woman blinked, took a breath, then said, "Fuck, I definitely should've thought this all the way through."

"Holy shit," Magnolia said, her heart in her throat. She recognized that face, half-crushed skull and all. They'd stared at it for hours as they planned the trip. "Cassie?"

Cassie gulped. "I didn't think it would feel this weird."

"Holy *shit!* I need—oh my gods—where's my..."

She patted her chest and choked on a noise of despair. Her comm pad was still on her desk! The ghost of Cassie Malone, right in front of her, and she wasn't wearing her gods damned comm pad!

"Just wait!" Magnolia put a hand out as she turned, as if she could hold Cassie in place. Cold shocked her hand as it passed through Cassie's chest, and they both gasped as a zap of energy passed between them. For a beat, Magnolia felt Cassie's emotions as her own, a terrible mix of fear and pain. She swallowed it down and scrambled for her comm pad.

She had it! A full body apparition! And she was going to...

Capture none of it, because as soon as she turned around,

Cassie blinked from view with a strange, blank look on her face. Magnolia ran back to the door and looked left and right, but found nothing. Nothing! Not even an inkling! Her emotions bubbled up inside her and overflowed into a frustrated yell. How? How could she fail so miserably at something so simple?

The door next to her opened, startling her. Korinne squeezed out as it moved, catching herself on the edge and nearly knocking herself over.

"What is it? Are you okay?" She came up to Magnolia and put her hands on her shoulders, then on her cheeks, cradling her face as she searched it. "What happened?"

"I just..." Magnolia squeezed her eyes shut, a flame of embarrassment crawling up her spine as a few tears leaked out. She sensed no presences around them, not a single one. Her pendant dug into her palm as she clutched it tight.

"Mags, what happened?" Korinne asked, tenderly wiping the tears away with her thumbs. Magnolia's mind raced as she played through the events of the last few minutes. How would she explain all this to Korinne, who didn't even believe in ghosts, let alone powers that allowed someone to see them?

"Nothing, it was nothing," she whispered, opening her eyes.

Korinne stood close, continuing to hold her and gently swipe her tears. "It's very clearly something," she said. Magnolia swallowed, then glanced down. Sure enough, Korinne had her comm pad in the harness, right where it was supposed to be. She must've misunderstood the look, because she said, "Don't worry, all of this is getting edited out. I wouldn't do that to you."

"No, I know," Magnolia said with a sniffle. Korinne made jokes, but she never aired anything unapproved. It was one of many reasons they refused to stream their investigations live.

"Then what's going on?" She looked so concerned, and

Magnolia felt nothing but chagrin and a healthy dose of vexation.

"I'm sorry I bothered you. I'm fine, really." She tried to step back, to put some space, but Korinne's hands only moved from her cheeks to her shoulders, keeping her close.

"Mags, talk to me," she whispered.

Faced with the opportunity to tell her everything, Magnolia suddenly doubted any of it actually happened. Maybe this was all some elaborate hallucination, and she hadn't actually seen Cassie. But she had, right? She'd seen her face, heard her voice. Cold still laced her hand where it went through her, particularly icy over the cuts on her wrist.

Korinne's brows furrowed. "Where's your necklace?"

"Huh?" It took a moment for her brain to catch up. Sure enough, she still clutched her pendant in her hand, so hard it left indentations on her skin. Hesitantly, she pulled it back on and tucked it beneath the collar of her shirt. With no ghosts around, she couldn't tell if it made a difference anymore.

Korinne let her hands drop then, but didn't step away. "I thought you weren't supposed to take it off?" she asked, making Magnolia scoff.

"You don't believe it's a protection spell," she said, sounding much more angry than she felt. Luckily, Korinne didn't take the bait.

"No, but you do," she said. "Why did you take it off?"

"I was just trying to see something." Magnolia created the space then, taking a step back toward her room. Korinne shifted like she might follow, but ultimately stayed in place.

"And that something made you cry?" Korinne asked.

Magnolia cringed. "I'm just tired and emotional. This is a big assignment, it's stressful," she said.

Korinne let out a huff of a laugh. "If you're going to lie to me, make it more believable than that," she said.

"I'm not lying," Magnolia said, dropping her eyes so she didn't have to look her partner in the face. That earned a full on chuckle from her.

"You sure aren't telling the truth. We've spent a million days together, Mags. I kind of know you. Just a little." She could tell Korinne crossed her arms over her chest, but refused to look away from her shoes. Gods, how could she get out of this conversation? "You know you can tell me anything, right? I won't judge."

It was meant to be sweet, Magnolia knew that. But this was past differing opinions on the legitimacy of ghosts. No way in hell could she say that not only did she see a ghost, but she only saw her because she apparently had some sort of secret powers.

Yeah, that was definitely a conversation she wanted to approach gently.

"I know. Thanks, Rinne," she said finally.

Korinne nodded. "And if any of those ghosts hurt your feelings, I'll kill them again," she said, with the cocky half-smile that charmed Magnolia every time.

Magnolia smiled and stepped forward, folding Korinne into a hug. She stiffened at first, then relaxed into it, wrapping her arms around Magnolia's waist.

"You're a good friend, Korinne," Magnolia said. An errant flinch went through her, probably because Magnolia hugged her so tight. But she didn't want to let go quite yet. "I have no doubt you'd find a way to kill a ghost just to make me feel better."

"And don't you forget it," Korinne said, her breath tickling Magnolia's neck and sending goosebumps down her arms. Magnolia stepped back once she had her fill; did she imagine it, or did Korinne's hands linger, just for a second?

"You ready to go eat?" Magnolia asked, putting on a brave

face even though she wanted to crumple to the floor and scream.

"Sure, that sounds nice and low risk. Just let me know when you're ready and we'll get going," Korinne said.

"Perfect, it's a date." Magnolia took two steps into her room, then leaned out into the hallway again. "Oh, Korinne?"

Korinne stopped halfway through, knocking into her door again. The girl would have a hundred bruises by the time this investigation finished.

"Yeah?"

"Thank you for running to my rescue again." Magnolia felt the blush on her cheeks and chose to ignore it.

Korinne smiled and saluted. "Anything for my liege," she said, and ducked back into her room.

Magnolia returned to her room, no less frustrated but at least less sad. She ran her thumb over her pendant, the familiar pattern scratching against her skin.

No pendant meant seeing ghosts. She flexed her cold fingers; no pendant also meant interacting with the ghosts. She thought of Baxter, and how she was able to give him some of her energy, but it exhausted her. But this time, she was able to touch the ghost and not get completely depleted.

Magnolia smiled. As long as she had enough energy, she figured she could make a full body apparition happen.

Good thing it was time for lunch.

CHAPTER 22
CASSIE

*From camera 53.2.9: [a rosary on the edge of a chair
starts swinging back and forth]*

THE WORLD WENT white as Magnolia's energy catapulted
Cassie into a memory.

She went from pod to pod through the engine room, filling
oil tanks with recycled lubricant and exchanging rusted and
dirty tools for freshly polished ones. Sweat poured from every
orifice and pooled in her gloves, the heat of the room boiling her
from the inside out. She hated it, hated this job, but it was the
first thing to come available and had the highest rate of inter-
ship travel. The sooner she became a full engineer, the sooner
she could transfer to the *Covenant*.

"Cassie, we need to move faster." Goss' harsh tone cut
through the clanging of the ship machinery, and for emphasis,
she smacked a metal hull with a tool. "He's being a real dick
today."

"Sorry, coming." Cassie exchanged tools faster and tried to

pour the oil without spilling a precious drop. She couldn't waste any credits replacing it if she wanted to get out of here.

"This thing is so damn temperamental," Goss said. She always sounded so angry, and it brought out the worst in Cassie. "If you wanna maintain it, you gotta be quicker than that."

"I could also help on the mechanical side." Cassie scrambled to keep up with the foreman, which was difficult considering the woman's tall stature. She had broad shoulders and short, steel gray hair, and despite her size, moved across the catwalks with deft agility. "I've been studying for the exam—"

"Make sure you finish your job first." Goss pointed down another row. "Walk eight looks a little dry."

Cassie growled under her breath. Goss always ignored her ambitions, and Cassie was quickly growing tired of it. The woman's arrogance made Cassie want to punch her old face to see if there was any blood left in the bag of bones.

"Yes, ma'am," she said through gritted teeth.

It doesn't have to be this way, she thought, anxiety rolling in her stomach at the idea. There were other avenues to achieve her goal.

"Last ship is tonight!" A red-headed engineer yelled over the clanging of the machine, talking to his partner. "They're cutting off contact and the *Covenant* is splitting off!"

Cassie stopped, realized how obvious her eavesdropping was, then continued to the next pod, just close enough to hear as she swapped clean tools around.

"No shit?" The partner's voice was higher, easier to hear. "Damn, no wonder they're pushing down the list so fast. Think they'll make you go?"

"Nah, I've got Eva now. A newborn is a pretty good excuse to stay here," the first guy said. "You?"

"Probably not. There's plenty of us to go around, and

they'll need more from the water reclamation crew, anyway. Let those people have the fun."

The reclamation crew?

Cassie flew through her duties, still careful not to waste resources, and punched out an hour early while Goss was distracted. If the last ship was tonight, then she needed to be on it.

She didn't stop to change clothes, instead running through the halls and to the back stairwell that led directly to the water reclamation locker room. The place was empty, and Cassie cursed, sidling up to the door between the room and the reclamation tanks. If no one but her friends were on the other side, she'd be fine. But if she came at the wrong time and the foreman found her, she'd be fodder for the *other* reclamation tanks.

As luck would have it, the door slid open and three water reclamation engineers clomped through.

Cassie pressed herself against the wall, staying unseen to the room beyond, and waited until the door slid shut again before kicking off and scaring the living starlight out of Malone.

"Jesus Christ, Cass, the fuck are you doing here?" Malone jumped a klick in the air, much to the amusement of her colleagues. She punched Cassie in the shoulder, then sat on a bench to unlace her boots.

"I need to borrow your uniform." Cassie knew how rushed she sounded, how crazed. She didn't care.

"What, you trying to hop stations? I told you, I gotta get the chief to submit the order—"

"No, I'm going on that transport to the *Covenant* tonight."

Malone stilled, one boot off and one boot on, and looked at Cassie from beneath her bushy brows.

"Cass, that's the stupidest thing I've ever heard."

"Please, Malone," Cassie begged. "They only need water

reclamation engineers. The shuttle—it's the last one, the *Covenant* is splitting off, and she..." She stopped and glanced at the other two in the room, who busied themselves with loudly changing and preparing for the showers. Despite their attempts at privacy, Cassie lowered her voice. "She doesn't have much longer. I have to go, Malone. I *have* to."

"So you're gonna do something completely idiotic to go see a dying girl?" Malone asked. She was trying to be the voice of reason, Cassie could see that. But reason didn't apply when it came to matters of the heart.

"I'll do anything to see her," she said. When Malone didn't reply, she reiterated, "Anything."

Malone made herself busy with her boots and socks, then moved onto her jumpsuit, covered in sweat and grime from the reclamation tanks. For a second, Cassie thought she'd toss her the dirty uniform, and while that certainly would've been gross, she'd still be grateful. But Malone stuffed the suit in the laundry basket instead of handing it over.

"I don't like it, Cass. It's way too risky."

"But it's not your risk."

"It *is* my risk," she said, pointing to the name patch ironed onto every jumpsuit.

Panic shook Cassie's voice as the emotions she so desperately wanted to hide spilled over. "If I get caught, I'll say I stole it from you. Malone, *please*."

She stared at Cassie, long and hard, before asking, "She's really that bad?"

"A couple of weeks." Tears pricked the backs of her eyes and blurred her vision. "Last time I talked to her, she had a couple of weeks at most."

Malone bit her lip, glanced at her coworkers, and sighed. "What's your plan?"

"Don't worry about my plan." Hope threatened to choke her.

"Well, now I'm extra worried about it," she said, and Cassie groaned in frustration.

"I'm trying to give you plausible deniability here."

"Oh, I *hate* that you said that." Malone turned and put her hands on her hips, staring at Cassie with those dark eyes. "Makes me think you've made friends with that idiot trying to start something."

"We're not friends," Cassie said immediately, which was of course the wrong thing to say.

"Cass, his own sister hates him—"

"I swear. Nothing will come back to you, and soon I'll be long gone on another ship. It won't matter. Look, I'll transfer the credits for your uniform right now." She poked at her wristband, opening her account.

"You don't have to—"

"Done." She stopped and stared at her friend, silently begging for her to see the light.

The other two engineers left, and silence rang loud for ten heartbeats before Malone groaned loud enough to shake the walls. "Okay, fine."

Though she didn't look happy about it, Malone reached into her locker and pulled out a fresh uniform, handing it over.

"We're not quite the same size, but it'll do."

"Thank you, Malone. I owe you everything." Cassie snatched the uniform and leapt on Malone in a hug. She couldn't breathe through her gratitude and her excitement. She was doing this, she was getting over there to Rose.

"Whatever, don't mention it." Ignoring her current outfit of sweaty underthings, she hugged Cassie back tightly. "And please, Cass, be really fucking careful."

"I will," Cassie said into her shoulder. "Thank you."

"Say hi to Rose for me."

Cassie left the way she came, stopping in the stairs to change into Malone's jumpsuit. The fit was way off, but it was close enough to pass, which was all she needed. Now, for her next order of business.

Etienne LeBeau was exactly where she expected him to be, running a table in the corner of the cafeteria. She ignored all the people around him and marched right up, claiming the bench across from him and ignoring the angry man behind her.

"That was rude," LeBeau said.

"If I do as you ask, can you get me on the shuttle?" she said.

His eyebrows shot up, and he made a show of lacing his fingers in front of him.

"Are you ready to do as I ask?"

"Yes." No hesitation.

"Are you sure?" He spoke low, preventing the others around from hearing him. "You know it'll be no small task."

"I'm positive." Cassie was never more sure in her life. "Whatever you need me to do, I'll do it."

His feral grin showed all his teeth. "Excellent, in a few days I'll get you—"

"I don't have a few days," she interrupted. "The last shuttle leaves tonight, and I have to be on it."

LeBeau exhaled slowly and spread his hands on the table. "I don't know if you're in the position to be making demands, considering you're depending on me to get you what you want."

"LeBeau." She couldn't beg like she had with Malone. That would only entice him to torture her more. "Whatever you need me to do, I will do it in the next hour, and I need you to hold up your end of the bargain."

"These things take time—"

"No, they don't." Cassie might not know much about rebellions, and this man definitely wasn't someone she respected, but he had a certain power she needed. "Whatever you had in mind for me is ready, because that's how you operate. I can give you my wristband to do whatever stuff you need to get me on the shuttle. Now, are you following through, or are you breaking your word?"

The stress made her want to throw up on the table between them. Boldness like this didn't come to her often, but all she had to do was hold on to it for a few minutes longer. Let him call her bluff; she'd walk away and find someone else who needed a favor.

LeBeau ground his teeth. "Fine. I'll have an associate meet you at stair E9. She'll give you further instructions."

"Pleasure doing business with you." Before she completely lost her lunch, Cassie rose and stalked away.

For an eternity, she waited at the proper stairwell, checking her watch every four seconds like that would make the associate move faster. Each moment she stood there decreased her chances.

"You Cassie?"

For all her impatience, Cassie startled at the voice, turning to find a short woman with hair and eyes nearly the same shade of honey brown. A blink later, she realized she was not a short woman, but in fact a kid barely into her teenage years. An adult by ship standards, but not by much.

"What're you doing here?" The girl should be in an apprenticeship, not down here with—"Is that a pipe bomb?"

"Shut up," the girl said, handing over the, yes, pipe bomb. "LeBeau told me to tell you to plant this next to where the delegation is meeting."

"The fuck? No, I—" She stopped, realizing whatever came out of her mouth would make it back to LeBeau's ears. "Wait, right, okay. Yeah, I can do that."

She snatched the bomb from the girl; a better person would stop, take time to talk to her, try to convince her to go into something else besides a life of crime. But at her core, Cassie was selfish, and didn't have the capacity to care about the kid's life choices. Besides, who was she to judge? She was the one taking the pipe bomb from her. She also had more pressing concerns, like where to hide a fucking bomb so that it threatened the visiting delegation from the *Covenant*.

This was, by far, her worst idea. By doing this, she was complicit in the damaging of her ship. People could get hurt, it would throw them into political turmoil, and if things slowed too much and they never reached another planet...

No, that wouldn't happen. Whatever the *Arkana* lacked in social support, it made up for in redundancy. This would send a message without hurting the true victims: people like her who scurried around at the bottom. People who were unable to be with someone they loved just because some zealots in charge decided to revive ancient ideals.

Rose. She had to make it to Rose, consequences be damned. If they wanted to lock Cassie up after finding them together, so be it. She would take the fall and take it gladly, as long as it meant seeing Rose before she died.

But what if the bomb killed someone?

Cassie swallowed and hoped she'd figure out the best spot to plant it.

As she wandered the halls around the delegation room, anger and self righteousness built in her chest. After all, what would it matter if someone got hurt? The ones who ran these ships couldn't care less about anyone besides themselves. They were the people who made these stupid rules, who would throw her out of an airlock if they knew about Rose. The rage took root in her heart, fed by the whirrs of the ship. No, they deserved a little taste of the uncertainty that every citizen below them held.

But did she have to hurt people?

Cassie let out a frustrated huff, catching the attention of someone walking nearby. "Sorry," she said when the man gave her an odd look. "Just realized I turned down the wrong hall."

She turned on her heel and walked as fast as her magnetic boots allowed. This was stupid, so stupid. What was she thinking? Surely she could find another way.

Something red flickered in her periphery, and she snapped her head toward it. Red? Red was never a good sign. But when she looked, all she saw was an exhaust pipe leading down from the engine room. Smoke curled from a seam in it; someone needed to repair that. She reached out and touched it, wondering what they were burning that made red smoke instead of black.

Heat burnt her fingers and shot straight to her heart. Anger wrapped around her again, springing from an unknown fountain within her that ran deep and pure. All her life she fought for every scrap, while others lived in luxury. No longer did they preach a job for everyone, and everyone for a job. *Loss of self for the success of all.* What bullshit. The elitist assholes at the top clung to their power and pearls and left everyone else in the cold.

No, no, that wasn't right. Plenty of people took care of each other, took care of her. It wasn't all bad, she was just... emotional? She'd never been this emotional before. It had to be the stress of the situation.

She wouldn't blow the room. But blowing part of an engine would slow their travel, enough to make a point. One engine was fixable, and it wouldn't hurt anyone. And maybe it would make the *Covenant* stick around long enough for her to get Rose over here. She left the wing and took the nearest elevator to the innermost level. She knew these engines like the back of her hand, knew where she could put it to make a point without causing injuries. She ignored the fury of the machines clinking around her and adhered the pipe bomb to the rumbling engine. Before she thought too hard about it, she pressed the button.

Good enough.

Time was not on her side, and Cassie bolted from the engine room. The borrowed uniform pulled and caught in weird places as she ran to the dock. Surely LeBeau would be waiting there with her manufactured credentials and her ticket to the *Covenant.* She would make it on board with moments to spare, a brand new water reclamation tank specialist with a job to do.

For the record, she was correct. LeBeau stood outside the entrance to the dock, hands in his pockets and a smarmy grin on his face. The expression would've scared her if she didn't have other priorities.

"It's done." Cassie stopped in front of him and held out her hand. "Wristband, please."

"Oh, you wanted that tonight?" His smile never changed. The rage Cassie felt earlier boiled up again, starting at her feet and moving up until she saw red.

"Don't *fuck* with me right now, LeBeau," she said. "I have five minutes to get on that shuttle. You promised."

"I promised you'd have your documents and ticket, yes. I didn't promise for tonight." The grin grew a sharp edge, and he crossed his arms over his chest.

"You knew what I meant, I don't—" She took a deep breath and tried to reign in her emotions. Blowing up wouldn't help. "I need to be on that shuttle, tonight. There's not gonna be another one. Why would I need those credentials later?"

"Well, should've planned ahead then." He lifted one hand and inspected his nails, oddly clean for someone supposedly working in sanitation. Grease covered Cassie's hands, staining the edges of her nails black.

"Look, I'm sorry, okay? Is that what you want to hear?" She was desperate now, and it was obvious in her voice, but she couldn't find it in herself to care. "I'm sorry I took so long. But I did what you wanted me to do, now please, *please*, tell me you have credentials."

The ground shook as the shuttle fired up. Less than a minute until launch now. And LeBeau did nothing but smile.

"Nope. You didn't fulfill your end of the bargain," he said.

"Yes, I did, I planted that—that thing," she said, glancing around for eavesdroppers.

"Planted it, yes. But wasn't it supposed to go off by now?"

Her stomach spasmed. Yes, it was supposed to go off by now. It was supposed to go off before the delegates left for the shuttle, which would depart in a few minutes. Engine malfunction alarms should be screaming. She'd set it right, she knew she had, unless...

"You were never going to help me," she whispered.

LeBeau shrugged. "Loyalty is earned, Cassie. Not freely given."

She learned then what it felt like to have all hope lost. No words came to her, no witty retorts or bolstering arguments. She gaped at him as the future she envisioned melted away.

"Better get going. Who knows, maybe that uniform will be enough. I heard they're looking for reclamation tank engineers."

Cassie's blood turned to ice, and then to fire.

She ran, faster than ever before, faster than she thought she could go. Her shoulders caught as she squeezed through the doors, which opened far too slowly. The inner airlock was already open, the shuttle inching its way through.

"Wait!" Her screech was high and ragged, the word barely recognizable. "Wait for me!"

A shuttle attendant spotted her, and her heart leapt to her throat. They saw her, they would stop the shuttle, she could still make it on—

The attendant stepped toward her, his hands outstretched to catch Cassie by the shoulders, preventing her from going further.

"No, you don't understand." She wracked her brain for an excuse, anything to stall. "I was just late, off shift, I'm sorry, my wristband—"

Except she didn't have her wristband. LeBeau did.

She stared at her empty wrist, and the attendant grimaced. "I'm sorry. No wristband means no pass."

"But I'm supposed to—I have to—" Panic gripped her, and the fist of grief choked her as the shuttle continued forward. "I have to be on that shuttle. I have to go to the *Covenant*."

"Everyone's accounted for. I'm sorry."

"No, let me—"

She wrestled from his grip and took off again. If she got there fast enough, they'd hold the outer airlock, and then she would have enough time to talk her way on.

A body slammed into her from behind, sending them both to the floor of the dock. Air rushed from her lungs, which instead filled with despair as Cassie watched the airlock doors close behind the shuttle.

"If I let go, are you gonna do something stupid?" The attendant held her down, but all Cassie could do was watch through teary eyes as the shuttle took off toward the massive ring ship waiting in the distance. Rose was so close, and yet she'd never felt further.

"No, I won't do anything stupid." Her voice cracked, the tears flowing freely now.

"Good, cause I'm already on overtime." He couldn't be bothered enough to call authorities or throw her in detainment. After preventing her escape, he'd done his job.

Cassie lay on the dock for a long time, a deep pain clawing her insides and consuming her whole. Around her, life went on, the dock workers locking everything and shutting down for the night. They left her in her grief, too concerned with their own lives to worry about one girl crying on the floor.

The lights dimmed to reserve levels. Cassie ran out of tears, though the deep, gnawing pain remained. With shaking hands, she pulled her handheld from her pocket and opened the inter-ship forum application; the *Covenant* was close enough for the signals to reach, as long as she patched into the extended comm circuit.

The video call showed how wrecked she looked, but she couldn't care less. After tonight, they would be too far gone.

"You look terrible," Rose answered. Rich coming from her, considering her skin held a yellowish tint, and she was hooked up to a multitude of machines.

"You look beautiful," Cassie replied. It wasn't a lie—despite the obvious signs of sickness, Rose was still the most gorgeous person Cassie'd ever seen.

"What's wrong, Cassie?" Her voice was soft and scratchy, her throat still irritated from intubation the week before. "Tell me, love."

"Someone might hear you," Cassie murmured, and Rose scoffed.

"What could they do to me now?"

Fresh tears came then, and Cassie wiped them away with the scratchy uniform sleeve.

"I'm sorry, Rose. I couldn't get on the shuttle."

Rose fell silent and still, and for a breath, Cassie wondered if she fell asleep.

Then, she whispered, "Oh."

"I tried, I did, I had to..." She shook her head. Let Rose keep the good impression of her. "I'm so, so sorry."

"It's not your fault, love," she said. "I know you would be here if you could."

Cassie choked on tears and Rose's patience. "They're saying that was the last one."

"Then we'll have to stay on here as long as we can." She brought the camera closer to her face. "Don't cry, my love. We'll see each other again someday."

"I just..." Cassie took a breath, but it did nothing to steady her. "I wanted to be there, to hold you, even if..." She couldn't bring herself to finish the sentence. Even if it wasn't for long, even if it wasn't forever. Even if they might get in trouble.

"I wish you were here too," Rose admitted. A sharp inhale told of her pain, but she smoothed it away from her face before Cassie could comment. "But maybe it's for the best."

"What?" Cassie froze.

"I'm dying, Cassie. We both know it."

"You don't have to keep mentioning it—"

"Hush, let me talk."

Cassie obliged, even when it took Rose a few minutes before she could continue. "If you were here, I could hold you, yes. But then they would see, and they would know, and while I would get to slip peacefully between the stars, you would deal with the aftermath, and I wouldn't be there to help you."

"I thought you were going to haunt me," Cassie mumbled.

"If I have the ability, I will." She grimaced and clutched her chest, only letting go to reach over and hit the button for her pain pump. "It won't be long, Cassie. But I couldn't die without telling you I love you, just one more time."

"What are you talking about? You have some time, the doctor said a couple more weeks."

"They withdrew treatment today," Rose whispered. She rested her hand on her abdomen now, giving an unflattering angle to the camera. Cassie still found her stunning. "I reached the end of the protocol."

"But you were getting better," Cassie said as another pain speared her chest.

"Not fast enough," Rose said.

"You just need a little more time," she said.

Rose gave her the saddest smile she'd ever seen.

"I'm out of time, my love."

"Don't talk like that."

"I have to talk like that." She gulped in air. "Cassie, you are the best thing to happen to me. Every day I thank the stars that you started that conversation about *Superheroes on Mars*. I love you more than anything, promise me you'll remember that."

It sounded too much like a goodbye. Cassie wanted to jump out of the airlock herself and hope she made it to the *Covenant*, but that would defeat the purpose. And so, despite the knife lodged in her chest, she leaned into Rose's words.

"You are the most wonderful person I know," Cassie said. "I love you so much. And one day, I'll find you among the stars, and our dust will combine or whatever shit you wrote that one night."

Rose laughed, weak and breathy. "At least you have all that poetry to remember me by."

Cassie's heart broke, over and over, the pain so deep she felt it in her very bones.

"Please don't leave me yet," she whispered, earning another half laugh.

"I wouldn't if I had a choice."

She was so pale. A rumble sounded from Rose's side, and Cassie dared to glance away from the screen to see the

Covenant's engines firing, slowing them down. Static spotted the screen.

"Wait, not yet—"

Rose's eyes were closed, her chest still.

"Rose? Rose! Rose, wake up, please—"

More static. Through the haze, she heard the screams of the machines. The handheld fell from the bed and landed on the floor, leaving Cassie to watch as medical personnel rushed to Rose's bed.

"No, no, no, wake up! Rose!" She was screaming, but no one seemed to hear her. Her voice echoed through the empty dock, the drop off next to her swallowing it whole. Pain the likes of which she'd never felt slammed into her as the connection cut.

Cassie screamed and screamed, but no one came. She stood and grabbed the handheld, rushing to the airlock door as if the proximity might reconnect them. It couldn't end here, she wasn't ready to say goodbye—

She slammed her handheld into the glass, which did nothing except hurt her fingers. The physical pain took attention from the anguish raging inside her, so she did it again, and again, ignoring the cracks on the screen and the crunching of her joints. Was Rose still alive? The *Covenant* was a speck in the distance now; it would take a few minutes for a message to reach her, and more minutes for her to respond.

The handheld slipped from her grip, her fingers bleeding and bruised from the assault. It hurt, everything hurt, how was she supposed to just go on like this?

She stepped back, searching for the handheld. Stupid, she wouldn't know if she didn't send a message. It sat at the edge of the dock, one corner hanging off. Everything shook as she reached down for it, then time slowed.

How far down was it?

No, she scolded herself. There was still a chance Rose was alive—she had to hope for that, had to believe that, because otherwise...

She didn't want to think about otherwise.

The pain was all consuming, but she couldn't give into it. She had to continue on.

Something grabbed her wrist, something strong and unseen. The pain in her chest multiplied until she was filled with nothing but despair. Any positive thought fled, and she no longer pictured Rose in their earlier days, but a strange, warped vision of her, stuck in the hospital as she was. The pain went beyond anything she'd ever felt, beyond any reasonable explanation. Why did it hurt so much?

The thing gripping her wrist tugged her, just slightly, toward the edge. Red smoke swirled from the depths and burned her skin.

Cassie dug in her heels, a whisper of fear barely touching the edges of her pain. Something was wrong.

Whatever held her tightened its hold and tugged. She watched her hand raise, her arm straighten, as the force led her to the edge.

"No," she said, and tried to jerk back. The thing held fast, pulled harder. "No!"

Something grabbed her right ankle, then her left. She tried to scramble back, her broken handheld long forgotten, but it was so strong. It leeched her pain from her and filled her instead with fear. What the hell was happening?

The thing pulled. Hard.

Cassie screamed as her feet went out from under her and her body slammed into the metal floor. The thing holding her slithered over the edge, dragging her along with it. She yelled, and thrashed, and scrambled for any sort of purchase, but she was deep in its clutches now.

With no one there to stop her, Cassie fell from the ledge.

Time passed. How much, Cassie couldn't say. With a start, she took a shuddering breath. But she couldn't feel the air going through her lungs.

What?

"Rose?" she said. But wait, who was that? "Rose?"

She was all twisted up. One limb at a time, she uncurled until she could stand straight.

The floor went through her chest.

"What the fuck?" She went to put her hands on the floor, but they passed through the metal. Energy buzzed around her and burned through her. "What the fuck, oh my God—"

"Hey there," a calm, gentle voice said.

Cassie whirled around to find two women. One stood tall and proud, wearing a maroon three piece suit and a sad smile. The other knelt, and had kind eyes on a round face. She leaned over, and the light caught on a round pendant as it fell from her shirt collar. Cassie barely caught sight of the symbol, like a sun with lines and wings.

"Rough one, huh?" the standing woman said. "Been there."

"Lottie, be nice," the other woman said. "I'm sure you remember what it was like to wake up."

"What the fuck are you talking about?" Cassie asked. "Who are you? Where am I? Why am I in the floor?"

"Calm down, hon," the one called Lottie said. "You're dead."

"Lottie!" the other woman scolded.

Dead? Cassie was dead? She didn't remember dying.

"It's no good to say it gently, Jocelyn, you know that," Lottie said. She knelt as well and offered a hand. "It's okay, I'm dead too. Have been for a long time."

"What's going on?" Cassie asked, taking Lottie's hand.

Jocelyn reached out as well. Her hand glowed with a

strange white light, and a slash in her palm leaked blood. When she took Cassie's other hand, a spark of energy passed through her. They pulled her from the floor so they were all standing on solid ground. Well, it was solid for Jocelyn, who was obviously very much alive. Cassie felt like she had to fight not to slip back into it.

"I'm Jocelyn, this is Lottie," she said. "You've been through a terrible ordeal, and we're here to help."

A terrible ordeal? What happened to her?

Lottie squeezed her hand, though there wasn't anything that could really comfort her in that moment. "C'mon, hon. You've got a lot to learn."

CHAPTER 23
MAGNOLIA

*From camera 22.4.5: [a piece of rubble slowly moves
across the ground]*

EVERY TURN THEY TOOK, Magnolia looked for Cassie.
She hadn't been a shadow, or a little glimpse like the person in
the hospital. They'd been so close Magnolia could see the blue
of her eyes and flecks of blood in her blonde hair. And the
energy that passed between them—it wasn't quite the same as
with Baxter. She almost felt like it lingered, making her skin
buzz.

Could she use it?

She could try at least.

Damn. If only all this could come about at a more conve-
nient time, like when she wasn't confined to a metal bucket
hurtling through space. It would be a lot nicer to end a day of
seeing ghosts with her comfy couch and a whole plate of food
instead of a lumpy cot stationed amidst the dead. After all
the days and nights she and Korinne spent in all those

haunted places, now she could legitimately *see the fucking ghosts.*

"What are you thinking so hard about?" Korinne asked, startling Magnolia out of her thoughts.

"Huh? Nothing," she said, much too quickly.

"Again, you're a terrible liar," Korinne said, with a look that made Magnolia's heart squeeze. If only she knew.

"It's nothing. Just thinking about Cassie." Her mind whirred as she tried to come up with a more convincing story, but each excuse felt less plausible than the next.

"That's it?" Korinne asked.

"That's it," Magnolia said.

She hummed, clearly not buying it. "Bet if I get some food in you, it'll get those lips moving," she said.

"You get me food, that's not all these lips will do," Magnolia replied. Korinne stopped walking, eyebrows raised in shock at the response. Magnolia was a little surprised too. "Eating, Korinne." She tilted her head. "Eating *food.*"

"Got it." She continued walking, forcing Magnolia to jog to catch up. Heat flooded her face, but not due to embarrassment. "Did you want to go back to her room?"

"What?" Magnolia said, unsure if she heard Korinne say "her room" or "your room," and which one she hoped for.

"Cassie," she said. "Maybe we should spend some more time in her room. We've already seen her funeral, and where she died, and where her body ended up. But maybe we should go find some more stuff in her room to talk about her life."

"That's a really good idea," Magnolia said as her heart warmed. "Maybe we'll even get to talk to her."

"How do you know she's still around?" Korinne asked. It was probably a joke, the same kind she'd made a hundred times before, but Magnolia stammered all the same.

"I mean, wouldn't you be? If that happened to you? Poor

thing, we didn't even know her real name until you found it," she said. Smooth, for sure.

"Nah. I told you, I'd only become a ghost to bother you for the rest of your life," Korinne said.

"Promises, promises," Magnolia said as they rounded one last turn to the dining room.

The small dining room was much the same as when they'd visited earlier, with the plain metal countertops and four square tables. It had all the old appliances, probably cemented shut after so much time unused. A meal prep machine sat on one counter, their lone modern amenity and the only way they could have a hot meal during this trip.

However, the room had one notable difference: Magnolia could now very much sense another presence there with them. The spirit had a sweet, grandmotherly air about her. She moved closer to Magnolia, bringing with her a swirl of curiosity. Magnolia grasped her pendant, ready to rip it off and say hello to the sweet woman.

"Go on, sit," Korinne said, pointing to one of the rickety chairs and knocking Magnolia out of her reverie.

"Or what?" Magnolia asked, just to be petulant.

"Or I'll make you, obviously." She didn't turn to make sure Magnolia sat, so of course Magnolia stuck her tongue out at her back. The ghost found that very amusing.

"I can get my own food," she said, even as she did, in fact, sit. If she calmed down enough, maybe she could sense the ghost even better. Korinne waved her off and went to the meal prep machine.

"I'm already going." She pressed a few buttons, and after whirring for a few minutes, the machine spat out a cup filled with tea and a plate of pasta. As it finished brewing the tea, Korinne sent it through the meal cycle again. This time, the prize was a pizza. The ghost crossed the room to the area right behind Korinne, and Magnolia tracked it with a smile.

"I think we might have a friend here," she said. Korinne whipped around and scanned the area, but of course didn't see anything. The ghost, startled, scooted back a few feet.

"Oh, right, ghosts," Korinne said, turning back to the machine. "I thought the captain decided to grace us with his presence."

The remnant of Cassie's energy simmered just below Magnolia's skin. With Korinne's back turned, she focused on her hand, seeing if she could control it again. A thrill went through her as the energy coalesced in her palm, emitting a soft purple glow. She tried to move it around, but the wrap on her wrist hindered her motion. Using the noise from the meal prep machine to mask the sound of the gauze, she ripped the bandage off.

The skin underneath was completely healed.

"The usual?" Korinne asked.

Magnolia clenched her fist, and the light disappeared. "Um, yes please," she said.

Korinne nodded and punched a few buttons for sugar and milk before bringing the offerings to the table. While she didn't seem to notice passing right through the ghost, the ghost certainly felt it. The sensation echoed in Magnolia's own chest, as if someone had reached out and grabbed her heart.

All of this was with her pendant still on. What could she accomplish without it?

Totally chill, Magnolia took a sip of her tea. "Ah, perfect. Thank you."

"I do pay attention sometimes," Korinne said, eyes on her pizza. She took a bite despite the obvious steam and seemed to regret it immediately.

"Do you remember anything about ghosts here?" Magnolia

asked, not waiting for her to finish the molten bite. Korinne breathed around it, head tilted up, until she could finally swallow.

"That's gonna sting for a while," she murmured. "Here specifically in this room? There's something, but I can't remember. It's on the list—I think we were supposed to do it yesterday."

"Let me check," Magnolia said, consulting her handheld. The ghost then shifted to her, evidently intrigued by the technology. She scanned the part of the file for the dining room, then laughed. "How did we forget this? We're supposed to ask Susan to make us cookies."

Susan, elated at hearing her name, flitted around the kitchen with her grandma energy in full force. Out of the corner of her eye, Magnolia could see the vague shape of her: short and round, with a nest of hair piled on top of her head. A headache started in her right temple, but it was a worthy price to pay for the validation of seeing the ghost. The energy from Cassie shifted through her body, following Susan's movements. Could she use it to make her fully form in front of Korinne? She tried to bring it together again, but it continued to follow Susan. On her sternum, her pendant warmed.

Ah, there was the limiting factor.

Korinne chuckled. "Oh, that's right! Finally, a harmless challenge. I could go for cookies right now," she said.

"Hey, you challenged yourself to get into that reclamation tank," Magnolia said, trying to focus on Korinne and not the ghost running around. How did her grandfather live like this? It was so hard not to stare. "Don't blame the audience for that one."

"True. Play stupid games, win stupid prizes and all that," Korinne said, ironically taking another bite of pizza without waiting for it to cool.

"I'm just glad you're okay," Magnolia said. She managed to keep her voice nice and even despite the fact that the memory made her want to cry again.

"Okay, Susie," Korinne said. The ghost bristled at that.

"Susan," Magnolia corrected. "Reports say that she prefers Susan." Lie. A small lie, but a lie nonetheless. Nothing in Zavir's report mentioned Susan's name preference.

"My bad, Susan," Korinne said, mollifying the ghost. "Word on the interstream is that you make some amazing cookies."

"Do we have any other information on her?" Magnolia asked.

Korinne shook her head. "Unfortunately, I think all we have is the cookie thing," she said. "I'll dig later, though. See if we can't find something else to add in post-production. Susan should be remembered for more than just her cookies."

"Perfect," Magnolia said, her heart warm at Korinne's commitment. "Speaking of which, Susan, would you mind making us some cookies?"

As she finished the question, a nearby oven beeped as the preheating cycle began. Something so blatant made Magnolia's heart soar for half a second before she caught Korinne's eyes.

"Let me guess," Magnolia said with a sigh. "Faulty wiring?"

"That one's too easy, if I'm honest. But I'll give it to you that the timing is odd," she replied. At least she had the decency to look a little sheepish about it. The act of influencing the oven apparently took some of the energy out of Susan, and her form faded. Magnolia could no longer see the distinct shape of her. But maybe, if she could give her a little...

"Mags," Korinne said, eyes narrowed. "What are you thinking?"

"Nothing," Magnolia replied quickly. "Just trying to figure

something out." She gave Korinne a tight-lipped smile, eyes wide and unblinking.

Korinne clearly didn't believe her. "What's going on? You've been acting weird all day."

"This is just a lot," Magnolia said, waving her hand around and fighting every instinct to divulge all her secrets. "I'm trying to keep up."

Korinne waited for her to continue, then sighed when she stayed silent for too long. "Is it..."

With those two words, Magnolia completely forgot about the ghost.

"Is it what?" she asked softly, her heart in her throat.

Korinne squeezed her eyes shut and twisted her mouth like she'd tasted something sour. "At the risk of sounding like a fucking teenager, are you mad at me?"

"What?" Where had that come from? Magnolia shook her head. "No, of course not. Why would you think that?"

"With everything that's happened yesterday and today... I don't know, it feels like you're counting down the minutes until you're done with this." She gestured at the ship, but Magnolia read between the lines.

"Which makes you wonder if I'm counting down until *we're* done," she said, and if Korinne didn't look so serious, Magnolia might've taken her by the shoulders and shaken her until she understood.

Korinne's jaw worked for a moment before she muttered, "Well, when you say it out loud, it sounds kind of stupid."

Magnolia reached across the table and took Korinne's hand in hers. "I'll never be done with you, darling. No matter what," she said.

"Promise?" Korinne asked, gripping her fingers tight.

"I promise. Whatever face I'm making, it's because I'm trying to figure out how to summon a full body apparition."

She smiled fondly and rubbed her thumb over Korinne's knuckles.

Korinne gave a dry laugh. "If anyone can make it happen on determination alone, it would be you." She didn't sound quite convinced. That was fine. When they were safe on solid ground again, Magnolia would make sure she knew exactly how she felt about her.

"That's the plan," she said with another squeeze.

Korinne squeezed back, then let go of her hand and returned to her pizza at least somewhat pacified. Good, Magnolia couldn't have her running around worried about their relationship when they had much more important things to do.

Like making a ghost appear.

She fidgeted with her pendant, running her fingers over the smooth lines of the protection spell. Susan moved around the table and hovered, as if she could sense Magnolia's hesitation. She got the feeling of a hand resting on her shoulder. The energy she got from Cassie gravitated there, and with a little push, Magnolia felt it flow from her into the ghost. It was just a touch, enough for her to know it worked.

Magnolia glanced at Korinne. She'd pulled out her hand-held and was scrolling, brows furrowed. Probably planning out the rest of their adventure, or checking on the cameras. A solid distraction either way.

Slowly, she peeled her pendant off and placed it on the table. Engrossed with her task, Korinne didn't notice. But Susan sure did.

As soon as she stopped touching the pendant, Susan's fuzzy details sharpened until Magnolia could see the wrinkles around her eyes and the gray of her hair. She wore a white apron over black pants and shirt, and oven mitts clipped to her belt. Concern colored her aged face, and her thin lips formed a small "o".

There wasn't a massive rush of energy, or a blinding light. Instead, the pressure of the spirits slowly descended upon Magnolia. She'd vastly underestimated how much ghost energy lingered in this place, and how much the pendant continued to dampen it all. One brick at a time, it threatened to swallow her up.

Magnolia glanced across the table. Even though Korinne wasn't paying attention, her comm pad camera remained dutifully trained forward. Perfect.

"Honey?" Susan asked, her voice pitched low. A purple light sparked as she yanked her hand back from her shoulder.

Magnolia met her eyes and smiled. She focused hard, gritting her teeth and willing something deep inside her to reach out to Susan. The energy she got from Cassie went crazy, mixing with her own—what, power? Was that what this was?

Susan, for her part, gave off tremendously nervous energy as Magnolia gripped the table. Magnolia felt something stir in the back of her mind and latched onto it. It tried to slip away, but she held tight. Cassie's energy jumped on it, further holding it. The power—definitely power—clicked into place.

Magnolia gasped as something buzzed behind her eyes. Susan's eyes went wide and she shook her head rapidly, her hands out as if trying to stop her.

"Honey, no," she said.

But Magnolia didn't listen. She tried to pull Susan to her, but that didn't work. A push then.

Faint purple light glowed around her hand as she reached out. Would it be enough to show up on camera? Magnolia grasped Susan's hand, her skin cool and dry and very, very real. She encouraged the energy to flow into Susan, but the ghost resisted.

"Don't do this." Susan tried to give the energy back, but

Magnolia was stronger—and more stubborn. She pushed more. Something popped in her chest; that couldn't be good.

"Honey, I think you're hurting yourself. You need to stop." Susan tried to sound stern, but Magnolia shook her off. "There's nothing you can do for us here. We're stuck."

Susan flickered, alternating between a clear picture and a shadowy version of herself. Could the camera pick it up? Magnolia couldn't be sure. Was she seeing with her eyes, or with something else?

She needed to give just a little more.

Black formed at the edges of Magnolia's vision. Her blood pressure skyrocketed, and her lungs no longer expanded fully. Sweat dripped from her temples and onto her shirt. Oh, wait. Sweat wasn't supposed to be purple.

"Almost..."

Magnolia barely got the word out, and dug a little deeper.

"Magnolia?" Korinne sounded far away. When did her ears get so stuffy? She heard Korinne's chair go sliding back, and felt the table shift as she bumped into it.

"Honey, stop." Susan shoved the energy back.

Magnolia's head split in two. At least, that's what it felt like. The power—and Susan—diminished to nothing.

"Mags?" Korinne said. She was closer now, and grabbed Magnolia's shoulder. In slow motion, she turned her head to find Korinne staring. Oh, she'd really done it now.

"What?" Magnolia asked, but the word never made it out of her mouth. Slowly, surely, breathing became more and more difficult. Magnolia willed herself to calm down, to inhale deep, but this wasn't a panic response.

Time slowed further. The world lost its color, leaving her with visions of blurry black and white. Korinne blinked, the movement so slow Magnolia could count her eyelashes—if only she could see them clearly. The tiny seed of energy pulsed weakly in her heart like a dying bird. What was happening?

Pressure built in her head, almost as if...

As if her powers were activating again.

"No." Magnolia shoved them down, but they spilled out anyway and raced through the ship. She gasped as the roots went further than she ever thought they could. Her energy plummeted, her head pounded, and cold enveloped her hands and feet. This wasn't supposed to happen. The harder she pulled, the more her powers pushed, drawn to something in the innermost levels.

Her power touched something in the engine room. Something big, something dark, something horrible. Something growling *mine* and *want* and *take*. Magnolia tried to scream, but all she could manage was a whimper as the world faded to black.

CHAPTER 24
KORINNE

"OH MY GOD, oh my God, oh my God—"

Korinne was so close to truly and absolutely losing her shit. One minute, she was sitting there wondering if this trip was the worst decision of her life. The next, Magnolia was sweating blood and passing out. Now she *definitely* knew this trip was a mistake.

"Mags? Oh God, are you dead? Mags, you can't die okay? You can't. Oh my God. There's so much I never told you, shit —" Did her words make sense? Probably not. All she could focus on was patting Magnolia's cheek. Her skin was so cold. Why was it so cold?

Magnolia's eyes twitched beneath their lids. "Rinne?" she croaked.

"Mags!"

Korinne's heart soared and relief crashed into her. She hadn't realized until then that she genuinely believed

Magnolia died, that she'd lost her forever before getting to tell her everything. Her emotions threatened to choke her, and she couldn't help it—she grabbed Magnolia by the face and peppered kisses all over it before holding her tight, not caring if the comm pad caught it or not. A few tears leaked out, falling into Magnolia's hair as Korinne pressed her cheek to hers.

"I thought you were dead! Oh my God!"

"I'm not dead," she said with a weak laugh, her breath tickling Korinne's ear. "Though if I knew passing out would lead to affection like this, I'd have done it a long time ago."

"If you wanted me to kiss you, you just had to ask. You didn't have to almost die," she said, leaning back and reaching out to wipe some of the blood from Magnolia's face. It didn't really work, instead smearing purple across her skin. Another drop seeped from her nose and slid down her cheek.

"Can you hand me my pendant, please?" Magnolia asked.

"Your... Fucking hell, Mags." Korinne scrambled to the table and found the pendant sitting there. With shaking hands, she put it over Magnolia's head until it settled against her sternum. "Why do you keep doing that?"

"Just seeing something." Magnolia sounded way too at ease, which made Korinne panic more.

"'Just seeing something?' Oh my God, I think I'm gonna throw up." Her panic pressed hard on her internal organs as her vision blurred. If taking off her pendant led to such a psychosomatic response as bleeding from her pores and passing out, why the hell would she try it?

"Just don't throw up on me," Magnolia said. Her dry laugh led to a coughing fit, and Korinne held her shoulders to steady her. It gave her something to focus on besides the bone-melting fear.

"What the hell happened?" Korinne asked, finally voicing

the question that had been rattling around in her brain the past few minutes.

"I'm fine—"

Coughs interrupted her, and Korinne pushed her to her side just in time for more blood to appear. She rubbed soothing circles on Magnolia's back and held her steady until the coughs subsided. Obviously, she was *not* fine. She looked like a goddamn horror movie, with blood all over her face and chest. When the coughing stopped, she rolled onto her back and placed a hand over her eyes.

"I'm fine," Magnolia tried again.

"You're very clearly not," Korinne said. "I'm gonna go get the med kit."

"Really, I'm okay. I just need to lay here for a second," she said.

Korinne reached out and smoothed the lavender flyaways from Magnolia's face. It killed her to leave her like this, but the bots would be way too slow, and it would probably be a bad idea to move her without clearance. Should she call the captain? They had to have medical training. But they were on the complete opposite side of the ship...

"I'll be right back. Don't move, okay?" She hated the idea, but what alternative did she have?

"Okay," Magnolia said.

Korinne placed one more kiss on her forehead, then got up and ran. Magnolia should take it as a compliment, really; Korinne never ran unless she absolutely had to. This became more evident as she skidded to a halt at the elevator and slammed the button, her knees nearly giving out at the fast change in direction. Her ragged gasping filled the quiet of the lift, and she counted her breaths in an effort to calm down.

It took so long to reach the area near their rooms that Korinne nearly pried the doors open herself and continued running. Damn this old ship with its slow, ancient technology. Didn't it know this was an emergency?

The med kit sat exactly where she left it, and she grabbed it and ran without bothering to close the door behind her. It took another thousand years to get back to the dining room. Thank God Magnolia was exactly where she left her, and looking a little less like death warmed over.

"Are you okay?" Korinne asked, kneeling next to her.

"Yeah, I think so," Magnolia said. She turned her head sharply, then sighed. "Damn it, I keep seeing things."

"That's the physical manifestation of my anxiety, just ignore it," Korinne said. She popped open the med kit and placed the sensors on Magnolia's forehead and chest. The machine whirred, running its tests as Korinne tried to calm her racing heart.

"Don't worry, I won't die on you," Magnolia said.

"You better not. That would really ruin my day," Korinne said. The med kit beeped, and she checked the display. "Seriously? Nothing wrong?"

"See? I'm fine. I just need some rest." Magnolia pushed herself up, and Korinne helped her into a seated position.

"You hacked up blood, you're not fine," she said. "I'm running this thing again."

"Rinne—"

"Nope, you're not talking me out of this one." She readjusted the sensors and pressed the button. Once she was sure Magnolia could sit unassisted, she jumped up and got a cup of water, returning to gently hold it to Magnolia's lips. She grimaced as she swallowed, but Korinne thought she looked a little more lively afterwards.

"Thank you. And I'm sorry about all this," Magnolia whispered.

"Don't apologize, it's not your fault," she murmured.

Magnolia bit her lip, and ice slipped into Korinne's veins. "But Mags, are you... I mean, is there something you're not telling me?"

Magnolia laughed, which made Korinne's cheeks burn with either embarrassment or fury.

"Yes, but it's not whatever you're thinking. I'm okay, I'm not sick, I'm not dying, I'm not mad at you. I'm just trying to figure something out, and once I do, I'll tell you everything, I promise."

Korinne's mind raced. What in the actual hell could she be talking about?

"Or, you could tell me now," she said, because somehow *knowing* Magnolia had a secret was worse than just *thinking* she had a secret.

Magnolia reached out enough to place her hand over Korinne's. "It has nothing to do with you, or with us. I need you to trust me on this one, okay?"

Every cell in Korinne's body told her not to agree. What could Magnolia possibly be trying to "figure out" that led to her coughing up blood and passing out? No, she had to know now—

The machine beeped, and once again said there were no problems.

"See? Fine. Just need a nap," Magnolia said.

"This thing must be broken. But I do agree you should be in bed," Korinne said. Maybe if she got Magnolia nice and comfy in her room, then she'd break down and talk to her. "Do you think you can walk? I can call the bots with a stretcher."

Magnolia wiggled her feet. "I think I'm okay. I just may need some help up," she said.

That answer wasn't good enough. "I changed my mind, let me ping the bots."

"No, gods no," Magnolia said, waving her off. "I don't need a stretcher."

"Yeah? You sure?" Korinne said, a challenge in her voice.

Magnolia glared, which in that moment Korinne took as a good sign. On her own, she pushed herself to her feet, slapping Korinne's hands away any time she tried to help.

"See? Fine," she said, leaning with one hand on the table.

"You're so damn stubborn," Korinne muttered, pulling Magnolia's arm over her shoulders and wrapping her own arm around her waist.

"Seriously? I'm okay," Magnolia said as Korinne gripped her hip.

"Of course you are. I'm just gonna hold you nice and tight cause I'm a good friend like that," she said.

"You're getting blood all over you," she pointed out.

"All my clothes are black. You can't even see it," she said. "I will say, you're really killing it with the spooky aesthetic right now. I appreciate the dedication."

"Anything for the show," Magnolia said.

They limped their way back to the elevator, and then back to their rooms. Korinne wondered if Magnolia realized how much she was leaning on her. She held her the whole way, only letting go when they reached the door to Magnolia's bathroom.

"How can I help?" Korinne asked.

Magnolia pulled away, and Korinne didn't miss how she kept a hand on anything solid as she made her way in.

"I can handle it," Magnolia said, though she didn't punch the pad to close the door. "I'm a big girl, I can clean myself up."

"Mags, you can barely stand," she said.

"Are you just trying to see me naked?"

Korinne never hated their cheap brand of flirting for the cameras more than in that moment.

"I'm just worried about you, that's all," she said as warmth flooded her face again. She held up both hands and took a couple of steps back.

"I appreciate you. And I'm sorry I scared you," Magnolia said.

"Don't apologize, just tell me how I can help," she said.

"You can help by going and getting cleaned up yourself. Don't worry, Rinne. I'm going to shower, then lay down for a while, and then we'll get back to it." Magnolia didn't realize Korinne could see her struggling to breathe.

Absolutely not. After her shower, Korinne would tuck her in and forbid her from leaving this room. But she would let her believe her plan—for now.

"Are you sure?" Korinne asked, taking one step back, then another.

Magnolia paused, her expression thoughtful as she leaned against the bathroom wall. The seconds ticked by as Korinne waited. Magnolia opened her mouth—

The palm pad sparked, and the door slid shut between them.

"What the fuck?" Korinne said. She hit the pad, but it didn't register. "Damn it, stupid faulty wiring—"

"It's okay, Rinne," Magnolia said, her laugh muffled by the door. "I'll shower, and if it's not working after that, then we'll panic."

Korinne, who'd been panicking nonstop for the past hour or so, let out a shaky breath.

"Do you have your handheld in there?" she said, running her fingers through her hair.

"Yes," Magnolia said. "I promise, I'll call you if things go awry."

That didn't really help her feel better, but it was the best she would get.

"Okay. I'll be just next door if you need me."

She heard the water turn on and, when no sounds of a body hitting the floor came, she sank onto the edge of Magnolia's bed. A pastel blue pillow fell, and she picked it up, making sure to return it to its proper place. Even if it had only been a day and a half, the whole room smelled like her.

Tears came to Korinne's eyes, and she allowed a few to fall as her adrenaline crashed. None of this was worth it if Magnolia got hurt. And it seemed like the more she went around the ship, the more things went wrong.

That settled it. Maybe Magnolia would tell her what was going on, maybe she wouldn't. Either way, Korinne wanted her to stay in this room until they landed. Nothing else would happen to her, not on her watch. Forget the portal to hell or all the other nonsense their viewers wanted; anything else the show needed, Korinne could get on her own.

She pulled herself together and wiped her tears before going to her own room. Only a couple of walls separated them, but it felt like a million miles. For fifteen minutes she paced the tiny area, waiting until her handheld buzzed with a message. Magnolia sent a picture of herself in bed, cuddled up with all her pillows, and said she was ready for her nap. Korinne let out a breath and sent a reply, saying she'd work on editing until Magnolia needed sustenance. In reality, she packed her bag to go get the last bits of what they needed. It was just a little lie, that way Magnolia wouldn't feel left out or try and force herself to work. Korinne hated to hide it from her, but what was her alternative? Allow her to run around when something was clearly wrong? Absolutely not.

She'd be in the deepest of trouble for it later, but it would be worth it to keep Magnolia safe.

CHAPTER 25
CASSIE

From camera 1 3.8.7: [an oven turns off]

CASSIE WOKE to a dog licking her face. Specifically, her dog.

"Baxter, good to have you back, buddy," she said, doing her best to get her breathing under control.

Her body hurt. Every place she'd been hit or crushed as she died jockeyed for her attention. And what...what was it that grabbed her? It hadn't been a machine, or a person, it was...

The thing. The thing in the engine room. The Malevolence Jocelyn allegedly sealed all those years ago. Funny, it had the same energy as the shade in the reclamation tanks.

"Fuck me," Cassie said as she pushed herself to a seated position. Baxter immediately curled up in her lap, looking up at her with all the love and adoration dogs provided. Of course, she never met a dog while alive. Baxter wasn't even supposed to be on the ship to begin with, she knew that much. She wished she knew his owner to ask the story.

"I'm not even your favorite human, I'm just a replacement," she said as she scratched behind his ear. He grumbled and leaned against her torso.

"We gotta find our friends, Baxter. Do you know where they went?"

Baxter stared hard with his one eye, that little broken tail wagging a million times a minute.

"Yeah?" Cassie asked, pitching her voice higher. "Do you know where they are? Can you find our friends?"

Baxter took off running. Having no other lead, Cassie followed. But instead of leading her anywhere she'd seen the girls go before, he led her to the inner residential areas. It wasn't the same zone she lived in, and Cassie wracked her brain trying to figure out who else they might visit.

Baxter slid to a stop at a specific door, his tail wagging.

"Here?" Cassie asked. She paused, but heard nothing. "I don't think they're here, bud."

Baxter sat and stared expectantly. Maybe the girls just weren't loud enough for her to hear them?

"Okay, let's go inside then," Cassie said, and passed through. Reminded of this skill, Baxter followed. He bounded through the room, checking each corner faster than she'd ever seen him move. He even jumped on the bed and sniffed the whole thing. When he found it empty, he stopped and looked back at Cassie.

"There's no one here," she said, though she had an inkling who he was actually looking for. His tail stopped wagging, and he curled up on the mattress, letting out a high whine. Tears sprang to Cassie's eyes; there was too much happening at once. She couldn't handle her own death and a depressed dog all in one day.

"Come here, buddy," she said, sitting down and taking Baxter into her arms. She buried her face in his wiry fur and allowed a few tears to leak out. "We're gonna figure this out, okay? I'll get you back to your human someday, I promise. I'm sorry they're not as fully formed as me."

She held him for a few minutes as her emotions rose and fell. With a shaky breath, she looked up at the wall screen across from them. It would make a poor mirror, but worked well enough for her purposes. She waited to see the red glowing back at her; after all, every one of her feelings had gotten hurt today.

But her eyes held no red light. Her emotions, while painful, were her own. Whatever Magnolia had done, it must've knocked the hold of the Malevolence loose. And if she was a free soul again...

"C'mon, buddy." She thought back; what had Korinne and Magnolia been planning right before their little run in?

Oh, right. Food.

"Guess we have a good place to start."

A hop, skip, and a jump, and Cassie sank into the dining room to find Susan seated at the table, her head in her hands. Purple blood stained a portion of the floor, not enough to make Cassie think someone died, but enough to make her worry.

"Suze, what the fuck happened in here?" Cassie said, startling the older woman.

Susan shot up, her hand over her heart.

"Cassiopeia, you nearly killed me again," she gasped.

"Gotta stay vigilant," she said as Baxter went to work sniffing the area. "Now, are you gonna tell me what the fuck happened with those two?"

"Language, Cassiopeia," she admonished, crossing her arms over her chest.

"Ew, not the government name, Suze. We talked about this." She pulled some energy from the ship, then sat on the chair across from her. "What happened? Where did all this blood come from? Baxter, ew, don't lick it."

Baxter stopped licking but continued his exploration. Susan glared for a second longer, then her face fell and she sagged. Her gray bun, normally frizzy at baseline, seemed even more voluminous than usual.

"She had some sort of energy. I haven't seen anything like it since the LeBeau woman was on board," Susan said. "Poor girl, she has no idea what she's done."

"No," Cassie said. They were officially in an area of ghost-hood outside her scope, but she understood enough to know that was bad. "Are you talking about the Malevolence?"

Susan nodded. "I'm afraid it's awake. And it knows they're here."

Jensen. Lottie. The shade in the reclamation tanks. Her own red eyes staring back at her. "It's been awake," Cassie said, unconsciously rubbing the wound on her arm. "Now it's hungry."

Susan ran a hand over her face. At their feet, Baxter evidently grew bored and trotted off, probably to find his damn ball. "The girl, she looked right at me. Tried to push enough energy into me to, I don't know, make me fully form? Or cross over? She... Have they been here before? She seems so familiar."

Oh, so Magnolia could possibly make the ghosts show? On her own? Why didn't she do that sooner, since that was the whole point of the cameras?

Cassie eyed the blood on the floor. That was probably why.

"She hasn't been here before, at least not that I know of." She tried to think back to how it felt when they'd made contact. There'd been something different about it, something that left a mark on her. And with her new memory... "She has Jocelyn's necklace."

"Oh, sweet girl. With energy like that, it almost made me think we'd be able to escape," Susan said.

"Really? That strong?" Cassie asked.

Susan nodded. "Like I said, I haven't experienced anything like that since Jocelyn."

Jocelyn. Jocelyn LeBeau, who sacrificed her brother's soul to the Malevolence. Who had some sort of ghost seeing abilities, though Cassie had been too freshly dead to truly understand them.

"Well," Cassie said, shaking off the thought. Long gone clairvoyants couldn't help them now. "Are you gonna tell them about the Malevolence in the engine room, or should I?"

"Do you really think they'll listen? The living are all the same."

Susan sounded too much like Jensen, and Cassie smacked the table.

"We have to try. We can't let anyone else get stuck like we are," she said. "Maybe we'll get lucky and they'll just stay in their rooms. I can try and trigger the lockdown mechanism. They have plenty of video footage to review, that'll keep them occupied."

Susan scoffed. "So that's what those tablets were. Hundreds of years, and there's still influencers. Ridiculous."

Cassie couldn't help but crack a grin. "I always forget how old you are," she said.

"August twelfth I'll be five hundred and sixteen," she said. "I still remember old Earth, if you can believe that."

"That's wild," Cassie said. What must it be like to remember everything?

Wait...

If Susan remembered everything...

"Suze, do you remember how you died?" Cassie asked.

Some of the ghosts found the question insulting, but luckily Susan laughed.

"So silly, really," she said, though her voice fell flat. "It had been a rough day. I'd been working for thirty-six hours straight. It was during the first flu outbreak, and people were dying by the hundreds. The rest of us picked up the slack. By then I hated everything about the ship, totally regretted volunteering to come. Even started thinking about taking a walk out of an airlock, just so I could be outside again. Anyway, I sat at the prep table and put my head down. In the few minutes I was asleep, they finally figured out the gravity generators. Everything went haywire, it set off all the sensors and red lights. Unfortunately, that's how we learned the magnets above the prep table weren't strong enough to hold the knives."

"Shit, Suze, that sucks," Cassie said, though a few things definitely stuck out in her story. Red lights? Ultimate feeling of despair? Sounded mighty familiar.

Susan shrugged. "Shit happens. We all have to die someday, even those two girls here now."

Oh, Cassie *really* hated hearing that.

"Yeah, but not yet," Cassie said. "The ship is supposed to dock tomorrow. We have to keep those girls safe until then."

Susan gave her a sad smile, and her eyes flashed red. Cassie waited for something to answer in her own heart, but she felt nothing but the little seed of energy Magnolia put there earlier.

"There's nothing we can do now, Cassiopeia. Their fate isn't up to us," she said.

Susan too? Fucking hell. How was she supposed to fix this when she was losing allies left and right?

"I've never been good at just accepting things," she said, somehow managing to keep her voice calm. "I'll go talk to them."

"Be careful out there," Susan said as Cassie jumped up. "I have a feeling it's only going to get worse."

"Cryptic and terrifying, thanks," Cassie said, throwing a wave over her shoulder as she walked out.

Faster than any elevator could take her, she passed through level after level until she found the girls' rooms again. The whole time, she tried to figure out the best way to explain what was going on. She didn't want to scare them. She just needed them to understand that a slightly sinister spirit might be lurking around the ship, and they needed to stay in one spot until they landed.

She poked her head into Korinne's and found it empty, then went to Magnolia's to find them both in her bathroom, certainly a bit worse for wear.

Magnolia looked terrible. Blood stained her chin, cheeks, hair, and shirt, and her skin was the palest shade of lavender imaginable. She leaned against the wall of her bathroom, doing a terrible job at pretending it wasn't the only thing keeping her upright. Her eyes never moved from Korinne; did whatever happened make her unable to see her now?

"Are you just trying to see me naked?" Magnolia asked, and Korinne flinched.

Cassie sighed. "Not this shit again."

"I'm just worried about you, that's all," Korinne said, and damn if her feelings weren't obvious enough for Cassie to hear a thousand miles away.

"You're just in love with her, that's all," Cassie said. She now recognized the look in her eyes—in both of their eyes. It was the same way Rose had looked at her on that tiny screen. "Just tell her, I'm begging you."

That would certainly be a good way to occupy them until landing.

"I appreciate you. And I'm sorry I scared you," Magnolia said tenderly.

"Don't apologize, just tell me how I can help," Korinne said.

They were so close to actually talking this out. Cassie could practically taste the confessions hanging in the air between them. They just needed a little push. Did they need to know about the Malevolence? Yes. But if this was happening now... Cassie could wait. Telling them now versus later didn't matter as long as they stayed in that room.

"You can help by going and getting cleaned up yourself. Don't worry, Rinne. I'm going to shower, then lay down for a while, and then we'll get back to it."

"Oh, no. Absolutely not," Cassie said as ire built in her chest. "You're staying right here. We're not playing this game anymore."

She reached out and tapped the palm pad. Nothing happened except a sting in the wound on her arm.

"Ouch, what?" She tapped the palm pad again. And again. The sting intensified, but the door didn't move. It normally took less energy than this; why wasn't it responding?

"Are you sure?" she heard Korinne ask, her voice barely registering. Cassie siphoned as much energy as she could without appearing and interrupting, then punched the palm pad. It sparked, and the door slammed shut.

"Yes!" Cassie said, until she realized Korinne was on the same side of the door as her and not inside the bathroom with Magnolia. "Fuck!"

"What the fuck?" Korinne said, hitting the pad herself. The door stayed closed.

"I swear to God..." Cassie groaned, pinching the bridge of her nose.

"Damn it, stupid faulty wiring—"

"It's okay, Rinne," Magnolia said. "I'll shower, and if it's not working after that, then we'll panic."

"Oh, I'll make sure it's working," Cassie grumbled.

"Do you have your handheld in there?" Korinne asked.

"Yes. I promise I'll call you if things go awry."

"Seriously?" Cassie said.

"Okay. I'll be just next door if you need me," Korinne said.

"Idiot, stop wasting time," Cassie said. Her anger waned as Korinne took a moment to cry, part of her considering appearing just to comfort the girl. But that would open an entirely new can of worms.

So much for a confession. Now Cassie had to go back to plan A, telling them about the Malevolence. But she couldn't do that while Magnolia was still in the shower, then she'd have to explain the whole thing again. And that was after explaining to Korinne that yes, ghosts were real, and had been the whole time. Good, this gave her a few minutes to figure out exactly what to say.

Except then Korinne left, like a fool.

"You've got to be kidding me," Cassie said. She followed Korinne to the room next door, and soon realized she would be doing nothing except pacing around waiting for Magnolia. Boring, and unhelpful.

Cassie popped back through the wall and waited. Magnolia showered relatively quickly, and Cassie respectfully turned her back when she came out of the bathroom and changed into clean clothes. True to her word, she got into bed and made herself comfortable, sending Korinne photographic evidence. Cassie shamelessly read over her shoulder; Korinne, it seemed, would be working on video editing until Magnolia felt better.

Okay, that was fine. Maybe she didn't need both of them in here. Maybe she could just tell Magnolia, who'd already seen her, and then she could skip the panic attack of the nonbeliever. If she needed to appear later to corroborate Magnolia's story, so be it. But until then...

Magnolia's pendant slid on its chain as she shifted position. The silly little circle, no bigger than an inch across, started all of this. But now that Cassie looked closer, she could've sworn she'd seen it before—on something besides the necklace.

If she still had blood flow, she would've paled. That symbol was the same as the one etched on the bars of LeBeau's prison, the one keeping him tethered to the ship in punishment.

"Okay, we definitely need to have a chat now," she said.

Cassie siphoned the energy from the ship, so much that the lights flickered and faded to a dim glow. Magnolia's eyes went wide in a way that said she could see every detail. Somehow, she managed not to freak out, which was pretty impressive. She looked Cassie dead in the eye, and it took everything not to shrink away from her reflective gaze.

"Hey there," Cassie said with an awkward wave.

"Hi," Magnolia said, breathless.

"Do you want to grab the camera?" she asked, pointing to the comm pad on the bedside table.

"Is that... I mean, is that okay?"

Cassie laughed. "Now you ask that? After you've been filming nonstop for the past two days?"

Magnolia winced. "Good point."

"You're not the first, and probably not the last." Cassie took a little more energy so she could grab the chair from the desk, and spun it so she could sit backwards and rest her arms on the back. "Would you prefer to call Korinne back so you can win the bet?"

"Weirdly enough, not yet," Magnolia said. "I kind of want to bask in this triumph for a minute first. Once she sees you, it'll be all screaming and crying and throwing up."

"Rude, is it my hair?" Cassie asked, touching the caved-in side of her head.

Magnolia's eyes went wide, and she straightened. "No! No, that's not what I meant. I just meant, because she so adamantly doesn't believe in ghosts, so it would be an entire reckoning for her—"

"I knew what you meant, chill out," Cassie said. "Honestly, I thought you'd do a lot of screaming by now too."

"I want to, trust me," Magnolia said with a shaky laugh. "But I'm trying not to scare you off again."

"You didn't... Never mind." They didn't have time to get into her lost memories. "Have either of you felt like, unreasonably hopeless today?"

"I mean, I can only speak for myself, but not that I know of," Magnolia said. "Although Korinne did seem sad earlier..."

"How sad?" Cassie asked. Did the Malevolence reach out to her first, an easier target? But Magnolia didn't seem worried.

"Situationally, it made sense. Nothing worse than I've seen from her before. Why?"

Cassie took a deep breath. "There's something you two need to know."

Magnolia's eyes lit up, and Cassie watched as she visibly forced herself to stay calm. "Is it the password to your tablet?"

"What? No," Cassie said.

Magnolia gasped so suddenly it made Cassie jump.

"What?" she asked, preparing to sink through the floor.

"Do you know who killed you?" Magnolia said.

"The fuck? You can't just ask someone who killed them," Cassie lied. Some ghosts were sensitive; she was not, especially since she didn't—

Oh, right. She did know how she died now. Weird, having that information after going so long without it.

"Oh, gods, I'm so sorry," Magnolia said.

"I'm just fucking with you," Cassie said. "That's actually why I'm here. I wasn't killed by someone, but something."

"Some...thing?" she said, her voice small. Her eyes widened, and her hand went to her necklace.

"Sounds like you know what I'm talking about," she said.

"I was hoping it was a hallucination," she said.

"Unfortunately, no," Cassie said.

"What is it?" Magnolia asked.

Cassie took a deep breath. How could she explain it when she herself didn't completely understand it?

"My friend Lottie called it a Malevolence," Cassie said. "No one's sure when it popped up exactly. Based on what I've heard, it's kind of always been here. I didn't really believe in it at first, 'cause Jocelyn sealed it with something like that." She pointed to Magnolia's pendant.

Magnolia shot up and grasped it. "What?"

"I don't know most of the story. I was still a new ghost, and she had better things to do than explain everything to me. Like keeping the ship in the sky and away from any source of souls."

"Hold on, I have so many questions about so many things you just said." Magnolia put up her hands and thought for a moment. "We'll start easy. You knew my Grandma Josie?" she asked.

"What? No," Cassie said. "How would I know her?"

"Her name was Jocelyn, and she gave me the pendant," Magnolia said. "Well, no, she didn't give it to me, my grandfather did after she died, but it was hers. She could see ghosts too?"

"Well, shit, I guess I knew your grandmother then," Cassie said. How many women named Jocelyn could see ghosts and wore a necklace like that on the ship? "She didn't tell you about the ghost thing?"

Magnolia shook her head. "No, she never said anything before she passed."

"Oh. She died on the planet?" Cassie said.

"Yes, twenty-something years ago," Magnolia said softly. Oh, right. Death was sad to living people.

"I'm sorry," she said, as sincere as she could make it. Damn it, so she really couldn't tag Jocelyn in to help.

"Thank you," Magnolia said. "But you said she sealed this Malevolence?"

"Yeah. I'm not sure on the specifics 'cause I was dealing with all of this"—she gestured to her head—"but I know she had some kind of energy like you do. She'd help me stay present while I learned how to use power from the ship."

"Okay, so she had ghost powers and could seal malevolent spirits, good to know," Magnolia said. "That could explain why all of this is happening now."

Even as she said it, a singular drop of blood seeped from her nose. She wiped it away without thinking, and Cassie grimaced.

"I mean, I don't know the first thing about your ghost seeing capabilities," she said. "But you look like you need a minute."

Magnolia reached into her bag and produced a package of tissues, which she used to gently clean her face. Cassie tried her best to stay patient; after all, there was nothing she could do right at this very moment to stop the Malevolence *except* talk to Magnolia.

"Wow," Magnolia said after a moment. "This is... Wow. All this time, I wondered if I dreamed the stuff that happened when I was a kid."

"Yeah, I can't really speak to that either," Cassie said. "Sounds like a great conversation to have with your alleged friend over there, while you two stay in here until the ship lands."

"Korinne? She's not just allegedly my friend, she's my dearest friend," Magnolia said.

Cassie rolled her eyes so hard she fell off the chair and landed one ring outward. After she took a few deep breaths, she jumped up and returned to her chair.

"I thought you left me," Magnolia said.

"And I thought you were smarter," Cassie said. "Look, just don't leave this area. Stay here where it's safe until the ship lands, okay?"

"But you said Grandma Josie sealed the Malevolence—"

"Well, the seal isn't as strong as I'd like it to be, so you and Korinne need to stay in here until we land. No more running around and climbing into things. None of that shit."

Magnolia winced. "You saw that, huh?"

"Who do you think helped you open it back up?" Cassie said. "Anyway, it's not safe out there. But I think we can survive another twenty-four hours as long as you two don't go running around with your living energy."

"What about the captain? We have to tell him," Magnolia said.

Cassie waved the comment off. "I'll take care of him."

She hesitated, running her thumb over her pendant. "I don't know how I can convince Korinne to stay in here though," Magnolia said. "She won't believe in a malevolent spirit. This is her dream. She's been looking forward to working on the *Arkana* since I met her. And she's supposed to defend her dissertation in a few weeks, so she needs to observe the landing—"

"Oh, cut the bullshit," Cassie said, throwing her hands up. "You don't think you can convince her to stay in here with you? Really? There's not a single thing you can think of that would keep her here in your bedroom for the next day? Nothing you can say or do that would encourage her to—"

"Okay, you made your point," Magnolia said, blushing furiously.

"Have I? Because, and I cannot stress this enough"—she leaned close enough to see the silver sparkles in Magnolia's violet eyes—"you two need to stop wasting your fucking time."

The hurt from losing Rose flooded her, nearly choking her. The backs of her eyes stung with tears, and she hoped Magnolia could feel the pain rolling around in her chest. Magnolia stared with wide eyes, her lips barely parted.

"Who was the girl from the *Covenant*?" she whispered.

Cassie swallowed enough of her feelings so she could talk around them. "Has my tablet turned back on?"

"Your... Let me check."

Magnolia crossed the small room and picked up the tablet. She held the button for a few seconds and, for the first time in decades, the screen lit up. The bright pixels washed out the lavender hue of Magnolia's skin and reflected in her eyes.

"What's the passcode?"

Passcode? Shit. Cassie hadn't thought of a passcode.

"Let me look at it," she said, hoping somehow a memory would return. In her mind's eye she could see herself using it, but what was the passcode?

Magnolia turned the screen toward her and Cassie held out a hand, remembering just in time not to touch it. Sure, she'd been able to interact with technology before, but with her luck, this time it would cause the tablet to spontaneously combust. She stared for a long moment before closing her eyes, the shadow of the screen imprinted on her eyelids.

"Try seven, six, seven, three," she said.

Magnolia tapped the screen, and the tablet unlocked. "You got it! What do those numbers mean?"

Despite not having blood, Cassie felt the burn of a blush. "It spells out Rose."

Magnolia was silent for a moment. "Was Rose the girl from the *Covenant*?"

"Yes. That green application has all our messages," she said.

"Do you want to read them?" Magnolia asked, her finger hovering over the square. Cassie thought about it. Did she? The pain was still very fresh, despite losing Rose all those years ago. Could she handle reading her words?

"Not yet. But she used to write poetry," she said. "Do you think you could show that? She was always too scared to post it anywhere, but I remember it being really good."

"Yeah, I can definitely do that," Magnolia said.

"You'll also, uh..." Should she tell her? Might as well. Better than her being surprised later. "You'll probably find messages with LeBeau too. Incriminating ones."

"Well, those can stay private," Magnolia said. She locked the tablet again and sat on her bed. "What happened with Rose? I have a feeling that's a better story than whatever happened with LeBeau."

Such a direct question. It made Cassie's insides squirm. "Shouldn't you be freaking out by now? We've been chatting for like, a thousand hours."

"Cassie, I've been waiting my whole life to talk to ghosts—not so I can prove anyone right or wrong, but so I can hear your stories." She settled into the pillows. "Will you please tell me?"

This was not how this conversation was supposed to go. Cassie was supposed to tell her about the Malevolence, then leave. But it felt good to talk to someone new, someone *living*, and if Korinne was content to hang out in her room and work while they had some girl talk...

Damn, it had been a *long* time since Cassie had an opportunity like this.

"We met in an online forum because we both liked the same stupid show," she started. "She was going to come here, because on the *Covenant* we wouldn't be allowed to be together. They'd gotten super religious over there. But then she got sick, and the ships reached the point where they were separating. That's why I got tangled up with LeBeau, and why I was at the docks that day. He said he could get me over there, so at least I could be with her when she died. But I couldn't get on the shuttle. I was so heartbroken... The Malevolence latched onto those feelings and pulled me over the edge."

"Oh, Cassie," Magnolia said, putting a hand over her heart.

Cassie leaned back, the pain replaced with revulsion. "Ew, stop that. I don't need your pity, I need you to understand. Time is limited, okay? Quit fucking around when it comes to someone you care about."

Magnolia mulled her words over, then nodded. "You're right. After everything we've been through the past couple of days, it's not worth it. We have more than enough footage for the show."

"I'm not talking about the show," Cassie said through gritted teeth.

"I know," Magnolia said, her eyes flashing. A touch of energy passed between them. "I'm coming up with my excuses. I know what I actually need to say to her, and it's something I should've said a long time ago."

Cassie sagged in relief. "Thank God. Okay, I'll leave you two alone to chat."

"Should I tell her about the Malevolence?" Magnolia asked.

"Do you think it would help?" Cassie countered, one eyebrow raised.

"Probably not," she said.

"That's what I thought," she said.

Magnolia nodded and picked up her handheld. Cassie watched as she typed out half of a message, then shook her head and instead started a call. Cassie couldn't hear the other line, but she knew when Korinne answered because Magnolia's entire face lit up.

"Hey, darling," she said, and she sounded so enamored that it made Cassie's heart ache all over again. "Can you pop over really quick? No! No, I'm fine. Just wanted to...show you something. I got Cassie's tablet to turn on."

Cassie's brow furrowed. Why were they still talking? Korinne was like, ten feet away. She could've been here by now. Magnolia's mouth turned down.

"What do you mean? I thought you were editing," she said. Cassie froze, and Magnolia's eyes shot to hers. "You're out in the ship? Alone?"

"Where?" Cassie asked, moving close so she could hear too. "Where did she go?"

"Are you just getting snacks?" Magnolia asked. Cassie inched even closer, close enough for a spark to pass between her and Magnolia, close enough for her to hear Korinne.

"I just wanted to see the jail and film that part about LeBeau we talked about. Don't worry, I have Efex here with me."

The jail.

The jail where LeBeau was.

Where he'd asked Cassie for living energy so he could break out, and let the Malevolence out with him.

"Get her back here," Cassie said, and took off.

CHAPTER 26
KORINNE

From camera 15.3.20: [something growls]

"IT'LL JUST BE A MINUTE, I promise," Korinne said, stepping off the elevator. She held her hand in front of the door so it wouldn't close on Efex, who moved a lot slower.

"No, Rinne, I don't want you out there alone after everything," Magnolia said, frantic. Why was she freaking out? Korinne knew she'd be pissed about being left behind, but the magnitude of her reaction surprised her.

"I'll be fine. You need to rest," Korinne said as they travelled down the hall.

"Korinne, please come back," Magnolia said, stressed enough that Korinne paused.

"Are you feeling sick again?" she asked, ready to turn and run back to their rooms.

"What? No, I just don't want you going alone."

Oh, she just wanted to be involved. That tracked; this was usually the point in the investigation where Magnolia got really invested in the results. With how high the stakes were for this trip, Korinne definitely understood why she'd want to be there for everything.

"You're not missing anything, Mags. I promise," she said, continuing on. "We have plenty of footage with you. No one will notice that you're not here for this part. And if I see a ghost, even if I don't capture it on camera, I'll still tell you. Promise."

"That's kind of my concern, actually," Magnolia said.

Korinne's heart sunk. "You really think I'd lie to you about that?"

"No! No, not that. I'm just worried you'll come across something dangerous," she said.

"If I do, I'll turn around. I already promised no more stupid stuff." She pulled her handheld away from her ear so she could check the map. Oh, she was a few hallways off. Oops.

"But running around the ship alone *is* stupid," Magnolia said.

Korinne laughed and backtracked to the right turn. "I'm keeping an eye out for anything. Nothing's gonna crush me, and I'm not gonna get stuck anywhere."

Magnolia muttered something imperceptible, which usually meant Korinne was close to winning the argument.

"Please, Korinne," she said. "I have a really bad feeling about this."

"I'll be super quick," Korinne said as she found the right door. She hit the palm pad and smiled as it slid open, quiet for once. "And I'll bring you snacks."

"But—"

Korinne's handheld shut off, and a small, empty battery blinked on the screen.

"Not again." She dug into her bag and found the power bank, but its little light blinked red when she pressed the button. Dead too. "Damn it. Efex, do you have a charging station hidden in there?"

Efex made a few beeps that sounded like a begrudging agreement. A second later, one of its docks popped open and a small port flipped out. Korinne smiled and connected the handheld before petting its binoculars.

"Thank you, what would I do without you?"

She stepped into the jail, which was remarkably well kept compared to the rest of the ship. Granted, it was just a series of cells with metal bars and minimal plumbing, so it probably had easier upkeep for the duration of the trip.

"So, as we talked about before, people usually report hearing a scream in here. The running hypothesis is that the scream belongs to one Etienne LeBeau, if you believe in that sort of thing."

She stopped at the first cell, taking a moment for the camera to record the cramped space. It was probably six feet on any side, with a metal bench welded onto the back wall right next to a commode and sink. Metal bars lined the front side, with just enough space for Korinne to slip her slender arm in between.

"The reason these cells are so small is because they weren't built for long-term use. With such a concentrated population, the judicial system moved at a rapid pace, and inmates were either transferred to a rehabilitative unit or, in the worst cases, executed. And then we have our friend LeBeau."

Korinne stepped further into the block and allowed for a dramatic pause, just in case Magnolia was right and something decided to talk to her. However, she got nothing but silence. That was fine, she could continue monologuing.

"LeBeau did his best to organize what could've ended up as the worst threat to the *Arkana*. It's possible our girl Cassie got tangled up in some of his schemes, though we don't know exactly how well she knew him, or what she did for the cause. After her death, though, is when things get interesting."

Efex dinged a few times, its eyes swiveling back and forth before settling on the far corner. It let out a long beep, then a few chirps, as if communicating with someone.

"Who're you talking to, Efex?" Korinne asked, remembering too late that her handheld sat dead on Efex's back and therefore the bot couldn't reply. "Never mind. Where was I?"

Efex chirped twice, the second longer than the first.

"Right, LeBeau." Korinne continued down the line, waiting for any of the cells to produce something interesting. Every one sat empty. "LeBeau got caught trying to plant a whole string of massive bombs in the engine room, which would've cut power and also blown a hole big enough to kill half of the population on the ship. The person who turned him in? His sister, Jocelyn. Note to editing Korinne, show a picture of the siblings here. Magnolia will love it."

Efex beeped six times in rapid succession as its eyes turned back and forth.

"Don't worry, they're not here," Korinne said.

Efex chirped and backed up a few inches, which was an odd response.

"Don't tell me you're having technical difficulties again," she said. Of course, Efex couldn't answer her, because her handheld was fucking dead. Damn it, she really should've gotten a new one before this trip. At least everything was falling apart at the end of the series instead of the middle.

"Anyway," she continued. "Jocelyn turned in her own brother, which got him thrown into this cell here." She stopped at the second to last one on the right and let the camera take a good look at it. "This was right as the *Arkana* found Vaela, and so his trial got delayed. You know earlier, when we said Cassie was the last death on the ship? That was a bit of a lie. She was the last before we found Vaela, but the actual title for final death belongs to LeBeau. Once the ship had a steady orbit and they began transferring planetside, they finally came up here and found LeBeau dead in his cell."

She moved right up to the bars and placed a hand on them, finding the metal ice cold. Weird, it wasn't cold enough in the room for it to feel like this. She scanned the area, looking for a vent or another reason for the temperature to change, but got distracted by a small blemish on the bars.

"What are you?" she asked. Once close enough, she saw it was a little symbol carved into the metal. It looked almost like a sun, with two lines coming out of the top and wing-like projections on either side.

The same as Magnolia's pendant.

"Okay, even I have to admit that's kind of weird." She reached out and touched the symbol and jerked back as it burned her skin. "Ouch!"

A low sound rumbled below her, almost like a growl. Korinne bent over and felt the floor vibrating.

"Also weird." She stood and rested her hand on the cold metal. "What was I saying? Shit, I must be getting tired. I can't remember anything else for this area."

Try as she might, the information didn't come to her. This wasn't an unusual occurrence—even her fact-filled brain had to short circuit every once in a while. That's what post-production was for.

"Whatever. Let me do the other half of my job, I guess." She turned to Efex. "Are you watching this?"

Efex backed up further and beeped like it didn't want to watch.

"Good. Hi there, is anyone here with me? My name is Korinne."

Silence. A chill went through her, and she rubbed her arms.

"Maybe I should turn on the thermal cam," she murmured, pulling out the comm pad just enough to do so. It caught the cold areas with the bars, and the hot spot with that symbol. And the cold area... She had to admit, it did have an odd shape. It wasn't a person, but it also wasn't some air vent path.

"Is that a ghost? Are you a ghost dude?" Korinne asked the cell. Of course, there was no response. "Come on, say something. Or do something. Can you open that door?"

The cold spot blazed hot, just for a second. The camera didn't catch anything else, but it caught that.

"Okay, even more weird stuff. I'll admit, there might be something going on in here," she said. No full body apparitions like she wanted, but more evidence than she'd seen before. "Magnolia is gonna be so pissed if all this goes down without her. Hey ghostie, you can talk to me. I'm a great listener."

Silence.

"You know you want to. Is it you, LeBeau? Are you stuck here forevermore thanks to your sister? That probably sucked, huh?"

The thermal cam didn't change this time, which made Korinne frown. So much for consistency and repeated results.

"Fine. Maybe you need a little more encouragement." She turned to Efex and pointed. "This doesn't count as stupid, because I'm going to leave the door open, so don't you go tattling to Magnolia on me."

As if summoned by her name, Korinne's handheld buzzed with an incoming call. Oh good, it had turned back on.

"Efex, can you answer that for me?" she asked as she opened the cell door. It clicked, and Magnolia's voice rang through the space.

"Why did you hang up on me?" Magnolia asked.

"I didn't, my handheld died. You called just in time,

though! Look, it's like you're here with me. Efex, switch to video chat."

Efex chirped and Magnolia's face showed on the tiny screen.

"Korinne, please come back," she said.

"I'm almost done." Korinne stepped in and waited, hands on hips. "LeBeau? Are you here with me? Am I encroaching on your space? I thought you'd like a visitor after all this time, since you got stuck in here and all."

How was the cell so much warmer than the outside? Especially when the bars were so cold? It made no damn sense. Compelled her, though.

"Korinne, is it?"

"Be glad you're there, Mags. You'd hate it in here," she said. Then, she realized the voice hadn't come from her handheld. It hadn't come from Magnolia at all.

She froze.

"Rinne, who's that?" Magnolia whispered.

Korinne slowly turned, the beam of her flashlight shaking as she shined it on the back of the cell.

An old man stood there, his gray hair slicked back and a menacing smile on his face. Korinne could've convinced herself he was the captain in his normal clothes, checking on a disturbance or something. Except for his eyes.

His eyes glowed red, with smoke curling from the edges. Now that she really looked, a lot of red wafted off of him. Heat sank into her.

"Korinne?" Magnolia's voice sounded far away. "Korinne, run. Run!"

"Yes, Korinne," he said, his voice low and rumbling. Adrenaline flooded her system, but she remained rooted to the spot as he took a step toward her. "Listen to your friend. Run."

"Korinne! Move!"

"Yes." His smile stretched too wide. Her adrenaline topped out, and her brain disconnected from her body. Distantly, she considered this might be a hallucination. But deep down, she knew exactly what was in front of her. "Move, Korinne. I dare you."

Heat wafted over her as he stepped close enough for her to count the hairs on his sparse mustache.

"I'm coming, Korinne," Magnolia said. "Just hold on."

"She won't get here in time," the man murmured, shaking his head. The heat built further, but Korinne almost felt cold. Her mind was just present enough to realize she was definitely, totally, completely going into shock.

"What are you?" she asked, her energy draining as the words left her mouth.

He smiled big enough for her to see every one of his teeth. Red smoke billowed out with his breath like a dragon warming its prey.

"I am the ultimate end," he growled, his voice layered a hundred times over itself. "I am what happens when death travels between the stars."

"Run, Korinne! Run, gods damn it!"

Korinne collapsed to her knees, her legs too weak to hold her anymore. The man inhaled deeply, as if smelling her, and somehow it made her so, so tired. Run? She couldn't run. She couldn't even stand.

"Rinne?"

Korinne wanted to move, wanted to turn back, wanted to see Magnolia's face and have everything make sense again. But she couldn't look away from the glowing embers of his eyes.

"You are mine," he said.

"I'm going to figure this out, okay? I'll save you," Magnolia's tiny voice said.

The man shook his head. "She won't be able to save you,"

he said, and the despair that washed over her threatened to choke her. "You are mine."

He placed his hand on her chest, and pain ripped through her, burning her from the inside out. She tried to scream, but it caught in her throat—no, it caught in her brain. She was trapped in her mind, watching as something else took over her body.

"I've got you, okay?" Magnolia sounded so, so far away.

The pain reached a new height, making her breath stop and her stomach churn. Her mind begged for release.

"Got you now," the man said.

Darkness formed at the edges of her vision as he sank his claws into her chest. Fire laced where he grabbed her, and she tried in vain to pull any oxygen into her lungs. He squeezed her heart until it stopped.

Then, mercifully, her mind went blank.

CHAPTER 27
CASSIE

*From Efex's camera: [Korinne slowly returns to her feet,
then sways back and forth]*

CASSIE HAD NEVER RUN SO FAST in her life or in her
death.

How could she have been so stupid? She should've talked
to the girls as soon as she saw Lottie's red eyes and LeBeau
made his request. He'd asked for one thing, and now Korinne
had unwittingly delivered it right to him.

A pulse that Cassie didn't have thundered in her ears as she
rounded the last corner and slammed through the door. Maybe
she had been fast enough, maybe she could still stop it all—

Korinne stood in the middle of the room. A red haze
covered the area, and a familiar heat circled her. Magnolia
screamed from the tiny handheld, all her words running
together in a jumbled mess. The bot chirped like a nervous
animal and shifted back and forth as if deciding whether or not
to flee.

The door to the second to last cell sat wide open.

"No," Cassie said as a rock settled in her stomach.

Korinne turned slowly. No, not Korinne. Not with those glowing red eyes.

"Hello, Cassiopeia."

The hairs on the back of Cassie's neck stood on end. "LeBeau."

He smiled, somehow making the expression look so wrong on Korinne's face.

"Thank you for fulfilling your end of the bargain."

"I did no such thing, and you know it," Cassie said. Could Magnolia hear her? She really hoped so.

LeBeau ignored her. "If you'll excuse me, I have a bargain of my own to fulfill."

He lifted Korinne's hand, and Cassie yelped as she flew across the room toward him. Pain erupted through her as he caught her by the neck. A second later, it faded—just in time for him to throw her into his old cell and slam the door closed behind her.

"No!" she gasped.

Without another word, LeBeau turned and walked out of the room.

"Fuck!" Cassie slammed her hand into the bars, recoiling as they pushed her back. "Shit!"

She paced the edges and poked every corner, hoping to find something, *anything* to set her free. Then she went to the bars and stared at that stupid symbol, the bane of her existence. She tried to reach through, but it stung like a bitch and left her partially drained.

"No, this can't be happening," she said, walking the room again for good measure. If LeBeau was out, then could he set the Malevolence free? If he could, then they'd all be doomed, and the girls—

The girls would end up like her, drowned in their pain and subjected to this for the rest of eternity.

"Fuck, okay, come on, Cassie." She ran her hand through her hair, remembering too late that part of it was brain and blood and skull. "Damn it."

She stared at the symbol. Hesitantly, she reached through the bars again. Making contact with the symbol sent a shock through her, with a special burn coming from the black wound on her forearm.

Okay, that was something. Something she could use, if she could just think. Maybe if she pushed into it?

Cassie placed her hands on the floor and pulled at the minimal electricity as hard as she could, filling herself to the brim. A tiny beat started in her chest, right where Magnolia's magic had zapped her earlier. Good, maybe she could use that too.

Locked and loaded, she returned to the bars. Before she could think too hard about it, she punched through, throwing a blast of energy at the symbol. It, in turn, threw a blast of energy back at her. She sailed into the cell wall and crumpled to the floor.

"Okay, so that didn't work," she muttered as she pulled all her parts back together. The ship's energy wafted off of her like steam, but the tiny piece from Magnolia stayed. It was different from the ship's energy—stronger. Cassie curled around it, allowing one moment of pure self pity as she cradled this tiny, pure nugget from...what, a friend?

"That's enough," she told herself. She'd seen good people die in life, she would *not* continue the trend in death. Cassie soaked up more energy from the ship, more than she even thought possible, and tried again.

And again.

She tried until burn marks coated the walls and the black

wound on her arm doubled in size. How did her hand stay attached? It was a miracle of the afterlife, apparently.

Each attempt, the little piece of Magnolia's magic kept her tethered. For a split second, Cassie considered depleting all of her energy so she could wake up on the docks again. But something told her that wouldn't work. If LeBeau stayed stuck here all these years, the cell could easily trap her too. What could she possibly try that he hadn't already?

Footsteps sounded at the doorway, and Cassie whooped as her current best ally stumbled in.

"Magnolia!"

"Cassie!"

She ran to the cell and pried open the door, her hand braced right where the symbol was. Cassie squeezed through the narrow opening and tumbled onto the floor.

"How did you know I was here?" Cassie asked.

"I watched it all happen," Magnolia said. "Were her eyes glowing because..."

Cassie swallowed and nodded. "LeBeau took over her body."

Magnolia's eyes widened. "He possessed her?"

"Yes, but what he said—I didn't take Korinne to him on purpose. I swear it. It was just bad luck."

"I know, it's okay." Magnolia leaned over, her hands on her knees as she gasped for breath.

"Why did you come to me and not to her? Come on, stand up. We've got to go." Cassie took her by the elbow and, out of habit, pushed some of her energy into her. Somehow, Magnolia absorbed it, straightening with wide eyes and a deep inhale.

"Wow, okay, that's refreshing," she said, shaking out her arms. "I'm still new to this whole talking-to-ghosts thing, and I don't know everything that's going on, but you do. I need your help, Cassie. You've seen stuff like this before, I can't save her without you."

Cassie nodded and set her jaw. Magnolia was right. She hadn't seen a possession like this, but she had seen someone throw an angry spirit out.

"Let's go get your girl," she said.

CHAPTER 28
MAGNOLIA

From camera 14.2.10: [sounds of footsteps running]

MAGNOLIA FIGURED NOW WAS as good a chance as any to learn how to use her new powers. The jump from Cassie certainly helped, refueling her after her earlier adventure with Susan.

She pulled up her handheld and locked onto Efex. "Efex, are you still with Korinne?"

They waited—Cassie reading over Magnolia's shoulder—until a ping landed from the bot. "Yes, and she's acting very weird."

"Okay, so we can track her." Magnolia strode from the jail and back to the elevator, Cassie limping to keep up.

"Do you know how to kick a ghost out of someone's body?" she asked.

"No," Magnolia said.

"Do you know how to wake Korinne up instead?" she said.

Heat crawled up Magnolia's spine. "No."

"Do you know—"

"Cassie, I hate to tell you this, but I don't really *know* how to do anything. I've been running on instinct for the past thirty-six hours," Magnolia said as a headache pierced her right temple.

The elevator arrived, and Cassie passed through the doors before they could open. She waited with arms crossed as Magnolia boarded the old-fashioned way.

"Okay, so we're flying blind here," she said.

"Didn't you watch Grandma Josie do it?" Magnolia countered as she found the closest elevator to Efex's location and pressed the right buttons.

"Yeah, but I didn't understand what was going on. That pulsey thing you've done a couple times seems similar though, and I remember Jocelyn usually had a cut on her hand for blood," she said.

Magnolia cursed. Those pulses had been reactions—could she actively choose to send one out? "Do you know anyone who can help?" There had to be thousands of ghosts on the ship, right? Maybe one of them had an idea.

Cassie thought for a long moment before shaking her head. "No, I can't trust any of my friends right now with all this going on. Hell, until you gave me that little zap earlier, my eyes were turning red too."

Great. Magnolia let out a long, controlled breath and squeezed her hands into fists. Blood, Cassie said. Her blood? Korinne's blood? She wasn't sure. But she'd figure it out one way or another.

"Where's your necklace?" Cassie asked a few minutes into the ride.

Magnolia reached up and rubbed the skin where it usually

sat. "In my pocket. I figured I wouldn't need it for this part. Not sure how much good it was doing me, anyway."

Cassie hummed in a way that said Magnolia wasn't wrong, but she wasn't completely right either. "It's still helping, that's for sure. And for the record, it was working really well at the beginning."

"Seriously?"

"Yeah. I touched it, and it flung me like, five floors away. I'd say it was rude, but it helped me regain some of my memories, so I'm not mad about it. It tossed the shade messing with you guys in the reclamation tanks, too." She sounded nonchalant, but Magnolia could see the tension in her shoulders and the way she tugged at a thread on her jumpsuit.

The pendant pushed her away? And the angry spirit in the reclamation tanks?

"We can probably use that."

Cassie grinned. "Atta girl."

They rode in silence until the elevator stopped next to the part of the engine room closest to the captain's bridge. The doors opened into a long hallway, an engine room entrance at the end. Efex met them by the elevator, whirring and chirping like a scared animal. They could see Korinne's outline facing the doors, her body standing with her hands on her hips. And the doors...

The doors, which should've been stationary like normal fucking doors, bowed slightly out, then back in. Red lights glinted through the middle seam as they moved apart and back together. A deep rumble sounded, then faded. A second later, the sound repeated as if something great and monstrous breathed.

"Well, I hate that," Cassie muttered.

"You can come closer, I don't bite," the thing puppeting Korinne's body said. "Not hard, at least."

Magnolia's arms tingled as her adrenaline kicked in. The little bit of energy she'd gotten from Cassie vibrated beneath her skin, waiting to be let out. "On a scale of one to ten, how bad is this?"

"Oh, like an eleven," Cassie said.

Magnolia's heart skipped a few beats.

"I don't know if I can bullshit my way out of an eleven," she said as she took a few steps closer to Korinne's body.

"Between the two of us, we can figure it out," Cassie said.

Pressure built in the back of Magnolia's skull as she moved, and her heart beat a heavy rhythm against her ribs. She had to do this, had to figure out how to save her dearest friend, the person she—

"Ah, there you are. I wondered how long it would take." It was technically Korinne's voice, but it didn't sound like her.

"Rinne?" Magnolia said, her voice cracking on the word. She cleared her throat. "Korinne Amaya Ramosa, you come back to me right now."

Her body turned, and her eyes narrowed as her mouth smirked. "No."

"Fuck you, asshole," Cassie said. Magnolia sent an elbow into her side. It didn't do anything, of course, but the sentiment remained. Another burst of energy had her seeing stars for a second, and when the light cleared, her head didn't hurt anymore.

Magnolia grit her teeth and steeled her resolve. She'd figured out how to see the ghosts and talk to Susan, right? Maybe even got close to helping her cross over? She could do the same thing here.

She took a breath. "And who do I have the displeasure of speaking with?"

There was power in a name, or so she was told.

Korinne's head tilted to the side as she considered her. "Do I know you?"

"No," Magnolia said. "Name?"

A mockery of Korinne's laugh escaped her mouth, and she took a bow. "Etienne LeBeau, at your service."

"At my service? Excellent," she said, bluffing with every fiber of her being. Faking it until she made it had worked well so far. "Leave my friend's body, please."

"Oh so polite," LeBeau said. "A tempting request, but no. It's a little small, but it'll do nicely once I clean it up a bit. Her soul takes up so much room."

"That body isn't yours, and you can't have it," Magnolia said. She pushed the energy to her hands, seeing if she could. It answered her call readily. "Let her go."

"Did my sister send you?" he asked. His tone was light, casual, as if he hadn't stolen her entire friend.

Out of habit, Magnolia reached for a pendant that wasn't there. "No, I don't know your sister," she lied.

"Huh. Strange, your energy feels kind of like hers. Thought Josie went and found herself an apprentice or something."

"Look," Cassie interrupted. "Your problem is with me, not them, right? Leave them alone, and I'll do whatever you want."

"Cassie—" Magnolia started, but LeBeau spoke.

"That's the thing, Cassiopeia," he said. "You don't have anything I want. These two do."

"Get out of her before I make you." She clenched her fists, and purple sparks erupted from them. How would she make him? She didn't know yet. But she would damn well figure it out.

Cassie took a step closer to her, and a jolt of energy went through her arm. It dulled any lingering pains and made her feel like she could throw a mountain. Purple energy crackled at her fingertips, and in her pocket her pendant heated. Something warm trickled from her nose, and when she reached up to wipe it away, her fingers came back purple with blood.

"You can't bullshit a bullshitter," LeBeau said. "Are you always this scared talking to someone on the other side?"

"You can't hurt me, and I won't let you hurt my friend." That part was true, at least she fully believed it to be. He scared her so badly she thought she might vomit, but she kept her face neutral.

"Your friend?" LeBeau chuckled darkly. "Yes, she's definitely only interested in being friends."

LeBeau jerked Korinne's head so her neck joints popped, and Magnolia cried out at the violent move.

"Don't!" she said. This only made him laugh again.

"Don't worry, I won't kill her. She's just had a crick in her neck all day."

"She didn't say anything," Magnolia murmured.

"Ah, yes, there's a lot of things she doesn't say." A smile spread across Korinne's face, too wide for her delicate features. "And I wonder how much you keep inside too."

How true were his words? How much could he see into Korinne's mind? Magnolia's traitorous heart thumped, daring to hope.

"Since when are you such a fucking gossip?" Cassie asked.

Magnolia reached a hand out, and this time felt resistance in the air as she made contact with Cassie's wrist. Energy flowed between them, and Magnolia snatched her hand back. The hallway seemed to brighten, and details sharpened. Now she could see Korinne, yes, but she could also see a red overlay where LeBeau's spirit hovered. Behind him, a symbol glowed on the engine room door. A symbol which matched her pendant.

"I'm not a gossip," LeBeau said, bringing Magnolia's attention back. "I just value information. You can leave, Cassiopeia. You're not relevant to this conversation anymore."

"As long as you're threatening them, then I'm relevant," Cassie said. Magnolia could feel her anger and pain coming off of her in waves, and had the distinct impression she would've tried to brawl with LeBeau if he wasn't currently squatting in Korinne's body.

"Oh? And did you tell them how we know each other?" His grin said he planned to use the information as blackmail. He was in for a disappointment.

"Yes, she did," Magnolia said. "We also know how your plans ultimately failed. Miserably."

His hot gaze turned back to her. "Be careful how you speak to me," he said, placing Korinne's nails over her own forearm and sinking them into the skin.

"Stop! Stop," Magnolia said, reaching out. He plucked the hand away, and blood seeped from the wounds. "Don't hurt her. Just leave her body, and we can figure something else out."

"Ah, but I can't do that." LeBeau took a step back, slow and deliberate. "You see, I made a deal when my sister locked me in that cell. A deal I intend to honor."

Magnolia wiped at her nose again, and more blood coated her hand. That was fine, that could work. She needed blood, right? Blood and her pendant. Idly, she dipped her hand into her pocket, hoping she didn't lose too much of the blood on the fabric as she grasped the necklace.

"You can just let her go. It doesn't have to be this way." Magnolia had no doubt he was past the point of negotiation. She just needed enough time to focus the energy rocketing around her body.

"I really need this body. I'd offer to trade, but something tells me yours wouldn't work quite the same," he said.

"You don't even know how to take care of a body anymore,"

Cassie said, gesturing to Korinne's arm. "Look at it, it's bleeding. That shit stays on the inside."

"She'll be fine. Well, physically anyway." He took another step back.

Another swipe at her nose gave Magnolia enough blood to cover most of her hand and some of the pendant. It burned so hot she thought it might leave a mark. "Here's the thing. You can't just hijack a body, it's very rude. And if you don't leave her alone, then I'm afraid I'm going to have to force you out."

LeBeau took a step back, and Magnolia took three steps forward. When she stopped, a pulse of energy shot out unprompted and knocked into him. The red shadow pulled away from Korinne's body, then sank back in. Okay, if she could just remember how that felt to do, then she had a real, viable plan.

"Don't bite off more than you can chew." His voice layered on itself, followed by a deep rumble from the engine room. The doors groaned, and with Magnolia's heightened senses she saw the symbol shine a bright white.

Cassie grew very still. "So we're not just talking to LeBeau right now, huh?" she asked. Magnolia twisted to look at her, but Cassie kept her sights on LeBeau.

"There's power in collaboration," he said, dark red smoke curling from Korinne's lips. "And I'm tired of you two wasting my time."

He turned, hand outstretched. Magnolia leaped forward and focused her energy on her hand, just like she had when she tried to give it to Susan. Her fingertips brushed Korinne's back, and her body went sailing forward, slamming into the doors and falling to the ground. Magnolia's heart leapt into her throat.

"Rinne!" Was she okay? Had she accidentally killed her? Or had that been enough to free her?

Her head snapped up. With the loss of power, Magnolia

could no longer see the red around Korinne's body, but could certainly see it glowing in her eyes. LeBeau stood and Magnolia mirrored him, her heart racing a mile a minute.

"Now, why would you go and do that?" he growled.

"Cassie?" Magnolia said, her voice shaking.

"I'm here." Cassie stepped next to her and put a hand on her shoulder, once again gifting her energy. The red outline returned, hiding some of Korinne's features and helping Magnolia focus.

LeBeau laughed. "You may have help, but it's not enough. Give up now, before someone really gets hurt."

"Don't act like you care," Cassie spat.

Magnolia reached out and took her wrist in an effort to stop her from goading the cosmic death force in front of them. Sparks flew from where they touched, and a current of power flowed back and forth until they reached some sort of equilibrium. Her world brightened until she could see every facet, every detail, every part of the unseen lying below the mortal surface. In her chest, a well opened, and she breathed in energy until it filled completely. The purple glow coating her hands spread over her arms until she too had power wafting off of her.

"Holy shit, you are like Jocelyn," Cassie breathed, a matching glow of white surrounding her.

"I guess so," Magnolia said, breathless. Truth be told, for every bit of power she felt twice as much fear. The energy flowed like a raging river: contained, but at an uncontrollable speed. She didn't know if she could manage it, and she didn't know if it would be enough to save Korinne.

"Fight all you want. It won't work," LeBeau sang, a thousand voices joining his own. Behind him, the engine room growled again, red light escaping from between the doors.

Magnolia shifted her pendant in her hand, the blood and

sweat making it difficult to hold onto. The metal seared her skin; that was fine, the more blood, the better.

"I will always fight for her," Magnolia said.

She marched forward, her eyes never leaving the red pools glowing where Korinne's usually held warmth. Cassie stayed right next to her, gripping her free hand.

"What are we doing?" she asked, but Magnolia ignored her. They had one shot.

LeBeau grinned and held his arms wide, red shining from his hands as he gathered power from the source beyond the doors. Did she have enough? It would have to be enough.

"Magnolia—"

LeBeau reached a hand back, preparing to strike. For Magnolia, time slowed. She could feel Korinne's life force fighting back inside her body, a tiny white light amongst the red. Her girl was still in there, and hadn't given up yet. Magnolia watched as it ate away at the red, which was taking longer and longer to fill in the gaps. LeBeau's hold was tenuous at best; it would just take one big push.

With a scream, Magnolia smacked her bloody hand and pendant onto Korinne's chest and forced as much energy into it as possible. Cassie gripped her wrist tight, giving her a steady supply as she unleashed the deluge. The well overflowed, pulsing through Magnolia's hand and into Korinne's chest. This close, she could see the place where LeBeau anchored himself, right where Korinne's soul fought him off.

LeBeau clawed at her arm, but the attacks glanced off her skin as if she wore armor. Cassie grunted, and another wave of energy crashed into her. Magnolia didn't try to control it, just redirected it to the tiny place where his soul latched onto Korinne's.

Behind him, the doors cracked open. That thing wanted to

eat souls? Fine, it could have this one. The other ones were spoken for.

Magnolia breathed. Focused.

Pushed.

With every ounce of power she had, Magnolia severed the last thread holding LeBeau's soul to Korinne's body. Something between a screech and a choke came out of Korinne's mouth as LeBeau's spirit sailed backward. Expelled by blood and commandment, the spirit tumbled back into the engine room. The doors slammed shut over LeBeau's scream. The floor shook, and Magnolia barely caught Korinne as she fell.

Silence. Stillness.

The light of her powers dimmed as the dust settled. Cassie flickered and faded to a vague outline as the last of Magnolia's energy dissipated. Her ears rang, and her whole body shook with adrenaline. She laid Korinne down, but her friend didn't move. Panic gripped her. What if she hit too hard and knocked her soul out as well? She couldn't see anymore to check.

Korinne gasped, and life returned to her eyes. Relief hit Magnolia like a brick, and she dropped her head onto Korinne's stomach.

"Oh, gods, Rinne," she said through her tears.

"What?"

Magnolia sat up and found Korinne staring, her brows furrowed. She looked legitimately confused.

"Rinne?"

"What are you doing here?" She sat up and winced slightly. "Mags, you're supposed to be in bed resting. How did you get... Where are we?"

"You really don't... You don't remember it? Coming up to the engine room?" Magnolia looked to Cassie, who shrugged.

"Did I pass out? I feel kind of woozy." Her voice shook, just enough for Magnolia to notice. Korinne glanced at the blood on her arm. "Did I cut myself?"

"A couple minutes ago," Magnolia said softly. Korinne paled, and sweat beaded along her hairline. Magnolia's purple handprint gleamed on her chest, bright and telling.

"Huh, maybe I need to go take a nap too," Korinne said. She likely meant for it to sound like a joke, but it fell flat.

"Rinne—"

"I think I even hallucinated someone. The captain, maybe?" She was grasping at straws, Magnolia knew it.

"Korinne—"

"Maybe we should go back to the room and run the med kit," she said. Her eyes turned to Magnolia's, and in them she saw the fear and uncertainty. "I probably just need to rest." She may have been trying to put up a brave front, but Magnolia knew her too well. She also knew how to handle her.

"Yeah, let's do that," she said gently, reaching out and taking Korinne's hand. She needed time to come to terms with the past few minutes. Cassie took one step back, then another, and Korinne looked over her shoulder.

Right at Cassie.

Magnolia waited for her to freak out, but Korinne just shook her head and dropped her eyes to the floor. "Come on, let's go."

Magnolia glanced once more at their ghostly companion, but Cassie simply held up her hands.

"Thank you," Magnolia mouthed to Cassie as she helped Korinne to her feet. Cassie gave her a thumbs up, and Magnolia appreciated the silence. No need to push things right now; they could talk later.

Once up, Magnolia refused to let go of Korinne's hand. She allowed it, following after Magnolia with a blank expression. Though her face gave nothing away, Magnolia could practically see the gears turning in her head as she reconciled the experience. She had a sneaking suspicion Korinne remembered far more than she claimed.

In the light of the elevator, Magnolia saw exactly how messy they looked. Blood and sweat covered the majority of their clothes, and their hair stuck out at gravity-defying angles. Oddly enough, she didn't feel nearly as exhausted as before. Perhaps she had Cassie's energy to thank for that.

Out of the corner of her eye, she saw Korinne give her body a once over, clocking every mark. Then, she looked straight down and spotted the purple on her chest that Magnolia was trying so hard to ignore.

"Is this your blood?" Korinne asked quietly.

"Yes, I'm sorry." Magnolia paused and tried to find the right words and ended up gesturing at her own face. "Nose bleed. I didn't notice until it was too late."

Korinne nodded, but Magnolia could tell that she didn't buy the story completely.

"Mags, do I want to know why your blood is on me?" It sounded like she already had an inkling.

"Probably not," Magnolia said, keeping up the charade.

Silence pressed around them, carrying them to their rooms. Cassie flickered behind them, barely perceptible.

"Do you need help cleaning up?" Korinne asked when they reached their doors. She looked fragile, which was so far removed from her normal presentation that Magnolia wanted to cry. Her girl—her tough, smart, soft-hearted girl—had nearly been lost to her.

"I'm fine, let me help you," she said, inwardly begging for Korinne to say yes.

"I'll be okay. Just need to run the med kit really quick and then wash all this off."

Magnolia wanted to shout, to scream, to tell Korinne how

she fought for her. She wanted to yell that seeing that thing take over her scared her more than anything they'd come across so far. How could she tell her that she found a power within herself and grabbed it with both hands, just to save her?

Turned out, she wouldn't get a chance to say any of it, because Korinne turned on her heel and went into her room. Magnolia stood, waiting for her to open the door again. But then the shower turned on, and she gave up.

Dejected, she opened the door to her own room. Alone.

CHAPTER 29
CASSIE

NOTHING? No confessions? Not even a hug? They barely even talked!

"Oh, I think the fuck not," Cassie said. She siphoned enough energy so Magnolia wouldn't have to work too hard to see her and barged into her room. "What the fuck do you think you're doing?"

"She clearly wants to be left alone," Magnolia whispered from where she washed her hands. "And keep it down, just in case she can hear you."

There was a non-zero chance she'd been way too loud. But what did it matter after she and Magnolia practically melded bodies?

Ew, gross visual. Joined forces? That was better.

"She's freaking out. She's confused. She's alone. She needs you," Cassie whisper-yelled. "Go in there and talk to her."

"But what if she—"

"Cut the bullshit," Cassie said. "I know you didn't just save her entire soul from an angry fucking ghost just to chicken out."

Magnolia opened her mouth, closed it, then nodded.

"You're right."

"Damn right I am," Cassie said. "Finally, you get it."

With purpose in every stride, Magnolia went and let herself into Korinne's room. Did Cassie need to follow? Maybe, just in case. After all, these two had proven time and again that they were fucking idiots.

Or she could admit she was just being nosy. That was fine too.

She smiled, emptied some of her energy into the ship, and followed.

CHAPTER 30
KORINNE

From camera 15.3.20: [silence]

"RINNE?"

Korinne jumped as she heard Magnolia's voice on the other side of her bathroom door. She'd had every intention of being in the shower by now, had even managed to take off her boots, but figured she earned a few minutes trying to come to terms with... everything. Magnolia knocked, but Korinne stayed silent. How could she face her after this? How could she look Magnolia in the eye when she'd been so wrong for so long? All those years talking about fighting ghosts, and when it came down to it...

Well, when it came down to it, she hadn't been able to fight one at all, had she?

"Rinne?" Magnolia called again, knocking again. "Rinne, are you okay?"

No, she was not.

Korinne gripped the sides of the sink and looked away from her own reflection. This only showed her how she had blood around her silver rings and caught in the beds of her nails. It matched the purple handprint on her chest, which pulled her skin with every movement. How had it all gone so wrong so fast?

Apparently, silence was not a good enough answer for Magnolia, as a second later her bathroom door slid open.

"Rinne?"

Korinne squeezed her eyes shut and took a steadying breath.

"Hey, sorry." She pushed herself up and turned to lean against the sink. She swallowed, and Magnolia tracked the movement at her throat.

"You didn't answer the door," she said quietly. "I was worried about you."

"I'm okay, I'm sorry I worried you." To emphasize how fine she was, she unhooked her belt and tossed it into the corner with her shoes, then peeled off her socks.

"You don't look fine," Magnolia said.

Korinne bristled at such a direct call-out. "Well, Mags, I'm covered in your blood, so I think *looking* fine is out of the question."

She grabbed a washcloth and went to the sink with every intent to scrub the handprint off, but couldn't bring herself to do it. Instead, she looked at Magnolia through the mirror. In the fluorescent lights, her violet eyes reflected just right, as if she glowed with that same energy she had when she...

Magnolia stepped forward and rested a hand on her back. Korinne shuddered at the touch, but didn't move away.

"Look, what you just went through—"

"I didn't go through anything," Korinne said as every emotion built inside her chest. "Just a little episode. The med kit said I'm fine."

"Rinne, you got—"

"Don't." She stepped away and pressed the heels of her hands into her eyes, trying to will away the tears threatening to form. "Please, don't."

"I know you don't believe in ghosts, but you can't just ignore this," Magnolia said.

"I have to." Korinne's voice cracked, and she dropped her hands. "If I admit something happened, that means I have to admit something took over my body without my permission, which means then I have to be afraid of every corner of this stupid ship. Not to mention, I can't trust anything I see or feel, and if that's the case, then I can't do my job. And I need to do my job, because if I don't, then everything we've worked so hard for will fall apart."

She took deep, measured breaths, trying to calm her racing heart. Magnolia held her gaze, strong and sure, and Korinne nearly crumpled beneath it. How could she still look at her like that when she'd been so weak?

"I'm supposed to protect you," Korinne said when Magnolia took too long to reply. "This whole time, I just wanted to make you feel safe. But if I couldn't even protect myself, how am I supposed to take care of you?"

There it was. Not an admission, not exactly. But if she was completely honest with herself, it wasn't the fact that ghosts were real that sent her spiraling. It was the fact that she had no control, that the one time a ghost appeared to them it took over her body like she was nothing. The whole thing felt like a terrible dream, one where no matter how hard she tried, she couldn't move.

"Oh, darling." Magnolia stepped to her and put her hands on her cheeks, forcing her to hold eye contact. "No one makes me feel more safe than you do."

Korinne couldn't help letting out an unamused laugh. She tried to look away, but Magnolia wouldn't let her.

"How can you still say that after today?" She'd been trapped in her own mind, watching through hazy eyes as someone used her hands to hurt Magnolia. It made it feel like *she* was the one who did it.

"Because I could see you," Magnolia said. She pressed her forehead against Korinne's. "And you fought the entire time. You, my girl, never gave up."

One tear leaked out against Korinne's will, and Magnolia swiped it away. Because while she was right, Korinne *did* fight the whole time, but she'd never felt more powerless in her entire life. How did Magnolia not see *him* when she looked at her now?

"And am I still me?" she whispered. She didn't feel anything in her heart like when that man took over, but obviously she couldn't trust herself anymore.

"Yes, you're still you." She moved one hand and placed it over Korinne's fluttering heart. It calmed her to hear the words. Magnolia may have secrets, but she never lied. "There's nothing here but you. I only see you, darling."

The pet names, usually just a fun kick in the teeth, felt like a balm to her bruised soul. Magnolia had seen her at her worst and pulled her out the other side. And Korinne wanted nothing more than to be next to her for the rest of their natural and unnatural lives.

"Thank you for saving me, Mags," she said, the rest of her confession resting on the tip of her tongue.

"Always. I will always be there for you," Magnolia said. She pulled away, and Korinne immediately missed her closeness. But it was all so Magnolia could direct her to sit on the closed commode. She took the wet washcloth and knelt between her knees, gently scrubbing away the blood on her arm to reveal smooth, unbroken skin beneath. Whatever happened, it had healed.

"Mags..."

Magnolia glanced up, and Korinne's breath caught at the look of warmth on her face. The rest of the world faded, leaving just the two of them in a pocket dimension. She didn't push her, instead waiting and looking at her with all the affection in the universe. God, Korinne adored her more than anything. Had she really almost died without telling her?

"Still me?" she asked again, just to be sure.

"Still you," Magnolia said with a smile. She finished cleaning Korinne's arm, then kissed the skin there. "Still my brave, smart, wonderful girl." She gently pried the silver rings from Korinne's fingers, cleaning the jewelry and setting it aside before wiping her fingers. She moved to her chest and softly scrubbed the blood away.

"I don't feel like those things," Korinne said. Her confession lingered on the back of her tongue, and her heart raced as she built up the courage to say it.

"Well, you are," Magnolia said as the last of the blood washed away. She leaned forward and placed a kiss right over Korinne's heart. Could she feel the heat of her feelings through her skin? The wave of them rose so strong she nearly choked on it. Korinne bowed her head, pressing her lips to the top of Magnolia's head.

She was done hiding it.

"I love you, Magnolia," she whispered into her hair. Magnolia moved back and fixed her eyes on Korinne's. Korinne tried to act as brave as Magnolia thought she was and continued. "I love you, I'm *in love* with you, and I'm sorry it took all of this happening for me to finally say something."

Magnolia's smile was absolutely radiant as she put the washcloth down. "And here I thought I'd march in here and say it first. But you always have to be one step ahead of me, huh?"

"What?" Korinne said, because some small part of her

brain thought Magnolia would leave in a fit of disgusted rage, and another part of her thought she imagined the words entirely.

"I love you too, Korinne. I love you in the forever kind of way," she said, resting her hands on Korinne's shoulders.

"In the 'grow old together' kind of way?" she asked, just in case she misheard her over her heart exploding.

"In the 'get a cute little house and live happily ever after' way," Magnolia said.

A mixture of joy and relief and crashing adrenaline made the backs of her eyes sting with tears. She'd done a fair amount of stupid stuff on this trip, but keeping her mouth shut was far and away the most egregious offender.

It was possibly the worst time for a love confession, but at least she said it. And thank every deity that might or might not exist, Magnolia felt the same.

"Say it again," Korinne said, because after everything she still needed repeated results.

"I love you," Magnolia said, eyes glistening. She rested her hands on Korinne's thighs and leaned forward to kiss one cheek. "I love you." She kissed the other one. "I love you." She paused and looked her dead in the eye. "I love you."

Korinne's hands went to Magnolia's waist, and before she could overthink it, she leaned forward and pressed her lips to Magnolia's. The kiss was deep and full of all the feelings she—evidently both of them—hid for too long. Magnolia kissed her back with every inch of her body, and God, why didn't she do this ages ago? Stupid, to wait until now to say something. She deepened the kiss, and Magnolia let out the softest noise in the back of her throat that bolstered Korinne's confidence. She kissed her again and again until they were left gasping, their breaths mingling in the minute space between them.

"We should probably slow down, right?" Korinne whispered, a lie to Magnolia and to herself.

"Whatever you want, my love," Magnolia said.

"I just—I don't want you to think that it's just because of what happened," she said, because despite everything, the thought of hurting Magnolia's feelings seemed the worst.

"I know you better than that, Korinne." She gave her another kiss, this one gentle and lingering. "If you want space, I can give you space. Or, if you want me to remind you that every inch of this body is yours, I would gladly do that too."

A shiver went down Korinne's spine. Even if she didn't want to let Magnolia out of her sight for the next century, she needed to say no, right? They'd just been through the worst experience of their lives. Sure, it was coupled with probably the *best* moment of her life, but after all this, Korinne wondered if she even deserved more happiness than what she already had. The thought made her heart ache, because after everything, all she wanted was to hold the woman in front of her and never let go.

Unprompted, the door slid shut. Another click echoed in the bathroom as it locked.

Magnolia stood and went to the door, and Korinne missed her presence immediately. She wasn't supposed to be over there, she was supposed to be here, in her arms. Korinne rose and went to her, placing a hand on the small of Magnolia's back. Magnolia pressed her palm to the pad, but the door remained resolutely shut.

Korinne loved when the universe made a decision for her.

"Good, I didn't want to wait, anyway."

She pushed Magnolia against the door and kissed her again.

CHAPTER 31
CASSIE

From Bitt's camera: [a blonde woman appears]

NAILED IT!

Cassie strolled out, dusting her hands off and celebrating a job well done. Outside of the room, she found one of the robots waiting. Was it Bitt? Or Efex? She couldn't tell the difference.

With a shit-eating grin, Cassie siphoned enough juice from the ship to appear fully formed in front of its binoculars. She waved, flipped it off, then sauntered away.

CHAPTER 32
KORINNE

From camera 1.1.1: [a giggle, followed by a moan]

AS KORINNE KISSED MAGNOLIA, she was forced to ask herself one very important question: why in the *fuck* had she waited so long to do this?

They'd joked about partners over the years, about how they'd need approval from the best friend before anything permanent. Over the last year, Korinne had stopped joking so much, because in her heart she wasn't sure she wanted to hear about Magnolia's partners anymore. And now, as they kissed in the bathroom of a haunted spaceship, she accepted the reason why. If she was honest with herself, she'd known for a long time.

Did she just get possessed? Maybe. Were ghosts real? Definitely. Did her entire worldview go up in smoke, as well as her sense of autonomy? Oh, absolutely. Which was why she wanted to take the moment with both hands and never let go.

Korinne slipped her hands into Magnolia's hair and pressed

her into the door, wedging one thigh between hers. Magnolia whined into the kiss, clutching at Korinne's waist and drawing her close. God, it felt so good to kiss her after all this time dreaming.

"Is this okay?" Korinne asked. Magnolia blinked, panting slightly, and took a second to answer.

"Was confessing my love for you and saying I want to remind you this body is yours not enough?" she asked with a self-conscious grin playing at her lips.

Korinne realized she never should've stopped kissing her, but was too far gone now.

"I just like verbal confirmation of things," she said as her heart hammered against her chest.

Magnolia responded by leaning forward and capturing her lips again. The kiss was warm, and tender, with the familiarity of coming home.

"That wasn't verbal confirmation," Korinne said as Magnolia pulled away.

Magnolia laughed and said, "Yes, this is okay. I want this. I want *you*. I have for a long time."

"'A long time'?" she asked, earning another chuckle.

"Yes. And here I thought I was so obvious," Magnolia said.

"To be honest, I think I convinced myself that you were just kidding," Korinne said. How long had they danced around the truth? How much time had they wasted? Stupid, both of them.

Magnolia leaned her head against the door with a dull *thump*. "Gods," she said. "We're such fucking idiots."

Korinne laid her head against Magnolia's shoulder. "We really are." She then took the opportunity to lay her lips against Magnolia's neck, which turned the giggles into a soft moan.

"Glad we're on the same page now," Magnolia said, her fingers toying with the hem of Korinne's tank top.

"That's for damn sure," Korinne said. She jerked back. "But also, I really don't want you to think... This isn't just because—"

"I know, darling," Magnolia whispered, violet eyes shining in the low light. "And you're still you, remember?"

Korinne swallowed. "Oh, right. Forgot for a second."

"And if you change your mind, we stop. No harm, no foul," Magnolia said as she brushed a curl from Korinne's forehead.

"As long as there's no more unnecessary pining," Korinne said, partially as a joke, but mostly serious. She couldn't take it if it happened again.

"Of course not." Magnolia sounded so sincere, Korinne had no choice but to believe her. "Now, do you want to kiss me again, or...?"

What a dumb question.

"Yes. Definitely, yes," Korinne said, and did so.

This time, the kiss was long and deep as Korinne decided to use her tongue for better things besides talking. Magnolia responded in kind, sinking in with a sigh. It was true, what all the songs said. It was different with someone she loved.

Magnolia slid her hands beneath the hem of Korinne's tank top, running her fingers over the soft skin at her waist. Inch by inch she raised the shirt until they had to separate for her to pull it off completely. She shivered as the cool air hit her, but Magnolia tugged her close and ran her warm hands over her back.

Korinne dropped her lips to Magnolia's neck again, leaving searing kisses beneath her ear, over her fluttering pulse, at the sensitive spot where her neck met her shoulder. Apparently this was one of her favorite places, as she gasped softly and rocked against Korinne's thigh. Korinne grinned in success and continued, sucking the skin just hard enough to make a wonderful noise spill from her lips. She nipped gently, then soothed the area with her tongue as Magnolia squirmed.

She unclipped one strap of Magnolia's overalls, then the other, backing up just enough so she could shimmy out of them. Korinne traced the strip of skin between her shirt and underwear, grinning when the muscles beneath tightened. With her minimal space, Magnolia reached out and undid the button of her pants, then the zipper. Korinne nearly tripped getting out of them, but managed to stay upright thanks to Magnolia holding her waist tight. Once settled, she unclasped Korinne's bra with devastating accuracy, the black, lacy thing falling to the floor with the rest of their clothes. Magnolia pulled back enough to see the newly bared skin, and the fire in her eyes lit something in Korinne's belly. Magnolia bit her lip and ran her thumbs over the pierced peaks of her, sending a jolt down her spine and a curse from her mouth.

"Sensitive?" she asked, looking at Korinne through her lashes.

Korinne gasped as she did it again and nodded.

"Very," she said. Magnolia gave her a wicked grin before ducking down and taking one nipple in her mouth. "Oh, fuck!"

She swirled her tongue, making Korinne swear again and place her hand on the door to steady herself. When Magnolia reached up to pinch the other side, she leaned into the touch and squeezed her eyes shut. She wanted Magnolia to touch her everywhere, kiss her everywhere, and she wanted to do the same in turn. Every flick and tweak sent spasms through her. The newness of it all heightened every sensation to a ridiculous level. It had never felt like this before. Too soon, Magnolia let go, leaving Korinne a panting mess. She kissed her way up until she could claim her mouth once more.

"We still need to shower," Magnolia said softly.

"Yeah, that's probably a good idea." Korinne grasped the edges of Magnolia's shirt and pulled it off. She took a moment to appreciate the ample cleavage the floral print bra provided before unclasping and discarding it. The view beneath was even better, and Korinne couldn't stop herself from saying, "God, you're fucking gorgeous."

"Thank you," Magnolia said, a blush spreading on her cheeks and chest. She shirked her underwear, and Korinne followed her lead, leaving them both naked as the day they were born.

To say Magnolia's body was stunning would be an understatement, but she didn't allow Korinne time to ogle her, instead pushing her into the shower. The water ran hot, and the first hit of the spray shocked her, sending goosebumps over her entire body. Then the heat sank in, and she relaxed.

Her body ached, and the warm water felt so soothing that for a moment she forgot what they were doing. A second later, Magnolia's hands were on her, but it wasn't the frenzied touches from before. She had soap and a washcloth in her hands, and gently scrubbed Korinne's skin, rinsing away the grime and the fear from the day. Over each freshly cleaned spot she pressed her lips, bringing awareness to every part of her body until it felt wholly hers again. Korinne watched from under hooded eyes as a goddess worshipped and cleansed her, fire building in her abdomen.

Next came shampoo, and deft fingers massaged her head and detangled her short curls, putting all her pieces back together. Magnolia seemed to know, instinctively, exactly what she needed to feel herself again.

Or perhaps it wasn't instinct. Perhaps she paid attention.

With the weight of the day washed away, Korinne took Magnolia's cheeks and brought her lips back to hers, the water coursing over them as their bodies moved together. Each gasp between kisses made droplets fly, but that didn't stop her, and Korinne ran her hands over every piece of skin available to her, catching each breath Magnolia let out at the contact.

Then it was her turn. Korinne gently scrubbed away the sweat and blood until Magnolia's smooth skin shone. She acquainted herself with every inch of her, taking note of every place that made Magnolia moan and tremble. She took care to gently detangle her long lavender waves, then swept them to the side to kiss that spot again.

"I love you," Magnolia said, her eyes burning as she said it. It felt so good to hear it again.

"I love you too," Korinne said, a massive ball of pressure unwinding in her chest. "God, Magnolia, I love you so fucking much."

To think, her soul almost got eaten before she finally had the guts to do something about these feelings for this woman. This perfect, beautiful, strong, possibly clairvoyant woman, who'd saved her life today. This woman who'd seen the very best and worst of her, and loved her anyway. Where would she be without her?

Korinne launched forward to capture her in a kiss, her feelings threatening to completely overwhelm her. Stupid, to wait this long. But she would remedy that situation quickly. She pushed Magnolia out of the water and against the shower wall, the cold metal making her inhale sharply. Korinne placed sloppy kisses over the plum blush covering her chest, not bothering to avoid the pendant hanging between her perfect breasts. She took one nipple into her mouth as she gently pinched the other, making Magnolia stiffen beneath her. But not quite in the right way.

Korinne looked up. "Not into it?" she asked, hand not moving. Magnolia faltered for a second before shaking her head.

"Doesn't do much for me, if I'm honest," she said.

Korinne catalogued the information away.

"You should get them pierced, it sometimes helps," she said

with a grin. She dropped her hand and slipped it between Magnolia's legs, smiling at the wetness she found there that had nothing to do with the shower. Magnolia bit her lip and shifted to meet her as Korinne gently circled her clit. "Would you prefer my mouth in other places?"

"This was supposed to be about you," Magnolia said, though she continued to move her hips in time with Korinne's fingers. "About making you feel present again."

"Oh, trust me, I feel very present," she said. If she focused on Magnolia, she didn't have to think about the day. "Can I taste you?"

Magnolia thought about pushing back, Korinne could tell by the look on her face. But her body won the argument, and she nodded. Korinne dropped to her knees, and Magnolia's eyes went wide.

"We have a bed like, ten feet away," Magnolia said.

Korinne responded by guiding one leg over her shoulder.

"Too far. I want you here," she said, pressing a kiss to her inner thigh. The view alone nearly sent her to the edge. She paused. "Unless you don't want it like this."

"I don't mind this one bit," Magnolia said, running her fingers through Korinne's wet curls. "I kind of like seeing you on your knees for me."

"Happy to be here," Korinne said, holding her tongue to keep from saying something about making Magnolia her religion. She found a better use for it, kissing up her thigh until she reached the apex. Magnolia exhaled sharply and jerked, more of her weight sinking onto Korinne's shoulder. She took it easily as she licked, the taste of Magnolia even sweeter than she imagined. When she sucked her clit into her mouth, Magnolia spasmed, her hand coming to the back of Korinne's head.

"Gods, that feels so good, Rinne," Magnolia said through her gasps. Korinne hummed, practically glowing with the praise, and zeroed in. She moved her tongue back and forth, and Magnolia whined. "Yes! Just like that. Fuck!"

"You taste incredible," Korinne said, not stopping long enough for Magnolia to respond. She said it because it was true, because if she could survive every day on simply eating Magnolia, she would. She slid one hand up Magnolia's leg. "Do you want more?"

"Yes, please, Rinne," Magnolia said, her hips rolling toward her face. Korinne listened, and easily—so easily—slipped a finger inside. Magnolia moaned loudly and clenched around her immediately. Korinne gently worked in and out until she relaxed enough for her to push in a second finger, just as seamless as the first. Magnolia called her name again, her voice lowering to a husky stream of yeses and curses. She leaned further on Korinne, who accepted this holy burden with great pleasure. It pushed her fingers deeper, and she crooked them just right on a spot that made Magnolia scream.

"Right there," she said, matching each movement with her own. "So good. Fuck, so good, you're so good—"

Encouraged by her words, Korinne continued, upping the pace slightly. Magnolia nearly lost her footing, but Korinne held her up without stopping. Her shoulder burned, her jaw ached, and she'd likely have bruises from the metal floor, but adrenaline flushed every thought of pain out of her mind. All that mattered was Magnolia panting above her, clenching around her, singing her praises as she coiled tighter and tighter.

"I'm...I'm gonna..."

She fell silent as she came, her head tilted back and her eyes squeezed shut. Korinne worked her through it, pressing tongue and fingers both hard and steady as she rode the wave. She felt the moment things became too sensitive and immediately backed off, though she couldn't help pressing one last kiss after removing her fingers.

Magnolia managed to move her leg off Korinne's shoulder, but didn't stay standing long, instead sliding down the wall to land on the floor in front of her, legs splayed wide and eyes dazed with bliss. With Magnolia spread before her like that, it took everything for Korinne to give her a minute and not dive right back in to repeat the process.

Sure, she had a running shower literally inches away, but she held Magnolia's gaze as she took her wet fingers and sucked them clean instead. Magnolia's eyes widened at the sight, and Korinne dissolved into laughter.

"What?" Magnolia asked, still breathless. Color tinged her cheeks, and Korinne kissed the hot spots to assuage the embarrassment.

"I'm just laughing because I'm a fucking idiot," she said. She let her eyes wander down Magnolia's body, taking in every stunning valley and curve, marking all the places she wanted to taste later. "Could've been doing this for God knows how long, but I had to be dumb about it."

"You weren't the only one, my smart girl," Magnolia said, and oh, turned out that name did something to Korinne's insides. "A thousand times I thought about kissing you, but held myself back like a fool."

"Well, you can make up for it by kissing me a thousand times now," Korinne said. Magnolia smiled and pulled her in for a sweet kiss. The next one, though, reignited the fire in Korinne's belly.

"Now," Magnolia said, taking Korinne's chin in her thumb and forefinger. "Do I have to fuck you in the shower, or can we move to the bed?"

"You could tell me to jump out of the airlock for it and I would," Korinne said, her heart already tripping at the idea. Shower, bed, whatever part of this massive ship Magnolia wanted to use, she was down.

Except the human reclamation tanks. They didn't need to mess with that again.

Magnolia crawled to her feet and cut off the shower. The ensuing silence threatened to swallow Korinne whole as the smallest seed of doubt appeared, but one look at Magnolia's mussed hair and satisfied smirk banished the thought.

They toweled off with gusto, sneaking in kisses where possible. Korinne wondered if the door would stay closed, but it opened with absolute ease. Their towels remained forgotten on the floor as Magnolia took her face and kissed her soundly. She walked her back, carefully dodging discarded equipment, until Korinne's knees hit the bed and she fell back.

Normally, being on display would make her nervous, but considering Magnolia looked at her like she was a feast, she felt a bubble of confidence form instead. She took a deep breath, satisfaction burning through her as Magnolia's eyes dropped to watch the rise and fall of her chest.

"Oh, darling," Magnolia said, an edge to her tone. "I want to devour you."

"Please," Korinne said, not nearly as sultry as she meant for it to be. Magnolia raised an eyebrow. "Want me to beg? I'll do it. I'm desperate for you, Mags."

Magnolia paused, obviously thinking about it. Korinne prepared herself to drop to her knees again, as if that would be some sort of punishment. But Magnolia shook her head.

"Maybe another time," she said. She crawled onto the bed, staying on all fours above Korinne before leaning down to kiss her. Korinne kissed her back, hungry, hands going to Magnolia's breasts and squeezing before remembering.

"Sorry," she mumbled, sliding her hands down Magnolia's arms instead.

"Does it do something for you?" Magnolia asked, moving

her lips to Korinne's neck instead. She let out a breathy chuckle.

"You're really asking if touching your perfect tits turns me on?" she asked.

"It's a fair question." She took Korinne's hands and placed them back where they started. "I want you to do what you like. Right now is about you."

"Feels selfish—shit." She swore as Magnolia found a sensitive spot just below her ear.

"You know better than that," Magnolia said, her hand coming up Korinne's ribs before taking a gentle handful. And Korinne did know. She whined as Magnolia's thumb ran over her, jostling the barbell piercing. "Does that hurt?"

"Not in the slightest," Korinne said as pleasure raced through her. Magnolia did it again, and Korinne squirmed beneath her. A sigh escaped as Magnolia shifted one of her legs, using her thigh to put pressure right where Korinne needed it. She didn't bother trying to stay still, instead slowly moving her hips and humming as the friction took the edge off the ache.

Korinne slid her hands around Magnolia's back and tugged until she lay flush against her, her weight pushing her into the mattress. She hooked her leg around Magnolia's waist, once again allowing the most delicious sensation. Their lips met once more, hot and wanting, and Korinne drank her down like water on a hot day. Each touch, each kiss, ignited her body further in a way that made her forget every scary thing that had happened on this trip.

Every second of footage could get erased, and she'd find it worth it for this moment alone.

"I want to make you feel good," Magnolia said, dropping her head so she could press a kiss to Korinne's throat. Korinne's hips moved of their own accord, the friction making her whimper. "Can I?"

"Yes, God, yes," Korinne said as she wound tighter and tighter with every brush of Magnolia's lips.

Magnolia tilted her chin up again and pressed a fervent kiss to her lips. Her other hand wandered down to her chest, once again flicking the little barbell and making her gasp.

"Keep moving," Magnolia whispered as she pinched lightly. Korinne obeyed, grinding against her thigh and trying in vain to keep kissing her as the sensations piled up. Each second pushed thoughts of the day away, until she couldn't focus on anything but the woman on top of her. "Do you want more?"

The question surprised her out of her stupor, and Korinne blinked. "Honestly, this is working really well for me right now." It felt good to be in control, to have Magnolia's whole body pressed against hers, keeping her together. She didn't want it to stop.

"Are you open to a suggestion?" Magnolia asked with a well-timed flick. Korinne let out a long breath.

"Yeah, I think so," she said. Magnolia grinned and moved away—how dare she—to lay on her back. She pulled Korinne with her, seating her with her legs on either side of one of hers. The change sent a jolt of pleasure down her spine, and Korinne understood. "Oh. Yes. Yes, this."

Magnolia grinned. "Keep going, darling," she said.

Her hands went to Korinne's breasts as she lifted one leg further, allowing them to slot together perfectly. Their wetness mingled as Korinne slowly ground against her, every movement pressing them together and steadily pushing her toward the edge. Magnolia wasn't immune, her lips forming a soft "o" with every roll from Korinne.

Magnolia moved her free leg out further to the side, and the next time Korinne rolled in, she gasped. Korinne repeated the movement, making sure to press with each go. Little noises escaped from both of them, mingling with the sounds of their bodies. Korinne couldn't move her eyes from Magnolia's torso, enraptured with how each thrust made the softer parts of her jump.

"It's supposed to be your turn," Magnolia said, dragging Korinne's attention to her face.

"You think I'm against watching you come again?" she countered as that telltale blush appeared on Magnolia's chest. "I get off watching you get off."

"Fuck," Magnolia said, tilting her head back so it rested against Korinne's one pillow, her brows furrowed and lips parted. "In that case, a little faster."

"Yes ma'am," Korinne said, following instructions. Sweat trickled down her back and Magnolia gripped her hips tight, which only helped her situation. She was in charge, she was in control, she was the one making Magnolia sound like that as they both wound tighter and tighter. Names and curses swirled together in the space between them. It became harder and harder to move as her muscles burned, and she was close, so close—

Magnolia tipped over the edge, this time coming with a cry and a harsh shudder that sent that sweet release rolling through Korinne just after her. Her movements slowed as she dragged it out, wringing every last bit from both of them before she finally stilled. They stayed there, panting and pressed together, as their heart rates lowered and previously tense places went boneless. Korinne collapsed against Magnolia, resting her head on her shoulder as Magnolia ran gentle hands up and down her back.

"I've got you," she heard Magnolia whisper as the blood rushing through her ears dulled enough for her to hear. "You're so good, I've got you, I've got you."

Korinne found a way to hold her tighter, burying her face in Magnolia's neck and letting out an unsteady breath. Tears pricked the back of her eyes, but she refused to let them fall. Things were good, *so* good. And not just the sex—though that was great—but everything else. The whole series finale could get zero views, and it would be worth it to have Magnolia in her arms.

The dust settled, and Korinne pulled back, untangling herself but not moving too far away. "Shit, we need to shower again," she said as the cool air hit her sweaty skin.

"Oh no," Magnolia deadpanned, a smile tugging on her lips. "What a travesty."

"You sound way too satisfied right now," Korinne said, only for Magnolia to put one hand behind her head and smirk.

"I'm incredibly satisfied right now," she replied. She reached out to take Korinne's hand and tangled their fingers together. "Are you?"

"More than you could ever imagine," Korinne said, bringing Magnolia's hand to her lips and kissing her knuckles.

"I've got an inkling," Magnolia said. Korinne made to move back, to go take said shower she'd mentioned before, but Magnolia tugged her back with a grin. "Hold on now. I'm not done with you here yet."

"Oh?" Korinne said as Magnolia laid her down on her back and pressed a kiss to her collarbone.

"Yep," she said, nipping the skin an inch lower. "After all, I still owe you at least one."

"You don't owe me anything," Korinne said, just happy to be there. They had forever to even things out. "Wait, 'at least'?"

Korinne wished she could take a picture of the smile Magnolia had as she shifted down, laying kisses to her sternum, her stomach, her hips.

"I said what I said."

And it all began again.

Korinne didn't think about the morning for a long, long time.

DAY
THREE

CHAPTER 33
CASSIE

From camera 15.3.20: [a machine clunks]

CASSIE SKIPPED AROUND THE SHIP, grinning and whistling and, in general, feeling pretty damn smug about the situation. The man who led to her death got thrown into another dimension, Magnolia and Korinne finally confessed their feelings for each other, *and* the Malevolence had gone quiet. It hadn't made a single sound all night, and even the weird black thing on her arm from its wraith had healed. Hell, she even had some memories back! She was currently winning at the whole dying game.

Every memory of Rose sent a deep pain through her, yes. She couldn't deny that. But actually getting to remember her? The opportunity to see her face again, hear her voice? Cassie wouldn't trade that for anything in this world or the next. And she had those dumb, lovesick girls to thank.

They stayed in Korinne's room the rest of the afternoon, only stumbling out to get some food later in the evening. Cassie gave them their space, watching like a proud mother as her idiot kiddos finally figured it out. They returned to Magnolia's room, and Cassie seriously considered checking the damage in Korinne's before deciding there were some things she was better left not knowing.

The ship rumbled as they approached Capa Emphara right at eight o'clock the next morning. Cassie floated up to the deck to find Captain Armand staring at the screens as cameras fed him the view of blue waters and green terrain—all things Cassie could've, but never, experienced.

"Do you think I can leave the ship once it lands?" she asked. Of course, he couldn't hear her. Only Magnolia could. Maybe Korinne, if she really tried.

"*Arkana* to Bellhaven, are we clear for landing?" the captain said, not noticing Cassie at all. The intercom crackled.

"Good morning, *Arkana*. Bellhaven here," came a calm, feminine voice. "We've got a nice open area for you. No living creatures for hundreds of miles."

"Okay, good," Captain Armand said. "Wouldn't want to accidentally hurt anybody."

Cassie hummed. "I didn't even think of that."

The woman laughed. "Don't worry, you're all clear. See you soon."

"All right, Armand," he said, flexing his hands. "Nice and easy, into orbit and into the gravity well."

"Don't forget to call Korinne," Cassie said. "Isn't she supposed to watch this?"

"Oh," Captain Armand said, as if he actually heard her. He clicked the intercom and said, "Ladies, if you'd like to make your way to the bridge, we'll be entering orbit now and soon beginning the landing."

Weird, usually she could hear when things got broadcast across the ship. Armand apparently noticed the same thing, and pressed the intercom button a few more times. On the middle-most screen, a blue dot labeled *Arkana* moved very close to a white circle. The captain looked back and forth between the screen and his handheld before sighing.

"I'll ping her in a second," he muttered.

"You've got this," Cassie said, trying to clap him on the shoulder and of course going right through him. He shivered. "Oops, sorry."

"Here we go," he said. What happened next, Cassie couldn't say—because she was, at best, a mechanic, not a ship captain.

Captain Armand got a very serious look on his face, then methodically flipped a bunch of switches and pressed a lot of buttons. If this wasn't the most stressful moment of his life, Cassie might've touched the equipment to mess with him. But she was in a new era of death, and she wanted to be a good ghost.

"How do you watch these all the time?" Cassie asked, strolling around the deck and eyeing all the screens. They held no signs of the girls yet, but she assumed they would pop up sooner or later once they got close to deploying the landing sequence. "How do you keep up with it all?"

Captain Armand didn't answer. He touched a few more spots on the screen, then pressed a yellow button. A vibration started as the ship entered orbit, sparks flying around Cassie's feet as the engine activity increased. Another few buttons, and they found the gravity well. A loud grinding echoed through the bridge.

"Oh, that's not good," she said.

"What—" Captain Armand hastily hit a bunch of buttons, and the ship lurched. For a moment, Cassie flew, weightless despite having no body. How could that happen?

Alarms screamed, and the captain touched every button he could reach in an effort to right it.

"I feel like it wasn't supposed to be like this!" Cassie yelled over the din.

"Just a...second..." A few more buttons, and the ship calmed, though the vibration remained. He rested his hands on the counter and heaved a sigh. Cassie watched as he took several deep breaths before touching the intercom. "Sorry about that."

His voice still didn't echo through the ship. He furrowed his brows, but ended up shrugging and moving on. It wasn't like he could help it.

"*Arkana?*" the woman said again. "You've gone off course."

"Sorry," Captain Armand said as his fingers continued flying across the controls. "I got knocked loose, I'm trying to get back in."

"Disengage landing sequence. If you try to land now, you'll take out a major metropolitan area."

"Trying!"

Cassie glanced up at the screens again. Still no signs of the girls, but...

It wasn't on every screen, but on enough of them she watched as random things fell or broke. The damages didn't match the timing of them arriving in orbit, nor did they match the rhythm of the ship. Heat built beneath her feet as more sparks flew.

"Oh, no," Cassie said.

The room shuddered. Red smoke curled from the ceiling, the floor, the door. The ship lurched again, exiting the gravity well and careening off course.

"No no no—"

"*Arkana!* Disengage landing sequence!"

The captain slapped at a hundred different buttons.

Cassie's eyes flew around, and she gasped as a familiar smoke poured from every crack and seam. How could this happen? They'd beaten it before, and now...

Despair filled her for a breath, then the bit of magic she shared with Magnolia flared to life, pushing it away before it could take hold. Cassie breathed easier until she remembered the captain. Red filled the room and coalesced around him until his hands went rigid and still.

"Captain—"

She ran over and went to put a hand on his back, hoping she could stop the Malevolence from grabbing him. Pain shot through her and tossed her back. The metal floor dug into her shoulder and hip as she skidded across the floor. With an eerie calm, the captain pressed a few buttons and sent the ship spinning through the atmosphere.

"*Arkana*, stop! You'll hit the city."

"Good," the captain growled in a voice that wasn't his own. He turned away from the controls and exited through the doors with long, deliberate strides. Cassie pushed herself up and followed on his heels.

"Where are you going? You have a ship to land," she said as sparks flew around them. He had to see her. There was no way he couldn't. "Stop! Go back and get the ship back on course!"

He continued down the hall to the engine room doors. There he paused, his shoulders hunched and his hands shaking. Above him, the seal burned white, but it wasn't nearly as bright as the day before. Cassie noticed, with abject horror, a crack along one side of it.

"Fight it, Armand. Turn around," Cassie said, putting her hand on his shoulder as a last ditch effort. The touch burned her, and her fingers came away crumpled and black. She screamed, holding her wrist to her chest as the pain sank in and spread through her entire arm.

The captain turned, his eyes smoldering red as he smiled.

"No," Cassie murmured, eyes wide and heart in her throat.

"I get what I want," he growled.

He reached into his pocket and pulled out a standard-issue pocketknife. With calm calculation, he flipped the blade open and sliced his opposite palm. Blood marked his movements as he went up and placed his hand over the seal.

The seal's white glow stuttered as the blood interrupted it, then went out completely.

The doors to the engine room blew open and sucked the captain in. The ground shook and heat blasted Cassie in the face as the captain disappeared into the machines.

"Oh, fuck."

Cassie ignored her pain and ran into the ship proper, trying to figure out the fastest way to the girls. Ghosts filled every area as far as she could see, their eyes glowing red in the flickering lights. As one, their gazes turned on her.

"Want," they said, thousands of voices in one. Cassie saw the kids, Jensen, Susan—everyone.

"You've got to be kidding me," she said, searching for an escape. The ghosts parted, and one walked forward from the sea of faces.

Lottie stared at her, eyes glowing and mouth leaking red.

"Want," she said, her voice layered with the rest. "It gets what it wants, Cassie."

The little seed of magic from Magnolia, still nestled somewhere next to her heart, pulsed. It made Cassie feel like she was about to throw up, but had the great effect of pushing the ghosts back. Lottie hissed, her fingers elongating into claws.

"Oh, fuck no," Cassie said, and jumped through the ceiling. Pain ripped through her as she did so, but she was able to pass. Floor after floor she traveled until she reached a quiet place, somewhere the ghosts hadn't reached yet.

Okay, so perhaps she spoke too soon about winning.

"Ouch, fuck." Her arm stung fiercely, and when she looked down, the black laceration had reopened and oozed sour red energy. "Oh, that's not good. That's not good at all."

The girls. She needed to warn Magnolia and Korinne, find a way to help them—

A growl emanated from the darkness behind her.

Cassie turned slowly. An eye glowed red, moving toward her with single-minded accuracy. The click of claws on the floor sent her heart into her shoes.

"No, please," she whispered as her last shred of hope fled.

The light flickered, and Baxter stepped into it, his eye burning and his lip curling as he growled.

"Seriously?" Cassie asked the ship at large. "My fucking dog?"

Baxter lunged, and she sank through the floor, dodging his attack. For once he didn't follow, his tracking skills apparently dampened by his contamination.

Cassie could cry if she had the time. For now, she had to focus on finding Magnolia and Korinne.

CHAPTER 34
MAGNOLIA

From camera 1 5.3.20: [one engine room door creaks partially open]

MAGNOLIA WOKE right where she wanted to be: nestled amongst her pillows and blankets, with Korinne's arms wrapped tight around her.

Forget everything that happened over the past two days. It was all worth it to come to this moment. Easy for her to say, of course. She wasn't the one who got possessed by a malicious spirit.

Korinne shifted and pulled her closer, letting out a contented sigh into her hair. Magnolia gently took her hand and intertwined their fingers, smiling as Korinne grasped back.

"You awake?" Korinne whispered.

"No," Magnolia whispered back, earning another tight squeeze.

"So this is all a dream?" she asked.

"Gods I hope not," Magnolia said. She rolled over—never

leaving her embrace—and tucked Korinne's head into her chest, their legs intertwining. "I hope this is real life."

"So no regrets?" Korinne asked.

"That's a stupid question for such a smart girl," Magnolia said. "My only regret is not saying anything to you sooner. To think I could've been waking up all nice and warm like this for ages."

Korinne's laugh tickled her chest. "Well, better late than never, I suppose."

A silence settled over them, and Magnolia was very tempted to try and go back to sleep. But she could feel the slight tension in Korinne's body, her fingers fiddling with the ends of Magnolia's hair.

"Do you want to talk about it?" Magnolia murmured. She placed a kiss on the top of Korinne's head and let her lips linger there.

A heavy sigh escaped her. "I probably should, huh?"

"It might help things," she said. "A lot happened yesterday."

"Yeah," Korinne said. "To be honest, I feel like I owe you a thousand apologies."

"What?" Magnolia leaned back so she could look her in the eye. "Why's that?"

"I made fun of you all the time for being scared. That was such an asshole thing to do. How could you even stand it?" Korinne said, her expression open and earnest.

"You made me *laugh* when I was scared," Magnolia said. "Yeah, maybe you made some jokes, but I never felt like it was at my expense. If anything, you made me feel brave."

"*I* made *you* feel brave?" Korinne sat up, and the blankets puddled around her waist. Magnolia did her best to keep her eyes on her face. "Magnolia, you're the bravest person I've ever known."

Heat flooded Magnolia's face, and she ducked beneath the covers.

"No, I'm not," she said.

"Yes, you are," Korinne said, peeling the blanket back. "This shit is legitimately terrifying. Thank God this is our last site. I don't think I could do another one. How did you live like this for the past five years?"

"In your defense, we never experienced anything like this before," Magnolia said. "The idea of ghosts running around isn't that scary. It's just the stuff we've seen here..."

"It's different," Korinne filled in.

Magnolia nodded. "It's different."

Korinne glanced away, her expression taking on that thousand-yard stare she got when she was trying to remember something specific. Magnolia shifted so she sat up again, the covers clutched to her chest. It would just take a few minutes, and then...

"So...how did you save me?"

There it was.

Magnolia inhaled and let the air out slowly, taking the time to figure out exactly what she wanted to say, and how to say it.

"Apparently," she started, giving herself just a couple more seconds to think, "my ghostly intuition is a little more substantial than I originally thought."

Korinne furrowed her brows. "I'm not following."

"Something happened when we got here," Magnolia said. "I don't know what exactly. But now I can like, see the ghosts. And talk to them, like when I was younger. Apparently, my Grandma Josie was the same way."

"So you could see what that guy did?" Korinne rubbed her sternum, right where Magnolia had placed her pendant.

"LeBeau," she said. "That guy was LeBeau."

"LeBeau like, the guy that got left up here? The one Cassie might've gotten tangled up with?" she asked.

Magnolia nodded. "And apparently my great uncle," she said.

"Whoa, what?" Korinne's eyebrows shot toward her hairline.

"It's a long story," she said. "But yes, I could see him. And then, when it came time to save you...I had some help." Magnolia picked at a thread, refusing to meet Korinne's eyes. It wasn't the full explanation, but she probably didn't need to lay all that on her right at that moment.

"From a ghost?" she asked with genuine curiosity.

Magnolia paused, but figured their helper wouldn't mind a little credit. "From Cassie."

Korinne took a pause so long Magnolia thought she'd become a ghost herself.

"Cassie. Like, *Cassie* Cassie? Like, the woman we've been talking about this entire trip?" she said.

"Yeah, that Cassie," Magnolia said.

Korinne groaned. "Oh God, so she heard everything? How does she not hate us? I'd flip shit if I had to listen to two assholes talk about my death for three days straight."

"She's fine," Magnolia said with a laugh. "She helped us, didn't she?"

"I guess that's true." She ran her hand through her hair, further messing up the already messy curls.

Magnolia reached out and laid a hand against her cheek. "How do you feel? Now that you know all this is real?" she asked, bringing Korinne back to the start of the conversation.

"Scared. Confused. A little sore that I lost our bet after all this time," she said, probably trying to deflect her feelings with some humor. But Magnolia knew her too well for that to work.

"It's very overwhelming, knowing that we can linger after we die."

"Yeah, it is," Magnolia said. "But it's like we said earlier. It's different here compared to anywhere else we've been."

"So you don't think I have to worry about more ghosts hijacking my body?" She said it casually, but her shoulders tensed, and she reached up to grasp Magnolia's wrist.

"No, I don't think you do," Magnolia said. "But I can get you your own protection pendant, if you want."

"That might not be a bad idea. We're already at the 'exchanging jewelry' phase of this relationship then?" Korinne asked with a cheeky grin.

"Is that your sly way of telling me you're hiding a ring in your bag somewhere?" Magnolia said, and while they were nowhere near ready for *that* conversation, the idea settled pleasant and warm in her abdomen.

"Well, now I wish I did." She turned and pressed a kiss to Magnolia's palm. "Any regrets from last night?"

"None," Magnolia said immediately. Then, amended, "Well, one."

Korinne went very still and tried way too hard to appear casual. "What?"

Magnolia drew her close and kissed her soundly, morning breath be damned. When they parted, she said, "I should've done that a long time ago."

"Thanks for that heart attack," Korinne said, pulling her into another kiss. Magnolia deepened it, sliding her hand into Korinne's curls and tugging slightly. When Korinne let out the tiniest moan, Magnolia grinned and slowly lowered them to the bed, pulling Korinne on top of her and intertwining their legs.

Things were just starting to get interesting when the ship tilted hard, sending them rolling into the wall.

"What the fuck—"

The ship dropped, and for a moment they floated weight-less above the bed before landing roughly, pushing all the air from Magnolia's lungs.

"We must've entered the atmosphere. Shit, I'm supposed to be up there," Korinne said, pushing herself up. "You okay?"

"Yeah," Magnolia said as her lungs reinflated. "I'm—"

The ship lurched, sending them tumbling to the floor in a tangle of elbows and knees. Magnolia let out a shout as something bony stuck her in her ribs, and a big *thunk* sounded from the direction of Korinne's head.

Magnolia waited to hear something from the captain, but nothing came. She detangled herself from Korinne and clambered to her feet, pulling her up too.

"I feel like it wasn't supposed to do that," Magnolia said.

"Could just be all the old equipment—oh shit!"

Magnolia spun toward the door to find Cassie standing there in all her dead glory, eyes wild and chest heaving. A charred stump replaced one of her arms, the sleeve of her jumpsuit burned away. Magnolia scrambled to grab the blanket and cover her and Korinne.

"We've got a problem," she said.

"Are you... Wait, how can I see you?" Korinne asked as she wrapped her half of the blanket around her. Magnolia had the same question—she just didn't have time to voice it.

"'Cause I want you to," Cassie said, as if the answer were obvious. "Look, the Malevolence ate the captain."

"What?" Magnolia and Korinne exclaimed at the same time.

"What's the Malevolence?" Korinne asked, looking between Cassie and Magnolia.

Cassie closed her eyes for a moment. "You didn't tell her?"

"I didn't have time!" Magnolia said. "We were discussing other things."

"Obviously," Cassie drawled, gesturing with her injured hand at the state of their undress. She turned her sights on Korinne. "Look, the guy that tried to take your body? We thought that by getting rid of him, we got rid of the entity that started this whole mess. But, uh, we were wrong."

"It's back?" Magnolia said as cold fear slithered through her veins. "How can it be back? It was sealed."

"The seal broke," Cassie said with a grimace.

"I'm sorry, this is a lot right now," Korinne said, gesturing to Cassie's entire being. "You could appear the whole time?"

"If I wanted to, yeah," Cassie said. "That's not important right now—"

"Hold on."

Korinne dropped the sheet and fumbled for her comm pad, which had disappeared with all the shifting of the ship. Cassie looked from her to Magnolia and back, blinking as she tried to compute.

"What the fuck are you doing?" she asked.

"Korinne—" Magnolia started, but Korinne let out a noise of triumph and emerged with the comm pad. "Seriously?"

"What? She's a full body apparition!" Korinne pointed to Cassie, who struck a pose.

"Korinne, we're naked," Magnolia said, clutching the sheets tighter. "And apparently a cosmic Malevolence is trying to take down the ship."

"Yeah, that's what editing is for," Korinne said.

"The Malevolence isn't your only problem," Cassie said, done with the show. "Remember ten seconds ago when I said *it ate the captain?*"

"It..." Magnolia couldn't finish the sentence. It ate the captain? It ate the captain. And with no captain...

"So how are we gonna land?" Korinne asked.

Cassie threw her hands up, wincing as her charred arm stretched. "That's the question of the hour, isn't it?"

Magnolia's mind raced for about four seconds before she locked onto Korinne. "You could land the ship, right?"

"Me?" Korinne turned and glanced behind her, as if someone else appeared in the back of the room. "You want me to try and land the ship?"

"You know the sequence! You studied how it was supposed to happen!" Magnolia said.

"That was a simulation!" Korinne said.

"And you got a ninety-seven percent," Magnolia reminded her. It had been one of Korinne's most stressful finals, and Magnolia took her out afterwards to celebrate.

"Ninety-seven percent means a three percent chance we crash and burn," Korinne said. "And that was ninety-seven percent when I studied!"

"Don't act like you didn't study it again before we came here," Magnolia said.

"Guys, can we..." Cassie pointed to the door.

"This is still weird as hell," Korinne said.

"It's weird for me too. But we don't have time for all the back and forth and existential crises," Cassie said. The ship dropped again, all of them going airborne for a second before crashing back to the floor. "I rest my case!"

"Korinne, you're our best option," Magnolia said.

"She's our only option," Cassie added. "The ghosts...well, you'll see when we get out there. It's just us, kids."

Magnolia's heart plummeted. Just them? What was she supposed to do when it was just them?

Cassie took a breath. "Magnolia, whatever power stuff you've got...we need it to hold off the Malevolence. At least long enough for Korinne to manage the landing sequence."

"Whoa, no, absolutely not." Korinne grabbed a t-shirt from the floor and tossed it to Magnolia before pulling on her underwear and a pair of black pants. "She doesn't need to go hold off anything."

"She does if we want this ship to land in the right place," Cassie said. "I think it's trying to land where there's a bunch of people. That was the original problem, back in the day."

"We're supposed to land in a big field," Korinne said. She found her bra but no shirt and apparently decided that was good enough.

Magnolia wrestled her way into her shirt and grabbed the first pair of shorts she could find. "But if it's running the ship, it can see that and change our course."

"So I'm supposed to be okay with you going alone—"

"Hey!" Cassie interjected.

"—to hold it off while I try to land this thing?" Korinne said.

Magnolia understood why she didn't like it. It was a risky plan with a lot of unknowns and more danger than she'd ever want to see in her entire life. But it was their only plan, and no matter how she tried to spin it, it was their best shot.

"We have to do this, Korinne," she said. "I'll fight it, and then you take us home."

"Absolutely not," Korinne said, her voice cracking. "Mags, no. It's too dangerous."

"Either you try and maybe die," Cassie said, "or we don't try, and you definitely die. That's how it goes, Korinne."

Korinne clenched her fists, and tears welled in her eyes. "I hate this," she whispered.

"I know," Magnolia said as her heart nearly broke in two.

She grabbed her pendant and pulled it off, just so she could lay it around Korinne's neck instead. Korinne grabbed Magnolia by the face and pulled her into a searing kiss, one that would've left her breathless any other time.

"Don't forget the cameras," Cassie said, sounding bored. "I imagine you'll want this for posterity."

At least someone remembered them. Magnolia had already forgotten again, distracted by the thought of a terrifying foe.

"You better win, you hear me?" Korinne said as she slid her comm pad into its harness one last time. She handed the other one to Magnolia, who copied her.

"I will, I promise," she said. "And I always keep my promises."

CHAPTER 35
KORINNE

From camera 75.4.1: [Korinne runs by]

KORINNE HATED THIS. Oh, she hated this so much.

How was she supposed to come to terms with ghosts and *getting fucking possessed* and then, ten seconds later, send Magnolia to fight the thing that possessed her? Magnolia, who didn't even like to kill bugs that got into the apartment and wouldn't even wrestle for fun? All while she herself tried to land the actual *Arkana*?

The ship shuddered and jerked as Korinne ran through the hallways toward the captain's bridge, making her bounce off the walls. Every step away from Magnolia sent a pang through her stomach. She'd had every intention of keeping her in her arms until landing, and now she and their one ally were off to try and fight some cosmic revenant hellbent on eating souls.

Her steps slowed, and she considered turning around. What was she doing, leaving Magnolia at a time like this?

The ship lurched, and Korinne fell hard, crying out as she

bounced on the metal floor. Magnolia's pendant burned where it touched her skin. Did that mean it was working, fighting off ghosts or whatever the hell was around? Korinne couldn't see them like she could Cassie.

And if she couldn't see them, she couldn't help Magnolia in the engine room. If she couldn't see them, she couldn't protect herself, and she'd just be a distraction. A liability. She'd be the last thing Magnolia needed at that moment.

Another bounce, and Korinne pushed herself to her feet. She couldn't fight ghosts, despite all her claims. But she could maybe stabilize the ship and make it an even playing field.

There was no time to consult her handheld, and Korinne was very glad for all the late nights spent pouring over maps while studying. While she still took a few wrong turns, she was able to find the captain's bridge in record time and collapsed into his chair.

"*Arkana,* what are you doing? That isn't sanctioned airspace—"

"Hi, sorry," Korinne said, tapping into the comms. Out of the corner of her eye, a red haze formed. On her chest, the pendant heated. The red slithered back like a scared animal. Oh good, so it was still working. She liked knowing that.

"You don't sound like Captain Armand," the woman on the intercom said.

"I'm his back up. We've had a bit of a situation," Korinne replied. It was only half a lie.

She took a deep breath and tried to push down every worry for Magnolia. She was a little worried for Cassie too, but since she was already dead, Korinne could only afford so much heart space for her. "Can you confirm our landing coordinates?"

That was step one. Magnolia had been right, she *had* studied the landing sequence before the trip, but only so she could annotate every moment when she *observed* the landing.

Because that's what she was supposed to do, not *actually* land the ship. At most, she thought Captain Armand would let her press like, a button or two.

And now, here she was.

The woman on the intercom rattled off a few numbers, and Korinne scanned the screens until she found the right place to input them. Once she locked in, she turned her attention to the keyboard and searched for the right switches to change the direction of the thrusters.

"*Arkana?*" the woman said.

"Sorry, I'm having trouble finding stuff," Korinne said, sounding like the least qualified person to land a ship.

"It's okay, I'm here with you."

There, the blue buttons associated with direction. Korinne pressed a few, cursed when the ship tilted in the wrong direction, and pressed a few more. When the ship turned the correct way, she let out a whoop.

"Great, *Arkana*! Now, we need you to—"

The woman's voice buzzed with interference.

"Sorry, could you say that again?" Korinne said.

More buzzing.

Then silence.

"Hello?"

Korinne tapped the intercom button, but nothing lit up. Above her, red smoke seeped between the cracks in the panels, falling around her as if the pendant kept her trapped in a little bubble.

She gulped.

"Manually then," she said as a hundred warning lights flashed in front of her. God, what she would've given for her notes.

Her handheld vibrated, and Korinne nearly leapt out of her

own skin. She pulled it out to find two pings from the bots. Not trusting her hands enough to type, sent them a voice note.

"Just hunker down and hold on," she said, hoping they understood. When she received an affirmative, she returned her attention to the screens.

She searched the wall until she found one with the most movement. Magnolia ran, obviously being led, but the cameras didn't pick up Cassie. Good, so at least for now she was still alive. Korinne selected the camera and highlighted Magnolia, glad that some interfaces hadn't changed so much in the past few decades. It allowed her to lock on to Magnolia and follow her through the ship by way of one camera at a time.

"Magnolia?" Korinne said, tapping into the all-ship intercom. Her voice didn't echo through the ship, and Magnolia didn't stop moving, didn't even acknowledge the sound. So, no communications then, at least from the ship. She grabbed her handheld again, just in time for the ship to shift.

"Fucking hell!"

The handheld dropped, and in the subsequent spin, went sliding under the desk. Korinne didn't have time to lament its loss, instead going back to the manual controls. This thing, this *Malevolence*, sure did fight dirty.

That was fine. She could fight dirty too.

CHAPTER 36
CASSIE

From camera 32.2.9: [Magnolia skids to a stop, changes direction, keeps running]

"OH, FOR FUCK'S SAKE."

Ghosts, as far as they could see. Not all of them had the telltale red eyes, but enough did to cause a problem. Cassie saw as the energy from the Malevolence spread from one to the next, slowly, insidiously, like a poison in water. Next to her, Magnolia shivered.

"I don't like this," she said.

"I don't either," Cassie said. "Let's try a different route."

Cassie led her through every twist and turn, every back way and shortcut. Poor Magnolia bounced off the walls as the ship fought against them, but she never stopped.

"Here we—nope."

Cassie popped her head through a door to find another sea of ghosts. Red eyes flickered as the group focused on them. She snapped back and pushed Magnolia toward the stairs.

"Run!"

They bolted up two flights of stairs, and Cassie stuck her head through another door.

"Clear," she said, pushing energy into the palm pad before jumping through. Magnolia followed, panting.

"Slow down," she gasped.

"Right, sorry."

It nearly killed Cassie again to reduce her speed, but what choice did she have? She couldn't exactly take down the Malevolence with just a little touch of magic, and Magnolia couldn't pass through the walls. They both had their flaws. She grabbed Magnolia's hand, wincing as power bounced back and forth between them. Purple sparks lit up at their touch, and Magnolia's eyes glowed.

"Oh, that helps," she said.

Cassie, who suddenly had a nice, whole hand again, had to agree.

She continued to drag Magnolia around, only losing grip when the ship moved too much. But then the ship stabilized, the jerks and bounces turning more into a heavy vibration through the floor.

"Korinne did it," Magnolia said with a goofy smile.

"Yes, and we're very proud of her," Cassie said. "Now focus."

It took four more path adjustments before they ended up at the long hall in front of the engine room. Here they found no ghosts, only a rancid heat that transcended the veil between life and death. Sweat beaded along Cassie's forehead, a sensation she hadn't experienced in decades. They both stared ahead, eyes trained on the place where there used to be a seal.

"Listen," Cassie said, trying to swallow her fear, "based on what I've heard and what I've felt, this thing can latch onto negative emotions. Everyone I know who died by it did so in a certain...state."

"Like, sad?" Magnolia asked.

"Let me put it this way," Cassie said. "Until yesterday, when I remembered how I died, I thought I'd killed myself."

"Oh," Magnolia said, squeezing Cassie's hand. The gesture was so simple and comforting it kind of hurt her feelings.

She cleared her throat. "Right. So keep your shit locked down, okay? One crack and it'll dig its claws in." She could cry later, after all this was done.

"Positive thinking, got it." Magnolia nodded. "And none of your friends can help us?"

Cassie thought of Jensen, of Lottie, of Baxter, and all of their red glowing eyes. "No. Even if you were able to fix them, by the time we found them all, we'd be dead and gone. Or in my case, deader and goner."

"How long have you been waiting to make that joke?" Magnolia asked with a dry laugh.

"Actually just came up with that one," Cassie said.

The heat grew. Sweat dripped from Magnolia's forehead and patches soaked through her shirt. Her beautiful lavender hair, normally so carefully arranged, now floated in a tangled mess around her as energy lifted it. She didn't go forth into the battle looking put together, but instead an angry and vengeful warrior.

Just like Jocelyn had been, back in the day.

The air thickened as they walked forward, pressing into Cassie as the sinister power ebbed and flowed. The metal doors shimmered in the heat; one remained closed, and the other opened just a crack. Smoke slid from every crack and seam. Beyond the doors, the Malevolence sucked energy toward it, the current flooding Cassie as it passed through her like a river.

"You ready?" Cassie asked. With all this, she felt so real, so *alive*. "We win, or we're gone."

"We're going to win." Magnolia set her shoulders, and a purple glow shone in her eyes and hands as power filtered through Cassie and into her. "I made a promise."

Drama queen. "Okay, here we go."

Past the doors, the machines clanked with awkward motions. Cassie watched as the bits and bobs she knew so well in life melted and stuck together. They needed to end this—fast.

"You aren't welcome here," Magnolia said, and God, Cassie wished it worked like in all the old movies.

A growl akin to a chuckle slithered from the room. If Cassie looked carefully, she could almost spot eyes glowing in the turmoil, numerous and terrible, all taking turns analyzing them. The room coughed and spat out two bodies: the charred remains of Captain Armand, his officer badge barely visible.

"You aren't welcome here," Magnolia said again, her attention still on the doors. "You need to leave."

Machines grumbled and clanked like someone clearing their throat. Fear tingled at Cassie's fingertips, and panic settled at the base of her spine. One eye stopped and stared, each blink drawing her emotions forward. This was a mistake, a futile attempt, they were headed for nothing but failure—

Cassie swallowed the feelings down and replaced them with determination. She *would* win this time. The Malevolence would not have her again.

The doors creaked all the way open, then melted away into molten puddles. Flames formed around two of the eyes, merging into a humanoid shape. A split in the fire looked almost like a smirk as it sized them up.

"Too late," it growled.

"It's never too late," Magnolia said. She held up her hand, which glowed and crackled with power.

The ship listed to the side, so fast it made Cassie's head spin. Down became up and vice versa, the artificial gravity generators fighting to keep a stable surface. Magnolia screamed and tried to ride the wave, but gravity and direction didn't have the same hold on Cassie, who recalibrated just in time to see a dark red tendril reaching for Magnolia.

"No!"

Cassie stepped forward and intercepted it, screaming as it latched onto her wrist. For the second time that day, her hand shriveled and turned black. It sucked her energy like a sponge, leaving her with all her anxiety and pain. Why did she think she could do this? She couldn't save anyone, couldn't avenge her love—

"Stop."

Magnolia grabbed the tendril in her glowing hand. The thing sizzled, and a deep, guttural screech echoed from the engine room loud enough to shake the floor. It snatched the tendril back, and Cassie stumbled away, chest heaving as she pulled at the energy around them. Bit by bit, she put herself back together.

"You okay?" Magnolia asked, laying a hand on her shoulder. That helped expedite the process.

"Yeah, I just wish it would quit doing that," Cassie replied, shaking out her hand as her fingers reformed.

The tendril wriggled back into the engine room, limp and bleeding red smoke. A smirk graced Magnolia's face; normally Cassie liked confidence in a woman, but something told her it wasn't earned quite yet.

"I said leave," Magnolia called, a wave of energy pulsing from her. The room crackled, belching heat and red spirit remnants. Faces and screams of victims bubbled out into the hallway.

"I think it's gonna take a little more than that," Cassie said.

"Right." Magnolia raised her hands and shoved, sending a force rippling toward the door. "Leave!"

The energy squashed the leakage and pushed the heat back. Even the volume of the growls lowered. But the man-shaped fire remained intact. It didn't even move.

Magnolia pushed again, and another wave crested and crashed past the door. This time, the Malevolence stumbled back a half step, its eyes wide in surprise. The screams on the other side faded, and the red haze dissipated.

Cassie put her hands on Magnolia's shoulders and funneled more energy into her. Magnolia yelled and let loose another wave, this one enough to push the Malevolence all the way back into the depths of the room.

Silence rang. Glowing and sweating, Magnolia grinned.

From the darkness, tendrils shot out and grabbed her. They circled her wrists, ankles, waist, everywhere. She screamed as they bit into her, strong enough Cassie could feel the disturbance as they siphoned from her. The lights in her eyes and on her skin stuttered and dimmed as she gasped for air. Her skin left the tendrils sizzling, but they squeezed tighter. No matter how she tried, Cassie couldn't get enough energy into her to stop them.

"Oh no you don't."

Cassie drew energy into herself, more than she thought possible, then seized a tendril with both hands. She twisted and tore at it until it ripped with a wet slurping sound. Smoke burned her nostrils and her arms, but she ignored the stench and the pain in favor of tearing tendril after tendril until Magnolia stood free.

Magnolia collapsed to her hands and knees. Burns covered

her arms and legs, and her blood wept from her skin in tiny rivulets. It pooled between her fingers as she tried in vain to catch her breath.

"Holy shit," Cassie said, kneeling next to her. She rested a hand on Magnolia's back, but this time her injuries stayed. "Are you okay?"

"Not in the slightest," Magnolia said. With shaking hands, she wiped at her face, which only served to smear the purple. "That seems like a lot of blood."

"It's okay, you've got more," Cassie said, because she had no idea how much blood a person could lose before it became a problem.

"Blood is what got rid of LeBeau," Magnolia said. Her eyes flicked up to the door.

Already, heat built again. Weakness settled in Cassie's muscles, and despair threatened the corners of her consciousness. She focused on Magnolia's face, on her breathing, and remembered their goal.

"Then blood is probably what we need now," Cassie said.

Two eyes appeared in the darkness. The Malevolence made another noise that sounded almost like a curse. The ship shifted again, tossing Cassie like a rag doll, ghost body or no. The Malevolence pushed energy into her every time she got close to a wall, making her just real enough to slam into it. Her body tried to fall apart and be sucked into the river, but she latched onto as much energy as she could and kept herself together.

The screaming and spinning slowed, then stopped, leaving Magnolia and Cassie both laying on the floor. One of them was significantly more banged up than the other. More blood streamed from a gash on Magnolia's leg, and a bruise blossomed under her left eye.

Something buzzed, but it wasn't from the engine room. It

took Cassie a moment to realize it was Magnolia's comm pad, which somehow managed to stay strapped to her chest with nothing but a crack on the screen. She groaned as she shifted it enough to tap the glass.

"Mags?" Korinne's voice came out echoey and warped.

"Yeah?" Magnolia's voice cracked.

"You okay? I'm trying to keep things steady, but the ship's fighting me."

Magnolia let out a weak laugh. "Yeah, same."

"I've got most of the alarms off though, and we're almost back in the gravity well to land. Are you two okay? Can you come back up here?"

At the suggestion, heat rolled over them, and the melting door between the hall and the stairs stretched to close the opening.

"What..." Cassie sat up and watched as the Malevolence sealed their only exit. She looked to Magnolia, who had her hand over her mouth as tears fell from her eyes.

"Mags? Are you—"

"I'm okay," she said, somehow managing to keep her tone even. "But we can't come back up quite yet."

The temperature rose further. The eyes reappeared.

"We can do this. We can finish this," Cassie said. She crawled to Magnolia and took her hand. This time their connection took, and Cassie drew from the ship and pushed energy into Magnolia. It couldn't heal all their wounds, but it at least patched a few of them up.

"I'll be there soon, okay, Rinne?" Magnolia said as both of them clambered to their feet.

"Okay," Korinne said, clearly not buying it. "Be careful. I love you."

"I love you," Magnolia said, choking on the words. More tears fell, and Cassie reached out to wipe them away.

"Keep it together," Cassie said, though she had none of her usual bite.

Magnolia squeezed her eyes shut and took a breath. When she opened them, they glowed once more. "It's going to fight her the whole time, huh?"

"Yeah. It wants to land around people. That's why Jocelyn sabotaged the landing sequence the first time around so they had to leave it in orbit," Cassie said. She'd watched the whole thing happen after following Jocelyn around like a lost puppy those few days after death.

Cassie kept her eyes on the engine room, and the engine room watched her in return. The flames came together again, warping her beloved machines as it siphoned from them.

"We're getting to it," she said. "We've just gotta hold on a little longer."

"Is this how you thought you'd spend the afterlife?" Magnolia smiled, showing off the blood smeared across her teeth.

"No, I thought there'd be more chains and crying," Cassie said. "Is this how you thought this trip would go?"

"No," Magnolia said. "I thought there would be a lot *less* crying."

"Well, we're almost done," Cassie said. "You've gotta make it out, otherwise Korinne will be so pissed at me."

"You're not the only one," Magnolia said. She rolled onto her hands and knees. With a trembling hand, she smeared her own blood across the floor until she made a recreation of the symbol on her pendant. It glowed faintly.

"That was a good idea," Cassie said, even as they watched her blood seep across the floor one millimeter at a time with the energy flow.

"Let's see if it does anything," Magnolia said, and clambered to her feet.

They both stared down the Malevolence as it finished forming, its bulk extending across the entire entrance to the engine room. There had to be something else they could do, something different.

"We've been playing kind of defensive," Cassie said.

"Speak for yourself," Magnolia said, affronted.

Cassie dug into the ship and took Magnolia's hand, letting the energy flow freely between them. Light appeared at her hands, and her eyes blazed like beacons. Straightaway, she threw another wave toward the door, slower and weaker than the first. A deep chuckle rolled from the engine room, and the eyes gathered in the door, fighting over one another to get the best view.

"It's gonna try and grab us again," Cassie said. "It's going to burn."

"Do you think we can burn it back?" Magnolia said.

Genius.

"Now you're thinking," she said with a grin.

The eyes shifted again, and the heat rose. A voice like rocks in a tumbler spoke. "You are mine."

Anger sparked in Magnolia. Cassie knew, because she could feel it rolling off of her.

"We are *not*."

Red tendrils shot out again, even more of them, reaching for both Cassie and Magnolia. But Cassie was ready this time, holding her arms up so she could still move despite the bondage. Instead of fighting the tendrils and the energy, she allowed both to pull and push and twist around her. The Malevolence could use its power to steal, but so could she. The symbol on the floor glowed, and smoke drifted from the tendrils above it. It helped, but it didn't completely cut them off.

They had to keep fighting.

Energy from the ship combined with the piece of Magnolia's magic. Cassie concentrated it on her ankles, burning the tendrils there. With her hands hot, she ripped the others, leaving the arms wriggling and dying on the floor. Magnolia changed her plan of attack as well, grabbing the tendrils like a rope and channeling sparking power into them. Bolts of lightning shot up the tendrils and through the door, making the Malevolence writhe and scream with a thousand voices.

"Keep going!" Cassie said.

She took two quick steps toward the door, the pull quickening her travel. The Malevolence learned from their attack and slowed the river of energy. It thickened the closer she got to the door, but she soldiered on until her skin felt like it was melting and her muscles and bones strained. Every step took all her effort to keep each post-mortem atom from breaking free.

"Fuck you," she seethed.

Lightning from Magnolia's powers shot around her. Cassie easily avoided them and crossed the threshold to sink her hands directly into the Malevolence with a battle cry.

Unfettered pain slammed into her, but she pushed back. As loud as she was, the Malevolence screeched above her, the sound of tearing metal and snapping rebar joining the cacophony. This close, elbow deep, she could feel its power and find its core—the pulsing crack in the wall where things blew on the first takeoff. Its heart beat there, a mangled, black, wretched thing. Nothing protected it except the being in front of her.

Cassie pushed.

The heart pushed back.

There wasn't enough dead air in her lungs for her to scream as she flew. She slammed into the wall, but the pain didn't end there. The Malevolence snatched both her and Magnolia in a vise-like grip and threw them around, spinning the ship until she didn't know what was up, down, or either side. Lights flashed around her, but whether it was Magnolia's powers or something else, she couldn't tell. Unable to latch onto the heart again, Cassie grabbed whatever she could and yanked, over and over until it stopped.

The Malevolence retreated, hurt but not defeated. It left the hallway hot and still, its anger simmering just beyond the door.

"Cassie?"

Magnolia was more than battered and bruised by this point. Blood dripped from her nose, her forehead, and her arms. While she kept her eyes on the ceiling, Cassie could see her stomach clenching in dry heaves.

"I'm still here." Cassie pulled herself together and moved next to her. She tried to put a comforting hand on her shoulder, but jerked the gnarled, chewed appendage back before she could make contact. The pain hit her then, pulsing with each wave of energy that passed through. She tried to grab onto it and heal, but it slipped like sand through her torn up fingers, carrying bits of her to the Malevolence on the ever present stream.

"Cassie, are you still here?" Magnolia swallowed heavily, and her breaths came in short gasps.

Keeping her hands tucked into her chest, Cassie scooted until she sat at Magnolia's head, then leaned down to rest her forehead against hers.

"I'm still here," she said. "I won't leave you."

Tears streamed from Magnolia's eyes, mixing with the blood and leaving clean tracks on her mottled skin.

"I don't know if we can do this," she said, her voice thick.

"We can. We can do this." Cassie hadn't truly cried in forever, but tears fell now, the draft dragging them away before they could hit Magnolia. They mixed with the purple flecks of

Magnolia's spirit departing too. "I'm here with you. We can do it together."

"Tell Korinne—"

"You can tell her yourself when we're done here."

Magnolia choked on a sob, clenched her eyes shut, and swallowed it down. A shudder ran through her.

"I don't know what to do. I can feel the power growing—any minute now it's going to lash back out. And I...I'm running on instinct, I don't actually know how to..."

Her eyelashes fluttered, and her eyes rolled. Cassie put her hand on her shoulder and tried to keep her tethered to consciousness. Energy slipped through them both without sticking. God, she was so *tired*.

"No, Mags, stay with me," she said, talking to herself as well.

Magnolia needed food, or water, or something. But Cassie couldn't even hold onto the energy, how was she supposed to use it to help? "Wake up." She shook her, as if that would help. She breathed deep, and even if she couldn't quite hold on to the energy, she could at least guide it to Magnolia. "Mags, wake up!"

Magnolia gasped and her eyes flew open, a sparkle of her prior energy in her eyes. Cassie startled and snatched her unburned hands away. Handprints stayed on Magnolia's shoulders. Part of them drifted away in the current, but the other part sank into her. The bruises beneath her skin faded from a dark purple to an iridescent green.

Eyes appeared in the door.

Cassie placed her hands on her shoulders again and pushed, earning another gasp from Magnolia.

"Cassie?" She looked her straight in the eyes.

Cassie nodded. "I have an idea."

CHAPTER 37
MAGNOLIA

From camera 15.3.20: [Magnolia stands; a blonde woman stands next to her]

"I HAVE AN IDEA."

Magnolia never liked hearing those words. Usually, they meant trouble. But at that moment, the sweet whisper of Cassie's voice lifted her spirit. Because for the first time in her life, Magnolia was woefully unprepared. And, if she was honest, outmatched.

"What's your idea?" The pain in her chest lessened, even if all the other aches persisted. At least one of her ribs had to be broken, and she continued to bleed from so many places she was surprised she had any blood left. Her head spun, and every breath hurt.

Cassie's hands rested heavily on Magnolia's shoulders, now more corporeal. Her voice sounded louder, more solid. "Its heart is at the back, close to the rift between this room and the outer floor. Did you see it?"

Magnolia had not. She hadn't even thought to look for it. "I think so," she lied.

Cassie smirked, as if she caught her fib. "Listen, you aim one of those big lightning bolts at that heart, and we're golden. I can see it, you can hit it."

"And what if we lose contact?" Contingencies were important, because if they failed one more time, Magnolia wasn't sure she had the gumption to try again—if she even survived the attempt.

"Well, that's the part I'm not sure you'll like," she said. "Remember how LeBeau sort of...combined with Korinne?"

"That's a very tactful way to say he possessed her," Magnolia said, somehow managing to find a bit of spite in her reserves. "But yes, I remember...oh. Oh, I see."

"Yeah," Cassie said with a grimace. "I'm sorry, I wouldn't say it if I didn't think it was our last chance. It won't be full on, but we'll definitely be very connected."

"It makes sense," Magnolia said. The air held a feeling of finality, and never in her life had she wanted to give up the way she did then. No amount of positive thinking could save them. Despite how much it hurt, she reached down and held the button on her comm pad. When it beeped, she said, "Call Korinne."

"Right now?" Cassie said.

"When else?" Magnolia said. It rang a few times before she picked up.

"You okay?" Korinne asked.

"I'm okay," Magnolia said. Another lie. "How close are we to the gravity well?"

"Super close. I know how to fight this son of a bitch now," Korinne said.

"Good. I'll see you soon then, just wanted to check in," Magnolia said.

"That sounds like you think you're about to die," Korinne said, and Magnolia nearly started sobbing all over again.

Cassie chimed in, "Not if I can help it."

"Take care of my girl, okay Cass?" Korinne said, and maybe Magnolia imagined it, but her voice sounded a little thick too.

"Oh, I'm your girl now, huh?" Magnolia asked.

"You sure are something," Korinne said. "Give it hell."

"Will do."

She disconnected the call and forced herself to roll onto her hands and knees.

"Note to editing Korinne," she said, hoping the video feed was live recording to the hard drive back in their rooms. "I love you. Don't forget that, okay?"

"Don't be so dramatic," Cassie said weakly.

"Fine. When we win, tell Korinne to sedate me," she said.

Cassie's hands moved to her back, right behind her heart. "Will do," she said. "You ready?"

"Ready as I'll ever be."

"I'll start slow."

Rumbles turned to vibrations which turned to shakes as the Malevolence gathered power, so "slow" was the last thing they needed. However, Magnolia was grateful for it as she felt the first flow of energy into her, making her heart rate spike and every hair stand on end. Pain lingered in her periphery, but it no longer choked her.

"Holy shit," she said. Her wounds continued to bleed, and her rib was definitely still broken, but the power calmed the pain enough so she could think.

"Okay, a little more..."

Cassie's voice rang in Magnolia's head, loud and clear. She could feel the pressure of her hands, and sense Cassie's body in the space behind her. It felt different, almost like Cassie was another living person and not a ghost.

"You have to hold it in," Cassie said. "Don't let it out."

Sure enough, the glowing bits shining on her hands broke off and flew through the door. The Malevolence gobbled them up as soon as they crossed the threshold. Magnolia took a steadying breath and concentrated, drawing the energy in.

"That's it," Cassie encouraged. The floor shook, hard, but of their own accord, Magnolia's knees softened and reacted to the movement with gentle, practiced ease.

No, those weren't Magnolia's reactions.

"Was that you?" she asked.

"Yep. Sorry, reflex," Cassie said. The ship swayed, and once again Magnolia absorbed the movement through Cassie's instincts.

The Malevolence grumbled. More eyes appeared, narrowed and fiery. It took a step forward, then another, breaching the doors and stepping fully into the hallway. The symbol glowed, and the Malevolence hissed, retreating past the doors. But it saw the same thing they did: Magnolia's blood chipping away, one piece at a time. Did she have time to redraw the symbol? She certainly had enough blood to do it.

Cassie cursed. "If we just—"

Magnolia never got to know what they should do, as tendrils shot out at an alarming velocity. Before she could move, they wrapped around her arms, legs, and torso, squeezing so tight they forced the air from her lungs. It didn't stop at one layer; more and more tendrils joined until a thick ring surrounded her, crushing her.

"Cassie!" she cried with what little air she had left.

"Working on it!" Cassie said in the back of her mind.

A surge of energy hit her heart. She felt alive, she felt like she was dying, she felt ready to fight. Her muscles clenched. Instead of trying to contain the power in her hands, she forced it from her every pore. It burned the tendrils, though they left their marks on her skin.

The stench of burning sulfur surrounded her as the tendrils withered away, the closest corpses fused to her skin from the rest pressing in. At that point, Magnolia couldn't tell if she simply felt the heat or if her skin was melting, but she continued until there was just enough space to pull her arms free.

She grabbed the two nearest tendrils, digging her fingers in until she felt the ghostly flesh break beneath her nails. Her hands lit up with power, and she forced it through. Feral cries of pain echoed through the space, and the Malevolence stumbled back beyond the engine room doors. The tendrils squeezed more, her ribs creaking and bending dangerously beneath the force.

"I can't see it," she said. The Malevolence was so encompassing, she couldn't get any details beyond its fire. Cassie continued to pour energy into her.

"It's in the back," Cassie said.

"I know, but I can't see it like you can."

So badly she wanted to lay down, to give up. But as the ship tilted again, she thought of Korinne, fighting to keep everything even for her.

No, she couldn't give up quite yet.

"You can do this," Cassie whispered.

A dip in the gravity hit, lifting Magnolia from the floor. Before the ship could right itself, the Malevolence lashed out.

They were ready this time. The tendrils wrapped, but Magnolia burnt them before they could take hold. Faster and faster they shot out, and together she and Cassie slapped them away one by one. Some managed to grab hold, but she pushed and pulled and yanked until they wrapped all the way up her arms, bruising the flesh and nearly pulling her shoulders from their sockets.

"Now!" Cassie said.

With a shout, Magnolia punched with all the force she could muster. Lightning shot up the tendrils. She tried to follow it as it slammed into the engine room, but there was no way for her to control it once it passed the door. Beyond there, her powers were unruly and wild. Even before the door, her control was tenuous at best.

"It's not working," Magnolia said.

In the back of her mind, Cassie grew still. "I have another bad idea."

"Oh, gods," Magnolia sighed.

"We just need to reach the door," Cassie said. "We reach the door, and we'll be able to see it."

"I'll need your eyes for that. Fully," Magnolia said. Which could only mean one thing.

"Are you sure?" Cassie asked.

"I welcome you with open arms," she replied. "Just don't steal my soul."

Cassie huffed a laugh. "Trust me, I'm fine just wrangling my own soul for the rest of eternity."

"Then let's do this."

Magnolia inched forward, making sure to control her progression. It wouldn't do to go through all this just to get swallowed up. Step by step, they moved until the door was right in front of them, the Malevolence itself staring her in the eye as if complimenting her audacity.

It was so hot, and there was so much power pulling at her. It tried to dampen her spirits and dislodge her soul. The thing wanted so badly to take her, but she couldn't—wouldn't—let it.

They were in the endgame now.

"Do it," Magnolia said.

"Yes?"

"Yes!"

Magnolia screamed as Cassie wedged herself fully into her. Her heart bucked, and her stomach rolled as a second spirit made room in her body. Even with her consent and concentration, her senses stretched beyond recognition. Cassie was a friendly ghost, but the possession still felt so wrong.

"Don't throw up yet, save it for when I leave," Cassie said, her voice as present as Magnolia's own thoughts.

"I hate this," Magnolia said.

"Me too."

Something locked down in her chest, deeper than her heart.

"I've got your soul. You're not going anywhere."

"That's a neat trick. Thank you."

Cassie scoffed. "Let's make sure it works before you thank me."

"Not the confidence boost I wanted." Panic flared somewhere in her middle, then simmered down.

"Sorry, forgot to control myself for a second there," Cassie said. "It won't be long, okay? Big shot with your powers, and then I can direct it to the heart."

The Malevolence tilted its head to the side, as if it could hear their conversation. A smirk cracked across its face. The heat was unbearable, the pain so complete Magnolia could barely think. But with the extra strength from Cassie, she held her stance.

"Let's do this."

It was so wrong, Cassie's soul scrunched in next to hers, but Magnolia ignored the sensation in order to focus on the well of power within her.

Everything paused. There was her, and Cassie, and the entity she needed to destroy. In her mind's eye, she saw

Korinne's face. She would do it for her, and for herself, and for all the souls this Malevolence captured.

She took a breath, gathered every bit of power she could, and pushed.

Lightning cascaded from her hands in great rolling waves. The violent eyes, so keen on watching, howled in pain at the bright light shooting through them. One by one they popped like balloons, shriveling into charred masses floating in the river of the Malevolence.

The Malevolence shot back, its piercing energy smacking into her left and right. But the conduit of energy Cassie created built a shield around Magnolia, protecting them both from most of the onslaught. Each hit sent sparks through her vision. The shield wouldn't hold forever, but it would hold long enough. It had to.

"Cassie?" She wasn't sure if she said it aloud or in her head.

"I'm almost there, keep going!" She sounded far away. There was a strain to her voice that Magnolia wanted to question, but the Malevolence fought against her with renewed fervor, distracting her. Magnolia hunkered down and battled back, holding steady with every clash and strike. A little longer now.

"Fuck!"

For a brief moment, Magnolia's shield faded as a remnant of Cassie's pain slipped into her. Seizing the opportunity, an errant tendril snuck in and sank into her leg. The pain was so deep Magnolia had to scream.

"Don't!" Cassie sounded clearer now, and there was an edge to her tone. "Don't you dare give up right now!"

Magnolia grit her teeth against the pain and tapped into the energy again. No longer did she try to harness it, instead letting it flow in and out without stopping. Her power concentrated, and a second later she could feel Cassie as she reached through

Magnolia and into the engine room. She pushed past the Malevolence, using its own energy against it as she searched.

"Almost there…" Cassie sounded so far away. More darts of pain shot through their bond, needling in an infuriating way. She was tired, so tired, and everything hurt on so many levels.

As Cassie moved closer to the heart, the Malevolence grew angrier, and fought back harder, but with her powers turned up to eleven, Magnolia sensed something else.

Fear.

The Malevolence was afraid.

Her body shook. Her muscles threatened to fail. She hadn't trained for this, had no idea what she was doing, wasn't ready—

"I'm here!" Cassie's voice sounded like an angel to Magnolia's tired ears.

"Kill it!"

Pain reverberated through her knuckles, an echo from Cassie. "Hold on."

"Did you just try to *punch it*?" The shock and distraction weakened her stance, and she slid forward an inch, nearly flush with the door now. If she fell in, she'd be done for.

"I need more power."

"I'm giving you all I have!"

"We need more, Mags."

Magnolia wanted to cry. Once again, she gave all she had, and it wasn't enough. Unless…

Unless she took the power from her shield and sent it to Cassie instead.

"Oh no, not like that." Cassie heard her thoughts, and knew her heart.

"It's the only way."

There was no fanfare, no declarations or messages. They no longer had the time.

"On three," Magnolia said.

"Mags—"

"You better be fast." Magnolia took a breath. The Malevolence reached out, its clawed hands aiming for Magnolia's heart. "One, two..."

She shifted the energy, dropping her shield and pushing it down the direct line to Cassie.

"Three!"

Pain ripped into her as the Malevolence lashed out. Cassie's fear lanced down the tether, but so did her determination. Magnolia dug her heels in and let her power go, no longer caring if it consumed her entirely.

Her light filled the room, past the door, latching onto every piece of the Malevolence. Its tendrils continued to wriggle around her, puncturing her skin, but the boiling power in the engine room froze in a brilliant stasis.

"Atta girl," Cassie whispered.

The Malevolence's eyes widened, its hand stopped in time.

"Give," it said, but its voice sounded weak and thin.

Magnolia didn't know if it lasted a few moments, minutes, or hours. She held the Malevolence in her grip, ignoring the pain and fatigue as Cassie dug into its heart with her bare hands and forced Magnolia's power through it.

Everything stopped. Then, the crash.

A shriek louder and deeper than anything a human could make exploded from the room. Cassie shot back from the heart and slammed into Magnolia, *through* Magnolia, landing as herself on the floor behind her. The power flooding from the room held Magnolia aloft as the Malevolence let out a dying breath.

Silence. Stillness. She crashed to the ground in a crumpled heap. Degree by degree, the temperature dropped. The ship stopped shaking, returning to a steady flight.

"Holy shit," Cassie said weakly. "We did it."

Magnolia didn't have enough breath to reply. She could feel the scrapes, the cuts, the stabs. More than one rib was broken now, she knew. There was so much pain in her body it almost numbed her. But she'd done it. *They'd* done it. Together.

She probably passed out, she wasn't sure. When she woke, she heard footsteps from behind her, audible now that there wasn't a cosmic revenant reaching for her.

"Mags?"

Rolling over was the hardest thing she'd ever done. There, at the door, stood Korinne. Eyes wide, face flushed, and the most beautiful thing she'd ever seen. Magnolia could see her gaze flicking between her and Cassie.

She smiled, wondering if her present state made this the creepiest moment Korinne had ever had with her.

"We won."

Her eyes rolled back, and she succumbed to unconsciousness.

CHAPTER 38

KORINNE

From camera 23.3.5: [the captain's chair swivels]

KORINNE REALLY NEEDED Magnolia to stop passing out on her.

Well, that wasn't fair. It wasn't like she could control it. But it would definitely make the next steps a lot tougher. Not to mention, she couldn't tell all the places Magnolia was hurt. She had a dark bruise under one eye and bled from a number of places. Did she have any broken bones? Korinne couldn't tell. Carrying her to the bridge would be a challenge. Luckily, she had a new accomplice to help.

Now that she got the chance to really look, she could see how it was hard to identify Cassie in life. She seemed skinnier than her morgue photo but didn't have any of the injuries, just long blonde hair and startlingly bright eyes. The stolen uniform fit poorly, even worse than the pictures from her investigation.

"So, uh." Korinne cleared her throat; it was still so weird to talk to a fucking ghost. "Can you help with this?"

"I'll try," Cassie said, holding up her ghostly hands, which were mostly opaque but shimmered between this layer of reality and the next. "I'm a little unstable though."

"Right, shit."

The ship shuddered and swung off course, which was a terribly inconvenient thing for it to do at that moment.

"Fuck!" The force shifted her insides. "We got pushed out of the gravity well again."

Clanks and crashes echoed from the engine room, and Cassie's eyes widened.

"The engines are giving out," she said. "The Malevolence was holding it together."

Between a ghost, a Malevolence, and her unconscious soul-mate or whatever Magnolia was, Korinne's mind threatened to implode. She would need *years* of therapy after this. Gravity dropped as the ship swung again.

"Cassie, if I find tools, can you help me fix whatever's going on in there?"

"Gimme a second." Cassie sprinted faster than light into the engine room. Korinne held her breath, waiting for news of the damage. Then, Magnolia stirred.

"Hey, take it easy. I got you," Korinne murmured, forgetting anything about the engines as she reached out to hold Magnolia's hand.

Magnolia knit her eyebrows and grimaced. "Fuck," she groaned.

"I'm gonna get you up to the bridge in a second, okay? There's a first aid kit. It's bound to have painkillers."

A boom sounded from deep within the engine room, followed by a muffled curse.

"What was that?" Magnolia asked, suddenly much more awake.

"Just Cassie, I think." Korinne smoothed her hair away

from her face and tried to stealthily wipe the blood from her cheeks. "Nothing to worry about."

"Cassie?"

"Yeah. Wild work, honestly," Korinne said.

Magnolia smiled. "She's nice."

"She's all right."

Cassie reappeared at the door. "I heard that," she said. "Kind of agree with the assessment. But we have bigger problems."

"What's it look like?" Korinne asked.

Cassie shook her head. "Bad. Really bad. Five out of seven engines are out of commission. Only way you guys are gonna land is if I can hold at least one of the last two together."

"Tell me how to fix it and I can do it," Korinne said. "I've got a working knowledge of the machines—"

"No," Cassie interrupted. "It would take too long. I can siphon energy from one engine and use it to power the other."

"That might take you out," Magnolia said, pushing herself up. Korinne moved to support her. "Cassie, you've already expended too much."

"I'm getting you two to the ground," Cassie said. She turned to Korinne. "This is the only way. Can you pilot it?"

Question of the day. "I can at least manage a crash landing," she said.

Cassie grinned. "If you can survive a Malevolence, you can survive a crash landing."

"I think I liked it better when Korinne couldn't see you," Magnolia said. Korinne and Cassie shared a conspiratorial grin, and for a second she forgot the other girl was dead.

Korinne's stomach leapt into her throat as the ship dropped from another wave in the atmosphere. She looked to Cassie, who had a grim expression of finality.

"It's our only shot," Cassie said.

Korinne nodded. "Let's do it then. Come on, Mags."

"No—"

Magnolia voiced her discontent, but Korinne hauled her to her feet and through the rapidly cooling hallway to the elevator. She just had to hope the electricity survived long enough for them to get to the bridge.

"So, like, do I have magic ghost powers now too? Or is Cassie just above her peers?" she said, trying to distract Magnolia from leaving their friend behind.

"You can only see them if they want you to see them," Magnolia said. She slumped against Korinne, and Korinne felt as blood seeped through her shirt. She needed to find a way to stop all the bleeding.

"You said that too fast. I think you're lying and you just want to be special," Korinne said, tugging her up higher so she could take more of Magnolia's weight.

Magnolia hummed, the closest thing to a laugh she could make. "Considering you haven't commented on anyone else hanging out here with us, it's an easy assumption." A smile hovered on her lips, which were a terrifying shade of mauve and swollen in two places.

"Mags, how bad are you hurt right now?" Korinne asked. The elevator finally arrived, and she hauled her onto it.

"Pretty bad, honestly," Magnolia said around a shallow breath. "Everything hurts."

"Anything broken?"

"So many things," Magnolia said.

"Well, we'll get you to the bridge, and then you can collapse until we land," she said.

"That sounds nice," Magnolia said as her eyelids drooped.

"Oh no, not yet," Korinne said, shaking her slightly. That must've hit some unseen injury, because Magnolia gasped and straightened. "No passing out."

"I'll do my best," Magnolia said.

The elevator slowed, and the doors opened, allowing Korinne to drag her to the waiting bridge. More alarms and flashing lights greeted them, but at least there wasn't any ominous red smoke circling the room, whispering that Korinne wasn't good enough and would likely kill them all.

"Thank you for coming to get me," Magnolia said as Korinne heaved her onto one of the chairs.

"I couldn't just leave you down there with Cassie. Did you see how hot she was? Ghosts might be your type, I don't know."

"Korinne," Magnolia said, not quite energetic enough to be a reprimand.

Korinne buckled the seatbelt over Magnolia's chest and lap. "I know the jokes are bad, but I'm very stressed right now, and you look like you almost died. Plus, there was a motherfucking ghost talking to me, so I have to cope the only way I know how." Korinne clenched her teeth to keep additional words from spilling out. One more weird thing and she'd lose her goddamn mind. "Not to mention, I have to land the *Arkana*."

"You can do it. You're the smartest person I know." Magnolia didn't comment on any other part of her statement, only leaned in to press a gross, semi-bloody kiss to her cheek. Korinne decided to wear the print as a badge of honor.

"Keep that confidence up. One of us needs it."

More alarms sounded, and new alerts flashed on the screen. Korinne was forced to leave Magnolia sitting there and return to the command center.

"I know, I know!" She slapped at the buttons to silence them, knowing the problem was unfixable. If she didn't cut the sound, she couldn't concentrate. Next, she grabbed the first aid kit from under the main desk and hooked it up to Magnolia, who sagged in the chair under her exhaustion. The bloodstains on her clothes were significantly wider now.

Before anything else, Korinne needed to stabilize her. If she didn't do that, it wouldn't matter how rough their landing was.

Pretending like she wasn't one loose screw away from a full on meltdown, Korinne set the med kit to run while she retrieved two stabilization packs. Magnolia closed her eyes and tilted her head toward the ceiling, wincing as Korinne sank the two needles into her thigh to dispel the saline and electrolytes.

"Doing great. Don't fall asleep on me, okay?" Korinne said, her voice shaking nearly as much as her hands.

"I'm awake," Magnolia mumbled.

"That was not very convincing at all. Okay, here goes painkillers." She sank another needle in, watching as the clear liquid drained from the syringe and Magnolia visibly relaxed.

"Oh, that's nice." She sounded peaceful, which somehow didn't make Korinne feel better. The med kit beeped, and Korinne's heart seized.

Three broken ribs.

Multiple deep wounds and burns.

Mild to moderate concussion.

Signs of internal bleeding.

"That bad, huh?" Magnolia said.

"You'll definitely need some medical attention when we land."

Korinne rifled through the med kit and hit Magnolia with every injection the kit recommended, then went to work rinsing her wounds with saline. Problem was, she didn't know where all of them were, or how deep they went. And the longer she took, the more the ship rumbled and drifted from the gravity well.

"Do it after we land," Magnolia said. The displays showed the planet surface as the ship rotated above it, the system trying in vain to track back to the right location. Everything trembled as the ship traveled against the current, fighting the pull of the atmosphere.

"No, we have time for a few bandages." Korinne ignored the alerts on screen which said they did not, in fact, have time for the bandages.

"Call the bots, they can do it," Magnolia said.

Korinne ignored the suggestion and went to work wrapping her arms with the long gauze strip from the kit. It would hurt like a bitch later, but would at least keep everything covered now.

"Korinne?"

"Last I checked, they went offline," she said. Any form of communication after Magnolia's last call had shut down, and she didn't know enough to bring them back on.

"Oh." Magnolia inhaled, which turned into a groan of pain. "Maybe hit me with some more pain meds, then."

"Got it." She pulled another injector from the kit and sank it into a solid patch of skin on Magnolia's upper arm. Her pupils blew wide, silver sparkling in their depths.

"Whoa."

"Don't get too excited now, baby." Korinne grabbed the captain's pristine white jacket and wrapped it around Magnolia's torso, hoping it applied enough pressure to keep everything secure. All she got from Magnolia was a low hum of discomfort as her gaze struggled to follow the movement.

"So strong." She poked Korinne's bicep.

"You're the one who beat an unholy horror," Korinne said. She rifled through drawers and cabinets until she found a stash of spare jumpsuits. That would have to do. She used the arm of it to wrap the hole inMagnolia's leg, which seemed to go all the way through.

"So smart," Magnolia said.

"You're high as fuck right now," Korinne said, grabbing another jumpsuit.

Magnolia giggled, then stopped as her ribs hurt. "Ow."

"I know, we just gotta get this ship on the ground and then we'll get you to a hospital."

Magnolia licked her dry, cracked lips. One drop of blood welled on the lower one. "You're scared."

"Of course I am, Mags. I'm depending on a ghost to hold a ship together, and I have to land it despite having nothing but theoretical knowledge. If I fail, we die." Korinne stood and went back to the command center, angry that once again her fear made her overshare.

"I had a similar thought earlier," Magnolia said. "If I can do that, you can do this."

"Yeah, well, you're tougher than me." Korinne glanced back to check and found Magnolia comfortable in the chair.

"No," Magnolia said.

"Yes." Korinne pressed a comm button for the engine room. Of course, it didn't connect. Shit.

She had to hope Cassie was ready.

Korinne took a deep breath, shook out her arms, and turned her head side to side, though her muscles were too tense for her joints to crack.

"Okay, ready Mags?"

"Are you recording?" Magnolia asked.

Korinne couldn't help it, she laughed and checked her comm pad. "Yes, I am."

"Good. I want the dissertation committee to be able to watch you do this," she said. "Wait! Come here."

In three quick steps, Korinne was back at her side. "What is it? Do you need another hydration pack? Or pain meds?"

"Shh." Magnolia grabbed her shirt and tugged until Korinne was close enough for her to place a kiss on her lips.

"Now is so not the time," Korinne said against her mouth.

"That was for good love, I mean luck," Magnolia said with a stupid grin.

Korinne blushed, and kissed her again for good measure. "Thank you, we're gonna need it. Now, hold on tight."

Korinne settled into the captain's chair and buckled her harness. She did her best to stabilize the alerts, then grabbed hold of the joysticks and circled the ship back into the appropriate zone.

Her class had been based on theory and reports. If anything went wrong, she'd have no clue how to fix it. She checked Magnolia one more time and found her utterly serene with hooded eyes and a gentle smile. If Korinne failed...

One last time, she had the radio sweep again, hoping for a response from someone, anyone. But whatever knocked their communications continued, leaving her to her own devices. She would cry, if she had the spare emotional availability.

On one of the engine room screens, she saw steam release and cloud the area.

Right. Time to go.

Korinne slid the ship into the gravity well. First step, alignment. Second step...

Shit, what was the second step?

Pressurize.

Without the Malevolence fucking around with the pressure and gravity generators, they worked nearly flawlessly as Korinne commanded them, stabilizing her in the chair.

"Ow," Magnolia said.

"Sorry!"

Now with everything stable, she located the thrusters on the upward side—the relative upward now—and fired them. Her organs lurched at the sudden movement. Next to her, Magnolia dry heaved, the pain meds not helping the nausea.

"Sorry, sorry."

She lowered the power. Steam covered another camera in the engine room. Oops.

Learning her lesson, she utilized short bursts at half power. According to her class, once they hit atmosphere, she could launch the auto landing, and they'd be fine. She just had to hit atmosphere the right way.

An alarm blared overhead. One of the remaining online engines was overheating. Korinne smashed the silence button and hoped it wasn't the one Cassie was running. They were close now, so close she could see the swirls of color from the atmosphere.

She'd grown acclimated to the vibrations of the ship, but they increased tenfold when it hit the first layer of gas surrounding the planet. Air squeezed from her lungs, and she fought to breathe, her fingers missing the controls more than once as she typed in the sequence for auto landing. How many times had she typed it for her exam? And now, it came back to her with ease.

A red error popped up, taking over the entire display.

Unable to support auto land. Return to orbit and run diagnostics.

Well, they could neither return to orbit nor run diagnostics. Even if one engine could support them for a full revolution, she wasn't sure Magnolia could go that long without proper medical care. She needed to land this thing, and land it now. Korinne's head swam, both with lack of blood and with the overwhelming situation.

She had to land the ship manually.

She hit the thrusters again, the resistance of the atmosphere sending flames licking up the side of the ship. Clearly this was the wrong move, as a separate screen popped up detailing all the bits and pieces of the ship sloughing off as they passed through. She was the worst anthropologist ever.

"Come on!"

She upped the thrusters again. A high-pitched whine preceded a deep boom as one went out, sending the ship into a spin. Through squinting eyes, she found the lever and lowered the thrust, then leaned over and vomited into the handy emesis canister next to the chair. Their spinning slowed, but they continued to careen through the atmosphere at breakneck speed.

An engine room camera went offline, overheated by the steam. Korinne had no choice but to keep faith in Cassie. Cassie could handle the engine, and Korinne could at least get the ship on land.

Korinne swiped her hands with grand gestures, clearing the screens so she could see the outside display. Flames blocked most of the cameras, but what she could see promised nothing but land for miles and miles.

"Hold on, Mags!"

More resistance fought them the deeper they went until they burst through the atmosphere in a shower of sparks and smoke. For a breath, she felt weightless in victory. Then reality —and gravity—set in.

The ship rocketed toward the ground. Korinne pulled back on the thrusters with all her might and swiped through the list, trying to find which ones she needed to slow their descent. But she was all turned around, and even if there was technically gravity around them, she couldn't decide up from down, left from right. They were going to torpedo themselves into an absolute nightmare, and it would be all her fault.

"L-4 and Q-9."

"What?"

Korinne whipped her head around, but no one was in the

room except her and Magnolia. It had to be her imagination, a panic-induced hallucination. But she checked the thrusters and those labels anyway, and found them online.

"Hit it."

Internal voice, she decided. Her subconscious, though it sounded like a middle-aged man.

She hit the thrusters, her body slamming into her chair as the ship slowed. In the corner of her screen, a countdown detailed their meters to the surface, plus their current velocity. She'd never been a math person, but something about the numbers didn't seem right. Even as the current velocity dropped, their distance to the ground decreased much faster.

"You'll have to change directions to slow it down more. Give yourself more space."

"Who the fuck—"

She turned around again, and at first Magnolia was the only person she saw. Then, a shimmer appeared at her shoulder.

"Cap...Captain?"

"Change direction, hit C-2 and G-6."

"Shit. Uh, okay."

So another ghost was going to help her. Cool. That was fine. Korinne hit the thrusters, changing their trajectory. Now, their speed and distance decreased at comparable rates, though the numbers were still red and an exclamation point blinked next to them.

"I took this job to land it like it was supposed to. We'll do it together," Captain Armand said.

"Glad to know pride kept you around long enough to help."

She was not going to think about ghosts right now, she was *not* going to *think* about *ghosts* right now—

"Cut C-2 and G-6, light up T-1 and P-9."

"That'll send us back—"

"Do it!"

"Okay!"

Korinne obeyed orders, full on freaking out and trying her best not to fall apart. They were close enough for her to see mountains now, and trees, and in the distance the skyscrapers of the main city in the area. The one the Malevolence wanted to get to so badly.

The ship swung back, like a leaf drifting to the ground, and once again Korinne made good use of the emesis container to her left.

"Back to C-2 and G-6."

Korinne groaned, but did it. "I hate this."

"This is how you live."

Back and forth they swung. Korinne kept an eye on the numbers in the corner, but they never left the red. They were going to crash into the surface, the ship would break into a billion pieces, and Magnolia was going to die, all because she wasn't good enough. This beautiful, glorious ship survived over four hundred years of space travel just to be destroyed by a post-doc with too much confidence.

"Don't stop!" the captain reminded her. Korinne pulled herself from her self pity and switched the thrusters. With each reversal, Magnolia flopped in her seat, barely contained by the belts. There was a green tint to her skin, but at least the pain meds kept her somewhat sedated.

"Almost there!" Korinne told her. She got a smile in response.

"You're right, we have to switch faster now," Captain Armand said. She could hear the warmth in his voice now, and the subtle accent.

"Faster? We're barely keeping it together as is."

"It's that or crash."

"Son of a—"

Korinne hated each change, but followed every instruction. They were a thousand meters from the surface now...nine hundred...seven hundred...

"It's not going to work!"

"Then you have to land at an angle and let the ground slow you the rest of the way."

"So crash land softer, that's what you're saying?"

"Pretty much, yes."

There was no way around it. At this point, a gentle crash was the professional recommendation.

If they survived, she was taking Magnolia on the longest vacation known to humans and Vaelish alike.

"Mags?"

No answer.

Korinne nearly broke her neck from turning around so fast. Magnolia's eyes were closed, and with the vibrations of the ship, she couldn't tell whether or not she still breathed.

"Focus!" Captain Armand snapped.

"But Mags—"

"If you don't land right, she's dead either way."

That was about the worst thing he could've said to her, though technically correct. Now she could see the tops of the trees and their individual trunks, as well as a winding turquoise river cutting through.

"I'm gonna destroy a forest!"

"There's grasslands over there!"

It was nearly impossible to steer the ship at that point, but Korinne leaned into it anyway, screaming as the structure rotated toward an open plain.

"Mags, hold on!"

"Hit A-1!"

Korinne did, and their trajectory shifted just enough to feel, though she still couldn't tell directions. She screamed, and

Captain Armand screamed with her as the vague masses turned into detailed landscapes.

A great, resounding boom blasted through the ship as they bounced on the ground, and her restraints squealed as they struggled to keep her in her seat. Captain Armand yelled letters and numbers in her ear, and she did her best to follow his instructions, her body flying in every direction as far as her harness would allow. Pain shocked her as her collarbones broke and her legs bruised. The harness made it feel like glass grew on the backside of her sternum, shredding her heart and lungs.

The restraints snapped.

Korinne flew. She did her best to cover her head, but it was nearly impossible as she slammed into the ceiling and then the floor. A bone cracked in her arm, and her head hit the metal so hard she saw stars.

Then the ship slowed. She slid across the floor and bumped into the chair as it stopped completely.

She'd done it.

With that thought in mind, she passed out.

CHAPTER 39

KORINNE

From camera 23.3.5: [Korinne groans]

IT DIDN'T EVEN HURT at first, to wake up. Sure, the ground was hard, and part of the chair dug into her hip, but she barely felt that. It wasn't until she attempted to move that the pain set in.

First, it was her neck, which caught and pulled as she straightened. Holding her breath, she wiggled her fingers and toes, exhaling once she felt them all move. This, of course, brought forth all the pain in her fingers and toes, which quickly spread to her arms, and legs, and torso.

She cracked open her eyes, then shut them quickly when assaulted by bright alarms and even brighter sunlight from the display. Despite being safely inside, she could almost feel the heat from the sun through the layers of the ship. Or perhaps there was a tear somewhere in the hull and she really was feeling the sun, and just hadn't noticed yet.

"Mags?" Turned out her throat hurt too, but she didn't

know if it was from injury or from screaming. "Mags, you okay?"

She braved opening her eyes again and turned her head a few degrees at a time, grimacing with the rapid onset whiplash. Magnolia was in her seat, but her eyes were closed, and her body sat very still. Adrenaline flooded Korinne then, and any pain she felt dissipated to a manageable level as she pushed herself up.

Her legs didn't want to hold her, so instead of running to Magnolia, she was forced to crawl and use the chair to stand up.

"Mags." She put a hand to Magnolia's cheek; her skin was warm, almost feverish. Once again she held her breath and lowered her fingers to Magnolia's neck, choking with relief when she felt a steady pulse beneath the surface. "Mags, wake up."

Magnolia, ever the contrarian, stayed dutifully unconscious.

"Okay, Korinne. You've got this," she said to herself.

She ran her hands over Magnolia, checking for any other injuries she might've sustained in the crash. While her wounds continued to seep, the bleeding seemed to have slowed. Korinne knew she should check herself for injuries as well, but if she found the injuries, then she would feel them, and she wasn't ready for that yet. So she stumbled to the console and used her one good arm to swipe away the alarms, finding the right one for communications.

She set the scanner running, hoping and praying they were back online. She sagged in relief when it picked up multiple nearby connections. She picked the first one and hoped it would suffice.

"Hello?" Her legs fatigued, the adrenaline buffering out of her blood now that she knew they were alive, and help was within reach. "Hello, my name is Korinne. I'm here on the *Arkana*."

She waited in the silence. Then, static crackled.

"*Arkana*, this is Onlow emergency services. We saw the crash and have help en route. How many injured?"

"Two, just me and Magnolia." Her hand shook as she held the comm button.

The comms crackled, and a new voice spoke to her. This person was gentler than the first.

"What's your name again, *Arkana*?"

"Uh, Korinne," she said. "My name's Korinne."

"Korinne, can you tell me how bad your injuries are?"

"Uh, I don't really wanna figure that out for me," Korinne said. "But Magnolia, she—she's got some...some...lacerations? Is that the word?"

"You can just say she's bleeding, it's okay."

"She's bleeding from multiple places. And has broken bones, and possibly internal injuries. And she's unconscious. I tried to patch her up the best I could, but I don't know if I did it right."

"You're doing great. Can you see us coming? Switch your display to east, you should have a visual."

Korinne did as instructed. The screen showed a wide expanse of plains, with tall green grass swaying in a gentle breeze. Large, boxy vehicles flew, kicking up dust with their turbines as they sped toward them. Korinne rested her head on the dash, dizzy with joy and relief.

"Korinne? Do you see us?"

She startled, having forgotten she was in the midst of a conversation, and fumbled for the comms button. "Yes, I see you. Thank you for finding us."

The person laughed. "Well, you're kind of hard to miss. Wasn't the smoothest landing."

"Yeah, well, I did my best. I'm sorry."

She didn't want to think about the damage they left in their wake. How many meters did they slide before stopping? She might've ruined a massive swath of forest with her inexperience.

"You did fine. No one was hurt, not even wildlife."

Korinne returned her forehead to the dash. The dizziness persisted, and when she looked down at her feet, she found a large gash in her calf and a pool of blood collecting on the floor. So that's why it was so hard to stand.

She slapped at the comms button again. "Hey, emergency?"

"Yes, Korinne?" They sounded far away.

"Turns out I'm bleeding too."

"From where?"

She swallowed, mouth suddenly dry, and reached down to put pressure on the wound. Blood normally didn't make her woozy, but feeling the muscle of her calf resting in her hand certainly did.

"Korinne?"

"What was the question?"

"Where are you bleeding?"

"My leg." She was so very tired. Maybe she could take a power nap, and then be ready by the time Onlow got to them.

"Rinne?"

Magnolia's voice was so quiet Korinne almost thought she imagined it. From far away, she heard the click of Magnolia's seatbelt releasing, and a thud as she fell to the floor.

"Rinne, you okay?"

"Don't..."

Unfortunately, she lost consciousness before she got the words out.

THE NEXT FEW hours passed in a blur. Emergency services arrived with great fanfare, yelling as they navigated the massive ship. Korinne woke up enough to greet them, then the next time she woke up, she was on a gurney with restraints over her body and a collar stabilizing her neck. She tried to turn her head to find Magnolia, but apparently her scream at the confinement meant she got a sweet dose of sedatives.

She faded in and out of consciousness, seeing the sky, and the ambulance, and the halls of a hospital. Every time she woke, she asked for Magnolia, and every time she was told not to worry, and to go back to sleep. If she didn't try willingly, they gave her assistance.

By the time she woke up fully, she was in a hospital room with a bunch of machines hooked up, and the world was dark outside her window. This unfortunate rise to consciousness was worse than the others, because it was accompanied by the pain again, and the sleep hovering at the edge of her brain for so long fled.

"Son of a bitch," she muttered. Her throat hurt to speak, and her lips cracked at the small movement. "Mags?"

There was no answer, but when she paused to listen, she heard other machines beeping off-rhythm to hers. She turned her head—they no longer restrained her neck—and found Magnolia in a bed next to her, looking pale and battered but alive. Korinne let out a long breath and relaxed for the first time in hours.

"Mags, you awake?"

Magnolia's eyebrows twitched, as did her arms on the sheets. Massive white dressings covered her forearms and hands, as well as a place over her eye. Green mottled her skin, evidence of healing bruises, and even though it all looked incredibly painful, she breathed deep and easy.

"Magnolia?" She tried one last time.

Magnolia opened her eyes. The violet irises were dimmer than usual, and the whites ringed in dark purple, but she was alive. Korinne grinned so big it hurt her lips and her cheeks, but she didn't care. She'd take the pain with the happiness any day.

"Hey there," she said.

Magnolia licked her lips slowly. "Hey yourself." Gravel rattled in her voice, but it was strong. She tried clearing her throat, but that didn't help. "How long have I been out?"

"Not sure, I just woke up too. How're you feeling?"

Magnolia paused, taking stock. "Okay, I think." Her eyes drifted to the IV pole next to the bed. "I think I've got some good stuff right now."

"Same." Pain crept up her spine and settled at the base of her skull. She tried rolling to her side, but that was even worse, so she stayed on her back.

"What happened? Did you land the *Arkana*?"

Korinne gave a dry chuckle, which quickly turned into the most painful cough of her life. Once she was stable, she said, "I didn't land it so much as crash it."

"Well, it worked. You got us here, and mostly in one piece too."

Korinne bit her lip, deciding whether to share the entirety of the story. In the end, how could she not? Especially to Magnolia.

"Captain Armand helped me," she said. "With the landing."

Magnolia's brows furrowed, then smiled as her meaning settled in. "He did, hmm?"

"Yeah. It was super weird, but..."

"You'll get used to it."

Korinne groaned. "I really don't want to. I'm fine with my two ghost sightings being the only ones I'll ever have."

"You may not have a choice."

"Now why would you go and ruin my day like that?" Her words didn't hit, since she still smiled so broadly.

"You're right. I'm just happy you agree now."

"That hearing ghosts can ruin a day?"

"That ghosts are real."

Korinne laughed again, and Magnolia joined her. "Yeah, yeah, yeah. You were right, I was wrong. And I'll tell the whole interstream about it."

"Good. It'll make the perfect ending to our series." Her smile faltered, as if she just heard the words she said aloud. Korinne's heart sank; after all they'd done together, and all they'd been through with this final trip, she suddenly feared the idea of the end.

"But *we're* not done, right?" Korinne asked.

Magnolia pressed her lips together, a purple blush appearing between the bruises on her cheeks. Her eyes shimmered with unshed tears.

"Do you mean you want to do another show?"

"You know damn well that wasn't what I meant." Spurred on by the need to be dramatic, she tried rolling over again, this time succeeding. Sitting up was a terrible idea, but she did it anyway so she could look Magnolia full in the face.

"What did you mean, then?" Magnolia asked.

"I mean that I meant what I said yesterday." She wished she could get up and pace, but had to settle for swinging her leg off the edge of the bed. "I love you, Mags. I want the tiny apartment and growing old and waking up every day next to you."

Magnolia's tears fell, and she gave a watery laugh. "Till death do us part?"

"Cheeky asshole," Korinne huffed. "Till death, and after.

I'll haunt the shit out of you if I go first. And if you go, then I guess I can talk to a third ghost during my lifetime."

Magnolia laughed. "You're terrible at romantic speeches."

"Did you expect me to be good?"

"No." Her smile was so big it looked like her cheeks might burst. "But it was still perfect."

"Does that mean you agree?" She didn't want to push anything, didn't want Magnolia to feel like she had to commit before she was ready. But it would be nice to hear for certain.

"Yes, Korinne, I agree." She said it with a hint of sarcasm. Then, with all seriousness, she said, "I love you, too. And I want to be with you, in whatever capacity life takes us."

"Oh, good."

She almost felt more relieved from that than by discovering Magnolia was still alive. She took a gamble and used her IV pole to stand, leaning on it as she limped the few feet to the next bed. Magnolia scooted as much as she could, giving Korinne just enough space to sit on the edge. Korinne sat gingerly, making sure not to jostle her body or press against her bandaged arms. Her muscles struggled to support her as she leaned over; she had to awkwardly rest her forearm on the pillow next to Magnolia's face just so she could bend over and kiss her.

Their lips were chapped and bruised, and both of them had a layer of grime the hospital couldn't sponge bath away, but the kiss was sweet, and pure, and everything Korinne hoped for.

"Just what in the seven hells is going on here?"

Korinne snapped back so fast it sent her head spinning and nausea climbing up her chest.

"I'm sorry, I—"

A tall man with dark skin and locs down to his shoulders stood in the doorway, his muscled arms crossed over a broad chest and one eyebrow raised in question. He wore a light blue medic uniform, but Korinne didn't know if that meant physician, nurse, or something else entirely.

"I don't care about the kissing bit." He waved that concern away. "I care about the fact that you're out of bed, without socks or an assistive device. You have to call for something like that."

"Calling you would've ruined the mood," Korinne said, earning a knee to the hip from Magnolia.

"You're getting back in bed."

He strode in, and for a second Korinne thought he might lift her like a sack of root vegetables, but the hand he placed on her back was gentle and respectful. "Come here, take my hand. The IV pole is not as sturdy as it looks."

"Uh, thanks." Korinne took one last look at Magnolia, who was struggling not to laugh.

"Unless you want to use this time to take a trip to the restroom?"

Korinne thought about it, and found her body wasn't making any requests. "Uh, no, I'm good..."

"Grayen," he said, pointing to a screen on the wall. Sure enough, it displayed his name under *nurse*. It also held other information, like their physician and their waiting messages.

"Thanks, Grayen." Korinne took his offered hand. Now that all her anxiety inducing events were over and she wasn't fueled by fear, it hurt a lot more to walk to her bed.

"Listen, I'll just move your beds next to each other, okay?" He sat her down and carefully helped her under the covers.

"That would be pretty nice, yeah." She glanced at Magnolia, who confirmed with a nod.

"Excellent. No more unsanctioned trips, okay? Not with that leg. Wait until the physios bring you an assistive device and teach you how to use it. If you fall, you owe me ten credits for the paperwork I have to fill out."

"Noted." Korinne couldn't help but grin. Grayen was good at his job, and she was very grateful for it. He did as he said, shifting IV poles and beds until Korinne could easily reach over and rest her hand on Magnolia's bandages.

"Hey, Grayen?" Magnolia asked, speaking for the first time since his entrance.

"Yes?" He stopped fidgeting with line placement, giving her his full attention. He might not see the turmoil within her, but Korinne certainly did.

"My hands, are they... Will I be able to use them again?"

Grayen gave a gentle smile. "You'll have some limitations, but should be able to do most anything. It's going to take a long time, and there's gonna be scars. There were some pretty bad burns all the way to your elbows, but luckily with your Vaelish heritage and some great skin grafts, you're gonna be just fine."

She exhaled and relaxed fully into the pillows. "Thank you."

"Don't thank me, you can thank your physician, who I'm gonna go grab now." He finished their set up, changed a few sections of the board, and made sure they could reach the call squares on their beds. "Now, do you need anything before I go?"

"No, thank you," Korinne said. He gave them a salute and left. "How're you feeling, Mags?"

"I can handle scars," she said, but there was still a layer of turmoil beneath her words.

"Are you wondering if I'll change my mind because of some scars?"

She kept her eyes on her lap. "Maybe."

Korinne rolled over, much closer now, and kissed her swollen cheek.

"You're stuck with me, Mags. Some scars aren't gonna change that."

A tear escaped, and Korinne kissed it away. Magnolia shifted so their heads rested together.

"I love you, you know that?"

"I do," Korinne said. "But it's always nice to hear."

The physician came later, detailing the specifics of their injuries and the steps of their healing. She wanted them to stay on Capa Emphara for the entirety of it, warning that space travel might not be in their best interest at the moment. After their most recent trip, they were more than willing to spend some extended time planetside.

"Oh, Doc, do you know where all our stuff is?" With all the downtime in their foreseeable future, Korinne wanted all their gear.

The physician paused. "I can ask around. It's either here in storage, or your assistant gathered it for you. But I'll find it."

Korinne smiled and shifted her elbow over, just enough so her and Magnolia touched. They'd get their gear back, and she'd be Magnolia's hands, cutting and editing it all.

They had one hell of a video to drop.

CHAPTER 40
CASSIE

From camera 3.2.9: [a dog barks]

IT TOOK three months for them to move the *Arkana* from her crash site to her final resting place, which was good since it took Cassie three months to stitch herself back together. During that time, Cassie's consciousness hung out in the engine room, listening and watching as a cleanup crew from Capa Emphara catalogued the damages and brought in expert after expert to hypothesize the source of the destruction. Since none of them would reach the actual conclusion, Cassie was happy to sit in the back and laugh at all their ridiculous measurements. Baxter showed up a few days later, complete with his ball and his shiny little eye, no signs of red anywhere. She carried him around for two days before continuing their eternal game of fetch.

With all the engines off, most of the ghosts faded back to the in-between or managed to cross over, but Cassie forced herself to stay awake, feeding on the energy of the little electronics the curators brought and the emergency reserve current they couldn't turn off. She listened for news of Rinne and Mags. They were alive when emergency services retrieved them, but she didn't know if they survived outside of the ship.

Once she could keep herself together enough to travel, Cassie floated up to the bridge, fully taking advantage of her ghostly abilities. It almost wrecked her to turn the display on, but it was worth it to see the rolling hills and brilliant landscape of a whole new planet.

Technically, Cassie had never set foot on a planet before. She'd been born on the *Arkana*, and died before it landed. Maybe she could try here; with the green grass and the shimmering sky, it seemed like a good spot to let herself drift apart for eternity if her plan went tits up. She was ready to die for real this time—

Until she saw the *Covenant*.

The *Covenant* wasn't as big as the *Arkana*, but she was prettier, gleaming in the sunlight like a brand new ship. Would the restoration crew do that to the *Arkana* too? Make her better than Cassie'd ever seen her?

That was when the really bad idea hit.

She didn't know if she could hold herself together out there in the world. Furthermore, she didn't know if she could hold herself together on the other ship. But she was sure as shit going to try.

The man in charge of the safety crew apparently didn't want her to succeed, and kept cutting the power manually so he could *assess circuitry and electrical* and *prevent the whole thing from blowing up*. Unfortunately this limited the energy she could steal, and she wanted to be at full capacity when she conducted her potentially lethal and final experiment.

Saving up felt like it took another entire lifetime, but then the day came. She had enough energy, she had enough courage, and the ship no longer held a living night crew that might be privy to her demise. She went to the loading dock, the site of her death, and gazed across the open area between the two ships. If this was the end, it would be a sweet, sweet irony.

She jumped.

Cassie didn't plummet to the ground, instead floating gently toward it. She held her breath, the breath she didn't need, as her feet touched the grass. Just like on the ship, she had to work to keep herself in one piece, but unlike the ship, energy was all around her. It was in the air, and the soil, and everywhere in between. The place was boiling over with it, and strengthened her as she took off toward the *Covenant*.

As she walked, she realized she no longer limped. When she reached up to touch her head, she felt her skull for the first time in decades. With this new information, she sprinted full tilt until she reached the wall of the *Covenant*. The nauseating sensation of passing through the wall didn't hit as hard as usual, but perhaps that was because of every drop of hope coursing through her.

The layout was just similar enough for her to move quickly and with purpose. A few other ghosts, all dressed in the same odd white garb Rose used to wear, glared and spat as she ran by. Whether or not they knew she was on the wrong ship didn't matter. What would they do, execute her?

The *Covenant's* hospital was much nicer than the *Arkana's*; if Cassie remembered right, they were much stricter when the influenza broke out, so perhaps they weren't overrun like the *Arkana*. Here the ghosts had a much more varied wardrobe, from the jumpsuits Cassie was familiar with to more traditional outfits from the very first Earth dwellers. Any other day, Cassie might've stopped and chatted, but she only had eyes for the beds, looking for the intensive care unit.

Even if every spot was built to be identical, Cassie knew

Rose's bed right away. There was the chip on the wall, and the red electrical outlet. Whoever was in charge of restoration even left her rosary, or a replica, looped on the bedrail. She paused at the door; there were no ghosts in sight. It occurred to her that she might have miscalculated. She had a Malevolence keeping her captive, but Rose didn't.

But then the air shimmered. A shadow appeared at the edge of the bed.

And then, she was there.

Rose was even more beautiful in person than online. Though illness took her from life, death became her, breathing an energy into her that the virus and machines sucked away. Loose, dark curls fell over slender shoulders, and when she looked up with those eyes—those beautiful, deep brown eyes—Cassie fell in love all over again. The white dress, which seemed so stuffy and old-fashioned, practically flowed off her frame. Her prosthetic arm clicked and whirred as she flexed the wrist, an old habit that her soul remembered, even when her mind forgot.

"Cassiopeia?" She had a musical voice, when not relayed over thousands of kilometers.

"It's me, Rose. I'm here." Cassie didn't have a heart anymore, but the space behind her ribs tightened painfully, and her eyes burned.

"Are you real?" Rose placed the prosthetic hand on her sternum, those pretty eyes sparkling. Her chest rose and fell in quick succession.

"I am." Cassie could see her own feelings mirrored in Rose's face. She'd been uncertain this plan would work, and even less sure the feelings they shared in life were real enough to transfer to death. "I'm real, and I'm here."

Rose stood, and in three long steps Cassie was across the

room and wrapped in her arms. She was also sobbing like a child, but she'd never admit that.

"How is this possible?" Rose cried as well, though she looked much better doing it. With tender fingertips she brushed Cassie's tears away. "Is this a dream?"

"No, my love," Cassie said, and God, it felt so good to say it out loud to her, without fear, and without a screen between them. "It's not a dream. We crash landed here, and I hoped... I didn't know if this would work, but I'm here."

"I can't believe it. I..." Her eyes flicked across Cassie's face, taking in all the details. "We finally have our time."

Cassie leaned forward, resting her forehead against Rose's. "We literally have forever."

And she kissed her.

Now, how a kiss could be even better in death than it had ever been in life, Cassie would never know. But that kiss felt like stars aligning, like the universe smiling, like the heavens opening up to bless them specifically. She just had to die and live as a ghost for sixty years to get her happy ending.

Reluctantly, Cassie pulled away, giving Rose space to ask, "What do we do now?"

"Well, I'm sure as hell not leaving you," Cassie said. At Rose's pained expression, she said, "What?"

"I just—" Rose glanced around the room, "I don't know if I trust them here. Any time I've come to, it's been difficult. Most of them were there the day I died."

The day they'd been on a call, the day they'd said too much to each other. Cassie paused and let the emotions of the ghosts around her sink in. Sure enough, there was judgment, and turmoil, and more than a little animosity.

"Then come with me," Cassie said. "Everything is fine on the *Arkana*. I even have a dog. We can..." She didn't expect herself to choke up, but here she was, strangling over some feelings. She cleared her throat. "We can be together."

Rose's eyes widened, and her lips parted. "Really?"

"Really. Will you come with me?"

Maybe it was wrong of her to ask Rose to leave the only home she'd ever known, but all she could think of was finally getting the forever they promised each other.

"Rose, come with me. Please."

More tears fell. Rose said, "I want to, but I'm not sure I know how."

"I'll teach you. I'll teach you everything."

Rose pressed her lips together, steeling her resolve. "I trust you."

"Good." Cassie smiled and stepped close again, holding her tight. She murmured against her ear. "Feel the currents in the walls and the lights. Picture it flowing into you. You won't need much to get across the gap, but you'll need more than this."

Cassie followed her own directions, gathering extra energy and pushing it toward Rose, teaching her how to feel for it and take it. As they stood there, Rose became more solid in her arms, her skin warmer, her hug stronger. Soon, she could feel her breathing against her, tickling her neck.

"You got it?" Cassie asked.

"I think so."

Cassie kissed her again, and this time she could taste her skin and feel every ridge of her lips. Rose responded in kind, kissing her fully, hungrily, making up for all the years they were left waiting and wanting.

Outrage rose around them as the bigoted ghosts of centuries past raised their concern at their love, but Cassie and Rose only had eyes for each other. And now that Cassie had hidden knowledge, she didn't hold back, grabbing Rose's arm with one hand and flipping the ghosts off with the other.

"See ya, fuckers!"

Rose didn't ask how Cassie knew the layout of the *Covenant* so well, she only laughed as they ran through the halls. They reached the loading dock and stepped to the edge. The *Arkana* sat so close, closer than it had ever been in space.

Cassie took Rose's hand. "You ready?"

Rose's smile was bright and perfect. "Ready."

They jumped.

She dragged Rose away. Away from prying eyes and bad memories, back to where Cassie knew the halls, knew the ghosts, and knew exactly where they could live—or die— forever.

CHAPTER 41
MAGNOLIA

From camera 87.5.1: [low battery error]

MAGNOLIA THOUGHT RETURNING to the *Arkana* would be scary, or painful, but once she entered she felt nothing but peace. They came without cameras or fanfare, with a simple goal in mind.

Most of the ghost activity had subsided with the ship powered down, but whispers of them followed her as she and Korinne walked through the hall to the elevator, her partner chattering away about her job on the restoration crew.

"—the guy formatting the recipe book is almost done, and he keeps bringing samples to... Are you listening?"

"Hmm? Recipes?" Magnolia had, in fact, *not* been listening. To Korinne, at least. Her attention was on the little ghost following them.

"Yes, recipes. So he's been baking everything and bringing it to the building apparently, and I tried Susan's cookies. They were incredible—you're gonna love them." Korinne touched the button for the elevator and sat back, idly reaching for Magnolia's hand as they waited. It still didn't feel the same as before the burns, between the damage and the silicone-laced elbow-length compression gloves, but she was happy for hands that worked, even if they were scarred.

"If I'll love them, why didn't you bring any home?"

Korinne shrugged. "Honestly wasn't sure of the protocol around it until the end of the day when I saw people loading their pockets. I'll bring you some next time, promise."

The elevator arrived and they boarded. Magnolia didn't know where they were going or what they were looking for; this was Korinne's trip more than hers. The little ghost joined them, and when the elevator hummed to life, she saw a glimpse of his form, specifically the wagging tail.

Baxter.

In the six months since their grand adventure, their videos had been viewed over ten billion times across the six planets of the system. On royalties alone, they had enough to retire on Capa Emphara with a cute little apartment, though Korinne had continued on to successfully defend her dissertation and join the crew. Then came the interview requests, and the psychological analyses, and the evergreen comments complimenting their acting and editing. But soon the hype would die down, and they could start their actual lives again.

"You okay?" Korinne rubbed the back of Magnolia's hand, gently smoothing the scar tissue beneath. She always helped Magnolia with massaging the scars, and the tickling tingle felt weird and good at the same time.

"Yeah, I'm fine. There's just a lot going on around us right now."

It wasn't a lie. Around them, ghosts came out of the metal-work, recognizing them as the two girls responsible for terminating the Malevolence in the engine room. They overwhelmed Magnolia with their feelings of praise and well-wishes, making tears prickle behind her eyes. But no matter how she searched, there was one presence she couldn't find.

"Do you need your pendant?" Korinne asked, her hand going to her pocket. Magnolia shook her head.

"Not yet." She was still learning how to use her powers on the day to day, and hadn't quite decided if she'd keep them or wear her pendant again. Maybe she could help the ghosts cross over, like her grandfather before her.

"Okay. In that case, back off, ghosts. We're doing stuff." Korinne swatted the air like trying to get rid of a fly.

The ghosts didn't back off, but Magnolia was fine with it. Their support helped her as they walked across the ship—had it always been this big?—to the dining room.

"Wait, do I get cookies now?" she asked as Korinne led her to one of the tables near the kitchens. It had a white tablecloth and sparkling silverware, as if they really were in the upper elite of the *Arkana* passengers.

"Eventually, yes," she said, letting go of her hand so she could pull a chair out for her. Magnolia sat with grace, smiling as Korinne took the seat next to her.

"You're enjoying this way too much," she said.

Korinne scoffed. "I believe I'm enjoying this a normal amount, thank you very much."

A server slipped out of the kitchen, dressed in a sharp black outfit and carrying wine and glasses. She set the glasses down before pouring their drinks, exchanging pleasantries like any fancy restaurant before returning to the back.

"There's no menus," Magnolia said, wondering if she'd missed something. Did Korinne ask her to review one before they came back here? She didn't remember.

"Correct, no menus," Korinne said. She reached over and took Magnolia's hand in hers. "Ages ago, I set up a nice, fancy dinner for us after we landed. Obviously, that plan went awry, so I networked a little and got them to make all your favorites for tonight."

Magnolia's jaw dropped. "You did?"

"Absolutely." She tugged Magnolia's hand so she could kiss her glove-covered fingertips. "We deserve a happy ending for this place."

"We do indeed," Magnolia said, her heart full to bursting.

As promised, the waiter brought out course after course of all Magnolia's favorite foods—and Korinne's, too—until both of them were stuffed to the point of discomfort.

"Come on, let's walk it off," Korinne said, once their plates had been cleared. Magnolia tucked her hand into Korinne's elbow and they strolled out. It felt so different, walking with real gravity instead of the fake stuff the ship had. Not to mention all the ghosts crowding around them.

She assumed Korinne had no route in mind for their walk, but as she led her further and further from the main entrance, Magnolia realized she had a plan. For one split second, she wondered if Korinne might propose.

Then, she saw the signs for the jail. Ice settled in her stomach.

"Can I have my pendant now?" Magnolia said. Wordlessly, Korinne dug into her pocket and handed it to her. But Magnolia didn't place it around her own neck; no, she clasped it around Korinne's, so the circle landed right in the middle of her chest.

Korinne swallowed and pulled Magnolia close, laying her lips against her temple. "Thank you," she whispered.

They fell silent as they entered the room. With the lights on, it felt smaller than it had in the dark. Korinne glanced at Magnolia out of the corner of her eye, and Magnolia shook her head with a smile. Only one ghost was here, and Baxter wasn't going to cause them problems any time soon.

One step at a time, they moved to the back of the room. In the light, the cell looked so small, so ordinary. The restoration teams couldn't quite get the seal off the metal bar, though now it just looked like graffiti.

One last thing, for closure.

"Still me?" Korinne asked.

"Still you." Magnolia squeezed her hand. "Always you."

Neither one of them had been able to stomach watching that part of the investigation, instead outsourcing it to their production assistants. Magnolia slipped her arm around Korinne's waist, tugging her close and holding her as they stared at the place that caused so many problems.

"I'm proud of you," she murmured.

Korinne nodded.

"Thank you." She let out a long sigh. "I can't believe we're really here, you know? After everything."

"I agree." Baxter came closer, trying to join in the affection. "I'm glad I'm here with you."

Korinne met her eyes and smiled. "I'm glad to be here with you too."

Magnolia kissed her lips this time, tender and warm. After all this, their job wasn't over. It was just changing.

"Come on, that's enough ghost stuff for today," Korinne said. "I'm ready to go back home."

Home. Oh, how lovely to think of their little nest together. Warmth spread through Magnolia at the very thought.

"Yes. Let's go home."

Baxter followed them all the way to the front entrance. Only then did Magnolia lower herself, with Korinne's help, and sit in front of him. He was a happy dog, of course, but he was also confused, and lonely. And a good test subject. Two other ghosts appeared, and she could just see the outline of Cassie and someone else.

Magnolia peeled her gloves off, displaying the raised, angry scars on her forearms. Korinne didn't comment, didn't ask what she was doing. She only shifted so her leg touched Magnolia's knee; she was there if Magnolia needed her. The dog wasn't afraid of her scarred hands, moving closer and wagging his tail with more ferocity.

"You're a good boy, hmm?" She tried to summon the energy from within, and felt it stutter. "You're just missing your person."

"He is." Cassie's voice was barely a whisper. "I took care of him as well as I could, though."

Magnolia tried the energy again, and this time knew where it got stuck. After closing her fingers a few times and stretching them apart, the energy trickled through her forearms and wrists and settled in her hands. When she pushed, the dog accepted it, and she could see his scruffy, white fur and name tag.

"What do you say, Baxter?" she asked. "Ready to move on?"

Baxter wagged his tail and rested his chin on her hand, his one eye closing with happiness. Magnolia inhaled so deep her ribs popped, then steadily released the air, along with the current to show Baxter the way. Technically, he had the choice to stay. But he would also sense his person on the other side, who probably looked for him the same way he looked for them.

His little broken tail moved at a sonic pace, his eye wide open and focused somewhere beyond her. Bit by bit, he faded away, running off to spend forever with the person he loved most.

When her adrenaline faded, Magnolia found herself sweating and exhausted. Her forearms ached something terrible, and the scars had changed to a dark purple, marbling over her skin. But pain meant nothing in that moment.

"You okay?" Korinne asked as Magnolia wrestled the gloves back on. They soothed the pain minimally, enough for her to reach up and take Korinne's offered hand.

"I'm fantastic," she said.

Korinne smiled. "Yeah, you are. Now come on, I know you need at least an hour nap after that."

She slipped an arm around Magnolia's waist, an affectionate gesture to help her mobility. Every injury she got from the Malevolence flared to life again, and she knew her body would complain for a long time about that small moment. But before they could leave, she paused and turned to Cassie.

"Who is it?" Korinne asked.

Magnolia couldn't help but smile, gesturing with her head at the two spirits next to them.

"Guess who's here."

"Oh. Oh!" Korinne spun, and technically looked a little to the left of where Cassie stood. "Cass! Glad you're still around. Never got to say thank you for holding everything together."

The lights flickered as Cassie siphoned energy. "Tell her she's a shit captain, and not to quit her day job."

Magnolia giggled and relayed the message.

Korinne barked a laugh. "Yeah, well, I wasn't aiming to put it on my resume, but shit happens."

The second spirit moved closer to Cassie and also soaked in some energy. There was enough for Magnolia to see long, curling hair, and the metal of a prosthetic limb. Her jaw dropped.

"Is that...?"

Cassie didn't answer this time, but the happiness radiating from the two of them was more than enough answer.

"What? What did she say?" Korinne asked. Magnolia's cheeks hurt from smiling.

"She went to the *Covenant* and spirited her girlfriend away." Tears prickled the back of Magnolia' eyes. There was so much joy it threatened to overwhelm her.

"Atta girl," Korinne said. "Happy for you two."

"She's happy for us, too." Magnolia took a step back. "We'll be around, okay Cass?"

There was a surge of emotion from the two ghosts, too muddied for her fatigued senses to distinguish. But she did know they were all positive. Magnolia turned to Korinne.

"Ready?"

Korinne smiled and kissed her forehead. "Ready. Let's go."

There was a lot of work to be done, and a long road ahead of them. They'd survived space travel, homicidal paranormal monsters, and judgmental internet comments, all to reach this point. After five years, they had nothing left to do but live out their dreams.

They walked down the ramp and left the *Arkana*, but it wasn't the end of their journey. This time, it was the beginning.

ACKNOWLEDGMENTS

Gah, where to begin?

This book has been the most fun to write, but also the most challenging. And without my friends and family, it would continue to sit in my hard drive instead of coming to life in the final form you see today. I wrote the first draft in a mad dash in 2022, and it has plagued me ever since. It is SO different compared to how it started, but the heart of it has always remained the same: *Buzzfeed Unsolved* meets *Tucker and Dale Vs Evil*. Cassie, Korinne, and Magnolia will always be so near and dear to my heart, and I'm so happy to finally share their adventure with you.

First, to my husband. Thank you for listening and giving me the space to work on this, as well as hyping up the concept. I couldn't do this without you.

Second, to my bestie Kaela. How many times did we have to whiteboard this story? Way too many. Thank you for your patience, your insight, and your impeccable editing skills. Without you, this book would literally not exist. Hell, without you EYE may not exist. Kind of like the first mate.

Third, to my writing group: Ali, Ana, Angel, Ariel, Jaci, Loren, Maia, Matt, Nic, Pat, and Tiffany. All of you play such an important part in my life, and I am completely obsessed with our discord. Thank y'all for always being in my corner and helping!

To the rest of my family, be it my mom, my in-laws, or my

work family, thank you for always supporting me. Thank you for listening to me, and for encouraging me to chase my dreams.

A special thank you to Averil (@bookishaveril) who made amazing character art for me and straight up designed Magnolia's pendant, Carmen Di Mauro (@carmen.dmdesign) who created the stunning cover, Charlie Arpie (@charliearpie) for the AMAZING title page and chapter headers, and Alicia MB (@alicia.mb.art) who delivered my first saucy art. These amazing artists took it upon themselves earlier in 2025 to host a giveaway for an OV indie author, and I was lucky enough to win and work with these beautiful humans. Y'all truly gave me the push to be brave and finish this book. Thank you.

Finally, to Ryan and Shane of *Buzzfeed Unsolved/Watcher*. They don't know it, but they inspired this 100%. This may sound like I ship them—I don't. They're real people, not characters. But the skeptic vs. believer hilarity that they have had me giggling for hours on end and kept me fueled as I edited this book from a hot mess to what we see now. So thank you for being two silly dudes chasing ghosts, and for sharing those adventures with the rest of us.

And to you, dear reader, thank you for taking a chance on me. It has always been my dream to be an author, and thanks to you, I get to live it out. Thank you.

See y'all for the next one!

ABOUT THE AUTHOR

Nico Vincenty is a science fiction and fantasy author from Texas. When she's not hanging out with her husband and dog, she enjoys baking, playing Gaelic football, and spending countless hours with Link and Zelda in any iteration.

To keep up to date with Nico, feel free to follow her on social media, or sign up for her newsletter via her website.

For more information, visit https://nicovincenty.com or scan the QR code below for socials, links, and other information.

ALSO BY NICO VINCENTY

A Swift and Sudden Exit

Bone Dresser